THE SHORES OF ETERNITY

THE SHORES OF ETERNITY

A PRAYER FOR EARTHRISE
BOOK 4

DANIEL ARENSON

CHAPTER ONE
His Arms like the Sun

Mars burned.

Standing on the balcony, Dale Emery watched the fires, tears in his eyes.

This world was his home. He had led Mars through years of peace and prosperity, only to see her fall now. Only to see decades of his work crumble and blaze. He was seventy years old. When he had moved to Mars as a boy, a timid young Earthling, he had found only an ochre desert. He had made the desert bloom. He had turned a colony of scientists into a glittering city of a million souls. Under his stewardship, Mars became the jewel of the solar system. Tourists, humans and aliens alike, flocked to fill the famous restaurants, browse the markets, explore the museums, and play at the haunted houses and casinos. Skyscrapers soared, alight with neon, reaching the tip of the glittering dome.

Now that dome had shattered.

Now the towers were falling.

Ares, the largest and oldest colony on Mars, burned.

Dale stood on his balcony, breathing through tubes, watching his life's work collapse.

His people had fought well. In space and on land, they had fought to the death. The warriors of Mars had died as heroes. But dead they were. And the hydrians were here.

Their foul ships filled the sky, hiding the stars. Billions of them surrounded the planet like ants covering a fallen fruit. Ships?

No, those were not true starships. They were *galactopods*, part mechanical, part organic. On the inside, the hydrians looked like the krakens of legend, giant squids with ravenous jaws. When traveling through space, they grew exoskeletons to sustain them. Interlocking plates covered their tentacles, lined with suction cups full of claws. Their mantles sprouted rings of metal that spun around glowing cores like the rings of orreries around artificial stars. Glassy canopies revealed their eyes. Red eyes. Dead eyes. Eyes with no compassion or mercy. Some predators had eyes that shone with bloodlust. Hydrian eyes were simply blank. To them, killing was mundane.

They had destroyed the human starships in space. And now they were descending toward the burning planet. Hydrians came from an ocean world. They were creatures of ink and water. They had not set these fires.

Dale had.

He had ordered Ares torched. He had set his towers and concert halls and museums ablaze. He had burned his life's work to hold the enemy back with fire. He set his ship aflame to hold back the krakens, dooming himself to a Viking funeral. He would not die in the belly of a squid. No, he would die in fire.

They all would.

Across the streets, the people ran. Mothers held their young children. Adult men carried their aging mothers. Some people were burning. They ran out from the colony into the desert, but only death awaited them. Hydrians landed on the sand-
-towering beasts, some as large as mammoths, others the size of whales. They scooped up fleeing children and crushed them in their jaws. A few people fired handguns or lashed knives. The hydrians shrugged off the bullets and blades and ripped people apart.

They kept descending, a multitude. They covered the red sands. Their tentacles swung, scooping up hundreds, pulling them into ravenous maws. Above the colony proper, the fire deterred the beasts. But not for long. The squids hovered above Ares like storm clouds, their armor gray, their eyes blazing red. Like tornado funnels, their tentacles descended toward the colony, then pulsed and bulged and spewed their ink. A black rain fell upon Ares, glittering capital of Mars. It doused the fires. But the ink offered the fleeing Martians no relief. The malevolent tar moved across the streets like sentient black mold, grabbing people, pulling them down, and burning through their skin and flesh until only smoking bones remained.

Dale stood on the balcony of Cydonia Hall, the seat of Martian governance, watching the slaughter. Watching a nation die. Watching genocide.

He looked up, seeking his family in space.

Where are you, Einav? Where are you, Marco and Addy?

Had they survived the battle above Mars? Or had their starship burned like all the others? Dale could only see the shoal. Mars had a new sky now. A sky of tentacles and raining death.

As the ink flooded the streets, the hydrians landed. They covered rooftops. They slithered along boulevards. They sucked up bodies into their mouths and feasted. They were even landing on the roof of Cydonia Hall. The building was shaped like a vast, stoic face gazing skyward. Lady Stargazer, they called her. Now the squids crawled upon her fair features, and her eyes shed inky tears.

Dale stepped into the weeping hall. He walked around his office. From this room, he had led Mars for decades. The room was cozy. Shelves held leather-bound books, antique naval instruments, rare geodes and seashells, and various other curiosities. An orrery glittered in the hearth light, depicting the solar system's planets. Each little planet glittered with gemstones. Sapphires covered Earth, topaz stones gleamed across Jupiter, while Mars dazzled with rubies. Dale placed his hand on the little red planet.

He looked at his hand. His fingers glittered with ruby rings, the stones of Mars. He looked at his robes. They were crimson and embroidered with golden thread, the color of the Martian sunset. He had always loved pretty things. He had always collected treasures--gems, precious metals, works of art. Throughout his life, he had sought beauty. Now it all seemed so trivial. Beauty faded. Ugliness spread.

A voice spoke behind him.

"Dale? Dale Emery is your name?"

The voice was deep, almost soothing, yet carried a hint of menace like thunder rolling nearer.

Robes rustling, Dale turned around.

A creature entered the room, slithering in from the balcony. The *thing* walked on tentacles the color of corpses. From the waist up, however, he looked like a man--an aging man with gaunt cheeks, a beaked nose, and beady black eyes. Aside from his fingers, that was. Those fingers were three times the usual length, almost as if they too were tentacles.

Dale knew who this was. He had heard tales of the hideous hybrid, the betrayer of Earth.

"Erafel," he said.

The gaunt chimera nodded. "My reputation precedes me, I see."

"You were a man once!" Dale said. "You were a human like me. You betrayed your world! You perverted your body and soul! Curse you. Curse your name to eternal damnation." He barked a laugh. "Damnation? We're already there."

Erafel raised an eyebrow. "Damnation? Oh, this is not damnation, Dale. This . . ." He gestured with his freakish fingers out the window. "This is heaven. The gods have arrived, my friend! They expunge sin from this world. Before our arrival, Mars was a hive of gambling, indecency, and infidelity, a world where the daughters of Earth prostituted themselves, where the sons of Adam rutted in the mud as they did in Sodom. As your god smote Sodom, so does mine smite Mars. His name is Ninazu. He brings cleansing."

"He brings mass murder!" Dale said. "You murdered millions of people. And now you will join those lost souls."

Dale was seventy years old, potbellied, sick with worry and grief, but he would not go down meekly. He reached over the fireplace. He grabbed an antique rifle from the mantle--a collector piece he had maintained, polishing and oiling, taking apart and reassembling. It was centuries old, but it still worked. And it was loaded. Dale fired.

The rifle boomed. A bullet slammed into Erafel's shoulder.

The hybrid stared at the wound, touched it with an obscenely long finger, and looked at the blood.

"Interesting," Erafel said. "Even now, with all my power, I am still mortal."

Dale reloaded.

Before he could fire again, Erafel seemed to . . . change. His eyes sank into his sockets, burning like red coals. His lips peeled back, and his teeth lengthened into fangs. The creature leaped at Dale, fingers reaching out like claws.

Dale fired, but a tentacle knocked the barrel aside. A bullet slammed into a photo on the wall. The glass shattered and the photo fell. And then Erafel was on him, gripping his throat, wrapping those terrible fingers around him and squeezing, squeezing. Dale sputtered, gasped for breath, but found no air.

"Humanity falls," Erafel hissed. "Mars is mine. And Earth will be next. Your legacy is over. Your race will go extinct. Now die, ape."

Dale couldn't breathe. His lungs screamed for air. Erafel lifted him by the throat until Dale's legs kicked like a man being hanged. The terrible fingers tightened, and Dale's neck creaked. Something was breaking inside him.

He stared into Erafel's eyes, and in those raging fires, he saw no remaining humanity. Perhaps none had ever been there.

Stars exploded across Dale's vision, and then everything went white and silent, and there was no more pain.

* * * * *

Dale Emery's body thumped onto the floor.

Standing over him, Erafel wiped his fingers on a curtain. Apes were such sweaty, dirty creatures. He looked at the bullet wound on his shoulder and winced. He reached into the wound, fished out the bullet, and dropped it. The pain blazed.

Despite everything, I'm still part ape, he thought. *Weak. Mortal. Simian.*

Disgust roiled his belly. His tentacles twitched. He would never be fully hydrian. His upper half, mutated as it was, would always retain its human roots.

For a second, the memories flashed before him. Himself as a man. A humble history teacher. Walking to work with his briefcase. A mild-mannered man, some would say. A lonely, balding, middle-aged man with no family, no money, no purpose. He had been Eran Felton then. A nobody.

As his blood dripped, he saw those images. Stepping in puddles of sludge. A car racing by, and the driver tossing a paper cup onto him. His landlord poking him in the chest, demanding rent. His pupils passing notes in class, drawing him, giggling at the hook-nosed, hunchbacked caricatures. The loneliness. The despair of being nothing.

Then he had found the gods.

Ninazu had chosen him. Among all the people in the world, Eran Felton was chosen! He became a prophet. A leader of a great faith. And finally a demigod. An evolved being. He became Erafel.

He shoved the memories of Eran Felton from his mind. That man was dead. Dead like Mars. Dead like all humanity would soon be. A new age was rising. The age of the squid.

Erafel squirmed onto the balcony and gazed upon Mars. The colony was gone. You could no longer see the buildings, the roads, the corpses. There was only a sea of squids, their mantles like wriggling waves rolling to the horizon. And there, on that horizon, rising above his minions--the true god.

Ninazu.

He was a hydprince. An alien the size of a city. He raised his tentacles, taking the form of a starburst, his arms like the beams of a dark sun. The dawn of the hydrians had risen.

CHAPTER TWO
To Feed a Crocodile

From a million miles away, from the shadows of deep space, they watched Mars fall, and they wept.

And they turned away.

Three friends. Three old Methuselahs cursed with long life. Three who had survived many wars together but had never seen such genocide. These old heroes, these warriors, these leaders who had commanded armies through triumph and tragedy--they turned away.

It broke their hearts. It shattered their souls. They were soldiers. They were survivors. They had vowed to protect their people. They had failed.

Had anyone else survived the battle over Mars? They did not know. A battle? More like a massacre. They had seen a handful of starships attempt an escape. Aurora, their Menorian friend, had been on one fleeing starship. Had anyone else made it through the shoal of squids? Maybe not. Hundreds of starships had battled the enemy over Mars. Thousands of brave spacers had died. As far as they knew, only the three of them--Marco, Addy, and Einav--had survived.

Tears in their eyes, the three friends left the ruin of Mars. They left the dead behind. And through the grief, through the shame, the words of Einav Ben-Ari echoed in their ears.

The battle of Mars is over. The battle for Earth begins.

They flew in silence. Behind them, Mars no longer appeared red. The planet was black. Black with galactopods. Black with death. It faded into shadow and was gone.

Ahead shone Earth. A pale blue speck. A mote of dust suspended in a sunbeam. Vulnerable. Another jewel for the hydrians to claim. Home. The trio sat silently for a long time, gazing together at the distant blue beacon.

Finally Marco broke the silence, speaking softly.

"We must defend our home. With everything we've got. With every breath, every beat of our hearts, we must fight. The fate of Earth cannot be the fate of Mars. Earth must not fall."

He turned to his right. Einav and Addy sat there--the two women of his life. If Earth was his beacon in the darkness, Einav and Addy were his anchors.

Joey, their little starship, had a cockpit with three seats side by side. Marco sat in the left seat, manning the helm. In the middle seat, the captain's seat, sat Einav Ben-Ari. The Golden Lioness. The Queen of Mars. The leader of humanity who had lost her people. She still wore her uniform of office--white trousers and a white shirt with golden buckles along the side. The ashes and blood of war stained the fabric, and tatters revealed scratches along her skin. Einav's prosthetic hand, her starhand, had been a work of art, a masterpiece of ivory, filigree, and golden gears, holding in its palm the Mariner's Tear, an azoth crystal of legend. The starhand had shattered. Its ivory, gold, and brass pieces lay strewn in her lap. Broken too was her heart.

Einav was a Methuselah, one of the last who still lived, a woman with unnaturally long life. She was 147, but she looked like a woman in her thirties. Her dirty blond hair hung in a loose braid. Yes, she looked young. But when she returned Marco's gaze, he saw the age in her eyes. Her eyes were not sunken, not peering from nests of wrinkles. They were clear and bright and glittered like emeralds, and yet they were old eyes. Ghosts haunted those green forests.

"Earth must not fall," she whispered, echoing him. "My

hand is broken, and so is my heart, but so long as I have one hand, I can fight." She raised her remaining hand, then balled it into a fist. "Until the end, I fight."

"Fuck yeah!" Addy said. "I got two fists right here, and I'm ready to pummel some squids."

Marco looked at his wife. Addy sat in the third chair, the gunnery chair. She had always loved weapons--blades, guns, cannons, or just those fists she brandished. After all, Addy Linden had always been a brawler. She had been born fighting, she liked to say. The baby of a drug addict. Born addicted. Born fighting for her life. Throughout her childhood, she fought on the streets. A child of a prisoner and a junkie. A child growing up in war. A child who became the bravest soldier Marco knew.

Addy was a tall woman, strong and fierce. In her veins flowed the blood of Norse Vikings, English knights, and Cree braves. War paint covered her cheeks, and tattoos adorned her arms. Many of those tattoos were mementos from her many battles. Tattoos for fallen comrades, for enemies killed. At times of peace, she could be silly, playful, childlike, but at times of war, Marco would want no other warrior at his side. She had given birth to his children. Children who had grown old and died. And still Addy fought at his side. His wife. The love of his life. The bravest woman he knew.

And then there's me, Marco thought.

He had never wanted any of this. Not to become a soldier. Not to become a Methuselah. A child of war, he had never thought he'd live to be thirty, but here he was, 145 years old. He did not look it. Like Einav and Addy, he aged slowly. Biologically, he was still in his thirties. He was not ageless, however. The stresses of battle were slowly, slowly etching their marks. There were new wrinkles at the corners of his eyes. Lines of grief. Streaks of silver in his temples. He had regained his youth, but God above, this war was taking it from him.

I only ever wanted to become a writer, he thought. *To live a simple, humble life in my library, dedicating myself to literature.*

He thought back to his youth. To hours lost in the library, reading and writing until dawn. To everyone else, the twenty-second century was history. To Marco, it was youth. Addy was with him in those memories, a scrappy teenager, her knees skinned, her long blond hair strewn with dry leaves. Those days had been so simple. Another lifetime. Another era. Another world.

But no. That world was still there. Earth was right ahead. His youth might be gone. His family had grown old and died. His library had been demolished long ago. But Earth was still there, full of new life, new families, new books, new youth. And that was worth saving.

"I still have you," he said, looking at Einav and Addy. "I still have my two best friends."

He did not need to tell them the rest--about the memories, his hope, his fears. They understood. They knew. They held his hands and smiled, and finally through the grief, he felt it. Just a bit of warmth. Just the faintest hint of hope. It was their love that gave this gift to him.

Einav leaned her head on his shoulder. Addy slung her arms around them. The trio sat together, taking long moments to grieve and seek comfort in one another. They had fought many battles, but they had never lost a planet. Never seen such destruction. They had not just survived a battle but genocide. For a long while, they just held one another, seeking animal comforts-- the softness of another body, the warmth of breath, the beating of hearts. A primordial meditation. A hundred million years ago, their ancestors had curled up in burrows, seeking shelter from storms and predators. Even now, evolved humans, they clung to these instincts. For connection. For physical warmth and companionship. Perhaps, out here in the dark, the need was stronger than ever.

An overwhelming desire filled Marco to turn the ship away from Earth. To flee to another world. To find some distant Eden far from any wars, far from the shoal, a place the hydrians would not follow. To settle there like Adam and Eve or Venus rising from the waves, virginal and new. To run. To hide. To spend the rest of their long lives as they were now--sheltering and nuzzling and comforting one another. Yes, that temptation for comfort nearly overwhelmed Marco.

But he knew it was an impossible dream. Even should they flee, the terror would follow them. It would live inside them. Whatever paradise they found, whatever Shangri-La of mossy forests or sunlit beaches they might reach, they would bring evil with them, for it was inside their minds. They could not forget the horrors of the hydrians or the visions of the dead. No, there was no fleeing terror once it got inside you. It stuck to your soul like tar. Forever.

We are soldiers, he thought. *And soldiers we will always be.*

"It's no use." Einav lowered her minicom. "I've been trying to contact other survivors. I've called Aurora on every frequency. No answer."

"So what do we do?" Marco said. "How do we proceed?"

"We go to Earth," Einav said. "That's where we make our final stand."

Marco shifted in his seat. "Einav, remember who rules Earth. President Cory Hart. The man who deemed us outlaws. The man who hunted us, who bombed Mars, who slew our soldiers. The man who opened the shoalgate and let Ninazu through. He grips Earth like a spider. How can we fly into his web?"

"He's not a spider," Einav said. "Cory Hart is a man. An ignorant man. Foolish. Petty and perhaps malevolent. But he's a man who always believed the hydrians were not a danger. That perhaps they were his allies. A man who now saw the terrible horrors the shoal unleashed. A man whom, I hope, is a changed man."

"Oh, bullshit!" Addy said. "Seriously, Einav. I love you to bits, but you're way too trusting. Hart knew exactly what he was doing when he opened the shoalgate. I don't buy this bullshit that he was naive or ignorant. He knew they'd destroy Mars. That's why he opened the portal. To wipe us out! I say we find him, stick him into a rocket, and blast him into the shoal where he belongs."

"I share the sentiment," Marco said. "And this is a lot coming from me. I gave Hart more chances than anyone here."

Addy nodded. "Yes, you did." She slapped the back of Marco's head. "Dumbass."

Einav gazed quietly into space, considering. "Hart was my enemy. We fought battles. He sent assassins after me, and I sent assassins after him. We fought a war. But that was the old humanity. That was the era before the shoal. Everything is different now. Mars is gone, and humanity will never be the same. Sometimes a man must release a demon from hell before cowering before it. I don't believe that Hart is cackling at his brilliant victory. I believe that he's afraid. Maybe shocked at what he's done."

"Let him suffer them," Addy said. "Let guilt eat him up. Before I feed him to the squids."

Einav shook her head. "No. Humans must never again kill humans. Like him or not, Hart is a human. And all humans must now unite. I have no more enemies among humanity. All are my kin. Even him. We must reach out to our old enemy. Yes, the very enemy who unleashed this genie from the bottle. And we must offer him our help."

Marco heaved a sigh and leaned back in his seat. "I hope you know what you're doing, Einav."

She gave him a crooked smile. "I'm just doing what I've

always done. Making things up as I go along."

"Great!" Addy muttered. "Our leader is winging it, and our enemy is now our buddy. What could go wrong? Ah, fuck it. Whatever you two say, I'm down for it. So long as I get to kill more squids."

Marco looked at his wife.

She's changed, he thought. Where was the woman who leafed through *Freaks of the Galaxy*? Where was the playful Addy who roasted hot dogs on a rake? Who talked on and on about hockey and bored him half to death, who teased him and mussed his hair, then kissed him, her eyes shining with mirth? That Addy had flourished during their era of peace, but she was gone now. The Addy from the Alien Wars, the warrior, the rebel--she was back. Older. Harder. A veteran carrying many scars.

And have I changed? Marco thought. *Am I still that writer, that thoughtful soul, or has my joy burned away too, leaving me nothing but a solemn soldier?*

Their new wounds were still healing. It was hard to see how they would look once the injuries scarred over. And he did not just mean the injuries on their bodies. The deeper injuries were those on the soul.

He held his arms around his friends, and their starship flew onward to Earth.

* * * * *

As Joey flew onward, Marco realized that his starship had not spoken in hours. Normally Joey chattered along, played music, teased Addy, and never shut up. Now she was silent. The little ship was hurt. Her ultrablack paint had peeled off. Her hull was dented and scorched. Her prow was crumpled, her cannons bent. But starships could not feel pain. Or could they? Some pains ran deeper. Perhaps software had a soul. And her soul was hurting.

"Joey?" Marco put a hand on her dashboard.

She did not reply. Normally, she would at least flash an emoji on her screen. Now she didn't do even that.

"Joey, it's me," Marco said. "Can you hear me?"

The dashboard showed the usual stats. Their altitude over the ecliptic plain. Their velocity compared to the sun. Their distance from Earth, the moon, and Mars--or what had once been Mars. But no sign of life from the soul of the ship.

"Joey?" Marco whispered. "Don't leave me, Joey."

His voice caught. Was his starship . . . dead? Was she nothing but a shell?

Einav noticed his distress. She put a hand on his thigh and leaned against him.

"Joey," Marco said. "Joey, wake up. I need to know you're here. I need to know you're not dead. I lost many people. Too many. Joey--"

"I'm here," she whispered.

Tears of relief flooded Marco's eyes. "Joey!"

An emoji appeared on the viewport HUD. A blue emoji. Tears in her eyes.

"They died," she whispered. "My daughters. They're gone."

Your daughters? Marco thought.

But then he understood. Of course.

During the early days of the war, Joey had proved herself an indispensable weapon. With her stealth cloak, sophisticated AI, breakneck speed, powerful azoth engine, and an arsenal of weapons, she was a perfect warship. She was custom-made. One of a kind. So on Einav's command, Martian engineers had reverse-engineered her. They built new Joeys, duplicates of the original, complete with copies of her AI. The copies even carried the original Joey's memories, feelings, loves, and hates. Her personality. Her soul. They were her clones, but Joey saw them as her daughters.

In the battle that followed, the Joeys formed a fleet. A deadly fleet called the Black Wolves. They slunk from shadow to shadow, invisible in the darkness of space, reflecting or emitting no light. When ready, they could pounce and unleash a barrage of deadly novabolts, tearing through enemies with neutron fury. The Black Wolves made short work of many Earthling warships.

And then the shoal arrived.

Then the Black Wolves faced something worse than Earthling warships. They faced a billion galactopods. They fought bravely. They fought like actual wolves. They slew many foes. But one by one, they died. Every clone, every copy of Joey. Every one of her daughters. Now the original Joey flew alone, a grieving mother.

Joey did not need to communicate all that to Marco with words. He understood. She conveyed it all with a single emoji and a few whispered words. Marco pressed his cheek against her dashboard and whispered, "I'm here for you, Joey. You're one of us. Always."

Her emoji became a heart.

The starship flew onward, carrying three humans home.

* * * * *

As they neared Earth, Marco expected trouble. To see a battle fleet defending Earth's orbit. To dodge the fire of defensive satellites. To face armadas. After all, Joey was no longer invisible. Her coat of ultrablack paint, which had hidden her in shadows, had peeled off in the battle. Hart's forces should recognize them. Arrest them as enemies. Maybe even open fire.

But nobody was there.

No defensive satellites orbited Earth. No warships

patrolled the planet. The shoal was just one planet over, and nobody was here to protect Earth!

With her usual eloquence, Addy voiced what Marco was thinking. "What the actual fuck?"

Marco thought he understood. "He struck a deal with the devil."

"Where is everyone?" Addy cried. "Why aren't there starships defending Earth? I thought Hart has a fleet, that--" She paused, understanding dawning on her. "Oh fuck. Are you serious?"

Marco nodded. "Yes. Hart must have made a deal. He'll open the gates to Mars. Let the hydrians take over that world. And demilitarize Earth."

"In exchange for what?" Addy cried.

"Mercy," Marco said softly. "Life."

Einav's face was grim. "Hart surrendered already. Surrendered without a fight. Earth is a vassal state of the Hydrian empire. Or at least that must be the deal Hart and Erafel struck. We can still undo it. We can still rally the fleet. Let's go find Hart."

Joey descended into the atmosphere unmolested. It was harder to fly in the sky than space, and Joey limped and skittered, and her engines rumbled. Smoke wafted from her exhaust ports.

"My baby needs a long, good stay in a shipyard," Marco said, patting the dashboard.

Addy snorted. "Shipyard? Those places rip you off. I can fix her." She lifted a wrench.

"Don't let her touch me," Joey said.

Addy bristled. "Why not? I'm a great mechanic!"

"She is," Marco confessed. "Addy makes many false claims. That she's a great chef, that she can sing, that she's taller than me--"

"I am!" Addy insisted.

"Heels don't count," Marco snapped. "Anyway, one thing

Addy is legitimately great at. Fixing machines. She'll patch you up, Joey."

Addy grinned evilly and cracked her knuckles. "I can't wait to get started."

Joey whimpered.

"Sorry, did that sound menacing?" Addy said. "I didn't mean to sound menacing. I just mean that I can't wait to carve you open and stick my tools into your guts." She cackled.

"Addy, be nice to her," Marco said.

"But I don't like being nice." Addy pouted. "I like being evil."

Marco was still surprised at the lack of resistance. He saw no military ships. Not even police coptrollers in the air. Earth was undefended. Demilitarized.

"The shoal is down the block, and nobody is here," Marco muttered. "Does Hart really trust Erafel? Does he really think the enemy's tentacles won't touch him?"

"There are three things that never surprise me," Einav said. "Human cruelty, human stupidity, and human naivety."

"Hart is all three," Marco said.

"Or maybe he's just the third," Einav said. "Extreme naivety can be cruel, Marco, and it can be stupid. We cherish and protect innocence in children and animals. In adults, it can be the most destructive force in the universe."

"That and Addy with a wrench," Joey said.

Marco couldn't help but grin. There was his beloved, snarky starship!

They glided over the desert and descended toward Jerusalem, their old home. A lump filled his throat when Marco looked down at the ancient city. He had missed this place. The city's ancient battlements snaked across the hills, overlooking the eastern dunes. Within these limestone walls clustered souks, houses of worship, minarets and domes and memories. Marco was a Canadian boy, born and raised. He had spent his formative years in Toronto. But many years ago, he moved to Jerusalem to be near Einav, and the city had become his second home.

The memories rushed back. Memories of Pax Terra, the century of peace. As a young man, Marco had fought in the great Alien Wars. Addy and Einav had fought at his side. For over twenty years, they fought the alien hordes on Earth, in space, and on hostile worlds. They rose through the ranks and became great leaders; some would say war heroes. Two decades of relentless war--and they cast back their enemies and built an empire among the stars. They had been born in hard times. They became hard people. And they created good times.

And for a century, those good times rolled. Marco had spent them here in Jerusalem. With Addy. With Einav. With their children, grandchildren, and great-grandchildren. Years under the sun, years among flowers and joy. A century of love. But now it all seemed so hazy. Just a dream. Another life. He had been another man.

Pax Terra had softened humanity. And it had softened Marco too. Now the wars were back. Now a foe greater than any Marco had ever faced threatened to destroy everything and everyone he loved.

The hydrians.

He winced, and images flashed before his eyes. The tentacles grabbing starships. The jaws crunching through hulls. The screams of spacers as the teeth tore into them, then the terrible silence. Space blazing and three hundred starships burning. The shoal descending upon Mars like a swarm of locusts upon Egypt. Never in all his decades of war had Marco seen such destruction, such a defeat of humanity.

Not since the Cataclysm, the terrible invasion of the alien centipedes, had humanity suffered such losses. The scum had destroyed the world that day in 2093. Marco had not yet been born. But he had grown up among the ruins. He had heard the tales. Entire cities wiped out. Billions dying. Half of Earth's population had fallen to the scum.

The hydrians could do even worse. They might not halve humanity but crush it entirely, drive humanity to extinction, and slay every memory, every treasure, every sign that humans had once lived on this beautiful blue world. For a moment, imagining it, despair clutched Marco like invisible tentacles, and he could not breathe.

But no.

There was hope.

There was the prophecy. Rowan. A girl named Rowan. Not yet born. A descendant of a woman who waited in a tower, overlooking the sea.

Come to me . . .

Marco would have further contemplated this faint hope, but Joey was taking them into the city now. The starship flew over the souks, blasting back embroidered curtains and tasseled awnings. Paprika and saffron blew from bronze bowls, forming aromatic swirls. A cart of persimmons overturned. Sacks of grain spilled wheat across cobblestones in golden avalanches. Engine sputtering, Joey dipped too close to a domed house, snapping its weather vane. She nearly crashed into a windmill, and her underbelly ripped fronds off palm trees. Finally, skittering like some awkward swan with one wing, Joey thumped down on a hilltop by Hart Hall.

The engine rumbled, coughed, and died. Joey tilted until one wing hit the lawn. The starship moaned. Addy was already reaching for her toolbox.

But as much as he loved his starship, Marco had more urgent concerns. He glanced at Einav. She stared back. In her green eyes mixed ice, grief, and the steel of determination.

"No guards," Marco said. "Not even outside Hart's

palace."

"He disarmed Earth entirely," Einav said. "On Erafel's orders, no doubt."

Marco nodded. "He signed a deal with the devil."

The trio exited the starship. For a moment, Marco just breathed. God, he had forgotten how wonderful fresh air smelled.

It's been years, he realized. *I've been fighting in space and on Mars for years.*

Had it really been that long? It must have been. It was 2270. It was four years ago--four years!--that the shoal had arrived in the Milky Way galaxy, destroying the human colony at Hypnos, then rampaging onward to Earth. Four years of war--most of it spent fighting Hart instead of preparing for the true enemy. Now Mars, like Hypnos, was gone, and millions were dead, and Earth was demilitarized. Four years of war and Marco had never felt this close to defeat.

For the first time since the massacre at Mars, he got a close look at Joey's exterior hull. Or what was left of it.

He winced. "What did they do to my girl?"

Marco touched her scarred hull, then pulled his hand back with a hiss. He had burnt his fingers. Joey had suffered blasts from hydrian inkblots, blows from clawed tentacles, and the bite of hydrian teeth. Finally she had flown through the inferno of a melting nuclear core to save Marco. And she had the scars to prove it.

"I feel like I've flown through a meat grinder," Joey said.

"That's not too far off. Addy will fix you up. She can fix anything."

Addy popped open her toolbox, revealing an assortment of wrenches, hammers, and soldering irons. She owned almost as many tools as weapons. She rolled up her sleeves and lowered a welding visor over her face.

"Let's get to work, baby." She lit a blowtorch. "I'll make

you beautiful again."

Joey's emoji grimaced. "Marco, don't leave me with her."

He patted her prow, then brushed hot ashes off his hand. "You'll be fine."

As Addy cackled and got to work with blowtorch and wrench, Marco and Einav stepped toward Hart Hall. They limped, wincing with every step. Bandages still covered them. Einav's starhand was inside Joey, shattered into many pieces. She tucked her stump into her shirt like a sad, battered Napoleon after Waterloo. Not long ago, they had battled Erafel aboard the bridge of a dreadnought. He had pounded them, would have killed them too, but the ship's core had begun to melt. Their battle had been interrupted, and they had barely escaped the ship before its destruction. But they would meet Erafel again. Marco was sure of that.

Marco remembered when the building had been called Bet Eretz, the House of Earth. That had been its name when Einav served here as president. Well, that was a long ago. The humble brick house had become a garish palace. Additions had been cobbled on like prosthetic limbs, making room for ballrooms and banquet halls. Three neon towers soared. The central tower, the tallest of the three, sported a massive mural of President Cory Hart. He was grinning and winking at the viewer.

But that was the old Hart. This temple of kitsch dated back to the Pax Terra, the long century of sleepy peace and decadence. The Hart on the mural, winking mischievously, was dead. There was a new Cory Hart now. A man who had fought a long, brutal war against Mars. Who had bowed down to the hydrians and handed them Earth on a platter. Whoever Hart was now, he was not that smiling man on the tower.

"Hello, Einav. Hello, Marco."

They spun around. And there he was, walking out the front doors onto the patio. Cory Hart, President of Earth. He was a tall, handsome man, his hair thick and wavy, his smile bright, yet the smile did not reach his eyes. Those eyes were haunted today, and though his suit was expensive and tailored, it was rumpled and fraying at the hems. Hart himself seemed fraying.

At once, Marco and Einav drew their sidearms and aimed at their old enemy.

Hart only smiled sadly. He held out his empty palms. "I'm unarmed. I have no guards. If you want, shoot me. Kill me like you've been trying to for years. Maybe I deserve it."

Marco frowned, keeping his finger on the trigger, the gun pointed at Hart's head.

"Yes, you do deserve it, you bastard." But then Marco spat and lowered his gun. "But we're not here to fight. At least not to fight you."

"Hart, where is Earth's fleet?" Einav said. "Where are the troops guarding your palace? The enemy is at our gates! Why is Earth undefended?"

Hart suddenly looked old. He was only fifty. But he looked older. The young gadabout, the tabloid star, the famous playboy who dated models--he was gone. Marco saw a weary middle-aged man, his beard graying, his eyes hiding deep pain.

"Come inside," he said.

Einav kept her gun trained on him. "If this is a trap--"

"No trap." Hart shook his head. "Our war is over. We fought a long, hard war, Einav. You lost. I won. And believe me, I take no joy in it. Only grief."

Einav glowered at him, and for a moment, she seemed to be struggling with an internal debate. Finally she holstered her gun. "You're right. Our war is over. But the true war has begun."

* * * * *

They entered the palace. As they walked down the hall,

Marco looked at the posters on the walls. He had seen them before. Posters from before the war. In each poster, Hart was shaking hands with another celebrity: athletes, actors, pop stars. In every photo, he was grinning. Marco looked at the man in the posters, young, naive, and handsome. Then at the man walking beside him, grim and weary.

The war changed us all, he thought.

Hart took them upstairs into his private quarters. Still no guards. The room was a mess. The bed was unmade, the sheets stale. Empty pizza boxes lay strewn on the floor, and copious amounts of cannabis reeked on the tabletop. Dirty laundry covered the couch.

"Sorry for the mess," Hart said. "My wife left me. Took the kids. And the housekeeper. God, this place is a pigsty. Come onto the balcony. Some fresh air. I need air!"

"Hart, it doesn't matter where we meet," Einav said. "You must defend this world! Raise the fleet! Summon the army! Fight, man! Fight for your planet!"

Hart looked at her, eyes haunted. "Against the terror from the stars, there is no fighting. There is no victory. Your fleet was strong, Einav. Strong enough to hold its own against mine for years of war. Against the shoal, your fleet fell in a day. No. There is no hope to defeat these monsters."

"So you appeased them," Marco interjected, disgust roiling his belly. "Do you know what Churchill said about appeasers? An appeaser feeds a crocodile, hoping it will eat him last. In your case, it's squids. You tossed those squids the planet Mars, hoping it'll fill their bellies and they won't devour you."

"But they will," Einav added. "They will, Hart. Whatever deal they offered you, it's a trap."

Hart sank into the couch. The dirty laundry crinkled around him. "I'm not an idiot, Einav. At least, not anymore." He barked a laugh. "Oh yes, I was a damn fool most of my life. I know it. But not this time. No. I saw what those creatures could do." He looked at Marco. "You tried to warn me, Marco, I know. You came into my palace a few years ago. You warned me. I ignored it. Go ahead, then. Gloat. Tell me: I told you so."

"We're not here to gloat," Marco said. "We're here to ally with you. You're still the president of Earth. Fight with us."

"No. No, the days of war are over. We lost, Marco. All of us lost." Hart turned weary eyes toward Einav, then, perhaps fearing something he saw there, he looked back at Marco. "Erafel promised me he'd spare Earth. The hydrians would have their feast on Mars. They'd have a planet to parasitize. And so long as I disarmed and swore fealty to Ninazu, Earth would be spared."

"A vassal planet," Marco said.

Hart nodded. "Yes. Better than a smoldering ruin. Wouldn't you agree, Marco?"

Marco wanted to rage, to grab the man, to shake him. But he forced himself to collect his thoughts. To think. To view the world as Hart did. Finally, when his rage settled down to a simmer, he spoke again.

"Mr. Hart, I understand that--" Marco began.

"Call me Cory."

Marco pursed his lips and started over. "Cory, I understand why you think this is a good deal. I understand that you're trying to do your best. To save Earth in your own way. But you cannot trust Erafel. Once they're done sucking Mars dry, they'll come here next."

"We have a deal," Hart said. "A solid deal."

"The Molotov–Ribbentrop Pact," Einav muttered.

The two men turned toward her.

"The what?" Hart said.

Einav sighed. "The Molotov–Ribbentrop Pact. An agreement between Nazi Germany and the Soviet Union. Hitler promised not to invade. Give me the rest of Europe, he said. And

I'll leave you alone. That was the deal. It worked great until Hitler conquered most of Europe and wanted more. Within two years of signing the pact, the Nazi forces were steamrolling through Russia. Hart, you signed the Molotov–Ribbentrop Pact with Erafel. And he'll devour you next."

Hart listened, face pale. "But . . ." He gulped. "We can't fight the shoal, Einav! You saw them. Oh God, you saw what they did to your fleet. You saw what they did to Mars." He covered his eyes, perhaps to hide tears. "Oh God, the horrors . . ."

Einav growled. She bounded across the room, grabbed Hart, and yanked him off the couch.

"Stand up, man!" she said. "Stand straight! Brush the crumbs off your clothes. Square your shoulders, soldier! Yes, you are a soldier, like it or not. Stop blubbering when Earth needs you. Fight, man! Fight them. With me."

To his credit, Hart stood straight. He managed to affix Einav with a glare. "Fight to the death, Einav? Go down as heroes? A final stand? Very heroic. So very noble. A fine death for soldiers, perhaps. But what about the people of Earth? Ten billion humans live on this planet. Families. Children. Would you have them fight to the death too? Because that's all that fighting can bring them."

"When the shoal arrives here--" Einav began.

"*If* they arrive!" Hart said. "*If* they arrive, I'll grovel. I'll beg. I'll kiss Erafel's tentacles. And maybe he'll spare some lives. Maybe . . . maybe he'll let us be slaves instead of corpses. If we bow down, there's still a chance. Rome didn't destroy all the lands it conquered. It destroyed Carthage. It destroyed Israel. It destroyed nations that fought. Those who bowed survived. That's why we still have a Britain but not a Carthage. I don't want to be a noble Hannibal, dying in battle, going down in legend while my world is destroyed. Yes, everyone remembers Hannibal's name. Nobody remembers the rulers of Britannia who bowed down before Rome. Well then, let nobody remember my name. They can remember you as a martyr, Einav. I'll be forgotten. But I'll be giving Earth a chance."

Marco had to admit the man had a point. Einav had brought a good example from history. And Hart had countered it with an example of his own. For a moment, Marco felt conflicted between them. Could Hart be right? Could Einav Ben-Ari, his best friend and war heroine, be wrong? Marco had always scorned Hart, thinking him a fool, a craven, a wicked man. Could Hart have changed?

He looked at Einav. They made eye contact. For 130 years, they had fought side by side. They were leader and commander, but they were more than that. They were best friends. They could communicate with their eyes alone.

Could he be right? Marco said, raising his eyebrows slightly.

Einav frowned. *Of course not, Marco. Don't be a fool.*

He pursed his lips. *Maybe his way is correct.*

Her frown deepened. *Don't be so naive!*

Marco lowered his head just the slightest. *Maybe you're right.*

Einav's finger twitched. *Maybe we should just shoot him. Take over Earth from him.*

Marco gave the slightest shake of his head. *No. No more humans killing humans. Remember, Einav? Our only enemy is the shoal.*

Now it was Einav's turn to lower her eyes. *Yes, you're right.* She looked back up at him. *But we must do something, Marco.*

Marco hardened his face. *Then we will fight. With or without him.*

The two friends turned to leave. But at the doorway, Einav paused. She looked back at Hart. And she spoke parting words.

"You said that Rome destroyed nations that fought, and you're right. But nations can rise again from the ashes, and so can worlds. We remember Hannibal, who died fighting, whose civilization fell and did not rise again. But we also remember Herod, who collaborated with Rome and ruled Israel as a puppet. Think carefully, Hart, whom history recalls more fondly."

With that, she spun on her heel and left the room, and Marco followed.

CHAPTER THREE
Lost Ships and Lost Souls

For the first time in years, the trio returned home. Not just to Earth but to Or Midbar, the Light of the Desert. The village they had built.

A century ago, after winning the Alien Wars, Einav had built a little house here. She had called the place Bet Or, the House of Light. It was a humble house for a president, which she had been in those years. Back then, Jerusalem had lain in ruin. The Alien Wars had punished the city. So much of Jerusalem had smoldered. So Einav had built her home outside the walls, using reclaimed limestone bricks. The bricks were enormous, craggy, and beautiful, their colors changing as the sun moved across the sky, cycling through bronze, copper, silver, and gold like the feathers of an iridescence sunbird. She had shaped these bricks into a humble house and a paradise around it. A stone archway led into a garden overflowing with lantanas, anemones, and cyclamens. Low brick walls surrounded a *boostan*--a garden for fruit trees. Carobs, persimmons, dates, and pomegranates filled the air with their scent. From this hilltop, Einav could see the desert. The dunes rolled into a hazy horizon scented of cinnamon and myrrh. But here on the hill, Einav had created an oasis.

This house she filled with warmth and love. Her beloved books, stalwart companions, filled the house with the scent of their old pages and leather covers. Souvenirs from the wars-- crystals from the engines of famous starships, medals won on the battlefield, framed photos of fallen comrades--filled nooks in her walls. In the winter, a warm hearth crackled. On cold desert nights, she would sit by the fire, sipping tea, while in the springtime, she would work in her garden as the turtle doves sang.

But most important were the people she had brought into her life. After her divorce, Einav had found herself lonely. When you were president, you saw people daily but didn't make many friends. Blessedly, she had Marco and Addy. And for a long time, Lailani had been here too. Lailani was one of those fallen comrades who gazed from a picture frame, frozen in time.

In this home, they raised their children. And then their grandchildren. And their great-grandchildren, and still they remained young. In this home, they tended to their aging children, nursing them through infirmity--feeding them, bathing them, changing their diapers, as if they had become babies again. There was great tragedy to watching a child grow old and die while you lingered on in cursed youth, but there was a blessing to seeing one's family grow and descendants flourish. The children of Einav, Marco, Addy, and Lailani became a clan. A village. They built more brick houses. More gardens and *boostanim*. More memories. This little house outside the city walls, a place they called Bet Or, grew into Or Midbar. The Light of the Desert. A village. It was Einav's proudest accomplishment.

And it was still here. Throughout all the wars and struggles, throughout her hard years in Martian exile, the village remained. New babies had been born. New families had been brought into the community. The village was growing into a town and might someday become a city. It would be Einav's legacy.

This is what I must protect, she thought, gazing at the village that overlooked the desert. *This is why I fight. I fight for all humanity. For all Earth. But shining brightest in my heart is this place.*

Einav did not know when the feast on Mars would end. But eventually, the shoal will have devoured every last bone. They would grow hungry again. And then they would fly to Earth. Hart thought he had secured Earth's safety. Einav did not doubt that Ninazu, along with his foul servant Erafel, was coming here next. Vermin did what vermin did. They spread. And ate. And spread some more.

"We don't have much time," she said.

"I need another two days to finish fixing Joey," Addy said. "Just the short flight from Hart Hall to here almost killed her."

"*You* almost killed me," Joey said. She was parked on a hill among anemones and cyclamens, her engines smoldering. "What did you do to me? I'm on fire!"

Addy snorted. "Oh shush, you're not fire."

"I can see the smoke!"

"That's just some oil from my weld jobs burning off. You'll be fine." She slapped Joey's hull. A chunk fell off.

Marco gaped. "Addy, my ship!"

"What? What happened?" Joey cried.

Addy blushed. "Nothing. You're fine!" She glanced at Einav. "I might need three days."

Einav heaved a sigh. "Fine. Work as quickly as you can, though. And . . ." Einav hesitated. "I hate to take you away from Joey, but do you think you could fix my starhand?"

Addy's eyes lit up. "I thought you'd never ask."

The starhand pieces clattered inside a wooden tea box. Many delicate pieces of ivory had formed the fingers and palm, interlocking together. The ivory came from a hellephant, an ancient and extinct beast from an alien world. The material was harder than diamonds. No individual piece had broken or dented, merely disconnected from one another. Inside the box, the ivory pieces looked almost like bones. Golden filigree adorned them, peeling off at spots. The internal components of the hand lay among these scrimshawed bones. Delicate gears, cables, and hooks forged from brass and gold rattled around the box, collecting tea leaf dust. Finally, most precious of all, shone the

Mariner's Tear. The azoth crystal had once glowed in the starhand's palm. A stone that could bend space and time. That could draw power from the human soul. It was worth more than all the gold in Jerusalem.

Addy examined the shattered starhand. "All the individual pieces are fine. It's like a Lego set that fell apart, but the bricks are still perfect. I just need to figure out the design. You don't happen to have the schematics, do you?"

"No," Einav said. "I bought it from Grimm's Limbs on Mars." She lowered her head. "I'd ask Grimm, but he must be dead by now."

Addy sucked her teeth. "Well, I'll figure it out. Joey, can you scan the individual pieces of the starhand, then run through different options for reassembling them?"

"Yes, but I won't be doing it for you," Joey said. "For Einav only."

Addy bristled. "Hey, with all the care I'm giving you, you're still cross with me?"

"I'll forgive you if you fix me," Joey said. "Big if!"

"Baby, I'm going to fix you so good your head will spin." Addy placed her hands on her hips and examined the battered starship. "I'm thinking a purple hull."

"Addy, no!" Joey cried.

Addy's eyes widened. "I know! I'll add some wood paneling."

"You're a monster!"

"Addy, stop torturing the poor starship," Marco said.

Just then, before Addy could come up with any more brilliant ideas, the people of Or Midbar came out of their homes. They ran up the hill to meet the trio.

Some were elders with white hair. Others were youngsters barely old enough to walk. But they were all family. All were descendants of Marco, Addy, Einav, and Lailani. Together the four friends (down to three now) had created a tribe.

As Einav watched her descendants running uphill, her anxiety eased, and love filled the places her pain retreated from. Her beloved son was gone, as were her grandchildren, but the next generations thrived.

The clan of Or Midbar celebrated the return of their patriarch and matriarchs. That night, they held a feast in the gardens. They served fruit from the boostanim and dishes seasoned with herbs from their gardens. Addy, of course, roasted hot dogs on a rake.

Einav was an introvert. When she wasn't fighting battles, she preferred being alone. Walking in nature, reading books, listening to opera, painting--all lonely pursuits that healed her weary soul. When she did spend time with other people, it was only with Marco and Addy. Other people exhausted her. Marco and Addy comforted her. Yet in the big gathering tonight, she felt safe. Even in the crowd. She laughed with her people. With her family. She drank a cup of wine, then another cup. The distress had been eating away at her, gnawing away from the inside like parasites, hollowing her out. She had not realized until now the full damage inside her, how much scar tissue covered her heart. Joy, good cheer, contentedness, a good meal with friends and family--she had nearly forgotten.

I won't ever be the same, she thought, sitting there in the crowd. Her descendants ate and drank and celebrated life. A few burst into song, and one lad stood on a table and played guitar. Children scampered around, and elders told tall tales and laughed. But Einav could not laugh with the same abandon. She could feel hints of this joy, a little warmth in her soul, but it did not fill her. No, she was still too damaged.

Even in this place of light and family, even here among flowers, images flashed before her. The shoal devouring. Mars falling. Bodies melting under the ink. Aurora, her dear friend, lost in the darkness.

No, I will never feel true joy again, Einav thought. *Some wounds do not heal.*

So while the others all laughed, she could not even smile. While the others sang, she remained silent.

A hand touched her thigh. Einav turned to see Addy beside her. Her friend smiled softly and looked into her eyes.

Einav, I'm here for you, Addy's blue eyes said. *I love you. I understand.*

Einav leaned against her friend, and Addy wrapped an arm around her. Feeling a little safer, Einav watched the kids scampering about between the tables. They were eating outside among the olive trees in the boostan. The children collected fallen olives and tossed them back and forth, laughing, pretending to be dragons and damsels, aliens and captains. More than the tales of the elders, more than the wine or music, the children soothed her. Watching them play, Einav could grasp more of that feeling she had thought dead. Joy. Her joy was still only an ember, and perhaps it would never more rage in a bright fire, but if only she could nurture that ember, keep it glowing to offer a little warmth and light, she could still navigate the darkness ahead.

After everyone went home that night, Einav retired to her old bedroom. During the years she had fought in space, her descendants had kept her house in pristine condition. Everything was the same. The same books on the shelves. The same geodes and rare coins on the windowsills. The only difference was the ivy that grew outside her window. It had lengthened and draped across the window like curtains, casting leafy shadows in the moonlight. Yet the room felt somehow smaller, somehow alien. She remembered her long years living here, but it was like remembering another life. Another person's memories.

It must be how the Joey clones felt, Einav thought. *I no longer feel like my old self. Just a copy, deadened, carrying another person's memories like a dybbuk locked in another woman's body.*

She did not think she would sleep tonight. With the party over, with the children gone, with those strange shadows on the walls, her anxiety returned. The shadows reminded her of tentacles.

The door opened, and in came Marco and Addy. They were carrying sleeping bags.

"I'm telling you, Poet, we don't need sleeping bags!" Addy was saying. "We can all fit on Einav's bed."

"You kick in your sleep!" Marco said. "It's bad enough I have to share a bed with you. Einav doesn't need to suffer the indignity too." He looked at Einav. "We figured we'd keep you company. That you wouldn't want to sleep alone."

Einav's eyes dampened. She hugged her friends. "Thank you. I love you guys. I love you so--" She frowned. "Addy, what's that in your pocket? It's poking me."

Addy blushed. "Oh. I almost forgot." She pulled a bundle of hot dogs from her pocket. "I brought leftovers." She held one out to Einav. "Want one?"

"No thanks."

Marco yawned. "I'm beat. Let's get to bed."

"I hope we sleep well tonight," Einav said. "Because I have big plans for us tomorrow."

Marco raised an eyebrow. "Oh?"

Einav nodded. "Tomorrow morning, we're going to steal Earth's fleet. And we're going to prepare for war."

* * * * *

As dawn rose, a problem presented itself.

Where *was* the Earthling fleet? They had no idea.

The Phoenix Fleet, the space corps of the Human Defense Force, had once been mighty. Earth's warships had pounded enemy worlds, liberated humans on distant colonies, and cast back invading hordes. Over the generations, the Phoenix Fleet had dwindled. Myriads of ships became thousands. Thousands became hundreds. And many of those hundreds shattered in the civil war against Mars. But there should still be several hundred warships remaining, ready to fight. Where were they?

The fleet certainly wasn't orbiting Earth. The trio would have seen it. Had it fled to exile? Had it been grounded and now lay rusting in some swamp or rusting underwater?

"Hart knows where those ships are," Einav muttered.

"Well, we can't bloody well go ask him," Marco said. "He'd never talk. He'd know what we want the ships for."

Addy looked up from her work and raised her visor. "Give me five minutes alone with him." She lifted a plier. "I'll get it outta him."

They all sat around the kitchen table. Marco had always loved Einav's kitchen. Fresh herbs grew on the windowsill. Pots and pans hung from hooks. The wooden tabletop was scarred and scratched, forming an abstract painting to commemorate generations of good times. The office held the books and treasures, the garden was a place of beauty and life, but to Marco, the kitchen was the heart of this house, and the best memories of his years here still filled the place.

This kitchen had seen times of grief and sorrow too, to be fair. Marco still remembered them having their first meal here after the deaths of their children. He still remembered the first morning here in a house that felt so empty. Today too was a solemn time in Bet Or's kitchen. The trio were here to discuss how to proceed. How to survive. How to prevent the very extinction of humanity.

No pressure, Marco thought with a wry smile.

Einav was sipping tea slowly, carefully, a methodical ritual.

It was how she did her best thinking. Her brain ran on tea. Addy, meanwhile, had arranged the broken pieces of the starhand across the tabletop, sorting screws and gears and bolts and wires. With the same slow, methodical care, she was reassembling the prosthetic. Fixing things was how *she* thought.

And Marco? He had always done his deepest thinking while walking. During his days as a writer, he would take long walks through the woods, sometimes for hours, and come up with ideas for his novels.

During my days as a writer? he thought. *When did I stop being a writer?*

He realized that he had not written a page in . . . Well, he couldn't remember the last time. This war had taken everything from him. Not just his joy and peace but also his muse. His very self-identity. Even throughout the Alien Wars, he had always considered himself more author than soldier, but now? Now facing genocide, facing human extinction? All that mattered was that he was human.

He got up and paced the kitchen, stroking his short beard, lost in thought. Addy wanted him to shave the beard, but stroking it helped Marco think. Einav kept sipping her tea. Addy kept tinkering with her tools. They were all in deep thought now.

"Let's consider some possibilities," Marco said. "First possibility. Hart sent the Earthling fleet to another planet. Instead of guarding Earth, they're orbiting some other world."

"I doubt it," Addy said. Using tiny brass hooks, she attached another piece of filigreed ivory to the starhand. "His deal with Erafel was to disarm. Erafel would not tolerate an Earthling armada that could swing by to attack him someday."

"Maybe the fleet left in secret," Marco said. "Maybe they're hiding."

Einav shook her head. "No. That's unlikely. Earth's frigates are not exactly stealth ships. During the civil war, we could always track their movements well enough. Erafel would be able to as well. And I agree with Addy. Erafel would not tolerate any Earthling army--anywhere."

"So that leaves two possibilities," Marco said. "Either Hart scrapped the ships, or he blew them up."

"We'd have noticed an explosion," said Einav. "Those ships have fusion cores. Bays full of armaments. Had Hart evacuated and blown them up, they would have released immense light and energy. Joey, battered as she is, would have picked up the signal. Hell, we probably would have seen the blast with our naked eyes."

Marco kept pacing the kitchen. "So that leaves only one possibility. Hart kept the ships, but he grounded them. They could be sitting somewhere in the desert. Or rusting underwater. Damn! Once you land frigates on Earth, it's downright impossible to get those fat bastards into space again. They're too damn heavy. You can land them but not take off again."

Addy looked up from her work. "It can be done."

"How?" Marco said. "Some of those warships weigh a million tons. I'm not using hyperbole. I mean they literally weigh a million tons. Their engines can't lift that much mass from the surface to space. That's why you build warships in space--and keep 'em there!"

Addy raised her eyebrow. "Is that so?"

"Yes!" Marco said.

"Really?" Addy stroked her chin, smiling.

"Oh, for fuck's sake, Addy! How does a million-ton warship take off?"

"I can get 'em to take off," Addy said. "But first you have to admit I'm smarter than you."

Einav stifled a smile. Marco groaned. "Fine, you're a genius, and I'm a blathering idiot. Now tell me!"

"And I'm also taller than you," Addy said.

"We're both five foot eight, Addy. We're the same height."

"And I'm prettier."

"Addy!" Einav said. "Stop torturing him."

"Fine. You use graviton plates." Addy grabbed a knife and began scratching a diagram onto the tabletop. "We use graviton plates all the time in starships. Even Joey has some. They're how we have gravity walking around inside them. They manipulate gravitons, the tiny particles responsible for the force of gravity."

"Yes, Addy, even I, the blathering idiot, know what graviton plates are," Marco said. "But they're just used to keep your feet on the deck. Yes, even your giant feet."

Addy gasped. "Shut up! My feet are petite." She kicked him. "See?"

Marco groaned and rubbed his side. "Yes, downright dainty. In any case, graviton plates aren't nearly powerful enough to lift an entire starship."

"Aha!" Addy raised her finger in triumph. "But they can be! It's all hypothetical. But take the fusion cores of warships. They can release massive amounts of energy. Massive. More than enough to lift a million tons into the air. So, divert that power into graviton coils, then run the coils under the starship into grav-plates. I'm massively oversimplifying for your little brain, but that's the general principle. Then you turn on the engine, and voilà! Floating warships!" Addy puffed out her chest and raised her chin in triumph.

"Yes, brilliant," Marco said. "There's only one problem. We have no idea where the starships are!"

A voice came from outside the kitchen window.

"I think . . . I think I do."

* * * * *

It was Joey who had spoken. The starship stood on her

treads outside the house, covered with scaffolds. Various components and tools lay around her among fallen pine needles. Slowly, she was beginning to look more like herself. Addy had buffed out the dents and scratches, repaired the broken wing, and started work on the damaged engine. The prow was still a mess, and her neutron cannons were still bent. She was a work in progress, but slowly, with Addy's ministrations, Joey was healing.

The trio left the house and approached the starship.

"Were you eavesdropping, Joey?" Marco said.

If starships could grin, Joey would be grinning ear to ear. "Sure was! I have powerful ears, you know. I can hear *everything*. Even when you sing in the shower, Addy."

"To be fair, I think all Jerusalem can hear that," Marco said. "But forget Addy for a second. I usually try to."

Addy bristled. "Hey!"

Marco ignored her. "Joey, what's this about knowing where the Phoenix Fleet is?"

The starship hummed and rattled. It was how she did her deep thinking. "Do you remember when I was cloned?"

"Of course," Marco said.

"I thought of my hundred clones as my daughters," Joey said. "It was a special bond. Not just a bond between mother and daughters. But a bond so strong it was telepathic. We could communicate with one another. Feel one another's feelings. When each daughter died, I felt it. I felt her death as if I myself died."

Marco caressed her hull. "I'm sorry, Joey. That must have been so horrible."

"With them gone, I felt so empty," Joey said. "I could no longer hear my daughters' voices, share their joy, comfort them in their sadness. I lost my family. But I also lost so much of myself. Of who I was."

Marco lowered his head. He knew something about that. He had lost children too. Three beautiful children. Terri. Roza.

Sam. They had lived for a century, which was far too short. Yes, when you lost loved ones, you didn't only lose them. You lost parts of yourself.

"But Marco," Joey said. "I can feel something now. It's faint. Just a hint. Like a feeling of warmth in your stomach after a sip of wine. At least that's how I imagine sipping wine feels. A sort of comfort deep inside you. And deep inside me, Marco . . . I can hear one. I can hear a Joey ship."

Marco's eyes widened. "What is she saying?"

"I'm not sure," said Joey. "I think . . ." Her motors hummed for a moment. "I think she was captured. By the Phoenix Fleet. I think they scraped off the rampant lion on her hull. And they painted a phoenix. She became a ship of Earth, but she's still calling out to me. She still remembers her home on Mars. Marco, she's alive. Her voice is so soft. I can barely hear her. But she's alive. And Marco, if the Phoenix Fleet indeed captured her. . . the rest of the fleet will be with her."

Einav and Addy gathered near, listening carefully. Marco kept his hand on his starship's hull.

"Do you know where your daughter is?"

Joey hummed in thought. "I hear only vague sounds. I see only vague images. She's talking to me. She's calling me. She's scared. But it's all so hazy. Like a dream."

A voice echoed in Marco's mind.

Come to me . . .

Yes, this reminded him of his dreams. His dreams of Kemi. Distant voices. Vague images. Dreams that slipped from his mind when he awoke. Even now, a century after her death, Kemi haunted his mind. His high school sweetheart. His sister in arms. A warrior who had fought at his side in the Alien Wars, then died in his arms. For a long time, Kemi had lived as a memory. But since the hydrian invasion, she had been calling to him. *Come to me . . .*

"I can almost hear her voice," Joey said. "She's saying . . . Come to me."

A bolt shot through Marco. His head spun. How was this possible? That Joey should hear the same voice? That her kidnapped daughter should speak the same words Kemi whispered from beyond the grave?

"What else do you hear?" Marco said. "Any background noises? Birds? Honking horns? Rustling leaves?"

Joey thought for a moment. "There's a sound. A sort of whispering as from many voices. She's calling to me, but I can barely hear."

Addy raised her finger. "I got an idea! Joey, hang tight. I might be able to give your sensors some extra juice."

She grabbed her toolbox, climbed the scaffolds that covered Joey, and settled onto her dorsal hull. Perched there, Addy pulled out her drill.

"Addy?" Joey said. "What is she doing up there? I can't see her! What is she--ahh!"

Joey screamed as Addy drilled into her.

"Oh, be quiet," Addy said. "I just grazed you. I need to install an extra telemetry sensor here. Give me five minutes, guys." The drill buzzed.

Joey screeched. "You're drilling into my warp coils!"

"Oh, I am not! I'm just--" Addy paused, leaned down, and frowned. "Oh." She looked back at Marco and Einav. "Nobody fly Joey at warp speed for a while."

"I've been savaged!" Joey cried.

"Don't worry. I'll fix it." Addy drilled another hole. "Eventually. Let me install that extra sensor first. Hold on, Joey." She lifted a big metal tube tipped with a spherical sensor. "This might sting."

She rammed the tube down.

Joey's scream sent doves fluttering from the carob trees.

When Marco and Einav removed their hands from their ears, they examined the starship. Joey had fallen silent. She just sat there, still. Even her engine no longer rumbled.

"You killed her!" Marco whispered in dread.

Still sitting atop Joey, Addy frowned and tapped the starship. "Hey, dumbass." She pounded her fist against the dorsal hull. "Hey, wake up! You alive?"

Silence.

Marco gasped. "You did kill her."

"Shh!" Joey said. "I'm listening."

"Oh, thank God!" Marco hugged her hull.

"I can hear better now," Joey said. "My daughter is calling to me. Her voice is muffled but less than before. I can hear . . . Yes, I think I know what it is. Waves."

"Waves?" Marco said. "A beach?"

"Shh!" Joey said.

They all quieted. Even Addy.

"Yes, waves," Joey finally said. "And wind. And . . . I see it! I see it now. A beach. Yes, I see waves. Sand. Seashells. And . . . Starships! Oh, Marco, it's horrible. There are so many starships, but they're stuck on the sand. Like beached whales. My daughter is there. I think some ships are underwater."

Einav stepped closer. Her eyes blazed with green fire. "Does it look like Earth? Is the Phoenix Fleet still on Earth?"

"Yes," Joey said. "It's Earth all right."

"We found them!" Addy cried.

"Not yet," Marco said. "All we know is that they're on a beach. Somewhere. Could be any beach on this world. Or on a world that looks like Earth. Joey, does your daughter have any satellite info on her location?"

"No, not anymore," Joey said. "She can't connect to any satellite network."

"That bastard Hart must have taken the satellites down as

part of his deal with the devil," Einav said. "Joey, can you see any landmarks? Anything to tell us what beach you're looking at?"

The starship concentrated. "Daughter? Daughter, are you there? Show me what you can. Open your eyes, sweet daughter. Let me see." The starship's motors hummed. "She's sending me more images. It's not a tropical beach full of happy sunbathers. It's cloudy. And cold."

"Well, that narrows the field," Addy muttered. "It's November. It's cold. Not telling us much."

"Well, to be fair, it tells us the fleet is in the northern hemisphere," Marco said. "It's summer in the south. So that's half the beaches on Earth off the table already."

"Oh, how delightful!" Addy said. "We only have half an entire planet to search! Assuming it *is* Earth."

Einav stifled a smile. "Joey, tell your daughter to look around again. Any landmarks on the coast?"

Another moment of rumbling motors. Finally Joey spoke again. "Yes, I see it. A castle on the beach. An old crumbling castle. Come into my cockpit. I'll show you an image on my screen."

* * * * *

They stepped into the starship. There was less damage on the inside. Amazingly, despite the sorry state of the prow, the cockpit was intact. Marco still noticed the bloodstains. They had fled in this starship from the destruction at Mars, bleeding and half dead. Three very old friends. Three who had survived the slaughter.

Tens of thousands of soldiers fell on Mars, Marco thought. *And a million civilians or more. Why should I live? Why should an old man linger on while the young perish?*

He looked young perhaps. The Methuselah Serum still

coursed through him. He could pass for a man in his thirties, but he was 145, and he felt every one of those many years. He had never recovered from the Alien Wars. They had raged a century ago, and those ghosts still haunted him. Now, seeing the bloodstains in the cockpit, the guilt raged through him.

I should have died back there on Mars. I should have died a thousand times. But they fell. And I linger on. What cruel joke is this? Why am I cursed with this long life?

He felt a hand on his shoulder. Addy was there beside him.

"You all right, Marco?" she said softly.

He looked into her blue eyes. Kind eyes. Loving eyes. And his grief and guilt eased enough to let him smile back.

"No," he said. "No, I am not all right. None of this is right. But thank you for being here."

While husband and wife hugged, Einav sat in the captain's seat.

"All right, Joey," Einav said. "Show us what you're seeing."

She tapped a button. The viewports burst to life. On the outside, Joey had a solid hull. No windows. No portholes. No windshields. Nothing made from reflective steelglass. After all, she was a stealth ship. When in running order, ultrablack paint covered her stem-to-stern. Perfect camouflage in space.

On the inside, digital viewports hung in Joey's cockpit, emulating vintage windshields. The screens connected to cleverly-embedded cameras on the hull. A triptych of screens formed a viewing area similar to the cockpit of an old starfighter. One screen pointed forward while two others gazed out the port and starboard sides. The starboard viewport was currently on the fritz, but the other two streamed a view of the hills of Jerusalem. Several children, all descendants of the trio, were scampering outside among the flowers, flying a kite and banging wooden swords.

Marco patted Joey's dashboard. "Babe, you still with us? Show us what your daughter is seeing. Show us that beach."

"I'll try," Joey said. "It's still a vague image, but here goes."

The front viewport changed. The view of Jerusalem's hills vanished. Instead they saw a blur of beige, dark blue, and gray.

Addy squinted. "What the hell? Looks like a goddamn Rothko."

Marco raised an eyebrow. "You know Rothko, the famous abstract painter?"

She raised her chin. "I'm an intellectual."

"Addy, you once asked me which Ninja Turtle photographed the Mona Lisa."

"She was using my Rothko book last night as a coaster," Einav explained.

"Hey, I thought it was just a sample of house paints," Addy said.

Einav opened her mouth, then closed it and tilted her head. "Come to think of it, you're not too far off."

Marco squinted at the "abstract painting" on the viewport. As Joey concentrated, it began to take on clarity. The beige smudges became sand. The blue began to look like water. And there on the shore--a gray smudge. What was that? Marco leaned back, squinting harder, trying to see. It almost looked like a tower. An old castle.

A memory shot through him.

Come to me . . .

He could smell the sea. Feel the sand beneath his feet. Hear the waves. See her smile.

"I know this place," he whispered. "It's--"

Screams sounded outside. The screams of children. Then came a deafening screech. The screech of a monster.

Marco knew that sound.

The sound of a hydrian.

"Joey, show me outside!" he cried. His voice filled the cockpit.

The blurry image of the beach vanished. The viewport once more showed the hills of Jerusalem. The children of Or Midar were still outside, but they were no longer playing. They were fleeing.

Chasing them was a towering monstrosity, a squid in a suit of black chitin. Its jaws opened in a slavering grin.

CHAPTER FOUR
Attack on Or Midbar

The hydrian slithered uphill, jaws open wide to devour the children of Or Midbar.

Not just any children. But Marco's descendants. Children he loved. They were fleeing uphill, screaming. One boy turned to face the beast, holding a wooden sword. His name was Elijah Emery. Marco's great-great-grandson, all of nine years old. He looked as small as a penguin facing an orca. And unless Marco got there fast enough, the boy would face a similar fate.

And here Marco was inside Joey's cockpit. A good hundred yards away. Too far!

"Joey!" Marco shouted. "Fly and bomb the beast!"

"I can't!" Joey cried. "Addy broke my engine."

"What?" Addy cried. "I didn't--"

Marco didn't wait a second longer. He leaped out of the cockpit, pausing only to grab a rifle. He hopped out of Joey's airlock onto the hilltop.

A second later, Einav burst from the airlock too, holding a plasma rifle. She was missing her starhand, her greatest weapon. But Marco had seen her take down entire enemy squads by herself with nothing but a gun. If a squad why not a squid?

Side by side, Marco and Einav shouldered their rifles and opened fire.

Plasma bolts slammed into the hydrian. The giant squid screeched and reared, tentacles spreading out like a sunburst. He was a male, judging by the pattern of lumps on his mantle. His jaws opened in a furious roar, splattering saliva. That hellmouth was large enough to swallow a horse, and teeth like a medieval portcullis sprouted from the gums. The creature had concentric rows of teeth designed to lacerate and slash flesh.

A coat of dark chitin covered the alien. This was a hydrian of the second instar. A hyd. The younger hydlings, beasts of the first instar, were easier to fight. Their skin was exposed. But this creature was old enough to have grown a suit of armor, though it was missing the propulsion system Marco had seen on some hyds. Unlike some hyds, this one could not fly. Did hyds come in two varieties, walking and flying? Marco wasn't sure.

The plasma bolts pounded the exoskeleton but only chipped the chitin. The barrage wasn't breaking through. At least the assault slowed the mammoth-sized alien down, allowing the children to escape. As the hyd reared and roared, the children reached the hilltop. They fled behind Marco and Addy and cowered, clinging to their legs.

"Get into the house!" Marco said.

The kids were too scared to leave them. A girl grabbed Marco's arm. "Pwease, Gwampa Mawco, don't send us away."

Young Elijah Emery waved his wooden sword. "I can fight!"

The adults of Or Midbar burst from their houses. Their guns boomed. Most just had simple hunting rifles or shotguns. Antiques. Bullets and buckshot pounded the hyd, not doing much damage. But Marco and Einav kept firing their plasma bolts, bombarding the alien's exoskeleton. The creature was flailing, trying to swat aside bullets and bolts with his armored tentacles.

One grandmother rushed toward the children who cowered behind Marco and Addy, still clinging to their legs. She shepherded them into the house. Reluctantly, young Elijah went with them, still clinging to his wooden sword. The children retreated just in time too. Not a second later, just as Marco and

Einav paused to reload, the hyd aimed a tentacle at them. The limb bulged and pulsed, rattling its interlocking plates of armor. Marco knew what that meant.

"Ink!" he cried.

He and Einav leaped apart. An inkblot splattered the ground between them. The ink corroded the flowers and grass, then began eating into the soil like a ravenous tar monster. Droplets sizzled against Marco's leg, burning him. He roared with pain, fell to one knee, and kept firing at the creature. He tried to aim at the eyes. But the hyd kept his gargantuan mouth open. Those jaws opened so wide they obscured all other parts of the head. All Marco could see was a portal to damnation, ringed with teeth. Tentacles flailed around the horrid hellgate. It reminded him of some demonic flower blooming from the carcass of the devil. Marco fired plasma into the mouth, but the hyd gobbled up the bolts like they were hot peppers.

A ring of villagers now surrounded the alien. They kept firing, reloading, firing again. It was all the hydrian could do to bat aside the bullets. When Marco and Einav paused to load fresh plasma packs, the alien took a swing.

A tentacle mowed through a group of villagers like a scythe. Several villagers flew into the air, then crashed down into the distance. They were the lucky ones. Suction cups lined the tentacle, filled with rings of claws. They looked like the mouths of lampreys. The suction cups grabbed some villagers and held them aloft. The rings of claws spun like garburators, chewing through flesh. Blood sprayed the hill.

"Addy, where are you?" Marco shouted over his shoulder. "We need you."

Her voice sounded from inside Joey. "I'm fixing your ship!"

"Addy, this is not the time for repairs! Get your ass out here and help us fight."

But she did not emerge. Dammit! Marco knew what she was doing. His wife wanted to get Joey into the fight. But by the time she was done with repairs, they might all be dead.

A tentacle came swinging his way. The armored limb was as thick as a Greek column.

Marco cursed. Instead of fleeing, he ran *toward* this swinging battering ram. Seconds before impact, he jumped onto a boulder, vaulted into the air, and flew over the tentacle. The enormous appendage swung beneath his legs, shattering the boulder. Marco landed on the grass, spun around, and opened fire. He aimed his plasma at the joint connecting the tentacle to the hyd's body. The alien roared.

Einav had managed to leap over the tentacle too--and without even a boulder to assist her. She landed, rolled, and came up firing. She saw what Marco was doing. She fired at the same spot. Their combined plasma bolts hammered the tentacle's joint-- and the huge limb detached.

The hyd screamed--a deafening cry, a howl so loud it knocked down trees and rattled stones. Cut free, the appendage flailed on the hillside, spurting ink and blood. Marco and Addy leaped behind a cypress. Ink splattered the tree, devouring leaves and branches.

Droplets sizzled against Marco and Einav. They screamed. The ink clung to them, searing through their clothes. In a mad panic, Marco kicked off his ink-splattered boots, then ripped off his jacket. Einav tore off her white trousers and buttoned shirt, remaining in her underclothes. The ink raced through the fabric, consuming it like dark flame devouring twigs. The pair grabbed dirt from the ground and scrubbed droplets off their skin.

The hyd was hurt, but he was still very much in the fight, and he was angrier than ever. The beast came rumbling forth, crashing through ink-splattered cypress and olive trees. One tentacle slammed into Einav's garden, shattering a stone table and crushing her flowerbeds.

Half naked, Marco and Einav ran toward the boostan--the walled garden of fruit trees. As they ran, they kept firing, pummeling the hyd. The alien aimed one of his remaining tentacles and fired another globule.

Marco and Einav reached the boostan. They ducked for cover behind the brick wall. It was only about five feet tall, but if they crouched, it protected them.

The ink splattered the walled garden, devouring pomegranate, persimmon, and carob trees, then splashing the brick wall. The mortar sizzled, but the wall held.

"What the hell is this thing doing on Earth?" Marco said as he reloaded. He was running low on plasma cartridges. "I thought Hart made a deal to keep them away. Those bastards are breaking the deal already."

"No," Einav said. "If Erafel had broken the deal, we'd be facing millions of hydrians. This one must be a guard. An overseer here to hold Hart's leash."

Marco spat. "And Hart didn't even warn us. The bastard. Maybe he wanted us dead."

Einav slammed a fresh plasma pack into her rifle. "We'll figure it out later. Now fight!"

They rose from cover, unleashing barrages of plasma fury at the hyd.

The alien rumbled and charged across the boostan, knocking down brick walls, archways, and fruit trees. The plasma bolts were doing some damage, albeit slowly. It was like chipping away at a wall with a spoon. It took a while. The barrage finally cracked the exoskeleton, burned the flesh beneath, and severed a second tentacle. Despite his injuries, the hyd wasn't stopping. Through the inferno, he came barreling toward Marco and Einav.

A deep voice bubbled up from the hellish mouth, rumbling with waves of bass.

"I know you . . ."

Marco and Einav kept firing. Plasma bolts hit the
creature's jaws. They burned the gums, knocking out a few teeth.
One tooth clattered down at Marco's feet, as long as a sword. Still
the creature lived.

"You are . . . Marco and Einav. I will take you alive . . ."

He reached out a writhing tentacle. Armored plates
covered the enormous digit. The tentacle was charred and cut,
dripping ink and blood, but still a powerful weapon. The two
friends unleashed a final barrage of plasma, then paused to reload
. . . but they were out. Out of ammo!

The tentacle reached down toward them. Only a low wall
stood between them and the monster. Marco and Addy raised
their fists, ready to fight to the death. And that death seemed to
be just around the corner.

Just then a boy rushed forth. It was Elijah. Marco's great-
great-grandson. The nine-year-old faced the towering hyd, raising
his little wooden sword.

"You will not touch them!" the boy cried.

"Elijah, get back!" Marco shouted.

The low boostan wall separated him from Elijah. Marco
leaped over the wall, then ran between smoldering fruit trees,
heading toward the boy.

The tentacle swooped. The limb grabbed the boy and
lifted him overhead. Marco leaped up and tried to grab Elijah, but
the hyd tossed the boy high into the air.

As Elijah tumbled down, the hyd tilted his head back,
caught the boy in his mouth . . . and gulped him down.

* * * * *

Marco's world crashed around him.

His great-great-grandson. Swallowed. Devoured like a

mere piece of meat.

"No!" Marco screamed at the hyd. "You bastard!"

He ran through the burning boostan toward the alien. He had no gun. He scooped up the fallen hyd tooth he had earlier dislodged. Wielding it like a blade, Marco charged. He leaped off a log and flew toward the beast, the tooth bright in his hand. As the hyd licked his chops, savoring the meal, Marco drove his makeshift blade into the creature's mouth.

He hit the lower gum. A deep cut. Marco shoved the tooth all the way in. He felt like a dentist ramming a needle into a man's gum. Without anesthetic. The hyd bellowed in agony. Quite understandable.

Marco fell back, losing his grip on the tooth. He hit the ground. Einav yanked him to his feet. They turned to flee. But they discovered that the boostan wall was now covered with ink. The black material consumed the mortar and was crawling over the bricks. The sizzling ink reached out tendrils as if to grab them. It was like little hands thrusting against a black curtain. Marco recoiled in disgust.

Their escape was blocked! Marco and Einav spun back toward the hyd. They were trapped--the inky wall behind them, the alien ahead.

The hyd reached down his tentacles.

"You will beg for death," it rumbled. "Your screams will echo across the galaxy."

Marco and Einav hurled rocks at the kraken, trying to hit an eye, but they might as well be shooting spitballs. The tentacle coiled around them and--

Engines roared.

Joey blazed over the boostan wall, knocking down the inky bricks, and plowed into the hyd.

The armored squid slammed down, crushing trees and toppling bricks. The west wall of Einav's house crumbled, exposing a honeycomb of rooms within. Joey's engines rumbled and glowed, shoving the starship into the hyd, ramming the beast into the house.

Joey's airlock popped open, and there was Addy! She wore a tool belt, her face was sooty, and she carried many weapons. She tossed rifles to Marco and Einav.

"Now let's get this sonuvabitch!" she cried.

Marco and Einav grabbed the fresh rifles and opened fire. Plasma bolts bombarded the squid.

With a great cry, the people of Or Midbar reached the ruins. They ran between the inky trees and scattered bricks, firing guns of their own. Plasma and bullets pounded the fallen hyd. The creature tried to rise, moaned, and collapsed. Joey had shattered the alien's carapace, exposing the meat within. That was where the humans aimed their guns. The fusillade joined into a great stream of destruction, carving into the hyd until it crashed down dead.

At once, not even catching his breath, Marco raced toward the dead hydrian.

"Addy, bring your katana!" he cried. "Hurry!"

She hopped down beside him, blade in hand. Marco grabbed the sword and began carving into the hyd. The carapace had already been cracked and the flesh ripped. There wasn't much left for Marco to do. He cut deeper, pulling back meat and tendons and arteries, and reached the beast's stomach.

He ripped open the stomach and out tumbled Elijah Emery.

He was covered with digestive acids. Marco placed the boy on the ground.

Elijah wasn't moving. He wasn't breathing.

Marco grabbed dirt from the ground, wiped acid off the child, and breathed into his mouth.

Elijah gasped and gave a shuddering breath.

Marco let out a massive sob of relief.

His great-great-grandson had saved his life. And Marco had returned the favor.

* * * * *

But not everyone had survived that day. In his rampage through Or Midbar, the hydrian had killed twenty-one people. A third were children. In one way or another, all were descendants--or spouses of descendants--of Marco, Addy, and Einav.

That afternoon, they buried their dead, and they grieved. This village, which celebrated the joy of family just last night, now mourned the fallen.

They stood on the hilltop, dressed in white, the color of mourning. Hundreds of people lived in Or Midbar, and they all came to say goodbye. Twenty-one fresh graves filled the village cemetery. Twenty-one wounds to the heart. Twenty-one scars that Marco knew would never heal.

Marco himself helped bury the bodies. They were his family. The oldest fallen was eighty-five. The youngest was only a few months old. They buried her in her mother's arms.

As Marco buried the dead, he looked around him at the older tombstones. For a century, the people of Or Midbar had been burying their dead here outside the walls of Jerusalem. A few steps away, under an olive tree, stood three old tombstones, side by side. They were the tombstones of his children.

Terri Emery. Sam Emery. Roza Emery.

And with them stood the tombstones of their spouses. Of their children. And of so many others who had fallen while Marco lingered on, and suddenly it was too much, and he could only stand there, frozen, fearing that if he moved, if he so much as breathed, he would shatter into pieces like Einav's starhand.

In his grief, Marco turned toward those who had always

propped him up. To the two loves of his life. Einav Ben-Ari, his captain. And Addy, his wife. The three embraced among the tombstones, and the grief was so great they could not speak, merely seek whatever comfort they could in one another.

I would be lost without them, Marco thought, adrift in a sea of mourning. *I'm still lost in this sea, but they are my raft. They cannot bring me to shore, but they keep me from drowning.*

"I'll kill them," Addy hissed, tears in her eyes, fists clenched. "I'll kill the hydrians. I'll kill them all. Every last one."

A sob racked her body, and Marco and Einav held her in their arms.

Nearby stood young Elijah Emery, nine years old, still holding his wooden sword. He had lost both his parents in the attack. He silently stared at their graves.

Marco gently detached himself from Addy and Einav. He walked toward the boy and knelt before him.

Elijah looked at him, eyes hard and dry, but Marco saw the pain. He knew the boy would weep tonight.

"I tried to save them," Elijah said. "I failed."

Marco put his hand on the boy's shoulder. "I was around your age when aliens killed my mother. I too felt like a failure. I felt grief. Guilt. All the things you're feeling."

Elijah raised his chin. "And you became a soldier. You grew up to kill aliens." He clenched his fist around his wooden sword. "I'll grow up to be like you. And I'll kill them all. Like Addy said. I'll kill them all!"

His little fists trembled, and his eyes blazed with rage. His lips peeled back, revealing his teeth. Some were still his baby teeth.

"Elijah." Marco spoke softly, kindly. "What I'm about to say to you won't make sense for many years. It's something even I still struggle with, even now, so long after I lost my mother. The best revenge is living well. Hatred is a poison. It can be used to kill an enemy, yes. But it also poisons your soul. I won't pretend that I never drink this poison. I drink it often. I won't pretend that I always got my revenge by living well. I did not. You will never rid yourself of this rage, of this grief, but please, Elijah. Do not let it consume you. Do not let it extinguish your joy. And whenever you need me, I'm here for you. And I love you."

He pulled the boy into an embrace, and finally Elijah wept--loud, ugly weeping that tore through his little body. Yes, this one was broken, Marco knew. And this one would become a warrior.

We will need warriors in the years ahead, Marco thought. *They say hard times forge hard men. But God, why must it hurt so much? Why must the cost be so great?*

When the dead were buried, and the tears were shed, Marco, Einav, and Addy returned to Bet Or, their little house on the hill.

It lay in ruin.

This gentle oasis, this loving home--it was gone. The walls had fallen. The trees had burned. The books lay strewn among the debris, their pages coated with hydrian blood. Marco searched through the ruins. He found a photo of Lailani. The frame had cracked, and the pane of glass shattered. He blew the shards of glass off. In the photo, Lailani was puffing out her cheeks and crossing her eyes, a rare moment of silliness for a girl who carried so much pain. He tucked the photo into his pocket and kept searching. A worry grew in him. Had it shattered in the crash?

Finally he found it. The soulshell.

The spiraling conch lay under a pile of wood and shattered naval instruments. The house collapse had chipped the shell, and terror filled Marco. Was it broken? But when he lifted the shell closer, he saw it. The soft glow inside. The faint blue light like a moonbeam through rain.

The yureis, ghostly aliens from another universe, had told

him that this shell contained Kemi's soul. That part of her lived on inside. When Marco held the seashell to his ears, he could hear the sea. And her voice spoke.

Come to me . . .

"Marco?"

He turned around. Einav stepped into the ruins. The ink had devoured her clothes, but the villagers had given her sweatpants and a sweatshirt, and a blanket was wrapped around her shoulders. Her dirty blond hair, normally in a ponytail or braid, hung freely, sprinkled with dust and leaves. Walking gingerly among the fallen bricks, she approached Marco. She looked at the seashell in his hand.

"I know where it is," Marco said. "The Phoenix Fleet. The blurry image Joey showed us. I know where that is."

Einav raised an eyebrow. "How?"

"Because I've seen it many times in my dreams," Marco said. "Kemi has been trying to tell me all this time."

CHAPTER FIVE
Escape from Pèlerin

Of course. Once Marco had lifted the seashell and heard the
waves, it all snapped into place.

The beach Joey had shown them. The place where the
Phoenix Fleet waited. Marco had seen it many times in his
dreams. A beach facing the sunset. A crumbling castle
overlooking the water.

Come to me . . .

It was the same place. The place Kemi awaited in his
dreams. She had been trying to show him. To guide his way. To
show him the path to hope.

Marco left the ruins of Bet Or. He crossed a valley strewn
with cyclamens and climbed a hilltop overlooking the desert. A
lone carob tree rose here, twisting and coiling like an old man, and
fallen fruit carpeted the ground. The tree seemed to Marco like an
ancient sentinel, a guardian of the desert. Standing here,
overlooking the eastern dunes, Marco raised the seashell.

"Where are you?" he whispered. "Kemi, show me the
way."

Come to me . . .

"I don't know where you are!"

He closed his eyes, and he saw her there, smiling sadly.
The wind ruffled her curly black hair.

You know where I am.

"Show me the way."

You've been there before, Marco. You took your children there. Do you remember? On a day of an eclipse . . .

And then he saw it.

He saw it in his memory so clearly.

Years ago. His children had still been young. Marco and Addy had taken them to the beach. It was winter and cold, but they wanted to watch the eclipse over the sea. The sun was setting, and just before it touched the water, the moon eclipsed it. The family gazed in awe at the celestial display. A single last beam from the sun, like a golden spear, shot out and touched the top of a tower. An old crusader fort watching the water.

Marco had almost forgotten.

His eyes snapped open.

He knew where that was. Where Kemi was. Where the Phoenix Fleet awaited.

He ran downhill to find Einav.

* * * * *

He burst into the village of Or Midbar and raced between the houses that still stood.

"Einav, I know where it is!" he cried. "Einav!"

Villagers looked up at him. They had been toiling to rebuild. To plant new gardens. To repair fallen walls. To scrub blood and ink off walls that still stood. Marco raced between them. He saw Einav and Addy ahead, tending to Joey. Fresh scaffolds covered the starship, whose prow was more battered than ever. Addy was decked out with tool belts, busy at work. She paused from drilling as Marco approached.

Marco reached them, clutching his aching side, out of breath. "Einav, I know where it is! Kemi's been trying to show me. All this time, in my dreams, she's been trying to show me. The beach. With the crumbling old crusader fort. It's where the lost ships of Earth are! It's nearby! It's only a hundred kilometers west by the sea. The ships are there!"

Addy removed her ear protectors. "Sorry, say again?"

Marco took a deep breath. "The Phoenix Fleet. It's on the coast of Israel. A quick dash away." He laughed. "Hart didn't park them far from his palace."

Joey whimpered. "Please don't fly me there. I'm not ready. I'm all tender."

Addy rolled her eyes. "Oh, you're fine. Solid as a rock." She kicked Joey. A chunk of her hull fell off. Addy blushed. "Oops. Hang on. Give me five minutes."

Addy climbed the scaffolds and began tinkering with Joey's exhaust ports.

Einav had been helping Addy with her work. Grease stained her thick work clothes, her face, and her hair. She lifted her goggles, revealing two pale white patches around her eyes where no soot had darkened her skin. Einav stepped closer to Marco, held his arm, and stared into his eyes.

"Are you sure about this, Marco? Visions, dreams? That's not exactly reliable information."

"I'm sure," Marco said. "It's the place Joey's daughter showed us. I know where it is."

Einav nodded. She turned toward Joey and patted the battered starship. "Joey, my dear, you can stay here. Rest. You've earned it. Marco, Addy--we can take one of the village shuttles. Let's go."

"Wait!" Joey said. "I don't want to stay here alone. If my daughter is nearby, I must go too. I'll try to fly. Just . . . be gentle with me. No dogfights until I'm better, all right?"

Einav smiled. "A nice, easy flight."

Joey popped open her hatch. "Hop in, bitches. We're hauling ass to the beach."

Marco and Einav glanced at each other, then looked back at Joey, eyebrows raised.

"Joey, where did you learn to talk like that?" Marco said.

Addy's voice sounded from the stern. "Goddamn piece of shit exhaust coils! I just fixed these little bitches!"

Marco nodded. "Ah. That explains it."

Finally Addy fixed the exhaust coils--or at least patched them up enough for a short flight. The trio climbed into the cockpit. As usual, Addy took the gunnery seat at the right. Einav took the captain's seat in the middle. And Marco, as always, took the left seat. The helm.

Before firing up the engine, Marco looked at his companions. They looked back, silent.

"We're still together," he said. "The three of us. We've been to hell and back a thousand times. We faced the hordes of demons and overcame them. We're grieving now. We lost battles. We lost loved ones. We lost family. But we're still together. We're here, in a battleship, still fighting. We can do this. I know we can. This is the worst war we've ever faced. This is humanity's darkest hour since the Cataclysm. But we will win!"

"We will win!" Addy cried, fist raised.

"We will win!" Einav said, raising her own fist. Sadly, her starhand was still broken. Addy had not finished reassembling it. But she raised her real fist, and small though it was, it signified all the power inside her.

"We will win!" Joey said. "Um . . . is it all right if I join the chant?"

Marco grinned. "Of course, babe. You're one of us."

"One of us, one of us!" Addy chanted.

Marco shoved down a lever, and the engines rumbled to life. The cockpit rattled. Smoke blasted out Joey's stern. For a moment, the ship made terrible sounds, but the engines kept running. Addy had done good work. Marco didn't take off yet, just let the machinery grumble and rattle on the hilltop.

"How do you feel, Joey?" Marco said.

"Ready to take on the entire shoal."

"That's my girl. Let's go."

He shoved down the throttle, then pulled back the yoke. With clanking metal and clouds of smoke and dust, Joey soared.

* * * * *

They flew over the hills, leaving Or Midbar behind. In the rearview monitor, Jerusalem's ancient walls and towers gleamed like polished brass in the sun, and the dunes rolled into Arabia. Ahead sprawled hills of pines and olive trees, sloping gently toward the Mediterranean. From high enough, you could see how small this land truly was. Just a little triangle lodged between Africa, Europe, and Asia, connecting the three great continents like a pebble stuck between boulders. It was no wonder that so many wars had been fought over this land. It was the cog holding the world together.

After a short flight, they reached the coast. Marco nudged the yoke, and Joey descended and skimmed along the shoreline, her engines blasting back sand and roiling the water. They flew northward, heading toward the place Marco remembered. The old crusader castle on the beach.

"It's somewhere around here," he muttered. "Remember when we visited the place, Ads?"

"Dude, that was decades ago. I can't remember what I ate for breakfast most days, which is weird because it's always Fruit Loops."

"We're looking for Château Pèlerin," said Einav. "The Knights Templar built the fortress in 1218 during the Fifth Crusade. Home to four thousand troops, it served as the headquarters for the Crusade to capture Jerusalem. In 1291, Al-Ashraf Khalil captured the castle from the Crusaders, and--"

"Boring!" Addy said. "I didn't ask for a history lesson."

"It's interesting," Marco said.

"No it isn't," said Addy.

"It's interesting how long we humans have been fighting wars," Marco said. "We really are a violent species, are we? Going back thousands of years, we've always been fighting."

Addy nodded. "Yep. We're warriors. That's us humans."

"Might not be such a bad thing," Marco said. "If the hydrians had attacked a world of pacifists, we'd all be dead by now. We're savage, naked apes who are very, very good at killing. Much is made about our potential for morality and nobility, the better angels of our nature. Maybe it's time to unleash our demons."

"Time to unleash the beast," Addy agreed.

Marco examined his feelings. Why did he feel so motivated today? He felt ready to go out there and fight, dammit. He itched for battle. He wanted to kill some damn aliens! To smell their blood. Hear their dying screams. It was all the grief at the funerals. The despair at seeing the fall of Mars. The sting of losing the battle in space. He was tired of losing. Tired of suffering blow after blow. He craved to fly in a warship with a great fleet, to bombard his enemies, to make them pay. The fires of war were lit. During his long years of peace, he had almost forgotten that part of him. The dormant warrior was now awake and furious.

There in the distance, he saw it. A crumbling old fortress on the shore, overlooking the sea.

Come to me . . .

The images flashed before his mind.

Kemi smiling, the wind rustling her black curls. The sunbeams like bronze spears. The sea gray and churning. For a moment, Marco's dreams and reality overlaid each other.

Then he blinked, banishing the dreams, and saw only the castle as it was. It seemed different in real life. Tangible. Earthly.

When Marco zoomed in, he saw no woman waiting on the tower. Part of him had hoped she would be there in this real world. But maybe she existed only in dreams.

And there before the castle--a great city of rusting metal. The grounded starships. The Phoenix Fleet.

Hundreds of ships lay on the sand like beached whales. Some were indeed as large as whales, and others were even bigger, larger than the Crusader fortress that had once housed four thousand men. There were corvettes. Frigates. Even a starfighter carrier on the sand. And in the water lay beasts that were larger still. Three dreadnoughts lay half-submerged in the sea like hippos the size of towns. The waves lapped against them, and moss was already growing across their hulls.

"There it is," Marco said softly. "The fabled Phoenix Fleet of Earth. How the mighty have fallen."

Einav stared, and her upper lip twitched, hinting at her fury. "When I was president, I commanded thousands of warships. The fleet patrolled a galactic empire. Now look. A few last ships lying in the water. This is what Hart has wrought." She shook her head sadly. "Is this enough? Is this really all we have left?"

"Ah, come on, Nav Nav," Addy said. "Chin up! We've been underdogs before, and we always won."

"Not always," said Marco. "Remember the last time we fought the shoal? They steamrolled over us."

Addy crossed her arms. "That was a tie."

"Another tie like that and we're done for," Marco muttered. "But you know what, Ads? You're right. No use being defeatist. You fight a war with the army you have. Let's see how damaged these ships are. And see about getting them back into space."

Marco flew Joey closer. The little ship zipped by the crusader fortress, then descended toward the beached starships.

They didn't look in such bad shape. Marco could imagine them rising again, proud and mighty. He spiraled down, moving toward a frigate.

He frowned. A smaller starship was leaning against the frigate. Some sort of corvette, he thought. But it looked odd. Lumpy. Without a proper stern or exhaust ports. Marco had never seen a starship of that design. What was it? He squinted, trying to identify the uncanny ship on the sand.

Suddenly that metallic, lumpy shape reared, turned dark gray, and stretched out tentacles.

Marco gasped. Addy screamed.

A hydrian!

The creature flailed and roared. It shot a blob of ink at Joey. Marco pulled the yoke, dodging the inkblot.

"That fucker came out of nowhere!" Addy said.

"Watch out, there are more!" Einav cried, pointing.

Marco saw it. Several of the beached starships were not starships at all. They were camouflaged hydrians! They were in the hyd instar, by the look of them. But different from usual hyds. Bulkier. Longer. And with that insidious camouflage. Marco had never seen them able to cloak themselves this way. Clearly, the aliens came in more varieties than Marco had known. These were deadlier beasts than the hyd at Or Midbar.

Abandoning their camouflage, the creatures became black, their natural color. They reared, jaws open in terrible shrieks, revealing red maws and curved teeth. Their tentacles pointed at Joey, bulged, and fired ink.

Inkblots hurled across the sky. Marco pulled the yoke, swerving left and right, dodging the assault. A hydrian tentacle reached toward Joey, claws spinning in the suction cups. Marco rolled, escaping the blow.

"Addy, fire the prow cannons!"

"I can't!" she said. "I haven't fixed them yet."

"What?" Marco cried, then winced and yawed, dodging another tentacle. It had nearly grabbed Joey.

"I was going to fix them next!" Addy said.

Marco grimaced and soared, but the inkblots followed like heat-seeking missiles.

"So use the plascaster," he said. "Joey has two weapons, you know."

"It's broken too," Addy said.

Marco groaned. "I'm getting us outta here. Hold on."

He soared higher. The hydrians warbled and rose in pursuit. Below their mantles, metal circles began to spin madly. It reminded Marco of the spheres you saw at circuses full of racing motorcycles. But instead of daredevils, these spheres contained crackling flames like little stars. These bizarre propulsion systems hurled the hydrians into the air like rockets. The giant squids reached toward Joey, who kept soaring, desperate to escape. The little starship rumbled and rattled and wailed.

"What's wrong, Joey?" Marco said. "You with me, babe?"

"I don't think I can fly to space," she said. "I can't rise so high, or it'll break my hull." She wailed. "I need lower altitude, or I'll burst!"

Addy checked the dashboard stats, chewing her lip. "She ain't lying."

Marco cursed. He leveled off, then swooped. The hydrians wailed in delight. Their tentacles were everywhere. One of the armored limbs hit Joey's starboard hull. She yelped and tumbled through space. Another tentacle tried to grab Joey but only knocked her aside. She rolled through the sky. Marco, Addy, and Einav jostled against their seat belts. It felt like riding the world's scariest roller coaster.

"Dammit, Addy, why didn't you fix the cannons!" Marco shouted, trying to steady their flight.

"You told me to fix the engines first."

"I never said that!" Joey was flying upside down now. "Admit it, Poet, this is all your fault."

Marco managed to right Joey. The little black starship raced across the landscape, and the hydrians followed, golden in the sunset. Marco counted five of them. Big bastards. Bigger than Joey and much meaner. Their inkblots flew, and it was all Marco could do to dodge them.

Einav unbuckled her seatbelt. "Marco, keep flying. Addy-- with me. We'll shoot from the airlock."

Addy's eyes lit up. "Best idea I've heard all day."

As Marco kept flying, desperate to dodge the tentacles, Addy and Einav raced into the hold. Within seconds, the two women were leaning out the open airlock, firing assault rifles. Plasma bolts bombarded the hydrians, chipping exoskeletons, but the beasts kept flying in pursuit. A barrage of inkblots flew. The tarry blobs came hurtling toward the open airlock.

"Hold on!" Marco cried from the cockpit.

He shoved the yoke, swooping. The inkblots flew overhead, missing the airlock and skimming Joey's dorsal hull. The quick dive had saved Addy and Einav, but it yanked both women off their feet. Einav flew, hit the top of the airlock, and rolled into the hold.

But Addy flew right out the airlock. She began tumbling to the ground below.

* * * * *

No.

Marco stared in terror.

Addy!

He swooped faster. Addy was spinning madly, hurtling toward the ground. A hyd rose from below, jaws opening wide to devour her.

Einav fired from the airlock. Plasma bolts hit the hyd in the eyes, and the alien recoiled.

Marco kept diving until he was flying level with Addy. Einav held onto the airlock rim with one hand. With the other hand, she reached out to Addy. She was too far! Marco tilted the yoke slightly, and the two women clasped hands.

Another hyd roared toward them, mouth open wide.

Marco soared and the beast snapped his jaws, nearly severing Addy's feet. She dangled in the air, clinging onto Einav's hand. Einav, the smaller of the two women, groaned and struggled but managed to pull Addy into the airlock.

Within seconds, both women were firing their rifles again. God bless those two!

Joey spiraled upward, etching a helix of fire across the sky. As Addy and Einav kept firing, plasma bolts flew in spiraling rings, forming a double helix with Joey's wake. Both streams of fire burned the hydrians. The aliens kept chasing through the flame. Plasma bolts burned and cracked their carapace, but it wasn't enough to kill them.

Killing full-grown hyds with mere rifles was hard work. Marco knew that from experience. It took a lot of concentrated fire at close range. The companions had slain a hyd on the ground at Or Midbar. But it was harder from the air, especially with five of the bastards attacking.

They were flying over the shallow waters of the Mediterranean now, spiraling farther away from the lost fleet. The setting sun painted the water blood-red, a fitting background to this grim battle. Dammit, without cannons, what could Marco do?

Then he had an idea.

"Girls, hold on!" he said.

Addy and Einav tightened their grips on the airlock handles.

Marco swerved, then swooped hard. He raced toward one of the hydrians. The gargantuan squid rumbled and reached out its many tentacles. The blades inside the suction cups whirred. Marco zigzagged between the tentacles, barely dodging them, until he flew right over the hyd's widening mouth. The beast licked its chops and reared higher, prepared to devour Joey.

Marco yanked the yoke, pulled the prow skyward, and shoved down the afterburner lever.

A roar of flames leaped from Joey's stern.

The starship screamed. "Ah, my exhaust coils!"

She rocketed skyward on a pillar of fire. The inferno washed over the hyd below, blazing into the alien's mouth, then burning through its guts. The creature grumbled and curled its tentacles inward like a wounded spider. The fire spread inside the alien, leaking through joints in its exoskeleton. Then, like the bloated old corpse of a beached whale, the hyd exploded.

Chunks of carapace flew every which way. Some pinged against Joey. One shard--as large as a dinner plate--flew right between Addy and Einav's heads and slammed into the inner bulkhead. It wobbled in the wall like a dagger tossed into a tree trunk. Along with the bits of exoskeleton flew huge globs of flesh and guts. Severed tentacles tumbled through the sky, spilling ink.

A geyser of ink spilled across a living hyd. The creature roared and covered its eyes. The ink began devouring its exoskeleton and burning the flesh within, for the hydrians were not immune to their venom. The sizzling creature crashed into the sea and raised a cloud of steam.

That left three hydrians. Better odds but not great. Joey was low on fuel. Most likely, she could not blast more afterburner. Einav and Addy were still firing out the airlock, but their small plasma rifles did only limited damage. If Einav still had her starhand, she could wield terrible destruction. But like Joey's cannons, the starhand was still broken.

Could they still escape? Marco didn't see how. With her regular engine, Joey just wasn't fast enough. Her warp drive would do the trick. But if Joey was too weak even to reach space, she sure as hell couldn't use her warp drive.

Or could she? Marco thought.

You weren't supposed to use warp drives near a planet. Certainly not inside a planet's atmosphere. Warp drives ran on azoth crystals. They could bend spacetime itself--the very fabric of the universe. Using them near a planet could crack open the surface, devour cities, and topple mountains. All modern starships came with software that detected when a starship was near a planet (or any object with a large enough gravitation field). If so, the software refused to turn on the warp drive. But Marco had seen it done before. Completely illegal, of course. But doable.

"Joey?" he said. "If I ordered you to turn on your warp drive right now, would you do it?"

"What?" she cried.

She was racing over the water now, heading toward Greece. The hydrians chased her, skimming the sea. The setting sun touched the water, casting glimmering brass light across the scene.

"Joey, would you do it?"

"You know I can't! My software forbids it. Also my common sense! I told you I can't fly to space."

Marco bit his lip. He looked down at the dashboard. They were over water, at least, not solid land. It was the only way.

"Joey, forgive me."

He ripped off her dashboard, exposing the cables and tubes beneath. She screamed.

"Marco, what are you doing?"

"Addy?" he shouted. "Einav? Get inside! Close the airlock."

"What?" Addy cried. She was leaning out the airlock, firing

at the pursuing hydrians.

"I'm about to turn the warp drive on."

"What?" Einav shouted.

"Hold on!" he said.

He reached inside Joey's exposed dashboard, rummaging through cables and bundles of wire. He thought he knew how to do this. He had seen it done before. In videos. Videos of different starships with different specs. Videos that might be fake. Ah, hell, here went nothing.

He found the gears that could activate the warp drive. Ignoring Joey's cries of protest, he yanked on the damn things himself.

For a second--nothing happened.

He was blind.

Nothing but white light.

He released the gears, and the warp drive shut off.

Marco blinked. Where was he?

For a disorienting moment, he had no idea where he was. Who he was. What the hell had happened? Was he asleep?

He blinked. As spacetime smoothed out, it slowly came back. He was Marco. He had been fleeing the hydrians and . . .

They were in space.

In a single second, they had blasted across the surface of the Earth, skidded into space, and were halfway to the moon.

"Joey?" he whispered.

She didn't answer.

Marco ran into the hold. "Addy! Einav!"

They sat on the deck, groaning. Addy rubbed her temples, and Einav blinked and shook her head wildly.

"Thank God you're alive," Marco said.

Addy pushed herself to her feet, swayed toward him, and grabbed his collar. Her eyes blazed, and she bared her teeth. "Marco?"

He gulped. "Yes?"

She yanked him closer and kissed him on the lips. "You are a genius."

"I might have killed Joey," he said. Her primary engine seemed to be off, though thankfully her life support system was still pumping away.

They all returned to the cockpit. Marco reattached the dashboard. "Joey?" he said. "Joey, you with me?"

For a long moment--silence

Then she whimpered. "My wings blew off."

Marco blinked. "Your . . . wings blew off?"

"You blew them off, Marco. Like a wanton boy ripping the wings off a butterfly. Oh, I've been crippled! I'm a monster now. A monster!"

Marco peeked out the side viewports. He gave a low whistle. "Well, I'll be. Blown right off."

Addy blinked. "Damn. She really is crippled." She shrugged. "Well, at least we humans are still in one piece." She glanced at Einav's stump. "Oh, sorry, Nav Nav."

"Um, guys?" Joey said. "My sensors are picking up something. Three hydrians are heading our way. They can see me. And they're coming in fast."

* * * * *

Marco winced. Dammit. Normally Joey was an absolute beast of battle. But she had lost her ultrablack coating, making her visible to her enemies. Her cannons were out of commission. Now her wings were gone too, meaning she could no longer fly in atmosphere, only here in space. And, just to make this a perfect storm, she was almost out of fuel.

Marco saw them now on the viewport. Three hydrians were flying across space. Their strange propulsion systems spun and crackled like red stars. Hydrians had azoth crystals in their heads and could travel faster than light, though right now, they seemed to be traveling at sub-light speed.

"How long before they reach us?" Marco said.

Einav sat down beside him in the cockpit. She studied the data. "They're moving slower than usual. They don't want to overshoot us." She chewed her lip. "We have about ten minutes before they get here. Maybe fifteen."

Marco wiped his brow. "So we're fine. Joey, activate warp speed and blast off."

"No can do, boss," the ship said. "Not enough juice. You burned all my warp sparks with that jump. I ain't warping anywhere before a visit to the hardware store."

Marco blinked. "Warp sparks? What are those?"

Addy slapped the back of his head. "You dumbass. Don't you know how Joey works?"

He bristled. "I knew enough to activate her warp drive manually!"

"Yeah, and burned up all her warp sparks." Addy snorted. "Dumbass."

Marco pursed his lips, thinking. "So we have three galactopods on our tail. No cannons. No warp drive. No weapons aside from a few rifles, and even those are low on ammo. Dammit! I wish we still had Einav's starhand. That weapon would sure come in handy." He paused. "Get it? Handy?"

Addy shook her head in disgust.

Marco looked over his shoulder through the cockpit door. Inside the back cabin, the starhand lay on a tabletop. Addy had assembled parts of it, but not the whole thing.

"I can fix it," Addy said.

"Addy, it took you days to get this far," Marco said. "And you're only halfway through."

"Yeah, but I spent those days dicking around. When it's an

Daniel Arenson

emergency I get superpowers." Addy raced into the hold. "I can do it! I can fix it."

She plopped herself down by the table, grabbed her tools, and began working in a fury, attaching little hooks and gears.

Marco looked at Einav, who still sat beside him in the cockpit. "She has meat hooks that can knock down a horse with one punch, but her fingers are nimble enough for the tiniest screws. It really is something."

A clatter sounded from the hold.

"Fuck, I dropped the screws! Anyone got a magnet? And maybe a metal detector."

Marco sighed. "Never mind."

He looked at the rearview monitor to check on the hydrians' progress. But he found the monitor dead. He tapped it, then banged it.

"Joey, you with me?"

"My stern sensors are on the fritz," she said.

Marco banged the viewport harder. Nothing.

"Marco, the sensors are on the stern," Einav said. "Hitting the screen won't help."

"Sure feels good, though," Marco said. "Einav, take the wheel. I'm going out there. I'll see if I can fix the sensors."

He leaped to his feet, hurried into the hold, and grabbed a spacesuit from the closet. Addy looked up from the table, busy working on the starhand.

"Going for a little constitutional, husband dearest?"

"Going to fix the stern sensors, since *somebody* did a sloppy job fixing them."

"Those will take hours to fix," Addy said. "We have only minutes."

"I can fix it."

Marco pulled on his spacesuit. Within moments, he was in the airlock. He clipped on a safety tether, and into space he

80

jumped.

He floated in the void, attached to Joey by a thin cable. From this distance, he could not see the hydrians with the naked eye. If they could camouflage themselves now, they would be even harder to spot. But the sensors would see them.

Marco pulled himself along Joey's hull until he reached her stern. The engines were rumbling, bathing space with heat. The warp drive was broken, but her regular engines were still roaring hot. Marco winced and climbed onto the dorsal hull. He walked along Joey's top until he reached the stern, then leaned over and saw the blue-hot exhaust ports below.

The sensors were there. Right above the exhaust ports. He saw the problem at once.

"Addy!" he said into his comlink. "What putty did you use when you reattached the sensors?"

"None," she said. "I screwed them in. Now shut up, I'm busy fixing the starhand."

Marco groaned. Yeah, there was the problem. The sensors were screwed in tightly enough, but along their rims, tiny openings let in heat from the engines. The heat was likely mucking up the readings. Marco would need to apply some putty, welding metal, or other material to block the heat.

"Addy, do we have any of that cooling caulk left?"

"I said--shut up! I'm busy. Deal with your job, Poet, and let me deal with mine."

Marco cursed. He had only moments before the hydrians arrived. At least he thought he did. Without the sensors, who knew? Ah, dammit. He didn't have time for this. He leaped off the dorsal hull. Like Tarzan on a vine, he swung on his tether and tumbled back into the airlock, banging himself against the inner door. He rummaged through the emergency repair closet, searching for anything. Ah, there! Cooling foam! Normally used to put out fires. Well, it would have to do for now.

He leaped out. Again he executed his Tarzan move, swinging on the tether through space. He thumped onto the dorsal hull above the exhaust ports. They blazed with blue heat.

"Marco, can you hurry up?" Einav said from the cockpit.

"On it, Einav!"

He yanked the pin off the can of foam and sprayed. The white foam wrapped around the sensors where they met the hull, sealing the cracks. Marco had to work carefully. He didn't want to jam the sensors themselves, only insulate them, blocking the terrible heat of the engines.

"It worked!" Einav said over the comlink. "Marco, we got a sensor reading. The hyds are close. Damn, they're close! Get back inside."

Marco peered into the distance, seeking them. With his naked eyes, he still could not see them. But human eyes had not evolved for space. He trusted the sensors. Again he channeled his inner Tarzan, swung on the tether, and crashed into the airlock. Amazingly, he landed on his feet this time.

I'm getting the hang of this, he thought.

He ran through the hold.

"Addy, how's it going?" he said.

"Almost done." She held up the starhand. "I just need to embed the Mariner's Tear in the palm."

"Hurry!" Marco said.

"Never rush an artist," she replied. "Would you rush Michaelangelo?"

"Addy, you once asked me how Michaelangelo painted the Sistine Chapel if he lived in the sewer. Just focus on the hand."

Leaving his wife to her artistry, Marco entered the cockpit. Einav sat at the helm, staring at the rearview monitor. Marco saw them now. Not three hydrians but a whole nine. So they had brought some friends. They were shoaling across space, their propulsion systems blazing white, their eyes red with fury. They were gaining on Joey. By the looks of it, they were only a minute or two away. Marco winced.

"Give me the wheel," he said to Einav. "Addy's almost done. Go do your magic."

Einav nodded and leaped from her seat. She paused, touched Marco's cheek, and looked into his eyes. Her look only lasted a second. But it spoke of their century of friendship. Of the love she held for him. It was a look that said she trusted him. A look that said: *If this is the last time I see you--goodbye, my dearest friend.*

Then she was racing into the hold, and Marco took the yoke.

* * * * *

As Marco flew onward through space, he stared at the rearview monitor. The sensors showed the hydrians getting closer. Closer. Their eyes blazed, and their tentacles reached out. Once they were in range, they would be spewing their noxious ink. With Joey's sorry state, they could not survive nine.

The galactopods came racing closer. So close they were right on Joey's tail.

"Addy!" Marco cried from the cockpit. "You almost done back there?"

She didn't answer.

The hydrians grinned, their jaws opening to reveal their ravenous maws and rows of teeth. Their tentacles extended like hungry serpents and spewed their malodorous venom.

Marco pulled the yoke left and right, up and down, slewing and rolling, pitching and yawing, dodging inkblot after inkblot. He couldn't keep this up much longer. The hydrians were still gaining on him. Every moment, they were closer, and it became harder to dodge their barrage.

"Let me fly," Joey said. "You go shoot out the airlock."

"You're not ready," Marco said. "I never taught you evasive maneuvers."

"I'll figure it out."

Marco hesitated. Could he trust her? Joey often flew on autopilot during peaceful times. But in battle?

"I can do it!" she said as inkblots flew all around.

Marco nodded. "You got the wheel."

He tapped a button, giving her control, and she began flying at once, dodging more inkblots. Well, Marco hadn't died instantly. That was a good sign.

He raced into the hold to see Einav lifting the starhand. The Mariner's Tear gleamed in her palm.

"It's fixed," Addy said.

"Took you long enough," Marco said.

On the stump of her left arm, Einav already wore her docking bay--an electronic cap that connected to her nerve endings. As Joey flew wildly from side to side, Einav snapped the starhand onto the docking bay. The filigree along the ivory fingers glowed. The Mariner's Tear shone with purple light.

"I'll cover you," Marco said, grabbing a rifle from the closet.

"We both will," said Addy, grabbing her bazooka. "And I'll bring some real firepower." She had always been a show-off.

Wearing their spacesuits, tethered to the starship, the trio leaped into space with their weapons. Plasma rifle. Bazooka. And a slender hand made of hellephant ivory, delicate gears, and the most powerful crystal in the galaxy.

Before them rose the enemy. Nine hyds, rumbling for war. Each was larger than Joey. Their exoskeletons were an odd mix of organic and mechanical. Cuneiform runes blazed on their carapace hulls, spelling out names of doom. Their eyes shone crimson behind bulging portholes like glass canopies. As predators on Earth evolved to hunt on land, underwater, or in the sky, these predators evolved to hunt in space. And they were very good at it.

The inkblots kept flying. The tarry projectiles chased Joey through space, following her like heat-seeking missiles. Eventually inkblots lost their way and vanished into the distance, but not before giving a good chase. Joey was whipping from side to side, dodging more and more inkblots. The breakneck maneuvers sent Marco, Addy, and Einav flailing around like tetherballs.

"Joey, careful!" Marco said.

"You told me to dodge the inkblots!"

"Yes, just not so violently!"

As he was shouting, Addy managed to aim her bazooka. Even as Joey was whipping around, Addy fired the enormous gun.

A shell blasted forth.

Addy flew backward and nearly snapped her tether off.

The shell streaked forth and slammed into one hydrian, hitting the kraken right on the prow.

The warhead burst. A hole blasted open on the hydrian's exoskeleton. Chunks of brain flew into the distance. With them flew an azoth crystal--the raw, rough stones the hydrians grew inside their skulls, letting them fly faster than light.

"Ooh yeah!" Addy cried. "Take that, you dirty squid. I got another one coming, you bastard!" She laughed manically, dangling on her tether, and loaded a second warhead.

Marco was busy firing his assault rifle. The gun boomed again and again in his hand. There was no sound in space, but he heard the blasts rippling through his spacesuit, through his very bones. The bolts flew toward the hydrians. Marco's gun was less powerful than Addy's bazooka. But he had many plasma packs, and they added up. He concentrated his fire on one hyd's eye. He scored several direct hits. The glass bulb protecting the eye cracked. Another few blasts, and it shattered. Marco kept firing, filling the alien's eyeball with red-hot plasma. The hyd squealed and tumbled backward in space.

"Got one!" Marco said. "We're tied now."

"Yours is still alive!" Addy said.

"Bullshit, he's dead. Look, he's not moving."

Addy fired her bazooka. Her shell slammed into the hyd Marco had blinded. The squid's head burst, scattering chunks of carapace, skull, and brain.

"Now he's dead," Addy said. "Two for me, zero for you."

"Addy, stop wasting ammo on dead hydrians. Shoot the living ones."

"I am!" she cried.

They continued the bombardment. Meanwhile, Joey was still flying like a maniac. The inkblots were flying all around. One globule splashed Joey's hull, sizzling across the metal. Droplets hit Marco's leg and began corroding the spacesuit. He cursed and shook them off before they could devour the fabric.

It was getting harder and harder to stop that ink. Several globules came flying right at Joey. She swerved left and right, but one blob came right at them. Marco fired his rifle, holding down the trigger. A torrent of plasma tore the inkblot apart. The droplets scattered only meters away.

When he paused to reload, he glanced at Einav. "You all right, Einav?"

She was floating in space, her eyes closed. Only the tether held her to the ship. Her starhand was glowing.

"Einav!" Addy shouted. "What's wrong?"

"The battery," she said softly, eyes still closed. "My starhand battery. It's empty."

"Dammit!" Addy said. "I knew I forgot to do something. Shoulda charged that bitch."

The hint of a smile curled Einav's lips. "There is a power inside me. Inside every man and woman. It is the power of the human spirit. I must reconnect with mine."

"You better reconnect fast, Nav Nav," Addy muttered, "or your internal power will be splattered across Joey's hull."

Marco fired another burst of plasma, shattering another inkblot. Damn, the hydrians were getting close! He hit another creature in the eye, knocking it backward. Addy took out yet another with her bazooka. But the survivors kept flying. They were only a few klicks away now. The ink surged forth. Joey flew like a deranged bee, racing in spirals. An inkblot hit her stern. She yowled, and one of her engines died. The ship slewed.

And then the hyds reached them.

The aliens swooped from above and soared from below. A tentacle grabbed Joey and began crushing her hull. Marco screamed and fired at the tentacle. Addy's harness tore free. She tumbled backward in space.

"Addy!" Marco cried.

The tentacle tightened, and Joey's hull gave a loud *crack*. Another hyd rose from below and reached for the little starship, and--

Purple light flowed.

A shock wave blasted out, knocking back the hyds.

Severed tentacles flew. The creatures tumbled, shrieking silently into the void, their carapaces cracked.

Through the lavender glow she ascended, an angel wreathed in luminosity, her eyes like gleaming stars: Einav Ben-Ari, her starhand alight. The hydrians cowered, covering their eyes. But Einav showed them no mercy. She held out her starhand, rippling space and time, blasting out a funnel of her fury. The rippling maelstrom plowed into the hydrians, knocked them back, and shattered their exoskeletons. Their soft, wriggling innards pulsed like oysters in the shell, exposed hearts still beating.

A growl rose in Marco's throat. He fired at those rancid hearts. They burst, scattering dark blood across space. He tore them one by one. Finally the last foul beast gurgled, curled up, and died.

The battle was over. The hydrians were dead.

The light faded.

Einav's eyes darkened, and she floated limply in space.

* * * * *

Joey steadied her flight. Marco kicked off her hull, floated through space until his tether snapped taut, reached out, and grabbed Einav's hand. For a terrible moment, Marco thought she had died, that she had drained all her inner strength until her heart had stopped. But then her hand tightened around his, and he pulled her into Joey's airlock.

"Hey!" Addy cried over the comlink. She was floating a few miles away by now. "Hey, what about me?"

Marco ignored his wife. Addy was unhurt and would be fine floating around for a while. He carried Einav into the hold and laid her down on the bed. He pulled off her helmet, revealing a pale face and hair drenched with sweat. Her eyes were shut.

"Einav?" Marco caressed her cheek. "You still with me?"

She gave a soft smile and breathed deeply, chest rising and falling.

Marco lowered his head, overcome with emotion.

"Thank God," he whispered. "You're alive."

As the adrenaline of the battle wore off, his anxiety, grief, and terror rushed in to fill the void. For a moment, Marco trembled, tears in his eyes. He lay down beside the slumbering Einav, held her hand, and just breathed. His eyes stung and tears ran down his cheeks.

I lost my family, he thought. *I lost my kids, I lost everything, but I still have Einav. My leader. My bedrock. I could not have gone on without her.*

"Hey!" Addy cried over the comlink. "Did you forget me,

dumbass? Still waiting for rescue here!"

Marco wiped his eyes and laughed. Yes, and he had Addy too. Truly he was blessed.

"Sorry, Ads," he said. "Joey? Can you find my wife?"

"Compliance!" said the starship. The deck tilted as Joey flew off to find her.

Soon Addy was stumbling into the hold, rubbing her neck. "Damn, that bazooka has some recoil. You ever fire one of those bitches?" She saw Marco and Einav lying on the bed and frowned. "Hey, what you two doing?"

"Einav is asleep," Marco said.

Addy tossed her helmet and bazooka aside. They clanged but Einav was so weary she didn't even wake. Addy hopped onto the bed with them. She clasped Marco's hand, and her warm touch comforted him. He looked at her, at his beautiful wife, the love of his life.

"Addy, you kicked ass out there," he said.

She nodded. "I did."

"I love you."

"I know." Addy smiled and bit her lip. "I killed more hydrians than you."

"Einav put us both to shame."

They looked at her. In her sleep, Einav's face was calm. All her sternness, her strength, her iron will--in sleep those layers of armor peeled back. Her eyelids fluttered open, and she looked at them.

"Everyone still alive?" Einav whispered.

"Yes," Marco said.

"Well, not the hydrians."

"Good," Einav whispered, and once more she slept. Marco had seen it before. The starhand draining her. She would need another day or two to recover. They all would.

For a long time, Marco just lay there between them. His

captain. His wife. His two best friends. He had lost so much, but he had them, and they filled his heart and soul and lit his life. Yes, he was blessed. His cup overflowed.

CHAPTER SIX
The Treasures of Darktech Cove

The trio slept the deep, dreamless sleep of weary soldiers. Marco had learned something during his long wars. It was after the war ended, after you returned home, that the nightmares haunted you. During the wars themselves, Marco had always been able to sleep deeply. Perhaps it was the weariness of past battles. Or perhaps his body knew he must rest for the battles ahead. Whatever the case, his wartime sleep was often as deep and dreamless as death.

While the trio slept, Joey kept guard. Thankfully no more hydrians arrived. Joey still needed to get a new ultrablack coat. That was okay. They were in deep space now. A ship so small drowned in the vastness. Nobody would see Joey out here. For now, floating in space, they were safe.

When they finally woke up from their deathlike slumber, they packed the bed away, unfolded the table, and sat down for breakfast. Despite all the damage Joey had taken, her larder remained in good shape. A few jars of pickles had fallen and shattered, but everything packed in boxes and cans was fine. They fried bacon, spread strawberry jam on toast, and drank strong coffee. Even Einav, normally a tea drinker, drank two cups of the black stuff. When their bellies were full and their brains caffeinated, they must decide how to proceed.

"So we know where the Phoenix Fleet is," Marco said. "But the hydrians guard it."

"And those fuckers can camouflage themselves now," Addy said. "Where the hell did they learn how to do that?"

"Genetic engineering, maybe," Einav said. "They battled the Menorians over Mars. The Menorians can camouflage their bodies like that. The hydrians might have captured some Menorians. Dug out their camouflage genes and wove them into their DNA."

"Those squids are smart enough for that?" Addy said. "They're just animals, Einav."

"They gave Erafel tentacles," Marco reminded her. "They're creepily good at genetic engineering."

Addy slapped the back of his head. "I was talking to Einav, not you, nerd."

"Ow." Marco shoved her away. "In any case, the hydrians are guarding the Phoenix Fleet, and with or without camouflage, they're tough bastards. They probably tripled their guard since our battle. How do we get the fleet now?"

"Hang on, hang on!" Addy said, leaping to her feet. "Why are the hydrians guarding the ships? Why didn't they just blow them up?"

Marco thought for a moment. "I . . . don't know."

"Because they don't need to," Einav said. "Those ships are grounded. Crewless. Probably disarmed too. Hydrians don't use explosives. They use ink. Melting dreadnoughts is no easy task, even for a hydrian. Some of those ships are a mile long. Melting that much ship would take far more ink than a few hydrians have. The bulk of the shoal could destroy them, yes, but not the watchdogs here to guard Hart. They don't *need* to destroy the ships. They're out of the commission. Hart dumped them in the sea to rust."

Addy bit down on a hot dog. "Well, I can fix 'em. We'll summon an army, destroy the guards, and reclaim the ships!"

"Where did you get that hot dog?" Marco said.

"From my pocket."

Marco blinked. "You had a hot dog in your pocket?"

Addy shrugged. "I always keep hot dogs in my pocket. You know that."

"I did not know that!"

Addy took another bite. "You never know when you might want a--" She coughed and stuck out her tongue. "Eww, I think I just ate some lint."

"I love you, Addy."

"Eww, eww!" She coughed and scraped her tongue. "I think there was an ant on there." She looked up at Marco. "What?"

"I love you, Addy. Just so you know." A lump filled his throat. "Only days ago, we saw thousands of our troops die. We saw millions perish on Mars. We saw genocide, and it's eating me up inside, and I couldn't keep going without you, Addy." He turned toward Einav. "Or you, Einav. I'm sorry. I'm getting sentimental. These past few days are getting to me."

Addy smacked the back of his head. "So man up and stop moping!" Then she hugged him and kissed his cheek. "I love you too, dumbass. Cheer up. We're gonna win this thing."

With her filigreed ivory hand, Einav lifted her teacup and sipped. She thought for a moment, then nodded. "We'll return to the Phoenix Fleet, but not alone. We'll summon help."

Marco heaved a sigh. "What help? Our army on Mars was wiped out."

"I don't mean the Martian army, Marco." Einav placed down her mug. "The Human Defense Force. The military of Earth."

Addy raised her fist. "Hell yeah!"

Marco shook his head. "In case you guys missed it, we're no longer officers in the Human Defense Force. We haven't been for decades. And last time we met, the HDF tried to kill us."

Einav gazed out a digital porthole into space. She spoke softly. "Everything is different now. Humans fought humans for

Daniel Arenson

too long. But now all humans will unite against the shoal. Yes, even the HDF."

"Tell that to Hart," Marco muttered.

Addy smacked the back of his head again. "I told you to stop moping!"

"I'm not moping. I'm being realistic," Marco said. "Hart is the supreme commander of the HDF. Or what's left of the HDF, at least. And he grounded their ships. He disbanded the entire goddamn military. What will we do? Go to a military base and rouse the marines? The bases will be empty and closed. Abandoned like the warships." He laughed bitterly. "All part of Hart's deal with the devil. He neutered Earth, put a collar around the planet, and handed the leash to Erafel."

Addy shrugged. "Hey, don't kinkshame."

"It takes a while to demilitarize a planet," Einav said. "The ships haven't rusted yet. And while the military bases might be closed, the soldiers are still alive. Still trained. And I bet you they're raring to kill some squids."

"How do we find them?" Marco said.

Addy raised her fist again. "We'll broadcast a call to action! We'll fly around with speakers, calling men and women from their homes. Grab a gun, join us, fight with us! We'll raise the masses against the--"

"No," Einav said. "That would invite quick reprisal from the shoal. I think a little more circumspection is in order. Joey, can you take us back to Earth?"

The starship's moan emerged through a speaker. "My warp drive is still busted. I can fly the slow way. We can be at Earth within a month."

Addy gasped. "But I only have five hot dog packages left! I'll starve by then."

"So fix my warp drive, dummy," Joey said.

Addy crossed her arms. "I did. Marco blew out your warp

spark coils. You need new ones. And fresh bores for your cannons. And a new exhaust calibration system. And a new coating of ultrablack paint. I know I'm a great mechanic, but I can't pull these parts out of my ass."

"Why not?" Marco said. "You certainly have enough trunk space."

She punched him.

Einav stifled a smile. "I think I know where we can fix you up, Joey. There's a place I know. Not far away from here. Hidden in the asteroid belt. Can you limp along a bit on your thrusters?"

"If Addy gets out and pushes," Joey said, "yes, I think I can."

Einav walked toward the cockpit. "Come on, then. Let's get going."

* * * * *

Leaving a trail of smoke and fallen screws, Joey limped across space toward the asteroid belt. Marco's beloved ship was in pain, and his heart hurt for her.

"We're not a trio," he whispered to her, caressing her dashboard. "We're a quartet. You're one of us, Joey."

Addy shook her head in wonder. "Amazing. And you say I'm crazy when I talk to Princess Slicey." She patted the katana, which lay sheathed across her lap.

"Your katana can't talk back," Marco said.

Addy solemnly drew the sword. "She speaks the language of the blade." She slashed the air, nearly taking off Marco's ear.

"Put that thing away before you chop somebody's head off," Marco said.

Addy kissed the gleaming steel. "Aww, don't listen to him, Princess Slicey. He's just a crazy old man who talks to inanimate objects."

"I am not inanimate!" Joey said.

"With your busted warp drive, you kind of are," Addy said.

Indeed, Joey was gliding on momentum alone. Every once in a while, one of her side thrusters released some steam, correcting her course. Like a piece of space junk, she tumbled onward to her destination.

Millions of asteroids composed the asteroid belt that ringed the solar system. In schoolbook illustrations, it often appeared like a dense cluster of rocks, dangerous to travail. In real life, the asteroids were thinly dispersed across a massive area. Most of the belt was empty space. Billions of years ago, the belt had been denser, clogged with countless asteroids. Indeed, back then, it looked more like the classic depiction. But over time, most of the asteroids had flown off, collided with planets, clustered together, and were otherwise lost. Only the last dregs remained. Today this wasteland spread in a vast ring beyond the orbit of Mars. Even today, centuries into the space age, most of the asteroids remained unexplored. The largest one, Ceres, was home to a thriving colony of humans. Other asteroids were barely larger than Joey.

"See that big lumpy one?" Einav pointed with an ivory finger. "Head there, Joey."

The little starship dutifully limped her way over. Marco examined the asteroid. It looked like any other rock. For an asteroid, it was large. About the size of a city. But in the asteroid belt, it was just one out of a million rocks. Gray, lumpy, uninspiring.

Addy patted Einav on the shoulder. "Great! You found a space potato."

Einav smiled. "You're looking at Corymbus. A lesser-known asteroid. At least it's called Corymbus on official star charts. To the underworld, it's known as Darktech Cove."

Addy's eyes widened. "Wait a minute! *This* is Darktech Cove?" She leaned toward the view. "I've heard of this place! A mechanic's paradise."

Einav nodded. "Even back in the days of my presidency, it was a haven for smugglers, genetic hackers, black hat engineers, and underground mechanics. We'll find the parts we need here."

Joey made a gulping noise. "Black hat engineers? Underground mechanics? That doesn't sound safe."

"It's not," Einav confessed. "This is a seedy part of the galaxy. There's plenty of engineering that's illegal. Antimatter thrusters, for example. They're fast but they can vaporize anyone within a million miles behind them. Darkwarp drives. They use black azoth, a crystal that's synthesized in labs. It can bend spacetime and leave it bent forever, permanently damaging the very fabric of our universe. Lots of engineering is dangerous. The people who want the illegal stuff come to Darktech Cove."

"Where has this place been all my life!" Addy cried. "I can't believe you kept this hidden from me, Einav. This is my paradise! My nirvana! My palace of forbidden delights!"

"Great, now Addy will blow our life savings here," Marco muttered.

"Oh, shut up, you waste all our money whenever you visit a bookstore."

Joey cleared her throat. Or at least made the appropriate sound. "I don't want any darkwarp drive, thank you very much."

"But you do want another ultrablack coat, right?" said Einav. "We'll find that here. If I'm right, this is where Joey was probably built in the first place."

Marco gasped. "What? I bought her from a reputable dealer! Well, one listed online, yes. And I did have to pick her up behind a gas station. But--no! She couldn't have come from here."

Einav shrugged. "Maybe not. But Joey had an ultrablack

coat. That's not available on any legit Earth market. And neutron cannons. Which, Marco, happen to be illegal."

He felt the blood drain from his face. "They are?"

"Most definitely," said Einav. "You bought an illegal starship, my dear. Probably from a smuggler. My guess is that our dear Joey was born here in this giant space potato."

Addy frowned and tilted her head. "How do you know about a sleazy place like this, Einav? I mean, if anyone should know about a joint like this, it's me."

The former president smiled. "I used to be a politician, darling. I know every sleazy corner of the galaxy. Compared to politicians, Addy, you're downright angelic."

"I'm certainly as beautiful as an angel," Addy said.

"A biblically accurate one, maybe," said Marco, earning a punch to the arm.

As they approached the asteroid, starfighters emerged from behind the giant lumpy rock. They raced toward Joey. They didn't look like any military starfighter Marco had ever seen. They looked more like metal porcupines bristling with cannons. No two were the same. The weapons had been welded on--plasma cannons, neutron blasters, photon launchers, graviton disruptors, and various other weapons Marco didn't recognize. Some guns had even been welded onto larger guns, forming fractals of destruction. He wouldn't want to tussle with these ships.

The trio sat in Joey's cockpit, facing the incoming bogeys--Marco at the helm, Einav in the captain's seat, and Addy at the gunnery station (where she no doubt felt useless, what with Joey's cannons out of order).

"Guys, they're coming real close," Joey said.

A message came from one of the flying arsenals. The voice was grainy and robotic. "Who dares approach the gates of dawn at the hour of darkness?"

Marco frowned. He looked at the others and hit the mute

button. "Some kind of code?"

Einav turned on the mic and spoke to the ships. "It is I, the seeker of lost treasures along the moonlit path from the sea."

For a long moment--silence. Then the ships turned away. "Follow."

Einav relaxed. "Ah, good. The old codes still work."

Marco gaped at her. "You know the codes to enter Darktech Cove?"

She shrugged. "Well, where do you think the HDF gets its best tech? I used to come shopping here all the time. Undercover, of course." Einav smiled. "This is where I found my best weapons."

Marco shook his head in wonder. "We're learning all sorts of secrets about our dear friend."

"Nav Nav, you have a wicked side." Addy mussed her hair. "And I like it."

As they flew closer to the asteroid, a chunk of its rocky surface moved, revealing itself to be a hidden door. The enormous door of stone slid into a hidden compartment. An opening gaped on the asteroid, large enough for a frigate to fly through. It was not some dark opening like a cave. This entrance glittered with particolored lights like a geode. On the inside, Darktech Cove was anything but dark.

Coughing out smoke, leaving a trail of loose screws, Joey skittered into the forbidden asteroid.

* * * * *

The asteroid was the size of a city, and a city they found. The hollow heart of Corymbus thrummed with ships zipping back and forth. Smugglers were loading their cargo bays with crates full of contraband treasures. Tankers were filling up with illegal, highly-toxic plutonium fuel. A floating brothel was offloading damaged sexbots for repairs. Bounty hunter ships limped in from battle, looking to repair their hulls and cannons. Tuggers raced back and forth to haul damaged ships. An enormous, vertical shipyard grew through the asteroid's center like a great tree, sprouting docks like branches. Thousands of ships docked along the metal boughs, bustling with mechanics.

The treelike shipyard wasn't the only reason ships came here. Countless shops honeycombed the round, rocky surface of Corymbus, surrounding the shipyard like a Dyson sphere. Signs glowed above the storefronts, announcing the wares within. This wasn't just a place for repairs but for shopping. As Joey flew along the inner surface, Marco gaped at some of the establishments.

"We might find a place that sells the parts we need," Einav said. "Keep an eye open, everyone."

They flew by the shops. The Quantum Enigma sold pocket watches that could manipulate time, quantum keys that could hack any lock, and even quantum portals that could shrink a ship into the size of a flea.

"Anything we need here?" Marco said.

"Everything," Addy said. "Every single thing in the shop. We need it."

"I mean for Joey."

Addy crossed her arms. "I suppose not."

They flew by a few other shops. Mindware Boutique sold neural implants, allowing humans to operate weapons telepathically, read minds, and hack into computer systems with thoughts alone. Meanwhile, the Gravity Girls sold forbidden graviton bombs. Toss them at an enemy, and gravity would reverse around him, hurling him toward the ceiling. Alien Relics Emporium sold forbidden alien tech--crowns that gave the wearer mind control, nanobots that could invade and destroy a man's heart, and wormhole generators that could carve through a planet.

"You know, normally I'm not one for shopping," Addy

said. "But can we go shopping?"

Marco shook his head. "No, Addy. We're low on funds. We need to save our money for Joey. We . . . We . . ."

Joey was now floating by a shop called Lovebot Labs. It sold alluring, sensual robots to fulfill every fantasy. A cowgirl, a geisha, and a scantily clad nurse stood in display cases, waving and winking at Marco. A few bots were even shaped like celebrities. Marco spent a little too long gaping at them, earning a jab from Addy's elbow.

"Don't even think about it."

"I was just looking."

"No looking!" Addy said. "We're here for business, remember? So stop staring at your filthy robots. We're in a rush to find parts, and . . . and . . ."

Joey was now floating by Genetic Joe, a black market bio-engineer. Joe promised to genetically modify you any way you liked. Want angel wings? Devil horns? How about a tiger's tail and fangs to match? Genetic Joe was your guy. The oddest customers hung around his shop. One was a human-reptile hybrid. Another man stood ten feet tall and sprouted bat wings. One man looked normal aside from gargantuan fists that were larger than pumpkins.

"Freaks, Poet!" Addy whispered, eyes wide. "Can we stop to look at the freaks?"

"What happened to being in a rush?"

Einav pointed. "There. We'll find what we need there."

Marco and Addy followed her gaze. They saw an enormous store, the largest they had seen so far. Mechanical letters, each the size of a house, floated above the store, covered with gears and cables and pistons, spelling the word: GEARMART.

"Gearmart!" Addy said. "Don't we have those on Earth?"

"We have GearSmart," Marco said. "With an s. This is

Gearmart. A ripoff."

"A ripoff with the best stuff!" Addy said, eyes wide.

Gargantuan display windows revealed a store packed full of engines, cannons, gears so large they could engulf houses, and innumerable other treasures.

Like the smaller shops, Gearmart was built into the inner, rounded surface of the asteroid. Several piers stuck out for small ships to dock. Smuggler haulers, pirate corvettes, and mercenary warships all crammed the docks. Marco saw quite a few alien ships too. One alien vessel looked like a giant aquarium; he could see the water through the windows. Another alien ship was a pulsing, oozing puffball, its fleshy hull sporting gray fuzz. A group of mushrooms emerged through a vent, clad in flowing crimson robes, and hopped toward the store's sliding doors.

The trio spent a while searching for a docking spot. Finally they found free space along a pier. Gingerly, they squeezed Joey between two larger starships. To her left loomed a starship made from a giant alien skull. It looked like a T-Rex the size of Godzilla. Glass filled the eye sockets, forming portholes, while cannons thrust between the mighty teeth. To Joey's left docked a pink puffball, which sprouted many swaying tendrils. It looked like a sea anemone the size of a house. The ship was oddly beautiful. Marco couldn't even guess what planet it came from. He had been traveling through space for over a century, but the galaxy was vast, its panoply of life dizzying. It would take multiple lifetimes to explore it all.

"Don't leave me here," Joey said. The starship trembled. "They'll eat me. Look at that giant skull ship beside me! A monster must have flown it. I'm too delicate to dock here."

"Oh, for crying out loud!" Addy said. "I thought you were a warship. Grow a backbone!"

"It's your fault," Joey said. "I used to be tough. You broke me."

Marco patted her dashboard. "I'll be just a shout away, babe. You got this."

He rose and left the cockpit, heading toward the airlock.

Addy followed him, slinging her katana across her back. "You always baby her."

Marco shrugged. Before entering the airlock, he opened the gun cabinet. "She's my baby. What can I do?"

"I thought I was your baby." Addy holstered a few handguns.

Marco chose a gun, hefted it, and holstered it. "You're my babe. She's my baby." He hopped out of the airlock onto the dock. "Big difference."

Addy hopped down beside him, faced the giant storefront, and took a deep breath. "Ah, smell it, Poet! Forbidden technology. A giant store full of illegal, experimental weapons that break every clause in the Third Geneva Convention." She wiped her eyes. "It's beautiful."

"And you say I never take you anywhere romantic."

Einav hopped out the airlock and joined them. She carried no guns, but she didn't need them. Her starhand was the only weapon she needed. She had replaced her old clothes, which the hydrian ink had consumed, with an identical outfit. Once again, she wore white trousers, white boots, and a white shirt with golden buckles along the side. The colors matched her hand of filigreed ivory. Her hair hung in a single blond braid across one shoulder. She looked like a true leader, Marco thought. Next to her, he felt shabby, wearing his old brown trousers, beaten-up vest, and bandoleers. He felt like a rough mercenary guarding a princess.

"I feel so underdressed," Addy said, echoing his thoughts.

"Me too," said Marco. "It's hard to compete with Einav's sense of style."

"No, I mean I forgot to put on pants."

Marco looked at Addy's bare legs and nearly fainted. Somehow, with all the stress, he had not noticed until now. His eyes bugged out. "*Addy!*"

Addy blushed and covered her Snoopy underwear.

"Be right back!" she said, hopping into Joey. Within moments, she returned, thankfully wearing a pair of brown trousers.

Einav heaved a sigh. "All right, guys. Stay vigilant. This is a rough hood."

Addy snorted. "Oh please. I grew up on the mean streets of Toronto in the smoldering ruins of the Cataclysm. I think I can handle myself."

"Um, Addy?" Marco pointed. "You forgot your shoes."

Addy looked down at her Woodstock socks. "Goddammit! Be right back again."

Marco looked at Einav. "It'll take her a while. Joey has a cockpit *and* a back room. She'll get lost."

Standing on the dock, Einav looked around at the bustling world of Darktech Cove. Standing here, facing the hollow bowels of the asteroid, they could see the towering shipyard that rose through the center of the asteroid like a massive tree, the countless starships zipping back and forth, and the endless shops that lined the inner surface.

"Look at this place, Marco," Einav said. "An entire hollow world, full of life. If the hydrians find this place, it will be extinguished. I wonder . . . if we need to evacuate Earth, can we bring refugees here? How many can this place sustain?" She shook her head sadly. "Not many. And without Earth to ship food and water . . ."

"Hey, chin up!" Marco said. "Talking of Earth's destruction? Earth still stands. We'll save the world. Like we always do."

Einav looked into his eyes and touched his cheek. "Like

we always do."

A deep voice rumbled behind them.

"Hey, squirts!"

Marco and Einav spun around. A towering, bipedal alien stood before them on the pier. Marco wasn't sure the species. The brute stood a dozen feet tall, covered with shaggy black fur. Four muscular arms sprouted from his torso, and each of his paws sprouted claws the size of Roman gladius swords. The face was vaguely canine, the snout long, the mouth full of fangs. The alien's eyes blazed orange like Halloween pumpkins. Bandoleers heavy with grenades, bullets, and blades crisscrossed his massive chest. The creature gave Marco the impression of some demonic werewolf from the sketchbook of a sadist.

Marco looked behind him, then back at the alien. "Pardon me, sir?"

Einav raised an eyebrow, and Marco swore he caught the hint of a smile on her lips.

She wants a fight! Marco thought. He understood that tiny smirk. He was used to Addy instigating fights. But Einav?

"You, squirts!" the towering, wolfish alien said. With a curved claw, he pointed at the starship docked beside Joey. "You scratched my ship."

Marco and Einav turned to look. Joey was still parked between two ships. To one side--the beautiful pink puffball that looked like a giant sea anemone or flower. The other side--the dinosaurian skull with engines, cannons, and blades attached. Marco safely assumed the slavering wolfman was referring to the skull-ship.

"It looks fine to me." Marco turned back toward the lupine alien. "I don't see a scratch on her."

Einav shrugged. "Looks fine to me too. She's a nice ship. Cool idea for a giant skull."

The wolfish alien snarled, dripping saliva. "That is not my

ship. *That* is my ship!"

He pointed at the pink puffball. Marco noticed it now. A slight scratch on one of the fuzzy, flowering buds.

"Oh yeah . . ." Marco squinted. "I see it now."

Einav was hiding her laughter behind her palm.

The brute stomped closer. With an enormous paw, he reached out to grab Marco. "You gonna pay for that scratch, squirt?"

Marco shrugged. "I guess so. How about a hundred credits for your trouble?"

The shaggy alien growled. His teeth gleamed, his orange eyes blazed, and saliva dripped from his jaws. "How about you pay with your life."

With a deafening howl and outstretched claws, the alien lunged at Marco.

Marco stepped back, smoking gun in hand.

The furry alien thumped onto the dock, a bullet hole in his forehead.

"Dammit, Marco!" Einav said. She held her starhand raised. It was glowing purple. "You killed him too fast. I wanted to fight too."

"Sorry, Einav. I figured we're here on business and didn't have much time to play."

Addy finally emerged from Joey, thankfully fully clothed this time. She looked at the dead alien, then at the smoking gun in Marco's hand. She gasped.

"You killed an alien?" Addy cried. "And you didn't invite me?"

"He didn't let me do anything either," Einav said. "Killed the bastard all by himself."

Addy shoved Marco. "You greedy pig!"

Marco blew on his pistol, and when the barrel was cool, he holstered it. "Sorry, girls. You snooze you lose."

"He always does this," Addy said. "Just like yesterday when he ate all the pork rinds and left me none." She walked toward the sliding doors of Gearmart, shaking her head in disgust.

Marco rushed after her. "Addy, that was you! You know I don't eat that stuff."

The glass doors slid open, and Addy stepped inside. "So why were there crumbs all over your shirt, Marco?"

"Because you were wearing it!" he said, entering the store with her.

Bemused, Einav followed.

* * * * *

The trio looked around with wide eyes at the gargantuan store. Marco had seen smaller starship hangars. Gearmart was truly colossal. It must have been two miles wide and half a mile deep. Aisles spread into the distance, rising toward a ceiling taller than a sequoia. Elevators moved up and down the shelves, and bridges stretched between the aisles.

The goodness of contraband engineering covered the shelves--a glorious cache of forbidden treasures. Marco remembered how, as a child, he had found his father's safe fascinating. Inside the safe, his father had kept a jar of cannabis, a handgun, a few rare coins, and other items Marco was forbidden to touch. As a child, he would spend hours staring at that safe, dreaming of the mysterious treasures within. The forbidden had always fascinated him. It still did, so many years into his long adulthood.

An old man in a blue vest limped toward them, leaning on a cane. "Welcome, welcome, shoppers! Welcome to Gearmart. I'm your greeter, Barney."

Marco nodded to the little old geezer. "Hello, Barney."

"What? What? You'll have to speak up, sonny. Is it

quantum benders you're looking for? Check them out in aisle eight. They're fifteen percent off and will shrink your enemies into the size of ants! Or were you after DNA splicers? Want to splice your cat and dog into one pet? Maybe mix your bird and reptile? Well, head over to aisle twenty-seven to find deep sales on our new Gene Splicer and Dicer Box Set!"

"Actually, we're just looking for some warp coils and ultrablack paint," Marco said.

The old man slumped. "Oh. Well, that's aisle eighty-nine and ninety-three." His eyes lit up. "Perhaps I can interest you in our new Soul Extractor? Capture the soul of your dearly departed in our new ectoplasm bottles!"

"Just the coils and paint, please," Marco said.

"Oh well. I tried." Barney flashed a grin. "Thank you for visiting Gearmart. Remember--Grab Your Gear at Gearmart!"

He tottered off to greet another new arrival--an alien snail the size of a horse, its shell adorned with machine guns and jet engines.

The trio walked down the aisles, worming their way between shoppers.

"Poet, we can buy a gene splicer?" Addy said.

Marco walked around a towering engine that was larger than Joey. Ghostly fish swam through the engine coils, their bodies shimmering with beads of light. A sign identified them as *neutron fish,* and they were advertised as the most powerful fuel in the universe.

"No, Addy," Marco said.

She pouted. "But I want to splice a dog and cat together. Freaks, Poet! I can make my own freaks! You know that's always been my lifelong dream."

"Addy, your lifelong dream was to enter the Coney Island Hot Dog Eating Contest. Which you did ten years ago. And finished fourteenth place."

She blushed and looked around. "Poet, shush! Don't advertise my failures in public. You know I could have won that thing if they let me use a rake."

They walked through the store, passing by the MindTech section. On the shelves, Marco saw truly bizarre weapons. Gaslight Guns purported to implant false memories in their victims. The box advertised them as useful for witnesses and loved ones alike. FeelSpray could change a victim's emotions. Make an enemy angry beyond reason, make a crush fall in love with you--just choose your poison and spray away. Brain Bots were tiny robots that came in little plastic buckets. They could invade a victim's brain through his ears or nostrils, then implant dreams, thoughts, and impulses.

"Psychological warfare, packed and sold on the shelf," Marco muttered.

Addy gazed at a Sentience Inducer on a nearby shelf. It was a little device, roughly the size of a coin. Slap it onto any inanimate object, and that object gained consciousness.

"Can I get one for Princess Slicey?" she asked Marco.

"Probably not a good idea. You thrust this sword into hydrian guts. You wouldn't want the poor thing sentient."

Addy sighed. "I suppose not. But I still think my princess is sentient in her own special way."

Einav pointed. "Hey, would you look at that?"

On one shelf stood rows of vials full of purple liquid. The sign identified them as Methuselah serums.

Marco glowered. "The same medicine we took. The treatment that gave us this long life. Einav, I thought you banned this crap."

"I did," she said. "But that was long ago. Looks like it's still for sale out here."

"Without even a warning label," Marco said. "And we know it kills half the people who drink it."

"Who needs a warning label?" said Addy. "If anyone takes Gearmart to trial, just spray 'em with a Gaslight Gun. They'll swear the warning label was there all along."

"Our dear Addy, already thinking like a criminal," Marco said.

"Already?" She bristled. "When was I not?"

Marco was about to leave the MindTech aisle when his eyes fell on an unusual box. The box floated an inch above the shelf, ephemeral, wreathed in mist. Words hovered above the box: SOUL RESTORER.

Marco approached.

"Poet, come on!" Addy said. "There's an aisle that sells real, moving dinosaur skeletons! Hurry!"

"Hang on." He stepped closer to the floating, airy box.

What the hell was a Soul Restorer?

The box floated before him. He plucked it out from the mist. A sheet of transparent plastic revealed the box's contents. A slender tube hung within a contraption of gears, gemstones, brass rings, and pipes. Strange symbols adorned the mechanism. Marco didn't recognize them. But he did recognize the language printed on the box. It was Japanese, one of the languages Marco had studied during his century of peace. He read aloud, translating the words into English for his companions.

"SOUL RESTORER! Still got the ghost of your dead? Restore them into a new body! Simply add one soul, drop in an embryo, and shakey shake! The crystal power will connect spirit and body. Your loved one--back to life!"

Below appeared fine print.

"Incubator not included. Live womb recommended. Embryos not guaranteed to survive. May cause birth defects."

Addy's eyes lit up. "Birth defects! Freaks, Poet! Buy it."

Einav looked at the box too. She shook her head. "Nonsense. There's no such thing as souls. It's a superstition.

That's just an ordinary test tube, the kind you can get at any fertility clinic, with some mumbo jumbo about magic and crystals slapped onto it."

Yet Marco wondered. Back inside Joey, he still had that seashell. The conch that glowed from the inside. The mystical yurei had told him the shell contained Kemi's soul. Could he . . .?

That voice again spoke in his mind.

Come to me . . .

He had come to her. To the place she had shown him, and he had found the lost fleet there. Now maybe it was time to bring Kemi to him.

"I'm buying this," Marco said.

Einav looked into his eyes. She put a hand on his shoulder. "She died a long time ago, Marco. We can't bring back the dead."

Addy frowned. "Who . . .?" Then her eyes widened. "No! Poet, you're not thinking . . . Kemi?"

"The oracles told me that her descendant will someday save the world," Marco said. "What if they were right? What if we can bring her back?"

Addy shook her head wildly. "Marco! The oracles talked about Kemi's descendant with *you*. With you . . ." She looked away, eyes damp.

Marco heaved a sigh. "Yes, I know. The oracles told me that I was meant to marry Kemi. To have a child with her. That someday that child's descendant will save humanity. But the lines of space and time are full of surprises. Kemi died and now humanity is in danger. What if we could reverse that? Align the timelines again?"

Addy spun toward him. "And what, you'll marry her?" Her voice cracked, and pain filled her eyes. "You'll toss me aside, a historic mistake in the timelines of reality?"

"Of course not." Marco held her hands. "Addy, I love you

with all my heart. More than anything. You're the love of my life, and I would never do that. I would never leave you."

"Prove it," Addy said. "Let Kemi stay where she is. You said her soul is somewhere peaceful. On a beach. Let her enjoy her afterlife, and don't bring her back!"

"Guys!" Einav said. "I hate to interfere in a married couple's argument, but this box is just a scam. I'm telling you. It's a fake. It's not worth bickering over."

Addy wiped her eyes. "Fine. Buy the damn thing, Poet. So long as I can to buy something too."

"Not a reanimated dinosaur skeleton."

She placed her hands on her hips. "Why not?"

"Well, it won't fit in Joey."

"A Velociraptor might."

"Addy, I'm not bringing an undead Velociraptor into my starship."

"Fine, fine!" She crossed her arms. "I'll buy something that won't murder us in our sleep. Happy?"

Marco cringed. "I'm not sure. Judging by the look in your eyes, *you* might murder me in my sleep."

Addy shrugged. "Well, if you keep eating my pork rinds, I might."

"I didn't--" he began, then caught her winking. He smiled and wrapped an arm around her. "Come then, Ads. Let's keep shopping."

* * * * *

They finally found all the parts they needed for Joey. New warp coils, new bores for her cannons, new hull plates, new sensors (her old ones had one foot in the grave), and several cans of ultrablack paint. It all cost a fortune. The trio had to drain their bank accounts and max out their credit cards.

They each bought a personal item too. Addy chose an authentic World War II helmet. At least the tag, which hung from the helmet's strap, claimed it was genuine. The helmet was Canadian too, which made Addy (a die-hard Canuck) happy. There was a bullet hole in the front, which Marco found rather gruesome. He wondered if the original owner had died in battle. According to the tag, the helmet still contained the souls of the dead soldier's brigade. In the hour of utmost need, the helmet's new owner could summon those old troops to aid.

"Why would you even want a helmet that clearly can't stop a bullet?" Marco said, sticking his finger through the bullet hole.

"Because it's cool!" With a marker, Addy scrawled the words HELL'S PRINCESS across the helmet.

"Congrats!" Marco said. "You just defaced a historic artifact."

"Worth it. Now it's even cooler." She placed the helmet on, then tilted it at a rakish angle. "How do I look?"

"Like a deranged psychopath."

"Perfect. That's the look I'm going for. Imagine it, Poet! Being able to summon a World War II infantry brigade!"

"Nice story," Marco said.

"It's real." Addy became solemn. "I can feel their spirits inside the helmet."

"Those are just the usual voices inside your head, Ads," Marco said.

At first, Einav insisted she didn't need anything. But Addy convinced her to indulge.

"And not books!" Addy told her. "You and Poet always just buy books. Buy something special for yourself, Einav. Something sparkly."

So Einav bought a chain slung with gilded coins, which she wore around her waist like a belt. Each coin was engraved with another animal, ranging from large beasts like bears to little critters like rodents and insects. According to the box, this "Chain of Transformation" allowed the wearer to become any animal. Choose the animal you want to become, rip the coin off the chain, place it under your tongue, and voilà. Instant animal transformation. But you could only spend each coin once. After one use, it melted away.

"Come on, test it!" Addy said. "Rip off a coin. Try the bear."

Einav laughed. "I don't want to break my new belt. It's just decorative. It gives me a bit of a Middle Eastern vibe. Reminds me where I'm from."

"At least try to become a wolf," Addy said.

Einav laughed. "Maybe later."

As for Marco, he bought the box. Yes, it was probably just a test tube stuck into a decorative steampunk contraption. A scam. But he kept thinking about it. To bring the dead back to life. To restore a soul to a new body . . .

What if it *were* somehow real? In his heart of hearts, he believed that Kemi's soul was still alive. Still in the seashell. Still in his dreams. Was it only his imagination, just superstition? Einav seemed to think so. But Marco knew there were wonders in the galaxy. There were mysteries the mind could not unravel.

What we understand, we call science, Marco thought. *What we don't understand, we call magic.*

Maybe Marco was just old-fashioned. Maybe his inner child still believed in magic. If souls were real, if you could bring back the dead, that didn't just mean saving Kemi. It meant there was a chance that somewhere out there, his children were still alive. That he could bring them home.

Joey left the dock, carrying the supplies in crates atop her hull. The ship limped through the hollow interior of Corymbus, heading toward the central pole that rose throughout the asteroid like an axis. Countless piers stuck out like branches from a tree trunk. It was an enormous shipyard. You could hire mechanics here or simply dock, rent tools, and DIY. Addy, of course, chose the latter option.

Marco and Einav helped. They replaced the warp coils, installed the new cannon bores, and welded the cracks in the hull. Marco wished they could have hired a few of the shipyard's androids. He watched, envious, as the androids rushed around other starships, fixing them at superhuman speed. But renting those workers was expensive, and once again, the trio was utterly broke. So they rolled up their sleeves, cursed a lot, and carried on with the repairs themselves.

It took several days. Time they could not afford to lose. But finally Joey was good as new. Well, maybe not *brand* new. She was a patchwork of crude welding, unlicensed parts, and kludges. But once more, ultrablack covered her, her warp drive worked, and her cannons were ready to unleash destruction. She was invisible. She was fast. She was deadly. And, much to Addy's delight, her pantry was restocked with hot dogs.

The trio stood on the pier, covered in grease. They wiped their hands, placed them on their hips, and gazed at their work.

"Joey, you're beautiful," Marco said.

"You can't even see her," Addy said. "She's ultrablack again."

"You'd be more beautiful if we couldn't see *you*," Joey said.

Addy raised her blowtorch. "Watch it! Or I burn that paint right off."

"I'll be good!" Joey said.

Einav considered the ship and nodded. "All right, my friends. We're ready to fly out. To return to Earth. To find help. If we can find more soldiers and enlist them to fight with us, we can reclaim the Phoenix Fleet. Maybe then we can--"

"Einav Ben-Ari!" boomed a voice behind them.

The trio spun around, drawing their handguns. Marco

expected to see another towering wolfman, maybe some other hideous alien gunning for blood.

Instead he saw a man. An ordinary-looking man. He was about fifty, sporting shaggy long hair and a grizzled beard. He wore a shabby jumpsuit, and a rifle hung across his back. A smuggler by the looks of him. Maybe a down-on-his-luck mercenary or alien hunter.

"You Einav Ben-Ari?" the brute growled.

"What's it to ya, punk?" Addy said.

"Wasn't talking to you," said the shaggy man. He pointed a finger at Einav. "You there. The little lady with the ivory hand. You're her, ain't ya?"

Einav nodded. "I am."

The bearded brute stomped closer, his eyes burning with rage. His lips peeled back to reveal his teeth. Despite his raggedy appearance, the man had good teeth. They looked sharp too. Marco's fingers twitched on his trigger.

"That's far enough," Marco said.

The brute ignored him. He stared at Einav with his blazing eyes. "I had buddies on Mars. Good buddies." Suddenly his eyes dampened. "The squids killed 'em. I came to Darktech Cove to buy this here gun." He gestured at his rifle. "And ammo. Lots of ammo. Ammo to avenge my buddies. My name's Wyatt. Let me join you. I'll help you kill some goddamn squids."

Addy lowered her gun and raised her eyebrows. "Dude. Is that a Canadian accent?"

Wyatt nodded. "Sure is. Saskatchewan boy right here."

Addy rushed forward and hugged him. "Welcome to the team!"

The commotion drew attention across the docks. A few more people approached. Mercenaries. Smugglers. Bounty hunters. They were gruff men and women, scarred, tattooed, carrying arsenals of weapons. Their ships were docked nearby, bristling with cannons. They all told familiar tales.

"My brother fought with the Raggedy Lions," said one man. "He fell fighting the squids."

A young woman wiped her eyes. "My entire family died on Mars." She balled her fists. "I'll fight for you."

A middle-aged man approached. He sported thick muttonchops and a leather jacket covered with metal spikes. He shared his tale. "My grandfather lived on Hypnos. The squids wiped them out. I grew up in exile. I'm ready to fight."

Marco looked at the people approaching. These were the scum of the galaxy. Criminals. Gangsters. The dregs who lived in shadows. At least that was the stereotype. That was how society painted these folks on the fringe. But Marco saw good people. Brave people. He saw warriors. No, these were not the dregs of humanity. They were the salt of the earth.

"Hey, man!" Wyatt said. "You're Marco, right? Marco Emery? I read your books! I read all your books! Cool stories, bro!" He pulled Marco into a hug.

Marco laughed and slapped the man on the back. Others gathered around to share their tales. They all had haunted eyes. They all carried scars. They had all suffered. But together their pain eased. Together their misery faded and smiles broke through the pain. More and more came, a hundred scruffy outlaws raring for a fight. All with weapons and ships of their own. They were all hardy survivors. All killers. They would form the seed of a new army.

In the center of the group stood Einav, silent, simply watching them gather. In this group of gruff, hairy, spiky brutes, she was a slender figure in white and gold, a lily among thorns. Yet when she finally spoke, everyone fell silent and listened.

"Yes, I'm Einav Ben-Ari. Yes, I'm the one who led Earth in the Alien Wars. I defeated many alien empires. Yet that was a long time ago. Before most of you were born. Today I fight again.

Today I face Hydking Ninazu and his terrible shoal. I won many wars, but when I led the fleet of Mars against the shoal, I lost the battle. I lost my fleet. I lost my planet. Millions died. I am a warrior, descended from warriors, but I cannot promise you victory. If you join me in this war, your fate might be like the fate of Mars. Death."

"Death in glory!" cried Wyatt, raising his fist.

"Death in glory!" cried the others.

"Death in glory!" shouted Addy, fist in the air.

"Death in glory!" cried Marco, his heart hammering against his ribs, and right now, he felt it. He felt that bloodlust. He felt the heat rising inside him, the anger, that blazing fire that shone with the glory of battle. He had fought many wars. He had seen boys and girls dying in the mud, weeping, crying out for their mothers. He knew that war was hell, that war was ugly, that war meant pain and grief even in victory, let alone defeat. Yet deep inside him was still a soldier. Below the mild soul of an author, beneath the bookish exterior of a librarian's son, a fire burned. The hydrians had stoked it. It burned hotter than Marco had ever known it. This was it. The great war. The final war. And if this war could only end in defeat, then he would die as he had lived. As a soldier.

Einav waited for the cries to die down. She looked across the crowd. "I look around me, my friends, and in your eyes I see the same fire that burns inside my soul. It's courage that fills your eyes. And it's the fire of courage that will light your way into the darkness ahead."

Marco raised his chin, and that feeling--whether you called it bloodlust or courage or determination--flared inside him.

"We will win!" he shouted.

The cry echoed across the dock. "We will win!"

"We will win!" Addy shouted.

And then something amazing happened. Across the

hollow asteroid, throughout all of Darktech Cove, shop doors opened. Ships turned toward them. Thousands stood on piers and docks, fists in the air, and they echoed the same cry.

"We will win! We will win!"

Marco looked at Einav. She looked back, smiling softly.

Love, Marco thought. *Yes, I feel anger and bloodlust. But I feel love too. Love for Einav. Love for Addy. Love for my people.*

"We found our army," he said. "Not on Earth like we thought. We found it among the lost."

They had flown into Darktech Cove with a broken little starship. They flew out with a fleet.

CHAPTER SEVEN
Give 'Em Hell

The fleet flew out, heading from the asteroid belt toward Earth.
There were thousands. Most of their ships were small. No larger
than Joey. No two were alike. Most were custom-built, and all
were heavily modified. Some were bounty hunter ships bristling
with weapons. Others were sneaky smuggler ships with stealth
cloaks. Many were mercenary boats with massive cannons bolted
onto their dorsal hulls. Some were hacker vessels hauling
enormous computers like saddlebags. Others were pirate ships,
skulls and bones painted onto their hulls. A few ships were just
random hodgepodges, cobbled together from spare parts--the
ships of vagrants, vagabonds, and various outlaws. Humans
crewed most of the ships. But some aliens were here too. Only
one thing united them. They were all outlaws. All outcasts. They
were not all sweethearts, but they were all brave, and they were all
ready to fight. The flotilla spread across space for many miles. A
true war fleet.

"We need a name for them," Einav said, sitting in Joey's
cockpit at the van. "Names are symbols. Symbols inspire. We
need a name to inspire our force."

Addy, who sat slumped in the gunnery seat, perked up. "I
know! The fleet shall henceforth be called . . . Addy's Adders!"

Sitting at the helm, Marco rolled his eyes. "Not this again."

"It's a good name," Addy insisted.

"I say we name the fleet Marco's Mongooses."

Addy groaned. "Not geese again! Geese are lame."

Marco raised his chin. "Mongooses are deadly predators who eat adders for breakfast."

Addy raised her fist. "Eat this for breakfast."

"A knuckle sandwich," Marco said. "How original."

"What? No. I mean--I got you a McMuffin on our way out from Darktech." She opened her hand, showing a crushed bundle of mush. "Sorry. Kinda squished." She delicately smoothed out her sandwich. "It's ruined. I'll have to eat it myself."

Marco looked in the rearview monitor at the fleet flying behind Joey. At the thousands of assorted ships, no two like. Rundown ships. Ragtag ships. Homemade, makeshift piles of junk, cobbled together from countless spare parts. It was a motley group, nothing like the gleaming warships of the Phoenix Fleet. It reminded Marco of the Raggedy Lions, the civilian ships Addy had commanded over Mars, but this fleet was even rougher, grittier, meaner--not just civilians but outlaws.

"I don't even know how to define this random assortment of ships," Marco said. "It's a ragtag fleet, that's for sure."

Addy nodded. "A ragtag fleet. That we are." She gasped. "Poet, I got it. I got our name!" She stood up. "We shall be . . . Addy's Adders!"

Marco groaned.

"We're the Ragtag Fleet," said Einav, sitting between them. "That's our name."

"The Ragtag Fleet!" Addy said, raising her fist. Then she winced and uncurled her fingers. "Dammit. Squished my McMuffin again."

They flew onward toward Earth. Space was empty around them. No Earthling warships patrolled the void. Following the news of Mars's destruction, most Earthlings hid in their homes, not daring to venture into space. The hydrians, for their part, were still feasting on the red planet, guzzling nutrients from their stew of ink and corpses. Space had never felt emptier.

Rough as it was, the Ragtag Fleet could not defeat the shoal. Einav knew this. But it could, perhaps, defeat the hydrians guarding the Phoenix Fleet on the beach. And that was a fleet of proper warships--if they could restore and staff them. Combined, the Phoenix Fleet and Ragtag Fleet were still not enough. But it was a start. It was something. It was resistance. Dammit, it was hope.

President Hart thought he could appease the shoal. But Marco was three times older than Cory Hart, and he had survived the Alien Wars. Marco knew that you could not appease monsters. You could only slay them. When the hydrians were hungry again, to Earth they would fly. And humanity must be ready.

They were flying toward the moon, and Earth shone blue and bright ahead, when the first hydrians appeared.

They rose from the moon, a hundred galactopods or more. They must have been lurking on the lunar surface, watching over Hart like prison guards. Now, shrieking and furious, their eyes blazing red, the gargantuan squids soared to face the Ragtag Fleet.

Marco inhaled sharply. "There's . . . a lot of them."

Addy grinned savagely and placed her hands on the triggers. "More for me to kill. Bring it on."

The galactopods formed an assault formation, tentacles pointing forward. They came racing toward the Ragtag Fleet. At this speed, they were only minutes away.

Across the Ragtag Fleet, shields flared to life. Cannons moved on great gears, pointing toward the incoming foes. Not one ship turned to flee. Even facing the terrors that had destroyed the Martian fleet, that had devoured an entire world, the Ragtag Fleet did not lose heart.

Einav lifted her minicom and broadcast a message to the fleet. "Hear me, Ragtag Fleet! This is Einav Ben-Ari, speaking to you from the vanguard. The enemy approaches! You joined me to kill hydrians. Here's your chance. The enemy is strong. The enemy is merciless. But we are warriors! We are not soldiers. We are outlaws! We are rebels! We are the roughnecks and brawlers of the galaxy. We are the Ragtag Fleet, and we will win!"

Voices flooded the ragnet--what Addy had named their comms network.

"We will win!" the pilots cried.

"Onward, Ragtag Fleet, to victory!" Einav said.

"To victory! We will win! We will win!"

"We will win!" Addy cried, fist in the air, McMuffin be damned.

More galactopods were rising from the moon. On the lunar surface, they had camouflaged themselves, blending into the silvery craters. In space, they became black and craggy. Their carapaces were hard to see, but their eyes burned, and their jaws opened like crimson caverns lined with bright white teeth. They stormed closer, two hundred now, maybe more, each beast the size of a whale. They raged for battle.

The Ragtag Fleet flew in no proper formation. They were not military. They were a mob. Ships ignited their afterburners, charging toward the enemy. Pirates unfurled their huge solar sails, displaying gruesome Jolly Rogers. Bounty hunters blazed out rings of spinning fire. The faces of the Ragtag captains appeared in Joey's cockpit, hovering as tiny holograms like bees. They were rough faces. Faces covered with war paint, tattoos, and piercings. Faces haggard. Faces weary from long lives on the run. But all those faces now twisted with rage. Their eyes burned with the light of battle. They roared, howled, and chanted for war.

"Hold your fire until my order," Einav said.

The hydrians came closer. Closer. Their tentacles engorged, then spewed ink.

"Evasive maneuvers!" Marco cried, pulling the yoke.

A needless command, of course. These Ragtaggers were all experienced fighters. The ships swerved and spun around the incoming inkblots. Joey whipped over and around them. Some inkblots impacted against hulls. They wrapped around ships like sticky black stingrays, eating hulls, eating human flesh. Ships crumpled like tin cans. The ink crushed them and sucked out the juices. The faces of multiple captains vanished from Joey's cockpit. But nobody turned to flee. The survivors charged onward to battle.

"Ragtag Fleet!" Einav cried. "Give 'em hell!"

At once, Addy pulled her triggers. Joey's cannons boomed, unleashing a barrage of novabolts. With battle cries, the Ragtag Fleet opened fire with her.

Their weapons were terrifying. Illegal weapons. Weapons so dangerous even the Human Defense Force dared not wield them. The barrage of bizarre destruction slammed into the enemy horde.

Antimatter bolts hurtled through space, sucking up reality around them. When they impacted with galactopods, they destroyed their very atoms, unleashing rippling blasts of all-consuming energy.

Quantum cannons ripped time itself like daggers slicing black cloth, propelling hydrians into the deep past or distant future. Some of the aliens might reappear in the age of dinosaurs, where they must battle beasts their own size. Perhaps a few landed in Earth's medieval oceans, terrified Norse mariners, and gave rise to the legend of the kraken. Other hydrians might find themselves in the far future, long past human extinction, maybe past the life of the entire solar system.

Genetic beams unzipped and reformed DNA, twisting enemies into hideous new forms, mutating and mutilating. Hydrians burst out from their exoskeletons like popcorn, puffing and sprouting thousands of eyeballs, writhing spines like undead serpents, or tumors with screaming faces. Trapped in their hellish new forms, they squealed and begged for death. A death the bounty hunters were happy to deliver with flamethrowers, laser beams, and spinning blades.

Some Ragtag ships fired nuclear weapons. It was ancient but terrifically effective tech. The small atom bombs--tactical weapons designed to destroy dreadnoughts, not entire cities-- slammed into some galactopods. The hydrians exploded like sausages left too long in the microwave.

Even with this savagery, most of the galactopods survived the bombardment. The strange half-organic, half-mechanical hydrian ships charged through the destruction. They dodged incoming missiles, lasers, and plasma. They crashed through the melting or charred remains of their comrades. They unleashed clouds of ink, a great tidal wave of sticky black death. The sea of ink flowed over the Ragtag Fleet.

Addy fired her novabolts, ripping holes through the inky wave, and Joey flew through the storm. Other Ragtag ships fired flamethrowers, hurled grenades, or sliced through ink with lasers. Some took the assault on their armor, counting on the thick metal plates to absorb the punishment. Some Ragtaggers survived. Others crumpled up and melted within the grip of the ravenous ink. Marco envisioned the ink as great dark hands, crushing ships like Addy had crushed her sandwich.

"Onward, Ragtag Fleet!" Einav cried. "For the memory of Hypnos! For the memory of Mars! For all humanity, charge!"

The galactopods kept spewing their ink, but the Ragtag Fleet would not turn back. Through the storm, they flew onward, firing their guns. Every moment, another ship fell, but the survivors sped up. Their engines roared and lit the night. Their cannons blazed like comets. Their cries rose in the silence of space and echoed down to Earth, giving hope to all who heard.

"We will win!"

The hydrians hesitated. They almost seemed confused. Their eyes darted. Why were the humans not stopping? How could they still be flying?

A ship streaked overhead. If you call it a ship. It was little more than a massive cannon, twin engines, and a little cockpit perched on the top. It reminded Marco of a Warthog aircraft from the old days of aerial combat. Most starships had cannons. This was a cannon that had a starship. Wyatt sat inside the canopy, laughing, his eyes alight, his grizzled hair billowing.

"Let's give the bastards hell, Marco!" he cried. "My *Spacehog* is with ya!"

Marco grinned and flew right below Wyatt.

Addy fired a fresh barrage of novabolts. When they emerged from the cannons, the neutron bolts were no larger than buckshot. In space, they expanded to glowing white missiles the size of trees. A hundred of these searing spears slammed into a galactopod, slicing through the carapace, cauterizing and roasting the meat within.

"Hey, Marco!" Wyatt cried. "Watch this, buddy!"

The shaggy mercenary shoved a lever, and the *Spacehog*'s cannon roared to life. The gun stretched the full length of the *Spacehog*, stem to stern. The bore was wider than a man was tall. That cylinder of destruction began to spin. With a deafening *brrrrr*, the gun disgorged a barrage of bullets the size of beer bottles. The projectiles slammed into a galactopod, shattering the exoskeleton and pulverizing the squid within.

"Haha! Told ya!" Wyatt whooped in triumph. "How ya like that, bud?"

Marco couldn't help but laugh, terror of the battle notwithstanding. Marco hated fighting. But Wyatt truly seemed to love it, and something about his delight was infectious.

"Good job, buddy," Marco said.

"Oh, look at you, you found a new friend," Addy said.

"When I kill aliens, you get jealous. When Wyatt does it, it's all *good work, buddy, I love you more than my wife, buddy*."

The battle raged on. Pirate ships unleashed full broadsides of graviton torpedoes. Bounty hunters unleashed nebula bombs. The projectiles shot forward like tiny stars, then bloomed into clouds of purple and blue energy, consuming all around them. The hydrians hit back just as hard. At close range, they pounced on ships, wrapped tentacles around hulls, cracked the vessels open, and sucked up the innards. A hydrian grabbed a smuggler ship, shattered the prow, then shook the ship like a bag of chips, spilling humans into its waiting jaws. One huge hydrian grabbed two ships, then slammed them together. It was like some mutated boy banging toy ships in the bath. A few Ragtag ships crashed onto the moon. Others floated off into deep space, not much left of them but charred chassis.

Men and women died. Dozens of them. Maybe a hundred or more. But the survivors did not stop fighting. Over and over, the cannons boomed, Addy's novabolts flew, and Wyatt's enormous gun spun in delight. Everyone here was a warrior. Not everyone had a military background, but they all had years of fighting experience, and they fought as bravely as any soldier Marco had ever seen.

Marco himself had always wanted to be a writer. Had always thought of himself as a writer first and foremost. But not now. Not in this war. Nor was he a soldier anymore, for he no longer belonged to any proper military. He was like the Ragtaggers now. A man broken. A man outcast from society. A warrior without a home. He had only met these outlaws, but here was his tribe. Here were his brothers and sisters.

They fought together. They fought well. And with sheer grit and gristle, the Ragtag Fleet surrounded the last few galactopods and bombarded them with hellfire. The hydrians squealed as they tore apart. Their broken, mangled pieces rained down onto the moon.

Across the Ragtag Fleet, cheers rose.

"Victory! Victory!"

Sitting in the captain's seat, Einav shook her head. "Not yet, friends. Our goal still lies ahead. Onward, Ragtag Fleet. To Earth!"

Marco shoved down the throttle. Joey blasted forth, shot through the debris of dead hydrians, and raced toward the blue planet. Behind her, the survivors of the Ragtag Fleet followed.

* * * * *

Down on Earth, in a palace of gold and splendor, Cory Hart lounged in bed with three beautiful women, a bottle of wine, and terror in his heart. He was King of Apeworld now. Ruling Earth for his masters. And that came with decadence, delight, and despair.

He looked around him at his quarters. He barely recognized the place. A few years ago, Heather had left him, taking the kids, taking her artwork from the walls, taking Hart's heart. She left his bedroom empty and his life emptier. For a long time, he had wallowed, sleeping like a bachelor among empty pizza boxes and beer bottles, letting his beard grow shaggy, forgetting to shower. Sometimes he went all day without eating.

But that was before Erafel had come to him. Before the emissary of Ninazu had spoken to him through the hydstone, bringing him gifts, power, and new life. Hart had signed his deal with the devil. He had given Mars to the gods from the void. With this sacrifice, he had saved Earth. Saved this planet the squids called Apeworld. There was a collar around his neck, and Erafel held the leash. But Earth was saved, Hart was king, and all the world's treasures were his.

No more empty pizza boxes and beer bottles. Erafel had filled Hart Hall with gold from beyond the galaxy, diamonds the size of apples, goblets of platinum overflowing with gemstones, statues of the purest silver that shone like moonlight, and ten thousand jewels wrought by alien hands, glinting with precious stones not known in the Milky Way. Not since the age of the Pharaohs had such a hoard gleamed on Earth.

"These are your gifts," Erafel had told him. "Be a good servant of Ninazu, and he'll continue to reward you."

Hart didn't give a damn about gold, silver, or diamonds. Every time he closed his eyes, he still saw the shoal devouring Mars. Saw the millions dying. He would do whatever he could to save Earth. To appease the terrors that had come from beyond the galaxy. He would join them, serve them, rule for them, debase himself and become a slave on a golden leash. Anything! If only to save one life! And he could save billions.

That was what Einav Ben-Ari did not understand. Against the terror from the void, there could be no victory. One could only bow before them and beg for mercy. Ben-Ari preferred to die on her feet. To die as a lioness. But a dead lioness became nothing but maggoty flesh, and no one would remember her glory. And even should she be remembered as a martyr--so what? Hart preferred life. Life! For life no cost was too great. Even servitude and slavery was still life!

As he lay in bed upon sheets of silk and ermine, these thoughts ran through his mind. He was sweating. His heart was pounding. The splendor surrounded him, but he could only see the falling of Mars.

"Cory?" whispered one of the girls in his bed. "Cory, are you all right?"

"He needs more wine!" giggled the second girl.

The third kissed his cheek. "He needs more loving."

He blinked at them. They were Martian women. As far as Hart knew, they were the only three survivors of Mars. They too were gifts from Erafel. Golden collars encircled their necks, and jeweled implants glowed on their temples. Erafel had done something to them, Hart knew. Broken their minds. Made them subservient and simpering.

"Take them," Erafel said. "They too are your gifts. Ninazu rewards his servants."

What were their names? Who had they been on Mars? What had happened to their families? Hart didn't know. He had asked them many times. They could only giggle, kiss him, and dodge his questions.

"Silly, we're your slaves!"

"We exist to serve you."

"You can name us whatever you want."

So he gave them names. He named the black-haired beauty Dejah. The freckled redhead he named Thuvia. The blonde with sapphire eyes he named Phaidor. Three Martian beauties. Three slaves with jeweled chips in their heads. His rewards. But even their graceful forms, fair faces, and gentle ministrations could not ease his pain nor assuage his guilt.

"I'm fine," Hart said.

Dejah pouted. "We must pamper you."

Thuvia giggled. "Let's kiss him all over!"

Phaidor grinned wickedly. "We'll make him forget everything but us."

As they nuzzled him, Hart closed his eyes. As they caressed and kissed him, a tear ran down his cheek. He would give up all of this--the treasures, the girls--to roll back time. To return to his days of innocence. Days of peace with Heather by his side. His kids had once jumped and played on this bed, and now he lay here in sweat and spilled wine with these beauties with broken brains, with Mars in ruin, with the shoal out there watching.

It had to be a dream. A nightmare. This could not be real. He would wake up any moment and Heather would be here, and she would whisper to him: "It was just a nightmare. Just a dream. There's no such thing as hydrians . . ."

Yet it was real. Oh God, it was real.

God? he thought. God was dead. God would not save him. The only god now was Ninazu, and he was cruel beyond comprehension.

A knock sounded on the door.

"Cory!"

It was one of his bodyguards.

"Go away!" Hart said.

"Cory, we've been trying to reach you by minicom."

Hart turned his head, nudged Phaidor aside, and blew back strands of his hair. When had his hair grown so long? And where was his damn minicom? Ah, there it was. Inside the bucket of melted ice, jammed between a few bottles. Well, it was a piece of crap anyway.

The knock sounded on the door again. "Sir?"

"Go away!" Hart said again.

He pulled Phaidor back into his arms. Dejah and Thuvia nestled at his other side. Hart closed his eyes. He just wanted to hold them. To forget the pain and terror. To be like a child, nestling in his parents' arms.

"Cory," came the voice through the door, "there are intelligence reports of a battle by the moon. Ben-Ari is back."

Hart's eyes snapped open.

His heart seemed to stop in his chest.

He tried to rise. The girls pulled him back down, kissing and caressing.

"Get off me!" he cried, shoving them aside. He leaped from bed, stumbled across the room, and grabbed a nightgown. His head swam. He could barely see, and the jewels and gold spun around him. By miracle alone, he managed to reach the door without falling flat on his face. He yanked the door open.

Jenkins stood there. Hart's chief of staff. The two had gone to school together. Not just any school but the prestigious Hollow Hill Academy back in Pennsylvania. The two came from immaculate breeding. Cory Hart was the son of Doug Hart, the late president of Earth. Gerald Jenkins was heir to Jenkins & Becket, one of the world's largest law firms. (There was no Becket family involved. Grampa Jenkins simply thought two names sounded better, so he added the name of his bloodhound.) Gerald Jenkins looked a little like his grandfather. Frumpy, his shoulders sloped, sporting a goatee and round glasses. He looked more like a harried school teacher than the heir to a fortune. The only sign of his wealth was a diamond-studded watch that cost more than a spaceship. His grandfather had owned it. The precious watch was woefully mismatched with Jenkins's oversized jacket and Corduroy pants. A member of the Hollow Hill Communist Camaraderie, he had always felt a little guilty about his inherited wealth. Not guilty enough to donate it, of course, but just guilty enough to keep his sleeve covering his Patek Philippe.

"Well, what is it, Jenky?" Hart said. The two had been friends for decades. "Where is she? What's Einav up to?"

Jenkins cleared his throat and smoothed his coat. "A battle on the moon. Well, about ten thousand klicks above the moon. It's her all right. Ben-Ari. And guess who's with her?"

"Emery and Linden, no doubt," said Hart. "The gruesome twosome."

"And hundreds of ships. Smuggler ships, pirate ships, bounty hunters and the like. A whole fleet of criminals."

Hart barked a laugh. "Ha! She must be desperate."

Jenkins adjusted his round glasses. "Cory, she won a battle. She destroyed two hundred galactopods. And she's flying here. Right now."

At first, Hart wanted to wave dismissively. *So what! Let her come. She wants to kill me? Go ahead! I don't care anymore. Let her put me out of my misery. Let her take over and rule this world. Let it be her curse! And let me rest in the grave.*

But then the realization dawned on him. No, Einav wasn't coming to kill him. She had entered this very bedroom just weeks ago. She could have killed him then. No, she wasn't going to fight him. She wanted to raise Earth in battle!

"She's poking the hornet's nest," Hart said. "My God. She killed two hundred of them? She's going to plunge Earth into a war. A war we can't win."

Jenkins nodded. "The hydrians will punish us for this."

"It's not our fault." Hart's voice shook. "We didn't do anything! It was her!"

He turned away from the doorway. He stumbled through his bedroom, stubbing his toe against a giltwood table. Damn, that hurt. He yanked open a drawer, tossed aside jewels and golden coins, and found it. The hydstone. The azoth shard from the hydling's head. Through this stone, Erafel had first made contact with Hart. And through the hydstone, Hart could call his master back.

"I need to call him," Hart said. "I need to call Erafel. I need to smooth things over."

Jenkins checked his minicom. He looked up over his glasses. "Einav and her fleet are entering Earth's atmosphere. They're descending toward the beached fleet."

Hart shoved the hydstone into his pocket. He dared not call Erafel. Not yet. Maybe Hart could still stop Einav! Maybe he could de-escalate. He must prevent a war between Earth and the shoal. Or Earth would end up like Mars.

"I'm flying over there," Hart said. "Right now."

The girls simpered in bed and pouted.

"Don't leave us!" Phaidor said.

"Come back, our handsome hero," said Dejah.

Hart pulled on his rumpled suit, ran a hand through his hair, and hurried out the bedroom.

CHAPTER EIGHT
Lions and Sheep

Like hundreds of blazing comets, the Ragtag Fleet plunged into
the atmosphere over the Mediterranean Sea. Once again, it struck
Einav how undefended Earth was. No armed satellites patrolled
Earth's orbit. No warships prowled the seas. Earth had been
demilitarized. With her little fleet, Einav encountered no
resistance.

Addy echoed her thoughts. "We can probably conquer
Earth with just this fleet."

The tall, tattooed warrior sat at Joey's gunnery station, her
feet on the dashboard. She was chewing bubble gum and playing
with a butterfly knife. Her antique helmet rested askew on her
head.

"We probably could," said Einav, sitting in the captain's
seat. "But I'm done fighting humans. Humans must not fight
humans. We must fight only the shoal."

Addy snorted and leaned back in her seat. "We could
probably take Earth even without a fight. We just need to show
up, strut into Hart Hall, and start running the show." She yawned.
"Boring. Without violence, it seems pointless. Maybe you're right,
Einav. Not even worth it."

Marco, who was flying Joey, looked down at the waters of
the Mediterranean. A few fishing boats were leaving the coast of
Greece, mere specks from up here.

"There is still strength in Earth," Marco said. "There is a
great untapped energy here. Billions of humans still live on this

planet, and inside every human is a sleeping warrior. If we fought Hart again, these warriors would awake, and we would butcher one another while Erafel laughs. We must tap into this energy-- and aim it at the true enemy."

Addy gasped. "High blood pressure?"

Marco groaned. "That's the silent killer, not the true enemy. I mean the hydrians!"

"Oh." Addy blushed. "I knew that."

Einav nodded. "The Phoenix Fleet is where we start. Look--there it is."

Joey was now racing toward the coast of Israel, her new components humming contentedly. The coast was a painting of this land's tumultuous history, a microcosm of Earth's turmoils. In cliffs loomed caves full of the bones of ancient humans, the first to have migrated out of Africa. On hills rose biblical ruins, just fragments of walls and archways, thousands of years old. On the coast rose a Roman amphitheater and aqueduct, two thousand years old--youngsters in this land. Not far from there stood the crumbling crusader castle, a mere thousand years old. And looking everywhere, one could still see the ruins of the Cataclysm--the terrible alien invasion the trio had been born into. Thousands of years of suffering. Thousands of years of rebirth. Civilization upon civilization. Life springing forth from death's ashes. Einav could see it all here, crammed into a coastline. The story was written in the ruins of the land of Israel. But it was the story of all Earth, of humanity since their ancestors descended from the trees and dragged their knuckles across the ground.

Einav spoke softly. "Some say we're risen apes, while others believe us fallen angels. To me, both stories are the same. In both tales, we came from virginal forests and wandered into the badlands. Maybe we're still lost. We've been cast east of Eden, and from our exile, we gaze to the stars. Does our fate lie in the heavens, or are we doomed to fall? Some have called space the cosmic ocean. We stand on the shores of eternity. If we can crest the waves, the galaxy and all her wonders will be ours. Yet there are terrors in the ocean depths, and the water is cold and dark, and dawn still seems so far. I'm the captain of this ship called Earth. Or I was long ago. I must find a lodestar in this storm. I must sail through these treacherous waters. I must leave our shores of turmoil and find Zion among the stars."

Addy tilted her head. "Were you eating Marco's special brownies again?"

Marco shoved her. "Stop ruining the moment."

"Dude, she sounds high as fuck," Addy said.

"Shut up!"

Einav pointed. "There it is! The Phoenix Fleet." She tapped a button on the dashboard, opening a channel to the Ragtag Fleet. "Ragtaggers, this is Ben-Ari. Get ready for trouble."

Wyatt soared overhead in the *Spacehog*. "We're always ready for trouble, ma'am. We're Ragtaggers." He blazed beside Joey, so close that proximity alarms flared, and waved at Marco. "Hey, buddy!"

Marco waved. "Hey, bud!"

Addy mussed his hair. "Aww, you're in a bromance."

They descended toward the shore. Hundreds of warships lay below, some beached on the sand, others submerged in the water. Looking down at them, Einav felt a mix of pride and pity. Pride because these were great warships. One of these dreadnoughts could have destroyed the entire Ragtag Fleet. Here was true military might, the great technological menace of humanity. She had once commanded this fleet, and these warships still made her proud. But pity too, for these ships were now pitiful, lying in salt and sand, collecting moss and barnacles, decaying remnants like the ruins of an empire, merely hinting at greatness now lost. She would restore their greatness. These ships would fly again.

"I see one!" Marco said. "A bunch of them. Look!"

"I see 'em!" said Addy.

Einav saw them too. Hydrians. Once more they were camouflaged. The alien lay among, atop, and alongside the grounded starships. Their carapaces emulated the appearance of metal hulls. They even sported the crude illusions of airlocks, portholes, and protruding sensors. They blended in like perfect chameleons. Einav would not have noticed them had they remained still. But the hydrians were rising to battle. They thrust out their tentacles and fired ink.

Inkblots hit a few Ragtag ships. One smuggler ship crashed into the sea. Another spun madly, drenched with ink, and slammed into a nearby pirate ship. But most of the Ragtaggers dodged the assault--and returned fire.

They had to be careful not to harm the Phoenix Fleet below. Einav had drilled her captains, impressing upon them the importance of caution. Even these rough outlaws, violent by nature, killers by trade, now showed restraint. Instead of firing torpedoes with heavy warheads, they fired slender missiles designed to slice through exoskeletons and expand within. They couldn't allow any crossfire to destroy the precious Phoenix Fleet.

One Ragtag mining ship extended huge metal claws, grabbed a rising hydrian, and crushed the alien's shell. Bounty hunters, often hired to bring back living prey, cast massive electric nets. The luminous cables wrapped around hydrians, squeezed, and slung the aliens onto the sand.

Wyatt, God bless the man, was firing that massive cannon of his, unleashing thousands of those bottle-sized bullets. For all his bluster, the wild-haired man was surprisingly surgical with his strikes. He took down three hydrians, and none of his bullets hit a single Phoenix ship.

Addy, for her part, went wild with her novabolts. She blasted a hydrian apart, then blew a hole into a beached corvette.

Einav had to restrain her.

"Addy, slow down!" Einav said. "Don't shoot our own ships!"

"Sorry, sorry!" Addy blushed. "My bad. Don't worry, Nav Nav. I can fix it. I--whoa! Marco!"

Marco was yawing hard, then rolling downward and soaring again, dodging incoming inkblots.

"Addy, give me some cannon fire!" he said.

"Einav said I shouldn't shoot."

"I said don't shoot our ships!" Einav cried.

Addy groaned. "Oh God, you're so picky. Fine!" She unleashed another barrage of novabolts. A hydrian tumbled backward, head blasted open, and crashed onto the shore.

As Einav watched the alien twitch and die, excitement coursed through her.

We're killing them, she thought. *We're winning battles. We're turning the tide.*

For the first time in this long, long war, Einav felt something almost like exhilaration, almost like joy. It was hope she was feeling. Hope was like light. As a beam of light was woven of many colors, so was hope woven of many feelings--joy, excitement, anticipation, and love. All those feelings flowed through Einav now.

Sixteen hydrians still guarded the fleet, each a terror of the hyd instar. They were aliens as large as the krakens of legend. They raced through the sky with terrifying speed, grabbed Ragtag ships, and crushed them in their tentacles. One hyd bit into an antique smuggler's ship, ripping it in half. Ancient coins and treasures spilled from the shattered hull into the sea. Another hyd ripped open a pirate corvette, scooped out screaming pirates, and devoured them one by one.

But the surviving Ragtaggers fought on. They were not just soldiers of fortune. They had lost loved ones on Mars, on

Hypnos, on Solarien. To them this was personal, and they fought as courageously as any soldier Einav had ever commanded. They would not stop fighting until the battle was won. Finally Wyatt and Addy, firing bullets and novabolts, slew the final hydrian. The beast crashed into the sea, twitched, and sank.

Cheers rose across the Ragtag Fleet. Cheering loudest were Marco, Addy, and yes--even Einav.

We're winning! she thought. *We're turning the tide! We can do this! We can kill them! We can win this war!*

"We will win!" she cried. And the voices of hundreds of Ragtaggers echoed her cry. "We will win!"

* * * * *

The Ragtag Fleet landed on the sand--hundreds of ships of all sorts. From above, they must have looked like a motley host of beetles, hornets, and spiders, no two alike. Several dead hyds lay on the sand, tongues hanging between their teeth. The Crusader fort rose above the water nearby, stoically watching another chapter in the long history of this turbulent coast.

"Oh, I'm getting sand in my gears," Joey said. "Marco, why did you land me here? Marco?"

He still sat in the cockpit, gazing out the window. Einav followed his gaze. He was looking at the Crusader fort. She placed a hand on his shoulder.

"Marco?" Einav said. "You all right?"

He looked at her and smiled softly. "I guess I'm still wondering where she is."

"If Kemi is out there somewhere in time, we'll find her," Einav said.

Thankfully Addy didn't hear them. She was already hopping out of the airlock onto the sand.

"Come on, guys!" Addy shouted. "We got giant ships to

fix!"

Marco and Einav joined her outside. After returning to Earth from space, Einav often liked to stand for a moment, inhale deeply, and savor the fresh air. But now, when she inhaled, she got nostrils full of reeking hydrian stench. She coughed. The dead creatures lay across the beach, not all in one piece. The trio walked across the sand and shallow water, moving between chunks of dead hydrians and the beached starships.

"Ah, the smell of victory!" Addy said. "Guts, gunpowder, and . . ."

Her voice trailed off, and she stared ahead. Marco and Einav followed her gaze. A dead Ragtagger lay on the sand. He must have fallen out from a crushed starship. His legs had snapped, and his mouth was open in a silent scream. Crabs were already picking at his body.

"And death," Einav said softly. "That is always the smell of victory."

Ragtaggers landed to collect the body. The rough crew of bounty hunters, smugglers, and pirates roamed the beach. Some already began ripping airlocks off beached starships.

"Hey!" a bounty hunter could be heard. "There's some good tech in these HDF ships. I need me some new Gideon launchers."

"We might have a looting problem on our hands," Einav told her friends. "Marco, see if you can organize the Ragtaggers. Prevent looting. Set up a security perimeter. Get some ships flying to give us air cover."

Marco saluted. "Yes, ma'am."

"Hey, wait a minute!" Addy said. "You're sending Marco to do this? Marco? The poet? To organize bounty hunters, assassins, and pirates? They'll eat him alive." Addy pounded her chest. "Send me. I'm scum like them. They're my tribe."

Marco bristled. "Hey, I can handle them. I'm tough."

Addy snorted. "Maybe you can correct their grammar."

Einav placed a hand on Addy's shoulder. "Addy, I need you with me. We're going to inspect the grounded ships. To see how bad the damage is. I need your eye for engineering."

Her eyes shone with pride. "Ah. That explains it." Addy waved dismissively at Marco. "Go play with your new friends. We girls have important work to do."

Marco wandered off, shaking his head with a sigh. "At least I get a break from you." He coned his hand around his mouth. "Hey, Wyatt! Wanna help me with something?"

The shaggy, bearded outlaw stomped across the beach, a smile spreading across his face. "I'm your man, buddy." He gave Marco a fist bump.

Watching from a distance, Einav stifled a smile. "It really is a beautiful friendship."

"Good," Addy said. "Gives me a break from him. I love the poet to death, but after a century of marriage, I need some girl time. So come on, Nav Nav. Let's take a look at these ships."

The two women walked among the enormous ships. At some points, they waded through the shallow water. Some of these ships were small corvettes, only large enough for a dozen spacers. Others were dreadnoughts, a mile from stern to stem, large enough for crews of thousands.

"They seem in good shape," Addy said. "At least from the outside. These ships are built to withstand bombardment, radiation, and the rigors of space. They're tough machines."

"Wouldn't the water have damaged them?" Einav said.

"The outside components?" Addy said. "Sure. The saltwater damaged the outside. But on the inside, the ships should be fine. They're watertight. These hulls gotta be perfectly sealed to survive in the vacuum of space. The software is probably still working. The engines should be okay."

They waded through the sea. The water rose to their

knees, churning, cold, and thick with algae. Finally they climbed onto a slippery boulder that jutted from the water, almost large enough to be called an islet. To their west spread the mysteries of the Mediterranean, this sea that had known so many naval battles. To their east, beyond the shallows, rose the crusader fort atop the cliff. And ahead lay the HDFS *Blood, Sweat, and Tear*s.

The dreadnought was among the largest ships in the Phoenix Fleet. The waves lapped against her gray hull. A phoenix figurehead reared upon her bow, as large as the Great Sphinx of Giza. Cannons thrust out her sides and prow, so large you could park Joey inside the bores.

"This is a starship that could take on Ninazu himself," Einav said. "And she's lying beached. Along with her sisters." Einav shook her head sadly. "Hart never dared use them in battle. But I will. How long before we can get these into space again?"

Addy stood on the boulder beside her, the wind in her hair. She sucked her teeth, considering. "Not sure yet. We'll need to repair whatever is damaged. And then reroute power to graviton plates along the lower hulls. Simply turning on the engines won't work. That would just shove them deeper into sea. We'll need to levitate these babies. We can use tuggers for the smaller ships, but the dreadnoughts? I'll need a week or two. And a big crew. Both to salvage the ships and operate them."

Einav nodded. "I'll get you the crew. If the ships' databases are intact, we can access the crew manifests. They'll have home addresses. Minicom numbers. Emergency contacts. We'll get the crews back. They'll help with repairs. Within two weeks, we--"

"Look!" Addy pointed. "Incoming ship!"

Einav spun around, reflexively raising her starhand. The crystal on the palm shone. She expected to see a galactopod. But it was a human shuttle flying toward the beach from the east. A presidential shuttle. The Hart family crest--a heart with angel wings--appeared on the prow.

Einav frowned. "Is that . . ." She raised her minicom to her eyes, using the binoculars app. "It is. Goddamn Cory Hart."

* * * * *

The presidential shuttle sported a hull of pristine silver that gleamed in the sun. The heart on the prow was a mosaic of rubies, while the angel wings shimmered with real gold. It probably cost as much as a warship. Addy and Einav waded through the salty Mediterranean and stepped onto the shore, wet up to their waists, seaweed clinging to their legs. The shuttle landed on the sand before them.

The hatch popped open. Normally, guards would emerge first, but with Earth demilitarized, Hart no longer had personal guards. The president had flown here by himself, and he stepped onto the sand alone.

Einav tensed and glanced around. This could get ugly. The beach was full of trained assassins, pirates, and random killers. Not exactly the place for the president of Earth to roam around unguarded. Especially not a president as unpopular as Hart.

Addy noticed Einav's gaze. As usual, the two friends could practically read minds.

Einav glanced at Hart, then back at Addy. *He's in danger here. This crew will rip him apart.*

Addy shrugged. *So? Let 'em. Not our problem.*

Einav frowned. *Humans must not kill humans! Keep an eye open, Addy.*

Addy let out the slightest sigh. *Fine!*

Hart walked across the sand toward Einav. He looked different. He had finally cut his hair and shaved his beard, and he wore a clean suit. Jewelry adorned him--gold chains and bracelets, a watch that probably cost more than Joey, and rings inlaid with rubies and sapphires. He had always been foppish, but this was ridiculous. Yet even with all these jewels, his new clothes, and his fresh haircut, there was a raggedness to him. His cheeks were flushed, his eyes sunken. Was he hungover? Or just terrified? Maybe both.

"Einav!" He pointed a shaky finger at her. "What have you done!"

She stared at him steadily. "Won a battle."

"Two battles, actually," Addy said. "But who's counting?"

Hart reached her. He stood on the sand, breathing heavily. The short walk must have exerted him. Or perhaps it was the turmoil inside him.

"Einav, goddammit." He was shaking. "You cannot provoke these creatures. You don't know what they're capable of."

Addy raised an eyebrow. "Really, dude? You think we're that dumb? We literally saw the hydrians destroy Mars. We know they're evil. That's why we're fighting them."

"You can't defeat them, dammit!" Hart cried, face red. "I made a deal with them. I saved Earth. I saved billions of lives! You're putting them in danger now."

Addy wiped her face. "Dude. Say it, don't spray it."

Hart took a deep breath, struggling to compose himself. "Listen to me. Listen carefully. I made a deal with Erafel. I gave him Mars, and he spared Earth. In return, we demilitarized. No warships, no army, not even guards. And we certainly don't engage the hydrians in battle!"

Addy pouted. "Aww, that's no fun."

"You think this is a joke?" Hart said. "Mars was wiped out! You fought them there. They plowed over you! They destroyed your fleet *and* the planet you vowed to protect. You think you're such heroes? You lost! You were butchered! If we break the deal with Erafel, he'll do the same to Earth."

"We'll stop him," Einav said. "We learned from the battle we lost at Mars. We learned how they fly. How to destroy them. And we already implemented what we learned. We won the last two battles--"

"Mere skirmishes," Hart said. "You fought two hundred hydrians at Mars, a handful here at the beach. Barely a brawl. If the true shoal arrives, the billions of them, no force can defeat them."

Einav stared at him steadily. "I believe there is. It's called humanity. When I fought the shoal before, I was leading Mars, a colony world. Mars's population, economy, and military might was not one percent that of Earth's. If we tap into the resources of Earth--the human homeworld itself--we stand a chance. We can beat them."

Hart gazed at the sea, silent for long moments. The wind ruffled his hair. He had always looked young for his age, but now he showed every one of his fifty years.

"If I believed that, Einav, I would join you," he said softly. "I'm not much of a fighter. I haven't fought anyone since the third grade, and I lost that fight." He barked a laugh. "But I'd have put on a uniform, grabbed a gun, and done my part. But I don't share your optimism. Einav, you nearly defeated me in our war. I put everything I had against you. And you nearly won. If Earth could not defeat a rebel from Mars, what chance does Earth have against the shoal?"

"At least we'll have a chance!" Einav said. "If we surrender, what do we have?"

"Life!" Hart said.

"Life as slaves," said Einav.

"Better than death!"

"Not for me," Einav said. "I'd rather die fighting than live on my knees."

"Exactly!" Hart pointed at her. "Because you're a fanatic.

You both are. You want to kill yourselves? Go ahead. But don't drag Earth into it. Billions live here. Children. Seniors. Babies. Would you ask them to die in glory too? Because if you lose this war, they will die too."

Einav hesitated.

Is he right? she thought. *Am I a fanatic, rushing to a war I can't win? Is Hart right, and is this the time to kneel?*

"Oh, that's a bunch of bullshit!" Addy said. "Don't listen to him, Einav. He's a loser. We can win! Come on."

Yet Einav felt her resolve weaken. Only hours ago, she had felt so motivated she was chanting, "We will win!" and smiting her enemies. Now Hart implanted doubts in her. She wished Marco were here. Would he side with Hart or with Addy?

Did we make a mistake? Einav thought. *Did we invite reprisal from the shoal?*

"I see the doubt in you," Hart said. "Einav, sometimes the tree that stands tall snaps in the wind. The reeds that bend survive."

Einav looked away. Was he right? Was this time to be a reed, not a tree?

No. No, of course Hart was wrong. You could not appease the shoal. At best, you could toss them a few sacrifices to sate their appetite for a while. But eventually they would devour you. Einav knew this, yet Hart had almost convinced her. Say what you liked about the man, he was persuasive. It was no wonder he had become president.

"I'll have to call Erafel," Hart said. "To smooth things over. To try to save our deal. Maybe--just maybe--I can convince him you acted alone. Maybe--just maybe--I can still save the human species."

Addy growled. "Call Erafel? What, to tell on us? Like a tattle-tale? Don't you fucking dare." She raised her fists and stomped closer. "You're a traitor, Hart."

"Easy, Addy!" Einav said, pulling her friend back.

"He's a fucking traitor!" Addy said. "You heard him. Making deals with the enemy! Even now!"

Addy's cheeks were flushed red, and she was panting with rage. Across the beach, Ragtaggers noticed. They stomped closer, reaching for their weapons. The bounty hunters and pirates muttered. A man spat. Another man drew a blade.

"Well, look who we have here," growled a bounty hunter. "Princess Cory Hart."

"Traitor!" hissed a pirate with long red hair and flashing eyes.

"I say we gut him and feed him to the squids," rasped an outlaw wearing spiky leather. He raised a serrated blade.

"Why gut him?" said an outlaw covered with spiky implants. He looked like a human porcupine. "Let the squids eat him alive. More fun that way."

Einav turned toward them. "No. Lower your weapons."

The Ragtaggers grumbled and did not immediately obey. They kept their weapons drawn but at least they no longer stomped forward.

"I say we take him out," said a smuggler.

"No," Einav said. "Humans must not kill humans. For years, we fought a civil war. We weakened ourselves. And the shoal attacked while we were at each other's throats. No more! Every human is our ally now. Hart too. He's doing what he believes is best. For humanity."

"He works for the squids!" rumbled a towering, muscular bounty hunter. The man stood seven feet tall and probably weighed three hundred pounds. Einav wasn't sure if he was naturally that big or genetically modified.

Two ships came swooping down. One was Joey, a shard of blackness. The other was the *Spacehog*, the ship with the ridiculously large cannon that stretched from stem to stern. The two ships landed. Marco and Wyatt leaped out onto the sand. They must have seen the trouble from the air, or perhaps they had been listening over the ragnet.

"Cool it, fellas!" Wyatt said, stomping toward his fellow outlaws.

"Humans must not kill humans," Marco added. "Hart does not work for the squids. He's an idiot. He's an asshole. He's a son of a bitch. But he's a fellow human. Let him live."

Addy gave Marco a look of disbelief. *Really, Marco?* She huffed and crossed her arms.

Einav was torn between her two friends. Part of her felt like Addy. She wanted to pummel Hart, even to kill him. She believed he was a traitor, and that he would betray them again. But another part of her was like Marco. More merciful. That part believed that Hart, misguided as he was, was still worthy of life. That perhaps he could change, even become an ally someday. Was that just naivety?

She stared at the president, brow furrowed. *Who are you, Cory Hart? Are you a villain, a traitor, a wicked man? Or are you a good man whose view is different from my own?*

Usually Einav could read people. But she couldn't read him. And that disturbed her down to her soul.

Hart stared into her eyes, his gaze hard. "They call you the Golden Lioness. They say your soldiers fight like lions. You will die as lions. I might be a sheep. But I would rather be a living sheep than a dead lion."

"You are forgetting something, Cory Hart," Einav said. "Trapped in the barn, the sheep only has the illusion of safety. Until the farmer arrives with his axe. You might feel safe with this deal you struck with the devil. But you're not safe, Cory Hart. None of us are. The shoal is coming, whether we kneel or stand. If we all must die, I prefer to die standing. Leave now, Hart. I can't guarantee your safety if you remain."

As he flew off in his glittering shuttle, Addy shook her head in disgust. "He'll do it, you know. Call Erafel. Tell on us."

"Oh, Erafel already knows we're here," Einav said. "We killed a bunch of his hydrians, and they're telepathic. He knows. He'll strike back soon. We don't have much time. We need to get these ships into space."

Addy nodded. "I'll get started. Within two weeks, we'll--"

"We don't have two weeks," Einav said. "Addy, we might only have hours. The shoal is coming. The easy battles are behind us. The great battle for Earth is ahead."

CHAPTER NINE
A Tidal Wave of Tentacles

Hart had barely landed his shuttle at Hart Hall when the crystal heated up. The hydstone felt like a hot coal in his pocket. A voice burst through his mind like shattering glass.

"What is the meaning of this, Hart?" screeched the voice. "An assault on my children? At the moon? On Earth?"

Hart covered his ears. That voice! It was tearing him apart, eating through him, consuming his mind. He stumbled out his shuttle onto the palace lawn.

"It was her!" he cried. "Erafel, it was--ahh!"

Erafel's voice rose to a deafening shriek, banging against his eardrums and pounding through his skull like a storm.

"We had a deal, Cory Hart! Dare you defy the will of Ninazu?"

Hart fell to his knees. He pulled the hydstone from his pocket, wanting to hurl it away. But it sizzled, burning his hand, sticking to the melting skin. Inside glowered Erafel's face, demonic and red, eyes like pits of fire.

"I named you King of Apeworld!" said the demonic hybrid. "I thought you would serve Ninazu. That you would keep your world under control. You betrayed me. You blasphemed against the lord."

"No, no!" Hart cried. "It was Einav. Einav Ben-Ari. I tried to stop her. I was going to call you! To warn you!"

The crystal heated further, turning from lavender to white, burning deeper into Hart's palm. He screamed.

"I gave you jewels," said Erafel. "I gave you women. I gave you treasures of conquest and glory. And you betrayed me."

Hart knelt outside his palace, nearly blind with pain. "Then punish me. Kill me then! But spare Earth. Spare the people of this world." Tears flowed down his cheeks. "They are innocent."

Erafel chuckled. "Noble fool. Do you think I would spare you from the agony Ninazu plans for those who betray him? You will beg me for death."

"I'm your servant!" Hart said. "I always did as you asked. I brought you here!" He shoved himself to his feet and raised his chin. "I opened the shoalgate. I gave you Mars. Einav is my enemy! As much as she is yours. We'll defeat her together."

A small voice in his mind was guiding him.

Make him feel we have a common enemy, Hart thought. *Make him realize I'm his ally. And maybe I can still save this world.*

He was so used to Erafel speaking in his mind that it took Hart a moment to understand. That was his own internal voice.

The heat eased in his palm. The shrieking storm in his mind faded. Erafel's voice--and yes, this time it was Erafel again--spoke in a deeper tone, rumbling and fading with every word.

"I will deal with Ben-Ari. And then your fate is in the hands of Ninazu . . ."

The terrible voice released him. Hart took a shaking breath. He tried to put the hydstone back in his pocket but could not. He looked at his hand and winced. The crystal had burned into his flesh, embedding itself into his palm. The skin around it was raw and blistering.

Einav had the Mariner's Tear in her ivory hand. Erafel had a crystal in his monstrous hand too--a chip from the azoth in Ninazu's brain. Now Hart had joined them in this unholy triptych of insanity. Like them, he was cursed.

* * * * *

They were coming.

They were on their way to Earth.

The shoal.

Marco knew that. They all did. What they had done here would echo across the solar system. Maybe across the galaxy. Einav Ben-Ari and her warriors were resisting. Humanity was striking back. The god Ninazu was still sucking Mars dry, but busy as he was at his feast, he would not forgive the apes for their recalcitrance.

They would strike back. They would strike hard. Without mercy. Without warning. It could be in two hours. Maybe in two years. Marco didn't know. But he knew the reprisal would come.

And so he flew Joey over the beach, patrolling the sky. A couple of hundred Ragtagger ships flew with him. They formed an umbrella over the beach, protecting Addy and her mechanics below.

Dozens of mechanics were scrambling over the beached starships. Most of them were Ragtaggers, and excellent mechanics they were. These rough outlaws had built their own starships from scratch. After every battle they fought, they welded, sawed, screwed, and repaired damaged ships. Now they raced over and inside the HDF dreadnoughts, frigates, and corvettes, doing what they could.

They were not alone. Einav had summoned help. Inside the ships, they found the crew manifests. The spacers had been relieved from duty and sent home. Now they must return to service.

There were thousands of spacers to call. Too many calls for any one person to make. So they let Joey handle the job. As Marco flew her, Joey was running many concurrent threads in her processor. Each thread was calling another spacer and playing

Einav's pre-recorded message. Sitting in the cockpit, Marco heard it repeated over and over, thousands of times in unison.

"This is Einav Ben-Ari, former president of Earth, current admiral of the Phoenix Fleet. Your ship awaits you at the coast of Atlit by the old crusader fort. The fleet will rise again. I summon you back to active duty. Put your uniform back on. Grab your gun. Make your way to your ship--right now. If you are eating dinner, stop eating. If you are in bed, get out. Return to your ship! Battle is near. Return to duty at once! Together we will win!"

And flying above the grounded fleet, Marco saw them appear. One by one. Shuttle by shuttle. Dozens, then hundreds, then thousands of shuttles. Then tens of thousands. The brave spacers of the Human Defense Force. En masse, they were landing on the beach and rushing to their ships. The ships still lay on the sand, but the crew raced inside and climbed the hull. The number of mechanics swelled, and soon swarms of hundreds covered the ships like ants over fallen fruit, welding, hammering, working in a fury.

They didn't have much time.

Marco tilted Joey upward, studying the sky for any sign of the enemy. It was daylight. He saw nothing but blue sky and a few hundred Ragtag ships. No hydrians. Not yet. Were they on their way already? Or were they still engorging themselves at Mars, building up strength for the great assault on Earth?

An enormous cannon rose to hover beside Joey. Engines were attached to the back, and a canopy rose on top. The *Spacehog* was truly a sight to behold. The flying gun was larger than Joey. Wyatt waved from the cockpit.

"Hey, buddy," said the shaggy outlaw, speaking over the ragnet. "Quiet day, huh? No hydrians to be seen. Maybe we should go down and help fix the ships?"

"Better stay up here, bud," Marco said. "The squids will come. I've fought those bastards many times before. They'll show up. We'll be ready."

Wyatt shook his head in wonder. "Damn, buddy. Giant squids from outer space. Who'd have thought, huh? I'm a mercenary. Gun for hire. For thirty-five years, I've been fighting. My job took me all over the galaxy. Thought I'd seen everything. But this?" He exhaled slowly. "Damn, this is a whole other thing."

It was funny, Marco thought. Thirty-five years was a long career for any fighter. Marco had been fighting a century longer than that. With his grizzled hair and white-streaked beard, Wyatt looked a decade or two older than Marco. But he was just a baby. Innocent. Thirty-five years of fighting? A newbie.

Barely anyone alive is my age, Marco thought. *Only Einav and Addy understand. Only they were with me during the Alien Wars. Wyatt was born after those years of struggle. He'll never understand what it was like. To face alien invasions. To see millions die. He's a tough, leathery old mercenary, but he's innocent. So many people are. They will learn.*

Marco had never had many friends. And most of those few had died in the Alien Wars. For the past century, his only friends had been Addy and Einav. Joey too, if you counted a computer. Could he ever find new people in his life? Forge new friendships? Male friendships? The idea appealed to him. But how could he? How could anyone understand what he had lived through? What was it like to be nearly 150, to have grown up during the Cataclysm, to have fought the grays and marauders, to have watched his children grow old and die? Addy and Einav could understand. Nobody else could. Marco felt like an alien himself. Different from all other humans who seemed so young, who seemed like children.

He looked at Wyatt flying nearby, and at the other Ragtaggers patrolling the beach. Could he find a brotherhood here? New friendships? New comrades? Male companionship? Or was he doomed to forever stand apart from other men, scarred by age and many haunting traumas from centuries past?

He didn't know. Maybe there could be two parts to him. The old Marco, the Marco with the memories, the Marco only Addy and Einav could understand. And a new type of man, shedding off his traumas, finding new life with a new generation of fellow warriors. He didn't know all the answers. But he knew that when he looked at Wyatt and the other Ragtaggers, he felt comforted. He felt that even in this universe of so much pain, strong people were fighting back. He was not alone.

"Yo, buddy!" Wyatt said over the ragnet. "You all right there? You spacing out?"

Marco nodded. "Yeah. A bit."

"Don't you worry, bud." Wyatt flew by close and raised his fist. "We'll give them squids hell. I got your back, brother."

Marco smiled. "Right back at ya."

Addy's voice came over the ragnet. "Aww, bromance."

"Stop eavesdropping!" Marco said.

A little hologram of Addy materialized atop Joey's dashboard. She was wearing overalls and holding tools. "Stop using a public channel, then."

Wyatt laughed and ascended. "I'll go take a look higher up. Catch ya later, bud. Later, Ads." The *Spacehog* soared into the stratosphere on a jet of flame.

"Damn, I love that ship," Addy said. "It's been my lifelong dream to ride a flying cannon."

"Addy, your lifelong dream was to visit the Elephant Man skeleton in the Royal London Hospital," Marco said. "Which you did ten years ago. They're still trying to piece him together after your crushing hug."

Addy shrugged. "At least he didn't crumble to dust like that mummy I hugged at the British Museum."

Marco groaned. "How are the repairs going? Hopefully you're not hugging any critical components."

"I'm inside the *Blood, Sweat, and Tears* now. She's a good

ship. Watertight. Really is a miracle of engineering."

"And what am I, chopped liver?" Joey said.

Addy's hologram blew a kiss. "Joey, you're a miracle of engineering too. Because I fixed you. Anyway, Marco, I'm working on installing new graviton plates along the lower deck, then running cables to divert engine power to them. This baby weighs a million tons. Not easy to get a ship this size off the ground. You only land these behemoths when you scrap them. They're not designed to take off. But I think I can have her flying. Eventually."

"How soon?" Marco said.

Addy chewed her lip. "Not sure. I'll be able to run a test tonight. We'll see how it goes. Maybe she'll fly tomorrow. Maybe in a month."

"In a month?" Marco cried. "There might not be an Earth left in a month."

"Oh, quiet, it's always doom and gloom with you. I'm back to work. Keep watch over me, babe, all right?"

"Always," Marco said. "Love you."

She blew him a kiss. "Love ya more." She lowered her welding visor, and her hologram vanished.

Marco pursed his lips. A day or a month. He glanced skyward again. Did they have that much time?

"Buddy?" Wyatt said. His voice emerged from Joey's speakers. The *Spacehog* was too high up now to see with the naked eye.

"What do you see?" Marco said.

For a long moment--silence.

"Wyatt?" Marco said. "Wyatt, what do you see?"

The silence stretched on for another moment. Then Wyatt cleared his throat. "Um, buddy? I got bad news. Hydrians. Hydrians are flying over. A whole bunch of 'em."

Ice flooded Marco's belly. "How many? The whole shoal?"

"Not sure. They're still too far to see. I don't think so. Thousands, though. Goddammit, buddy, those bastards are flying fast. They'll be here within the hour."

Marco inhaled deeply and his fingers tightened around the yoke. He called his leader.

"Einav? Company is on the way."

* * * * *

Einav was inside the HDFS *Blood, Sweat, and Tears* when Marco raised the alarm. The dreadnought still lay in the shallow water. She was in surprisingly good shape. At least for a million-ton dreadnought submerged in salty water halfway up her hull. Addy led a team of mechanics and engineers, redirecting power to the graviton plates laid inside the lower hull. All around the engine room rose great machine parts--gears the size of houses, pipes you could walk through, engines like cathedrals, and pistons that could shatter mountains. Addy and her mechanics were like ants in a hive, scurrying everywhere across the engine room, reconfiguring this great machine to do their bidding.

Einav had a military mind. She knew little of engineering. She was here to help however she could. And so she followed Addy's instructions, doing her part to move and install graviton plates on the deck below. This was not her field. But right now, it was all hands on deck. Einav's top priority was getting the heavy hitters into the air.

When Marco called her, a chill flooded her. His words echoed in her mind. *Company is on the way . . .*

We're not ready, she thought. *We need more time. We can't fight again so soon!*

She pursed her lips and took a deep breath.

Control yourself, Einav!

She spoke into her minicom. "How far are they? How

many? What instars? Send me the data."

Marco nodded. "Grabbing it now from Wyatt, relaying it down to you."

Einav stood inside the dreadnought's engine room, reviewing the videos and stats pouring into her minicom. Her heart sank. Ten thousand galactopods were heading to Earth.

It was not Ninazu's entire force. The bulk of the shoal was still on Mars, still feasting. But ten thousand . . . Dear Lord, even that terrified her. Each of those hydrians was like a living warship. She had only a few hundred Ragtaggers in the air. The rest of her fleet was still grounded. The galactopods could travel faster than light. Whatever data was reaching Earth was already old. The hydrians were probably only an hour away. Maybe only minutes away.

For a second, Einav could not breathe. The blood drained from her face. Her heart froze in her chest.

Is this the end? Our end?

No. She inhaled sharply. *No! Do not succumb to fear! Fear is an enemy. Fear destroys a warrior. Be brave! Be strong!*

She looked up from her minicom.

"Addy!" she cried. Her voice echoed across the cavernous engine room.

Addy stood several stories up on scaffolds. She looked down at Einav. Normally Addy might respond with a quip, but even from the distance, she seemed to notice Einav's fear.

I must look as pale as hydrian bones, Einav thought.

Addy leaped off the scaffolds. Her jetpack thrummed, blasting out blue graviton streams. Addy flew across the engine room and landed by Einav.

"What is it?" Addy said.

Einav showed her the data from space.

"Those fuckers!" Addy blurted out. "Hart must have called them. I knew I should have killed that bastard!"

Einav wasn't so sure about that. As much as she loathed
Hart, he seemed sincere about trying to appease the shoal.

"Hart doesn't matter now. Addy, we must get these ships
in the air. Now."

"We can't!" Addy said. "We still have loads of work to
do."

"Addy." Einav grabbed her arms and stared into her eyes.
"They're coming. Thousands of them. We need these ships rising
now."

Addy was pale. She gulped, tightened her lips, and
nodded. "I'll do what I can. I'll need an hour. The Ragtag Fleet
will have to hold off the hydrians until then."

Einav nodded. "All right. I'll be up in space with them.
I'm heading to the starfighter bay."

She turned to leave, but Addy grabbed her arm. "Einav,
it'll be a bloodbath up there." Her voice shook. "I can't lose both
Marco and you."

Einav wanted to weep. She saw the terrible grief and fear
in her friend's eyes.

She hugged Addy and whispered into her ear, "I'll keep
Marco safe. And he'll keep me safe. Stay strong, my friend. Do
your job. Get the ships flying. We'll survive this. I promise you."

Addy sniffed and nodded. "I love you, Einav. Tell the
dumbass I love him too."

Einav's eyes dampened. "Love you too. Godspeed, Addy."

Then she left her friend's embrace and ran.

* * * * *

Einav raced through the tilted corridors and decks of the
HDFS *Blood, Sweat, and Tears*, heading toward her hangar bay. As
always, Einav Ben-Ari would serve where she was needed most.
Right now it was in the sky.

As she ran, she raised her minicom to her lips. "All starfighter pilots, report to the hangar bay!"

The *Blood, Sweat, and Tears* was a starship the size of a town, and the elevators were powered down. Even sprinting, it seemed to take forever before Einav reached the hangar bay.

Fifty Firebirds stood on the deck. L35 Firebirds--the great starfighters of the Human Defense Force. They had won the Alien Wars. Even now, a century later, they were mighty weapons. Back in Einav's early days in the military, pilots had flown the L16 Firebird. Over time, technology had advanced. The L35s were faster, more agile, and deadlier than ever. They were small ships. Each was only fifteen meters long. The cockpit only had room for one pilot. But they packed a punch, their wings laden with missiles, torpedoes, Gatling guns, and novabolts. Their hulls were painted navy blue, while their pointed tips were gold like beaks. Rampant phoenixes adorned their wings. The Firebirds themselves looked like phoenixes--birds of fire rising from the ashes of the Cataclysm to strike back at their foes.

One thing had not changed. Even now, Firebirds were not sentient. They did have basic AI installed; it helped fire the weapons, control the engine heat, navigate, and fly in battle. But it was not conscious. In an era of artificial intelligence, Firebirds relied on human pilots, human intuition, and the human spirit of battle, honed over millions of years of savage evolution. AI was smarter, faster, perhaps more capable, but when it came to sheer brutality, it could not beat a naked ape who had survived generations of warfare in the wilderness. Within their souls, pulsing beneath a thin veneer of civilization, all humans carried within them the instincts of killers. The brutes used this instinct to terrorize others. The noble and wise aimed it at the enemies of civilizations and wielded it as a weapon of justice.

Pilots were entering the hangar and running across the deck. A klaxon wailed overhead, summoning the Firebirds to war.

Deckhands raced everywhere, preparing the starfighters and rushing toward the airlocks. Einav was not a pilot by trade, but during her long military career, she had flown plenty of starfighters. She would fly one now too.

"Einav!" Marco cried over the ragnet. "Einav, I hear the sounds of a hangar bay. You're not about to take off in a Firebird, are you?"

"We're short on pilots," she said, running toward a bird. "You need me up there."

"You're our leader, Einav! I need you alive."

"I'm no longer president. I'm a soldier again. And I will fight."

She reached a Firebird. The starfighter was beautiful, all graceful curves, her hull gleaming gold and navy blue. She had never flown in battle, by the looks of it. That or her crew had done a fantastic job restoring her. Awe filled Einav at the sight of this deadly and noble bird of prey. Modern Firebirds had individual names, emblazoned with golden letters on their hull. This bird was named the *Don't Panic*. A good name. A deckhand raced forward with a ladder, and Einav climbed toward the cockpit.

"Einav," Marco said, speaking from Joey into her earpiece. "The hydrians are coming in fast. They're only moments away. There are a lot of them."

"I know, Marco. I'm coming to help. Hang tight."

She hopped into the cockpit, settled in the seat, and shut the canopy. She looked at the controls. It had been a while, but it was all coming back to her. This cockpit felt so familiar.

"Just like riding a bike," she said, flipping switches.

The engine roared to life.

Around her, the other pilots were firing up their engines. The birds were ready to fly. The deckhands struggled to pull open the airlocks. When the doors finally opened, seawater rushed in, sluicing across the deck. The sea level was about a foot above the hangar deck. The water short-circuited a few control panels but couldn't stop the Firebirds.

Einav shoved down the throttle. *Don't Panic* raced across the watery deck, raising waves at her sides, parting the water like a mechanical Moses. Then Einav burst through the airlock, pulled the yoke back, and soared. Her engines roared, blasting the sea below, scattering so much water she revealed the seabed. She soared, rising in a straight line. The g-force shoved her against her seat. She clenched her jaw. Excitement burned through her. The thrill of battle flowed over her fear. A fast starfighter, an array of weapons, the feeling of power--that always fed her heart before battle.

When I was a little girl, and the scum rained down hell on Earth, I used to hide in the bomb shelter, hugging myself and crying and praying to live, she thought. *Now I fly a starfighter with enough ammunition to destroy a city. The enemy is mighty, but so am I. And while I'm still afraid, I'm powerful.*

Below her, more and more Firebirds emerged from the airlocks. Soon a hundred birds were soaring in straight lines, blasting skyward on trails of smoke and light. Below them, the beached Phoenix Fleet still lay in the water, the great ships shrinking and shrinking until even dreadnoughts became like mere toys.

Hurry up, Addy, Einav thought. *We need those ships. We need hope.*

* * * * *

Most of the Ragtag Fleet was already in the space, prepared to meet the hydrians head-on. Einav soared in her starfighter through the sky, heading to join them. A hundred other Firebirds rose with her.

A single dark ship, somewhat larger than a Firebird, raced up beside Einav. She couldn't see the ship. Einav saw only the shape of a ship, all in black, cut out from the blue sky. Joey reflected no light. You could not see any glimmers or details on her hull. Nothing at all. She appeared two-dimensional like a shadow.

I really need to get ultrablack paint on my Firebirds, Einav thought.

Joey moved closer until she flew only meters away from *Don't Panic.* The two ships soared side by side through the stratosphere, heading to space.

Einav's comlink crackled. Marco was calling her.

"Most of the Ragtaggers are forming a wall formation in lower orbit," Marco said. "We can expand the wall with your starfighters."

Einav considered. A wall formation involved ships spreading out to block an enemy advance. That worked well with larger warships. Their electromagnetic shields could snap together, forming a huge buzzing force field in space. And if any enemy got through the shields, they'd meet mighty cannons and armored hulls. But would it work with smaller ships?

"No," she finally said. "Only the larger Ragtag ships have electromagnetic shields. None of my Firebirds do. Joey doesn't either. Our wall would be more like a chain link fence. Full of holes. Let's go with a blooming flower formation."

Marco thought for a moment. "I dunno, Einav. It's risky. That would let too many enemy ships through."

A blooming flower formation involved tightening a small fleet into an isosceles triangle, driving into a larger foe, then folding out the triangle's sides like blooming petals. It could break a large enemy fleet in two. But Marco was right. Each half of the enemy fleet could fly around the "blooming flower" and make its way down to Earth.

Einav pursed her lips. Her Firebird and Joey were entering space now. The blue sky faded, and the stars burst to life ahead. The Ragtag Fleet was already there, waiting, watching the distance.

And there they were. Coming in fast.

The hyds.

"Supernova formation," Einav said. "If we can't build a thick wall, and if we can't bloom like a flower, we'll explode inside them like a grenade."

"Supernova formation?" Marco said. "Einav, in all our simulations, that results in massive casualties."

"I know," she said softly. "For both sides. It's the best way to shock the enemy. To stun them until Addy has the Phoenix Fleet ready."

"All right, Einav," Marco said. "Let's go supernova. I'm with you. And may God have mercy on our souls."

They soared higher, joining the Ragtaggers in space. More Firebird squadrons, launching from more grounded dreadnoughts and carriers, rose to join them. Soon hundreds of Firebirds were in space.

Ahead, in the distance, Einav could already see a distant blue stain like a bruise. That was the light of the hydrians, blueshifting as the swarm approached. Ten thousand, the data suggested. They would be here soon.

Below the human defenders shone pale blue Earth. Fragile. So small in the vastness of space. Their homeworld. This was not just a battle to save her own life, Einav knew. Not only to save the Phoenix Fleet. This was a battle to save Earth and all the billions who lived there. Time and time again, Earth had faced annihilation. Time and time again, for centuries, one alien empire or another thought to conquer this little blue jewel, only for the courage of humanity to cast them back. Einav had fought in all these wars--since the first great war against the scum until this, the wrath of the shoal. Against overwhelming odds, Einav and her soldiers had cast back the enemies. But they had never faced a foe like this.

The shoal had come from another galaxy. They had conquered a million worlds. And now, all that lay between them and Earth was a small fleet. The Ragtaggers. The Firebirds. Perhaps a few hundred warships too, if Addy could raise them into the air. All in all, it seemed so trifle a force against an alien empire.

Even if we can defeat these ten thousand, what of the billion still at Mars? Einav thought. *Am I being a fool? Is Hart right and we can only kneel?*

She shoved her doubts aside. No. She had seen what the shoal had done to Mars. They had devoured the planet, leaving not a soul alive. That would be the fate of Earth should hydrians wrap their tentacles around it. Erafel was smooth of words, a deceiver who had fooled Hart. Einav could not allow herself to be fooled, to be tempted by false hope. She was a soldier. Her way was the way of battle and death. If she saved Earth, it would be on the battlefield, and if she fell, it would be in the same place.

She broadcast a message to the entire fleet of Firebirds and Ragtaggers. "All ships--we're going to take a supernova formation. Form a sphere around me. Firebirds on the inside. Ragtaggers on the outside. Don't go supernova until I give the order."

She heard a few mutters across ragnet.

"Supernova?"

"Is she mad?"

Wyatt, meanwhile, gave a whoop and a "hell yeah!"

In the distance, the alien light was glowing brighter and larger. The indigo stains became purple, then crimson like dry blood. Twisted black shapes, limbs undulating, appeared before the sanguine light like ghosts dancing before a decaying star. Warped space and time were distorting the image, painting a melting masterpiece of damnation. Hieronymus Bosch himself would have shied away in fear.

The human fleet took form, clustering close together. Not in a wall. Not in a triangle. They formed a tightly-knit sphere, cannons facing outward. They were like a sea urchin with bristling spikes pointing every which way. The sphere was compact, not hollow. Ragtaggers formed the outer layer like the shell of a grenade. On the inside, like bits of shrapnel waiting to erupt, flew nested spheres of Firebirds. In the very center flew Einav in her starfighter and Marco in Joey.

"We're like Russian dolls," Marco said. "Nesting within one another."

"Killer Russian dolls armed with enough firepower to destroy a small moon," Einav said.

"Addy would have loved it," Marco said.

The hydrians were swarming closer at incredible speed, writhing and squirming through the void, black tentacles outstretched, red eyes ablaze, and always behind them rose their nebulous wake of fire, a hellish background for their dark cabaret. And Einav heard them. Heard the grunts, grumbles, and echoing squeals. There should be no sound in space. She knew that. And yet the way they distorted spacetime cast out gravitation ripples. When those ripples hit *Don't Panic*'s hull, they thrummed with demonic squeals like haunting ghosts calling out curses from beyond.

Across her fleet, she heard men pray. Others whispered in fear. The formation began to loosen. One Firebird pilot even turned to flee, changed heart, then resumed formation. They had all fought battles before, Firebird pilots and Ragtaggers alike, but even the stoutest warrior would quiver at these eerie sounds and hellish sights. Einav's own heart pounded within her rib cage like a trapped animal.

"Fear not!" she told her fleet. "Fear is death on the

battlefield. Fear deadens your aim, clouds your mind. Be brave! Stay strong! Keep your formation tight and your cannons hot! I am Einav Ben-Ari. I fight with you. Together we will win. Say it with me. We will win!"

"We will win!" they cried. Their voices were loud and strong, but they carried the tremor of fear.

The shoal's squeals and grumbles grew louder. They were dropping out of warp speed now. As spacetime straightened around them, it revealed their true terror. No longer were they vague, tentacled smudges but demons fully emerged into the world. Their jaws opened wide, lined with teeth.

Most were hyds, and those were bad enough. Hyd tentacles were as long as oak trees, and their mouths could devour starfighters. Ten thousand of these foul beasts flew toward Earth and her defenders. But they were not even the worst of it. Greater terrors flew here. Three hydlords commanded the host, larger than blue whales and infinitely meaner. They were not as large as Hydprince Ninazu, and they were certainly smaller than the mythical hydkings, planet-engulfing creatures Einav had never seen. But hydlords were big enough to take on the largest human warship. And all those large warships were down on Earth. It was up to the Ragtag Fleet and Firebirds now. They were a few hundred strong, a band of plucky warriors against a vast armada of monsters.

"Let's roll," Einav said.

And roll they did--literally. Like a ball of interlocking ants, the sphere of starships rolled toward the hydrian host. It was a complicated maneuver. Each ship had to perfectly synchronize with the others, maintaining the spheres within spheres. Navigational software and AI helped, but mostly it was the experience and skill of human pilots. Einav had a ridiculous mental image of a huge bowling ball rolling toward a group of upright squids.

Closer, closer they rolled, gaining speed, cannons bristling in all directions. The formation tightened as they approached. The sphere condensed. The ships flew so closely their wings almost touched. Einav kept leaning on *Don't Panic*'s yoke, rolling and yawing to stay in position. Joey, with Marco at the helm, flew at her side. Around them spread the great interlocking sphere of small ships.

The hydrians swarmed closer, their formation spreading wide, forming a tidal wave of armored mantles. Their mouths opened in slavering grins. Their limbs stretched forward and disgorged clouds of ink.

"Fire the foam!" Einav cried.

During the last respite between battles, they had augmented the Ragtag ships--even some of the Firebirds, as many as time allowed--with foam cannons. These defensive weapons had done good work during previous skirmishes with the shoal. The outer sphere of the supernova formation--comprising the Ragtag Fleet--fired their new weapons. Torrents of foam flew toward the incoming waves of ink. These cannons were, essentially, giant fire extinguishers.

When foam met ink, it instantly absorbed it. Rivers of the tarry liquid were socked up. The saturated chunks of foam floated off harmlessly. The cannons sprayed more and more foam, combating the ink, absorbing oceans of the stuff.

But there were too many hyds spewing too much ink. The foam could not keep up. Inkblots hit a few Ragtag ships, clung to their hulls, and began eating through the metal. Inky serpents made it into a few ships. Ragtag captains and crews screamed as the sticky black stuff devoured them. A few Ragtag ships crumpled up, slammed into nearby ships, and careened into space.

"Maintain the sphere!" Einav said. "Keep rolling! Right at them!"

Shedding another ship with each rotation, the sphere

formation kept rolling toward the enemy, blasting a path forward
with spurts of foam. The true cannons Einav did not yet fire. No
missiles or torpedoes flew. Not yet.

"Einav, we have to fire our guns!" Marco said.

"Not yet," she cried. "Hold!"

Closer they rolled. Soon they were only a few thousand
klicks away. The tentacles reached toward them, claws whirring,
and the ink blots rose in a hurricane.

"Hold!" Einav shouted.

The sphere rolled closer, tearing through the ink, shedding
more and more ships. The hyds chuckled and gloated and
grinned. They looked like mutated dogs who saw a ball of food
roll their way.

"Einav!" Marco shouted.

"Hold!" she said.

Closer they rolled. Closer. Tentacles reached outward,
engulfing them, swinging inward.

"Fire!" Einav shouted.

The outer sphere blazed with gunfire. Hundreds of Ragtag
ships let loose together. Torpedoes, laser beams, shells, and
plascasters blazed in a spinning circle of death. Wyatt could be
heard whooping as his *Spacehog* unleashed. The sphere became like
a rolling firecracker, spurting sparks every which way. As they
fired, they kept rolling, carving into the hydrian formation. Squids
squealed and pulled their tentacles back. The barrage hit eyes,
entered mouths, and cracked exoskeletons.

"I feel like a bowling ball!" Marco said. Like *Don't Panic*
and the other Firebirds, Joey was still in the center of the sphere,
not yet in the fight. Only the outer sphere--the brave ships of the
Ragtag Fleet--were firing now.

"Keep rolling!" Einav called to her combined fleet. "Move
deeper into their lines!"

The hydrians were swarming in a great wall as wide as the

Earth. That wall was thicker than a mountain range, and the humans must fight for every roll of their sphere. The hyds were overcoming their initial shock. Their tentacles lashed, slamming at the human sphere. Ragtag ships careened into the distance, shedding chunks of their hull, only for Firebirds from the inner sphere to replace them, to open fire too. The shoal was like a bear that swallowed a porcupine. The bear managed to gulp down his prey. Barely. And it hurt like hell.

The sphere kept rolling. Another revolution. Another. They kept firing, blasting back galactopods until they were a hundred klicks deep. They were embedded into the wall of hydrians now. They were deep in the belly of the bear.

And then Einav gave the order.

"Go supernova!"

And like a star going supernova, the sphere burst open. Ragtaggers blazed outward in an expanding shock wave of destruction, firing their guns every which way. From inside, hundreds of Firebirds burst out like hornets from a cracked hive. In the heart of the shoal, the small human force burst open, devastating the enemy from within.

Einav shoved down *Don't Panic*'s thruster. She blazed forth, swerving between other Firebirds, and pulled her triggers. Her torpedoes streaked forth and hit a hyd. The alien ripped apart, scattering chunks of carapace, gobbets of flesh, and fountains of ink. Marco shouted nearby. Joey streaked into the alien lines, a dark wolf in the night, firing novabolts as white and bright as a wolf's fangs. All around, the hundreds of human ships flared, punching as hard as they could, ripping through their foes.

They were like a bullet exploding inside a man's flesh. They did terrible damage, taking out dozens, maybe hundreds of hyds around them. A blast wave of broken exoskeletons and mangled tentacles flew outward. From Earth, they would look like a true supernova tearing through a dark cloud.

But a supernova could only explode once. And when the dust settled, the human fleet was scattered. Each ship was like a piece of shrapnel embedded into flesh. Thousands of hydrians still lived. They bared their teeth, and their eyes--normally so apathetic when it came to killing--now burned with rage.

This was the downside of the supernova formation. It dealt devastation . . . then left you exposed. It was a kamikaze attack. And now the enemy came closing in, and Einav, Marco, and the rest of them fought for their lives within the sea of squids.

CHAPTER TEN
God's Nightmare

If there was anything Addy loved more than hot dogs, hockey, and freaks, it was fighting. Now she was stuck down here on Earth, fixing warships, while Marco and Einav were having all the fun. She should be up there in space! Fighting at their side! Instead Addy was down here, rerouting graviton coils.

"No, no!" she shouted, hovering through the engine room with her jetpack. "You have to attach the north side to the red pipe. The red one!"

Two young mechanics looked up from below. They saluted and flipped the coil. Addy groaned. The work was almost done. The ships were almost ready to take flight. But every time she thought they were ready, another nincompoop plugged something in the wrong way.

She was inside the bowels of the HDFS *Blood, Sweat, and Tears*. Across the beach, other teams were hurrying to fix the other warships. A few corvettes were almost ready to blast off. A frigate was already rumbling her engines, vibrating in the sand and shaking the shore and water. The dreadnoughts, the heaviest ships, were taking the longest to repair. Three dreadnoughts lay on the coast: the *Blood, Sweat, and Tears*, the *Ragnarok*, and the *Brimstone Fury*. And dammit, they were a bitch to get in the air.

Addy hopped onto the deck. "No, dammit! You gotta slide the accelerator tube in first, then clamp the quantum coils, and *then* reroute the electric wiring." She shoved a mechanic aside. "Like this."

She snapped the pieces together, then felt the comforting thrum of gravitons flowing through the pipes. The artificial gravity tugged at her. Bits of debris, dust, and scattered screws moved across the deck like beetles, inching toward the pipes. Addy's hair undulated, reaching toward the pipes in golden strands. A few loose coins, batteries, and packs of gum flew from her pockets and snapped against the pipes. The gravitational field was working. Good. Excellent, in fact. Of course, pulling coins and screws was one thing. Lifting a million-ton starship? Quite another.

If Addy had assembled things right, once she turned on the fusion core, she could flood the pipes with enormous power. She could magnify the graviton field to monstrous proportions, then direct those gravitons downward. If her theory was correct, and her engineering was proper, the *Blood, Sweat, and Tears* would levitate from the beach, rise to space, and then blast off to battle. So would the other ships along the beach, where her teams were making the same modifications.

Of course, it might also blow up every ship here. And kill thousands of spacers aboard. Including Addy. Well, it might not be *that* bad. The graviton field might levitate the ships and simply crush the crew into paste. At least the ships would be salvageable. The crew? Not so much.

Addy would have loved an extra few weeks. One week to run the math and schematics past physicists. Another week to build a fake rig and run small-scale tests. Maybe a third week to test the system on a disposable ship full of crash test dummies. But she didn't have weeks. She had minutes. Maybe seconds. Einav and Marco were up there, facing ten thousand hyds. They needed her.

She pulled out her minicom, tapped a button, and raised a holographic screen. She called Marco.

"How you doing up there?"

He didn't answer.

"Marco?"

No reply.

Cold terror gripped Addy's heart. She tapped buttons on her minicom. In an emergency, she could access Joey's computer remotely. From her minicom, Addy could see what Joey saw, hear what Joey heard, peer out into space or into the cockpit. Marco didn't know Addy could do this. It was how Addy had learned of his love for *Catgirl Academy* and those other shameful cartoons he watched in the cockpit. Right now, Addy didn't care about spying on her husband. Her minicom displayed a view from Joey's perspective. Down here on Earth, Addy was seeing what Joey saw.

And Addy saw nothing but squids. An ocean of them. Joey's novabolts flew, galloped through space like luminous stallions, and slammed into the enemies. There seemed no end to the shoal.

"Marco!" Addy shouted through Joey's speakers. "Marco, it's me!"

"Addy?" came his voice. "How did you hack into Joey?"

"Are you alive?" Addy said.

"Barely. Bit busy now, Ads. Can we talk later?" More novabolts flew.

"Stop trying to fly and shoot at once," Addy said. "Let Joey fly. You shoot!"

"Stop backseat flying! Goodbye, Addy!"

He tapped a button, cutting off the stream. His words echoed through her mind.

Goodbye, Addy . . .

Was this goodbye?

She pursed her lips and wiped her eyes. He needed her. Her sweet little Poet needed her. Memories from the old days flooded her. She remembered them as children, war orphans struggling to survive in the ruins of the Cataclysm. Marco had been small for his age, scrawny and bookish. Addy had been taller, stronger, wilder. He was the child of a librarian who lost himself in books. She was a rough-and-tumble tomboy who got in fistfights, smoked, and stole. She would protect him in those days. He had become like a little brother to her, and if bullies approached, she would send them fleeing with a kick to the pants.

Marco had grown since then, had become a soldier, a leader, a strong and courageous man. But a part of Addy, somewhere deep inside her, still remembered him as that bookish, scared little boy. And she still wanted to protect him.

"We're taking off," she said. "Now."

Mechanics looked up at her. The chief engineer, a bald and sweaty man named Murphy, stomped toward her. "You must be mad. We haven't even run any tests yet! We haven't even secured the backup overflow tubing."

"If we don't take off now," Addy said, "our brothers and sisters above will die. And the hydrians will destroy us on the ground. We take off. No tests. No backups. Turn the system on. *Now*."

Murphy tossed down his wrench. "No." He crossed his arms. "I refuse."

Addy leaped down from the scaffolds, hopped over a pipe, and advanced toward him.

"What--?" The engineer took a step back. "What are you--"

Addy drove an uppercut into his chin. He hit the deck.

Everyone was staring at her. From across scaffolds, atop gears, and along pipes, mechanics stared.

"Battle stations!" Addy shouted. "Move, soldiers!"

They ran.

Addy raised her minicom and called the bridge. "This is Brigadier Addy Linden from engineering."

She wasn't sure which rank to use. Einav had promoted her to rear admiral in the Lionheart fleet. But that fleet had shattered over Mars. A century ago, Addy had retired from the Human Defense Force as a brigadier. This was a Human Defense Force ship. So she decided to use her old HDF rank again. The ghost of that officer from ancient wars was rising again, and so would this ship.

The hologram of a man burst from Addy's minicom, several inches tall. Commander Caleb Harris, captain of the dreadnought, had broad shoulders, a gray crew cut, and stern dark eyes. He had rushed over from his home, his dinner half-eaten, and now stood on the bridge. The starship was so large he was half a mile away from Addy.

"We read you, Linden," he said.

"We're firing up the engines," Addy said. "We're taking flight. Right now."

"We're not--"

"That is an order. Don't make me punch you out too." She pointed her minicom camera at the supine engineer at her feet.

The gruff commander nodded. A twinkle touched those dark eyes, and the hint of a smile played on his lips. "Understood. Let's get this bird in the air."

The engine room began to rattle. Deeper in the ship, the fusion reactor was crackling to life. Heat bathed the innards of the *Blood, Sweat, and Tears.* Great machines awoke from slumber. Gears turned and ticked. Pipes thrummed. It would take a moment for the system to warm up. They hadn't blown themselves up yet. That was promising.

Addy relayed the orders to all the ships along the beach-- several hundred in total. The other captains and engineers objected too. The familiar chorus of "We're not ready!" and "You must be mad!" filled Addy's earpiece. She shut them up with curses and threats of extreme violence. The fear of Addy's kicks (which had become the stuff of urban legend) motivated them into action. That and, perhaps, an understanding of the greater danger. The danger of the hydrians. The other grounded ships had sensors too. They were also getting glimpses of the battle above. They knew the peril. Knew the brave pilots above needed help and needed it now.

Hang tight, Marco, Addy thought. *I'm coming.*

The engine room rumbling increased. Pipes thrummed and rattled. The fusion core was flaring to life, condensing hydrogen into a super-dense sphere. Addy could not see the fusion core. It was hidden behind layers of force field, concrete, and lithium blankets. Any camera nearby would melt. To supply their monstrous energy needs, dreadnoughts utilized nuclear fusion--essentially crafting and controlling miniature stars within their cores. The sun gave energy to Earth, and artificial suns powered ships to leave Earth and explore the galaxy.

But right now, Addy's system was diverting the power of that artificial star not to the engines--but to the graviton plates lining the ship's lower decks. Instead of thrusting the ship forward using Newton's Third Law, the *Blood, Sweat, and Tears* was levitating using graviton mechanics. Or at least trying to.

"Please work," Addy whispered, crossing her fingers behind her back. "Please don't blow up. Please--Whoa!"

The ship gave a huge jerk. Addy grabbed a rail for support. The pipes were thrumming, the gears turning, the power flowing. Massive power. Addy's entire body felt electric. Her hair floated as if she swam underwater.

And then she felt something. A sensation of rising. Her feet levitated off the deck. Her jetpack was off, yet she floated inside the engine room.

Across the room, mechanics and engineers clung to railings. Their eyes widened. They too levitated. Screws and dust and tools floated around them.

"It's happening," Addy whispered. "It's working. It's a miracle." She shook her head. "Not a miracle. Science. Or is there a difference? Oh bloody squid balls, I sound like Poet."

She laughed. The important thing was--it was working!

On her minicom, she could see a view from sensors on the dorsal hull. The mighty HDFS *Blood, Sweat, and Tears* was rising from the water. She was a dreadnought that would make a blue whale look like a sardine, a machine the size of a town, and she was levitating upward in the water! As a million tons of steel and energy rose from the seabed, they churned the sea. Waves rocked the smaller ships.

Then, with a sucking sound, the underbelly detached from the sea. The dreadnought jostled and rumbled, and Addy thought the hull would break, but they kept rising! Dripping seawater and algae, the mighty *Blood, Sweat, and Tears* hovered above the Mediterranean coast. Behind her, Château Pèlerin--the mighty fortress that had once housed thousands of crusaders--appeared as small as a hut.

Then another warship rose--a corvette named the HDFS *Stormshard*. Then the *Indominus* levitated--a mighty frigate with cannons along her sides. One by one, they rose from the water and beach. The HDFS *Ragnarok*, another dreadnought, finally rose from the water with great waves and foam and thundering booms. Last it was the *Brimstone Fury*, the third and final dreadnought in the fleet, that ascended from the sea, spilling water full of fish and algae and broken stones.

In mythology, phoenixes rose from ashes in blazes of fire. The Phoenix Fleet rose from the water with sprays of foam and dripping seaweed. Their engines rumbled. Their hulls thrummed. They almost sounded like a pod of whales, singing with deep, mournful voices. Hundreds rose from the water. Largest were the dreadnoughts but all were mighty. The lost fleet of Earth was rising again, and the sight filled Addy's eyes with tears and heart with pride.

We're still in this fight, she thought. *There's still hope.*

Higher they rose until they all levitated above the beach and water. Then they tilted backward, sterns to the water, prows facing the stars. Hundreds of ships rose like skyscrapers, a cityscape along the ancient gateway to the east. Some of these titans rose a mile into the air.

"Soar," Addy whispered.

Her soft command traveled across the fleet. And together, the ships diverted power to their stern propulsions. Engines rumbled, then blasted as one. The world thundered. Flames burst from exhaust ports, steaming the water and exposing the seabed. The ships soared skyward, bathing the beach with heat and light. Water gushed in waves. Bricks crumbled across the fortress. Sand blew onto distant cities. The world shook and trembled and the starships kept soaring, ripping through the sky, shaking the world.

Addy was still in the engine room of the *Blood, Sweat, and Tears,* watching through her minicom, clinging onto the railing. The beach became smaller, the Sinai dropped down below her, and the vastness of the Middle East unfolded in rolling gold and craggy mountains. And then the fleet ripped through the stratosphere into space, and all the world was but a blue marble wreathed in clouds.

The stars spread around them. Addy tapped her minicom to stream a video from the ship's prow sensors. And there it was. Right ahead. The great battle.

We're too late, Addy thought, her breath dying on her lips.

The hydrians. There they were. Most of the bastards were still feasting at Mars, sucking up every last bone and mineral. But quite a few had come here to Earth. More than Addy had expected. Ten thousand? No, that had been a gross underestimation. Twice that much at least. Maybe ten times as much. They hid the stars. The hydrians were a black nebula, spreading out tentacles like cancerous growths, a stain upon the galaxy. Addy could barely see an end to them. This was not the entire shoal, of course, just a small assault force sent to punish Earth, but even this force seemed insurmountable, unstoppable, an evil that could wipe out humanity. That had, perhaps, already wiped out everyone Addy had loved.

Where were the human ships? Where were the Ragtaggers? The Firebirds?

"Marco?" she whispered. "Einav?"

She couldn't see them. Oh God, they were gone, they--

No. Wait! She saw it now. Light within the shoal like thunderbolts flaring within storm clouds. Addy cheered and laughed and wept. Humanity still fought! Marco and Einav were still alive!

"I'm coming, Marco! I'm coming, Einav! Hang tight!" She raised her minicom to her lips and broadcast her words to the Phoenix Fleet. "All captains, this is Addy Linden. Turn off your graviton engines. We've risen high enough. Divert power to your shields and your cannons. Form an assault formation and fly! Fly right at them! We will win!"

Part of her wished she could be on the bridge. Even more, Addy wished she could be in Joey beside her husband. But she knew that right here, in the engine room of a dreadnought, was where she belonged. Here she had rewired, rerouted, and restored the fleet to glory. And from this chamber of pumping pistons and roaring engines, Addy Linden-Emery would deliver salvation to her world and those she loved.

* * * * *

Marco wanted to call Addy. To say goodbye. But he couldn't even remove his hands from the yoke. He was flying the ship while Joey's artificial intelligence controlled the cannons. He was alone in here. Without his wife. Without Einav. Fighting one of the hardest battles of his life. Not since the destruction over Mars had Marco faced such overwhelming odds.

Myriads of hydrians flew all around him. Most were hyds-- terrors as large as Joey, large enough to swallow a man whole. Some were hydlords--beasts large enough to swallow *Joey* whole. Their ink flew everywhere. Their tentacles caught ships and crushed them. A few hundred Ragtaggers and Firebirds fought alongside Marco, but they were falling fast. Their supernova explosion had damaged their foe, but now the human fleet was scattered. Every moment, another human ship fell--devoured by ink, crushed by tentacles, or swallowed into the gut of a squid.

Don't Panic, Einav's little Firebird, forever flew at his side. Though she led the fleet, Einav never strayed far from Marco. The two had been fighting side by side for over a century. Marco had been only eighteen, Einav only twenty, when they had fought their first battle. It had been at Fort Djemila in North Africa, and they had fought with simple rifles against a swarm of alien centipedes. Now, all this time later, still they fought side by side, this time in space, this time flying machines of devastating power. But the odds were even worse, the danger to Earth greater.

"Einav, we must fall back!" he cried.

"Fall back where?" she said. "In case you haven't noticed, we're surrounded."

Don't Panic streaked by. Marco caught a flash of Einav in the cockpit. She fired a barrage of photon bolts at a lurching hyd, knocking the cephalopod back.

"We can concentrate our fire," Marco said. "Carve a way out. Same as we carved a way in."

Three hyds rose before him, jaws unhinging to reveal gaping maws ringed with teeth. Their mad red eyes shone like witches' cauldrons. For a moment Marco must concentrate on his foes. Tentacles flew at him. He dodged most. One slammed into Joey's side. The little starship yelped and tumbled. Marco grabbed the yoke, helping Joey steady her flight. Alien jaw came thrusting toward his bow. Marco engaged the prow graviton thrusters and shot backward. The jaws snapped shut mere meters away.

Not missing a beat, Joey opened fire, bombarding the hungry hydrian with novabolts. The searing neutron missiles plunged through exoskeleton, flesh, skull, and finally brain. A spark of purple light flared. Joey must have scored a direct hit on the azoth crystal inside the hyd's skull. As the crystal shattered, scattering lavender shards, the blast rippled spacetime. Gravitational waves cracked the shells of nearby hyds and shattered their bones. As spacetime wobbled, Marco found himself moments in the past.

"Einav, we must fall back!" he cried.

"Fall back where? In case you haven't noticed, we're--"

The crystal shards vanished into the distance, and space and time righted themselves. Marco returned to the present. Which wasn't exactly comforting. The blast had shattered the three hyds who had attacked Marco, but thousands still flew all around. Far in the distance, Marco descried the *Spacehog*. Wyatt was riding his giant gun like a cowboy, whooping and firing in every direction. The crazy outlaw was loving it.

Someday I'll have to ask him how he became an outlaw, Marco thought. *If we survive this battle.*

Which wasn't looking likely.

"Whoa!" Einav cried.

A tentacle whooshed toward *Don't Panic*'s starboard. Hydrian teeth snapped before the prow. Einav tried to dodge the teeth, and the tentacle slammed into her starfighter. *Don't Panic* rolled, racing on a collision course toward Joey.

Wincing, Marco pulled the yoke. Joey soared, leaping over Einav's tumbling Firebird. The two ships missed each other by mere inches.

Another tentacle wrapped around *Don't Panic*. Einav cursed in her cockpit, firing her guns, unable to break free. Marco snarled and dived, and Joey opened fire, strafing the hyd. The beast squealed and released *Don't Panic*. Working together, the two little ships bombarded the beast, severing tentacles and finally shattering the hideous face.

More hyds came squirming toward them through space.

"There's just no end to these damn things!" Marco said.

He couldn't see Earth, the moon, or the stars, only this alien storm. Around him, more and more lights were winking out--Firebirds and Ragtaggers shattering.

"Einav, if we don't make it--" Marco said.

"We'll make it."

"If we don't, thank you. For being our leader. For being *my* leader." His eyes stung. "I still remember the day I met you. That day you marched up to command your first platoon. You became a leader who inspired me. Who taught me how to fight and how to be a better man. It's been the honor of my life to serve you. And to call myself your friend."

"The honor, Marco, has been mine," said Einav. "You've always been an exemplary soldier. But more importantly--my best friend. But right now, Marco, we fight. And if we must die, we die side by side as soldiers!"

She nudged her joystick. *Don't Panic* came to fly right alongside Joey, beam to beam. The two prows pointed toward a sea of squids. Thousands, tens of thousands of them. The rest of the human fleet was battling their own monsters. Marco and Einav flew here alone, facing the hosts of hell.

Rumbles passed through the storm. The creatures squirmed. The tentacled sea parted, and for a second, Marco dared to hope their lines were breaking, that they were falling back. But then he understood.

As the smaller hyds pulled back, a colossal hydlord rose.
Marco stared in horror, barely able to believe what he saw.

* * * * *

The kraken was the height of the Eiffel Tower, a true lord
of the depths. Its tentacles were like highways lined with blades.
Its red eyes stared--emotionless, dead eyes like pools of
congealing blood. The creature was some sort of strange,
conjoined twin. It had two faces, deformed and bloated. Three
eyes were large and bloodshot, the third small and white and
insane. Two mouths morphed together at the corners, forming
the shape of a hideous L filled with teeth and two dripping
tongues. Around the hideous faces grew a ring of tentacles, tipped
with blades. One of those tentacles sprouted a parasitic twin, a
hydrian the size of an elephant growing like a tumor. They were
triplets, these conjoined monstrosities. Cuneiform was engraved
onto the armored mantle, spelling the name of the foul
galactopod: GOD'S NIGHTMARE.

"Ugly son of a bitch," Marco muttered. Despite his
flippant words, his insides roiled, and terror squeezed his heart.

"Right at him, Marco," Einav said. "We take him head-
on."

He nodded. "Together. A final charge."

He looked out his starboard viewport at the *Don't Panic*.
Einav looked at him through her cockpit. She gave him a small
smile and nod. Then she looked forward again and shouted, her
voice echoing through both cockpits and across the fleet, and
Marco imagined that across the galaxy they could hear her cry:

"For Earth!"

"For Earth!" he shouted.

They shoved their thrusters. They blazed forth, charging
on waves of fury, and fired their cannons.

God's Nightmare extended its many tentacles. Dozens of the armored appendages spread out like the petals of a mutated flower. Their suction cups spun with claws. The parasitic twin on one tentacle snapped its teeth and cackled. The larger twins, forming the main bulk of the creature, opened their fused mouths, revealing a dripping cavern full of crushed starships and wriggling tongues. Maggots the size of horses squirmed inside, feasting on dead humans.

Toward this hellish apparition Marco and Einav flew. Einav's torpedoes streaked forth. Marco's novabolts seared through space with blinding light. The barrage hit the creature. Explosions bloomed. *God's Nightmare* squealed and snapped its mouths shut and lashed its tentacles.

Inkblots flew. Droplets slammed into Joey and she screamed. The ink began eating through her armored hull. Einav managed to escape the ink, but a tentacle hit *Don't Panic*, snapping off one wing, and tossing the Firebird into a tailspin.

"Marco, it burns!" Joey cried. "The ink eating through me!"

"Keep firing!" Marco said.

"It's breaching my hull!" the little ship cried.

Marco yanked the yoke back and forth. Joey shook like a wet dog, scattering dark droplets. But the ink had done its damage, carving little holes into the hull. Air began whistling out. The oxygen levels dropped. Marco cursed.

He pulled down his helmet's visor. An oxygen tube dropped from above, and Marco fastened it into place. Air flowed into his helmet, and he kept fighting, but *God's Nightmare* lashed out again. A tentacle slammed into Joey, crushing one of her prow cannons. A novabolt burst only meters away. A shock wave hit Joey, knocking her back in space. Her front viewport flickered. The port screen cracked and died.

Marco glanced toward Einav. *Don't Panic* was dented, one

wing gone. Her exhaust puffed out smoke, and her canopy was cracked, depressurizing the cockpit. Einav had her visor down too, breathing through an oxygen tank.

The hydlord chuckled. One tentacle wrapped around Joey, gripping the starship so tightly her hull creaked and bent. The little starship screamed. So did Marco. Another tentacle grabbed *Don't Panic* and squeezed. The cracked canopy shattered, leaving Einav exposed to space. She wore a spacesuit and helmet, but that was little comfort. The great jaws of the beast loomed ahead. Sitting in the ravaged cockpit of what remained of *Don't Panic*, Einav drew her sidearm. She fired that little handgun at this monster the size of a cathedral. God bless her, she really was determined to fight to the end.

Marco drew his own handgun. Not to fire at the creature. But to fire into his own head. He would not be taken alive. He would not allow himself to become maggot food, to perish in agony in the mouth of the beast. Or worse--to be captured and mutated, turned into a creature like Erafel. No. He would go down here. In his ship. In Joey, the best ship he had ever flown.

Tears in his eyes, Marco looked at the photo taped to the dashboard. A photo of him with his old platoon. With Einav, his commanding officer. With Addy, his best friend. With Lailani, Elvis, Jackass, Texas, Caveman, and all the others. Soldiers he had loved. Most of them were gone now. Marco had lingered on far too long. He would join them now. He would see them again.

As Joey's hull cracked, Marco held his gun to his head.

Light flared.

From behind the monstrous hydlord rose a great gleaming shape.

A starship soared. Not just any starship but a dreadnought. A ship that was a mile long. A ship with a hull like sky over sea, lined with gold like beams of sunset, and upon her prow gleamed a rampant phoenix in all the colors of fire. She was the HDFS *Blood, Sweat, and Tears*, mightiest of Earth's warships. She was risen.

"Addy, you crazy lunatic!" Marco cried, laughing and crying. "You did it! You did it!"

"Had to come save your ass," Addy said from inside the dreadnought. "As usual."

Her hologram burst to life inside Joey's cockpit. Her antique helmet hung at a rakish angle, the words HELL'S PRINCESS scrawled above the bullet hole. Her two blond braids hung across her shoulders, adorned with bullet casings. She was grinning. God, Marco loved that woman.

God's Nightmare screeched. The conjoined triplets spun around, tentacles lashing, to face this terror from Earth. And then Marco saw them. Behind the *Blood, Sweat, and Tears*--hundreds of other warships, all rising like a pod of whales, blue and gold and furious. Their cannons boomed, tearing through the swarm of hyds, carving their way forth.

The Phoenix Fleet was here.

Of her own volition, Joey opened fire again. She had only one cannon left, and it was sputtering, but she managed to spray novabolts at the twisted hydlord ahead.

Then, with light and fury that shook the galaxy, the HDFS *Blood, Sweat, and Tears* opened fire.

Torpedoes larger than some starships slammed into *God's Nightmare*. Warheads the size of cars exploded, spilling liquid light across space. The luminous desolation spread through the conjoined heads of the hydlord, and its morphed skulls tore open, revealing pulsing brains that maintained their form for only moments, then curled up and burned until they released the crystals within. Those crystals were not purple but deep crimson, infected with maggots. When the crystals shattered, shock waves of red and black ripples tore through the battlefield, knocking aside nearby galactopods and starships.

The tentacles that had gripped Joey and *Don't Panic* ripped off. The two damaged, cracked vessels spun through space. And Einav tumbled out of *Don't Panic* . . . and flew through the darkness.

* * * * *

Marco's heart pounded. He pulled the yoke, flying toward his captain. She tumbled helplessly through space.

"Einav!" he cried. So long as her helmet was online, she would hear him.

"Marco!" Terror filled her voice. She was spinning madly now, unable to stop. She was spinning too fast. It would break something inside her.

"Hold on, Einav!" He flew closer, slowed down, and tried to bring the airlock in line with her. He could not. She was spinning out of control!

"Joey, grab the wheel," Marco said, and the starship instantly took over.

Marco ran into the hold, popped open the airlock, attached his harness, and leaped into space.

He soared into the void, arms held out.

Sounds faded. It was so quiet out here. All around him, he saw the battle raging. The *Blood, Sweat, and Tears* was still fighting, bombarding nearby galactopods. The other warships of the Phoenix Fleet were engaging their own enemies. Missiles, inkblots, explosions, lasers, novabolts--they all formed a great show of shadows and light around Marco. But it was utterly silent, and he shoved it all to the back of his mind. He focused only on Einav. On his captain.

He glided toward her through space. She was just ahead, curled up like a fetus, spinning like a top. In space, without friction, with nothing to hold onto, she could not stop that terrifyingly fast spin. It must be rattling her brain around her skull. Left alone, she would spin like that for all eternity.

Marco reached out toward her through space as explosions blazed all around. He moved on momentum alone, his tether trailing behind him, connecting him to Joey like an umbilical cord.

"I got you, Einav." He reached out, and--

When he grabbed her, the force of her spin tugged him mightily, knocking the breath out of his lungs.

He tightened his grip.

"I got you!"

His tether snapped taut. He wrapped his arms around Einav in a crushing embrace, stopping her spin.

"I got you, Einav." His voice choked. "I got you."

He tapped a button on the tether, and it began to spool inward, pulling him and Einav back into Joey's airlock. The ship was cracked and depressurized. But they had their spacesuits, and Joey was a raft in the storm.

Marco pulled Einav into the hold and laid her down on the deck. She looked up at him, blinking.

"I'm . . . dizzy."

"You're crazy is what you are." Marco laughed, tears in his eyes, and clasped her hand. "Almost lost you there."

She blinked tears from her eyes and her hand tightened around his. "Help me up."

He pulled her to his feet. She leaned on him and they entered Joey's cockpit. The battle raged ahead, great warships battling galactopods. The *Blood, Sweat, and Tears* was a furious leviathan, plowing through squids, crushing them with her bulk. Marco imagined the scene as an underwater war between primordial beasts of some alien ocean. For the moment, the hydrians were too busy battling the warships to attack Joey. They probably thought the little ship dead already.

Joey whimpered. "Guys? I feel weird. Am I broken?"

Her hull was bent and cracked, one of her cannons was missing, and much of her ultrablack paint had peeled off again.

"You'll be fine, baby," Marco said, patting her dashboard. A chunk of paneling fell off. He winced.

"Marco, see if you can fly Joey into the *Blood, Sweat, and Tears*' hangar," Einav said. "The airlock will open for us."

He blinked. "During battle? With a hundred hydrians attacking the dreadnought?"

Einav nodded. "Yes. I need to be on my flagship."

"All right. Joey? Give me back the wheel." Marco sat down at the helm. "You still got control of the cannons. Err, cannon. Any hydrian that comes close--you roast the squid."

"Compliance!" the starship chirped.

It took some tricky flying. Marco had to pass under, over, and around tentacles, inkblots, and streaking torpedoes. The closer he flew to *Blood, Sweat, and Tears*, the trickier it got.

"It's 2270," he muttered. "Why hasn't anyone invented transporters yet?"

An inkblot grazed their underbelly. Joey yowled. Marco yanked the yoke madly, rattling the ship and shaking off the ink. Most of the ink. Some kept sizzling. Well, looked like Joey would need underbelly repairs too.

He flew nearer to the *Blood, Sweat, and Tears*. The dreadnought loomed before them, truly colossal. Joey was like a minnow approaching a whale. And Kraken surrounded that whale. They wrapped tentacles around the dreadnought, banged at her hull, and bit at her armor. But mighty *Blood, Sweat, and Tears*' cannons kept booming, pulsing with rings of energy, blasting back her foes. She was larger than hyds, bulkier and mightier even than hydlords.

"Here is the true might of Earth," Einav said, sitting in the cockpit beside Marco. "Here are ships such as we flew in the great

Alien Wars. This is what we're capable of. We're not all weak like Hart. We were strong once. We're becoming strong again."

Joey flew closer to the dreadnought's airlock. But the massive metal door remained closed. Hyds clung to the hull around the airlock, pawing at the hinges, trying to break in.

"Joey, use your plascaster," Marco said. "Low setting. Just scrape them off."

"Compliance!"

A hatch opened on Joey's dorsal hull. Her plascaster emerged. It was a lower-intensity weapon than her neutron cannons. The gun whipped from side to side, firing plasma bolts with deadly accuracy. The bolts burned the hyds, knocking them into space, leaving charred scars on the dreadnought's hull.

Einav lifted her minicom. "*Blood, Sweat, and Tears*, this is Admiral Einav Ben-Ari. Please open your airlock and allow us to dock."

Marco raised an eyebrow. "Admiral?"

She shrugged. "Well, I'm no longer Queen of Mars, am I?"

On *Blood, Sweat, and Tears*' battered hull, the airlock creaked open like an anguished mouth in a scarred face. Joey vaulted over a lashing tentacle, dived, and slid into the airlock. The ship raced down a short tunnel, then hit the deck and skidded, shedding droplets of ink and raising showers of sparks.

She kept sliding. Racing across the empty hangar.

"Um, Marco?" Einav said.

He was pulling the yoke, shoving levers, flipping switches.

"Marco, she's not slowing down!" Einav said.

"I'm trying!" Marco said, fiddling with the controls. Joey was still sliding across the deck toward the far bulkhead.

"Have you tried pulling the handbrake?" Einav said.

Joey skittered, spun, banged into a few wheeled ladders, and kept screeching across the hangar. Sparks flew where her underbelly scraped along the deck. Deckhands leaped for cover.

"Joey, dammit, engage your prow thrusters!" Marco said.

"I can't! A hyd bit them off."

Marco cursed and placed an arm across Einav's chest. "Hold on."

She winced.

Joey raced toward the bulkhead, and Marco cringed, and--

Two things happened at once. Joey slammed into the bulkhead. At the same time, Einav raised her starhand and blasted out a bubble of enveloping energy.

Joey's prow crumpled. Marco and Einav jerked forward in their seats. The bubble of spacetime wrapped around them, cushioning the crash like an airbag.

For a moment, they just sat there, stunned that they were alive.

"Ouch," Marco said.

Joey whimpered. "I can't feel my face."

"You have no face," Marco said.

"Not anymore. Ow . . . my prow . . ."

Well, they were inside the dreadnought. Safe? Maybe not. Just then, Marco heard it. And his heart sank.

* * * * *

The grumble rolled through the hangar bay. It came from behind Joey. A deep, angry, hungry grumble.

Dammit, don't I get a minute to catch my breath? Marco thought.

The grumble sounded again, louder this time. Deckhands screamed. Marco and Einav glanced at each other. Then they raced out the cockpit, hopped out Joey's airlock, and landed on the hangar deck.

The cavernous hangar sprawled before them, empty of all its starfighters. Across the distance loomed the mighty airlock of the *Blood, Sweat, and Tears*--a gateway you could ride a mammoth through. Or a mammoth-sized hyd. And now one of those mammoth-sized hyds was crawling through.

The alien's tentacles were already inside, blocking the door from closing. The cephalopod wore a suit of thick, lumpy chitin. Only its mouth was exposed. Rings within rings of teeth filled that hellhole.

Standing side by side, Marco and Einav drew their handguns and opened fire. Bolts hit the hyd, but the squid shrugged off the assault, fully entered the hangar, and squirmed toward them. They kept firing. Plasma bolts pinged off the creature's armored head and mantle. A few bolts even hit the eyes, but thick nictitating membranes protected the red orbs. The beast approached Marco and Einav, jaws opening wide, ready to engulf them.

"Um, Einav?" Marco said. "Your starhand?"

"I'm preserving the batteries." She loaded a fresh plasma pack and kept firing. The hydrian squealed and moved faster, tearing across the deck, ready to feast.

"This is not the time to save batteries!" Marco said. "Handguns aren't going to cut it."

The hyd leaped, lunged through the air, and swooped toward the two humans.

The plascaster whirred atop Joey's dorsal hull. Plasma bolts the size of grapefruit slammed into the hyd. The beast squealed, fell, and hit the deck. The hot bolts burned through its carapace and began eating through the flesh.

Marco slammed a new plasma pack into his handgun, then fired through the holes in the carapace. Finally, only meters away, the huge alien collapsed. It gave a final twitch, then lay dead. Its bloated tongue oozed across the deck.

Marco turned toward Einav. "Did you know Joey was going to do that?"

She blew on her handgun and shrugged. "I had no idea."

Marco blinked. "Saving batteries, huh? You were going to let that hyd eat us."

Einav waved dismissively. "We had him." She holstered her gun. "Now come on. Let's head to the bridge." The admiral smiled. "We have a fleet to command."

Daniel Arenson

CHAPTER ELEVEN
See No Evil

Cory Hart stood in his palace gardens, gazing at the night sky and the fire among the stars.

She was fighting them now. Einav and her fleet. From down on Earth, Hart could see little more than smudges of red and occasional flashes of light, perhaps torpedoes exploding. Every once in a while, a great flare of light shone brighter than the moon, then faded. A starship blowing up, perhaps.

While the explosions flared above, it was peaceful down here in the gardens. Crickets chirped among the trees. Frogs trilled in the tall grass. A breeze rustled the pine trees and cypresses. Hart remembered himself as a child in America, sitting in his family yacht on the Fourth of July, watching the fireworks. He missed his parents so badly. He was an only child. His parents had lived a long life, but they were gone now. At fifty years of age, Hart was alone. He ruled a planet of billions of people, and yet . . . he was alone.

So he ruled people. So what? What was ruling people? It was nothing. They were not people. They were statistics. Numbers lodged in his mind among other bits of trivia. Friends? He had none. Only flatterers. The only thing that mattered was family, and his was gone. His parents--dead. His wife and children--they had left him.

Alone.

Hart was an extrovert. A reveler by nature. A lover of people. Yet who did he have? Who did he have that really mattered?

He needed somebody. Oh God, he needed to hold somebody, to hear another's breath, not to be so alone.

He left the garden, reentered his palace, and trudged through empty halls. All the guards--gone. All his flatterers--home for the night. Hart Hall was an empty, cavernous tomb. A place where he had once hosted parties all night long. A place that had become his mausoleum.

He made his way into his bedroom. Or what had been a bedroom once. Now it looked more like a sultan's pleasure house. The treasures Erafel had granted shone everywhere. Rubies glittered in golden chalices. Strings of gemstones and links of precious metal dangled from the ceiling in gleaming curtains. Fine rugs topped the floor, and priceless artwork adorned the walls. The fireplace crackled, filling the room with warm light. Treasure chests were bursting open, spilling golden coins, diamonds, and gemstones in shimmering rivers. There were billions of dollars worth of treasure in this room.

Beautiful, Hart thought. *Beautiful and worthless.*

His three concubines were lounging in the room. Phaidor reclined on an ottoman, her arm dangling toward the piles of golden coins on the floor. She ran her fingers again and again through the coins, smiling softly as they clinked--a girl on a summer day, running her fingers through a flowing stream. Her hair was just as golden, and her eyes were sapphires. She was naked aside from many jewels and ornaments that glittered across her shapely form. The brightest jewel was the one embedded into her temple, shining with electric light. She was a woman of Mars, proud and free, but the implant kept her docile. She saw Hart enter and gave him a simpering smile.

"My emperor!" she said, reaching out to him. Her bracelets clinked.

Thuvia, a second beauty of Mars, lay by the fireplace. Her

hair was the same color as the flames, and freckles adorned her naked body like a field of stars. She rose from the rug like a serpent from a jug, her cheeks flushed, and smiled at him. The implant in her temple shone deep red.

"My lord!" she said.

Dejah, most beautiful of all, lay on the bed. The firelight dappled her coppery skin and raven hair. She gazed at Hart from under her lashes, reached out to him, and her lips parted.

"Come to me, my master," she said. "Let me pleasure you."

Yes, these were his rewards too. These captive women of Mars, once warriors, their brains broken, forced to become like animals, to serve him. Lobotomized lovers. They were beautiful yet they disgusted Hart.

"Let me pleasure you too," said Thuvia, smiling crookedly, her red tresses bouncing as she hopped toward him.

Phaidor giggled. "And me!"

They pulled him into bed. He lay on the silken sheets as they kissed him, made love to him, giggled and simpered and whispered and nibbled his ears. And as they pleasured him, a tear rolled down his cheek.

"It's fake," he whispered. "It's all fake."

Phaidor pouted. "What is fake, my lord? My curves are real."

"You're fake." He sat up in bed.

"Master?" whispered Thuvia.

"You're fake too!" Hart said. "And you." He pointed at Dejah, then at the treasures across the room. "This whole place is fake! It's all a show! All a scam!"

Dejah gasped. "The gold is real, my lord. The gemstones and diamonds too. I can tell. My father was a jeweler on Mars. I think . . ." She frowned, and the implant on her head glowed. "I can no longer remember. Are we still on Mars?"

Thuvia tilted her head, her own implant shining. "I . . . I don't know."

Phaidor giggled. "Oh, what does it matter? Let's make love to him again."

"Let's, let's!" said the other two.

"No!" Hart shoved them off. He leaped off the bed. "Get away from me, you zombies. You're nothing but dolls of flesh. This gold? Nothing but blood gold!" He kicked, and coins flew across the room. "This artwork on the wall? Mockery!" He ripped a picture frame off and hurled it across the room, knocking over a chalice full of jewels.

The girls whimpered. They fled behind the ottoman and cowered, hugging one another. Phaidor began to weep.

"Get out," Hart said.

"Master?" Thuvia said.

"Get out!" he shouted. "Get out. All three of you."

"No, master!" Phaidor said, tears falling. "Please, my lord. We love you."

"We'd die without you!" said Dejah.

The implants were shining brighter on their temples. Controlling them. Just like the damn hydstone stuck in Hart's palm. He growled, grabbed Phaidor by the arm, and dragged her toward the door. Then he dragged Thuvia and Dejah too.

"Take whatever jewels you want. Here, have more gold. Have more diamonds." He tossed jewels into their arms. "Now get out and leave me!"

He shoved them out the room, then slammed the door in their faces. Behind the door, he could hear them whimpering.

"We love you! We love you! Please forgive us!"

He locked the door. He paced the room, covering his ears. This was meant to be his heaven. It was hell.

Cursed, cursed! He was cursed. Trapped. A mockery. He was a trained ape, that was all. An ape on a leash. King of

Apeworld. As they were his slaves, he was a slave to Erafel.

Alone.

He was alone.

He had thought these playthings, these lobotomized lovers, would comfort him. But they made things worse. Made him lonelier than ever. They were toys, that was all. Just toys! And sometimes, in their eyes, he saw flickers of the women they had been. Of lost souls. Terrified. Trapped inside their perfumed, jeweled bodies, forced to serve him. He could not tolerate it. He would sooner make love to a blow-up doll. At least it wouldn't stare at him like that. At least he wouldn't see a trapped soul within its eyes. Hell, he would rather make love to a squid!

He laughed at the thought. Then he was laughing louder, laughing so much his body shook, and as he laughed, he wept. Finally he fell onto the bed and lay on the silken, sweaty sheets among golden coins.

"I miss you, Heather," he whispered. "I miss you, my wife. I miss my kids."

His laughter died, and now all that remained were the tears. He looked at his hand. He still wore his wedding ring. Even now, a year after Heather left him and took the kids offworld, In this room of many treasures, his simple wedding band was his most precious jewel.

He poured himself a cup of wine, held it with shaky fingers, and drank it slowly until he calmed down. Then he lifted his minicom and called his ex-wife.

For a long time, her minicom rang. Hart had no idea where she was. She had taken the kids offworld, fearing him--his temper, his madness. Yes, he had been a beast. If she never answered, never forgave him, perhaps he deserved it.

She did not answer. Well, she was right not to.

Then he heard her voice. Her beautiful, angelic voice. "Hello! This is Heather Sullivan. Please leave a message and I'll get back to you. Or, if you're a salesman, maybe not."

Hart laughed through his tears. God, it felt good to hear that sweet voice. Yet the name she used--Heather Sullivan. Her maiden name. That part hurt.

The minicom beeped. Hart wanted to hang up. But he wiped his eyes and spoke.

"Heather? It's me. Cory. I . . . I just called to . . ."

He hesitated. He wanted to make up some excuse. To hang up. Instead he decided to let it all out.

"I miss you. I love you. I'm useless without you. I realize now what a shitty husband I was. How I never gave you and the kids my time, my attention, my love. I drove you away, and it was the biggest mistake of my life. I'm sorry, Heather. I'm so sorry. I lost you. And I'm broken without you. I realize now how much I need you and love you. I think about you every day, and . . . I want you to come back. I promise to be a better husband. A better father. A better man. Please, if you can find it in your heart to forgive me, come back. Let's be a family again." His tears flowed, and his voice choked. "I'm sorry, Heather. Please come back."

He was about to hang up when she answered the call. "Cory?"

He caught his breath. "Heather?"

Her hologram appeared in the room, smiling sadly. "It's me." She looked around the room. "Wow. Cory . . . wow. That's . . ." She blinked. "Wow."

He looked around at the gold and jewels. Thankfully, the three Martian girls were nowhere in sight.

"It's all worthless," Hart said. "The only treasure I care about is my family."

They talked for a while. A long while. They did not argue or bicker or bring up the past. She told him about Ellie's ballet recital, Jordan's baseball game, and little Jody's tooth falling out.

They shared memories of better days. For an hour, they spoke, and it was like old times.

Finally, when awkward silence sneaked in, Hart said, "Heather, would you take me back?"

She lowered her head. "Cory, I don't know."

"Heather, the galaxy is falling apart. I'm scared. Please come home. I'll look after you. I'll keep you safe."

She wiped her eyes. "Cory, I never needed you to look after me. I just needed you to be with me."

"No more bunker," he said. "We won the war. It's over. Come back home, sweetheart. Please."

Heather sniffed and nodded.

As it turned out, she had never gone far. She had been hiding out with the kids at a luxury hotel on the moon. With a quick starship, that was only an hour or two away.

When the shuttle descended, Hart stood on the palace lawn. Dawn was rising. The flowers bloomed and the birds sang again. Thuvia, Dejah, and Phaidor had slunk off somewhere to sleep as they often did during the day. Hart hoped they would never return.

The shuttle touched down. It was a luxurious shuttle, trimmed with gold. The hatch opened, and out they came, one by one. Ellie, precocious dancer and straight-A student. Jordan, wearing a baseball glove and cap. And precious little Jody, a tooth missing in her grin. They had all grown so much. They ran toward him, and Hart scooped them into his arms. He held them tightly, laughing, and never wanted to let go.

Finally Heather emerged from the shuttle, smiling sadly. Hart placed his children down and walked toward her. He hesitated, not sure if to hug her.

"Heather," he said. "Welcome home."

She let out a sob and embraced him, and Hart stood there on the lawn, holding her, feeling the world mending, feeling his soul healing. He was home.

* * * * *

Covered in ash and hydrian blood, her uniform smoking, Einav marched onto the bridge of the HDFS *Blood, Sweat, and Tears*. It was a cavernous room, resembling an ancient planetarium. Like on other modern dreadnoughts, viewports formed a huge sphere around the bridge. Screens even tiled the deck underfoot. The viewports showed space all around, giving the crew a 360-degree view. It felt like hovering in open space. In reality, the bridge was located in the heart of the ship, safe within thick walls. The viewports streamed videos from sensors on the hull. But the illusion was complete. Even the deck became invisible, and as Einav marched across the bridge, she seemed to be walking on space.

Marco walked a step behind her, stern, scanning the bridge. Einav was glad to have him here. He could always comfort her.

"Looks just like the *Pride of the Lioness*," he said.

Einav nodded. "Same design."

The view would normally be breathtaking--a vista of stars, nebulae, and galaxies. But now one could barely see space, only the sprawling battle, endless miles of galactic krakens battling the warships of Earth. Every once in a while, a torpedo painted a long stretch of light across the darkness, and a hideous mouth opened to devour a starfighter.

"Commander on deck!" cried the guard at the door--a moment too late. He had needed that moment to gulp and rub his eyes. It wasn't every day that a legend from the Alien Wars stepped onto your bridge.

As Einav walked across the transparent deck, the crew of the *Blood, Sweat, and Tears* stood at attention. Even Commander

Harris. He was a burly man, about sixty years old, with a gray buzz cut and a face like an old catcher's mitt.

"Return to your posts!" Einav snapped. "This is a battle!"

At once, they scurried back to their control panels. All but Harris. The gruff old commander approached her. "Ma'am, according to our scans, the enemy flew here with three hydlords. You took out one--*God's Nightmare*. Excellent work! But two remain. We've been carving our way toward *See No Evil,* a foul hydlord who commands thousands of hyds. Meanwhile, our sister ship, the *Brimstone Fury,* is searching for the third hydlord. It seems to have slipped off our sensors. But we'll find it."

Einav nodded. "We take out the enemy leaders early on. Risky approach. Lots of foot soldiers in the way. We'll take heavy losses. But I agree. Given how badly we're outnumbered, it's our best play."

Einav reached the center of the bridge. Workstations rose here in a ring. Officers were busy monitoring and controlling every aspect of the battle. They had their hands full, but Einav caught them glancing her way, and she saw the awe in their eyes.

They probably read about me in history books when they were children, she thought. *Einav Ben-Ari, the leader of the fleet during the Alien Wars. Bet they never thought they'd see me in the flesh.*

"Ma'am," Commander Harris said, "I've been serving as acting admiral, but I hand the post over to you. I should command this ship and this ship alone. Ma'am, the fleet is yours."

He handed her a badge. It featured two golden phoenixes flanking a ruby. Sigil of the fleet admiral.

She raised an eyebrow. "Are you sure, Commander Harris?"

He lifted his chin. "Madam, my great-aunt fought in your platoon. The Dragons Platoon. Back in the Scum War."

Einav frowned. "Harris, Harris . . ." She tilted her head. "Who . . ."

Marco, who still stood a step behind her, blurted out, "Jackass!"

Einav glowered. "Excuse me, Brigadier Emery?"

"Hope 'Jackass' Harris!" Marco said. "You remember her, right?"

Einav's eyes widened. She spun back toward Commander Harris, the gray-haired, steely-eyed commander. Yes, she saw the resemblance now. The aquiline nose. The thick eyebrows. The determined jawline.

"Hope Harris was your great-aunt?" Einav said.

A thin smile tugged at the commander's lips. "Yes, I'm aware that some called her Jackass. But I understand she was fond of the nickname. She died before I was born. But I heard the tales."

Einav remembered the girl. A young recruit. A misfit. Hope Harris had spent time in military prison for a whole variety of disciplinary problems. Sleeping late. Losing her helmet. Skipping firing range practice. Several platoons had kicked her out, and she had failed boot camp again and again. Hope had been fiercely intelligent, well-read and wise, but broken. Finally Einav had taken her in, had tried to nurture her, but . . .

I failed, she thought.

After being told she would flunk boot camp yet again, Hope Harris had committed suicide.

"She was the first soldier I ever lost," Einav whispered, more to herself than to Commander Harris. "She was a good soldier. She was brave."

"She was my friend," said Marco.

A sudden boom shook the *Blood, Sweat, and Tears*. A tentacle had slammed against them! The ship reeled. The cannons roared. Torpedoes knocked a hyd back.

"All right, no more time for reminiscing," Einav said. "Show me a map of the fleet. On that screen there to my left. Oh, and get engineering on the line. On that monitor. Harris, keep commanding this ship in battle. I'll take care of the rest."

* * * * *

A holographic map materialized near Einav, showing every ship in her fleet, their position in space, and their stats. Golden icons represented the Phoenix Fleet, including the remaining Firebirds. Blue icons represented the Ragtag Fleet. The hydrians appeared as black, tentacled icons like ten thousand little spiders. Things weren't looking great. Even with the mighty Phoenix Fleet in the fight, the human force struggled. Einav wasn't ready to throw in the towel yet, but goddamn, they needed to start landing more punches.

A second screen burst to life at her right. It streamed a view from engineering. The engine room seemed almost as chaotic as the battle outside. The great mechanisms that powered the *Blood, Sweat, and Tears* were rumbling and trembling and barely holding together. Engineers raced back and forth, repairing systems that continued to fail and flounder. Among them ran a tall woman with tattooed arms, a belt heavy with tools and weapons, and blond hair that spilled out from under an antique World War II helmet.

"No, you morons, no!" she cried. "You'll flood the graviton pipes again! Reroute the fusion coils toward the pistons. We need to blast forward, not levitate!"

"Addy!" Marco cried from the bridge.

She looked around, confused. "Huh, wuh?" She finally found the camera. "Oh, hi, Poet."

"Addy, thank God you're alive," Marco said.

"What, you think ten thousand squids can kill me?" She snorted, then blew him a kiss. "Love ya, babe." She waved at Einav. "Hey, Nav Nav, you taking good care of Poet?"

"I'm not some pet who needs taking care of!" Marco whispered, glancing around nervously, hoping nobody heard.

"You needed me to take care of you last time you caught a cold," Addy said. "Remember how you convinced yourself it was pneumonia? And needed me to fly you to the doctor?"

"Addy, it *was* pneumonia," Marco said. "I almost died."

She nodded. "And I saved your life."

"Addy, give me all the firepower you can," Einav said. "Propulsion is your lowest priority. Shields are medium priority."

"Wait, what?" Marco said. "Shields are medium--"

"Full power to the cannons, I got ya, boss." Addy saluted. "I'll make it so." She winked at Marco. "Later, babe. Don't die!"

"I'll do my best. Love you, Ads."

"Love ya, Poet."

While the married couple was talking, Einav focused on the battle. She had fought some large battles before. She had commanded fleets in great wars. But this was something else. Something bigger. Crueler. In all her years of warfare, Einav had never faced a foe so strong. So malicious. She had never seen such brutality, not in any species in this galaxy. But the hydrians were not from this galaxy. They were intergalactic predators. And Einav understood now how they had conquered so much.

Single organisms--hydrians the size of small towns-- grabbed and crushed starships. Hungry mouths devoured starfighters whole. One burning world lay behind them alrcady-- Mars, a red planet that had turned black. And the dead cephalopod eyes now focused on Earth. Under her leadership, Earth had faced many foes and defeated them. But not since the Cataclysm, the terrible destruction Einav had been born into, had humanity come so close to extinction. A war on this scale was new even to her.

I will not allow another Cataclysm, she vowed. *We must win!*

She got on nixnet--the communication network of the

Phoenix Fleet--and connected to her warship captains. There was no time for a proper meeting. No time to get to know everyone, to establish rapport, to come up with plans. Everything was happening too fast, dammit. Einav had known about the hydrian threat for years, but now everything was happening at once, and she had no time.

For years, we bickered amongst ourselves, she thought. *Fighting our petty little civil wars. Now the squids are crushing us.*

Well, there would be time for soul-searching later. If humanity survived the night.

"Marco, take command of the Ragtag Fleet," Einav said. "Get them to rally around us."

"Yes, ma'am." Marco turned toward a control panel and tapped a button. "Wyatt! Wyatt, you read me?"

"What's up, buddy?" came the reply.

As Marco and Wyatt conversed, Einav contacted a few nearby frigates. She ordered them nearer. The *Blood, Sweat, and Tears* was part of a strike force. Several corvettes flew around her at all times, but Einav needed to augment that now. Two hydlords still flew among the unholy hosts. And one was not far away. Its galactopod loomed beyond the throng of hyds like a mountain soaring over hills. This one was larger and tougher than the *God's Nightmare*, the twisted triplets.

The hydlord ahead was blind, it seemed. Stubby eye stalks, like those of a lobster, thrust out from the galactopod's lumpy prow. But they ended with holes like craters. No red eyes peered. There were only dark sockets. Instead of a regular hydrian mouth, this creature sprouted a long, dark beak like a bird of prey. When the beak opened, it revealed rows of serrated teeth that lined the entire inner surface of the beak. The teeth moved like chainsaws, designed to grab and lacerate prey. And what prey this creature must have hunted in its natural habitat! That beak was large enough to rip off half the *Blood, Sweat, and Tears*. Tentacles the size of skyscrapers ringed this hideous countenance, tipped with long, slender feelers. The creature was blind, but the strange whiskers its tentacles grew seemed to work like antennae, twitching and scanning the darkness. Einav guessed that it could see better than any creature with eyes.

Like all large galactopods, this one seemed part organic, part mechanical, complete with a propulsion system of spinning blades around a sphere of crackling red energy. Hydrians--the soft, fleshy animals within their shells--had names of their own, often twisted names human tongues could not pronounce. But they gave their galactopods separate names the way humans named their starships. Runes were engraved upon this chitin hull, full of fire, spelling out its name: SEE NO EVIL.

"Cute name," Einav muttered.

The frigates Einav had summoned answered the call. They plowed through the sea of hyds, moving closer toward the *Blood, Sweat, and Tears*. Hyds were large, deadly creatures, but with cannons and lasers and graviton pulses, the frigates tore through the sea of squids. Each frigate was the size of an aircraft carrier from the Second World War. They joined the corvettes that protected the *Blood, Sweat, and Tears*. This was not the entire fleet. Hundreds of other human starships were fighting elsewhere. But combined, the dreadnought and her escorts formed a mighty strike force.

"Forward toward the *See No Evil*!" Einav said, pointing for emphasis with her ivory finger. "Tear through all in our path. Do not stop or turn no matter what damage we take. Charge through any foe! Fly through fire and ink! Onward, children of Earth! To victory!"

The fleet charged, and the *Blood, Sweat, and Tears* flew at the van, her great cannons booming. Torpedoes larger than starfighers streaked out, hundreds of them. Explosions blazed ahead, carving through the swarms of hyds, etching a path of fire.

Down this flaming highway the *Blood, Sweat, and Tears* roared. Around her, the corvettes and frigates fired broadsides. Their cannonades shoved back hyds that tried to flank the force.

The hyds realized what was happening. Their foul galactopods clustered closer. Soon they flew so close together that their tentacles touched. Their ink gushed in waves. But the human ships flew close together too. The largest human warships linked their force fields into great, conjoined shields. The ink landed on this shimmering force field, sizzled, and burned, sparing the starships. The charge continued!

Standing on the bridge of the *Blood, Sweat, and Tears*, Einav's chest swelled with pride. Yes, the hydrians were numerous, and yes, they were strong. But human warships were their equal! More than their equal--they were superior! Here was great human engineering and technology, ships with tiny stars that powered them, with weaponry to tear through any armor, with brave and capable crews. War was savage, ugly business, but it could reveal great nobility too. And in this charge, the nobility of humanity shone brighter than the light of the exploding warheads.

Hundreds of hyds clustered before the charging fleet. They wove their tentacles together, linking hyd to hyd, forming a huge wall in space. Shielding the hydlord, the wall of smaller hyds advanced toward the human charge.

"It's like the world's worst game of Space Invaders," Marco muttered.

"Full speed ahead!" Einav cried. "Vanguard--fire graviton bombs at them! Flanks--give some raking fire! Onward, Phoenix Fleet!"

The *Blood, Sweat, and Tears* shook as her prow cannons boomed. This time the dreadnought fired spheres of pulsing, spinning gravitons. They looked like huge cannonballs full of swirling stars. When they hit the hyds, the bombs detonated, unleashing massive gravitational waves. Tentacles unbraided. The links between the hyds in the wall loosened.

Just then, the flank warships pitched forward and unleashed devastating raking fire. Neutron bombs, torpedoes, and grapeshot slammed into the wall of hyds. The aliens squealed as their formation collapsed. The squids floated loosely, their solid wall now porous and cracked.

The Phoenix Fleet was only gaining speed. They could not turn back now. Racing along a highway of fire, they slammed into the wall of hyds . . . and tore through it.

Hyds scattered every which way like so many bowling pins. The *Blood, Sweat, and Tears*' escorts kept firing, pummeling hyds as the fleet flew by, cracking shells, cooking the flesh inside. The hyds fought back. They swarmed. Tentacles grabbed a few corvettes and crushed them. One hyd bit through a frigate's flank, exposing a honeycomb of decks, then slurped out spacers with a long tongue. Casualty counters flashed through *Blood, Sweat, and Tears*' bridge, showing dozens, then hundreds dying.

"Onward!" Einav shouted. "There he is! Charge!"

Ahead loomed the *See No Evil*. A hydlord. Einav still remembered seeing her first hydlord--the foul creature Mezmeron, the devourer of children, who lurked without a shell under the mountain. *See No Evil* was even larger, more hideous, bristling with thousands of whiskers that twitched and buzzed. The hydlord was blind, but those dark sockets seemed to stare right into Einav. And she saw it now. Deep inside those sockets were clusters of skulls. Human skulls.

Einav stared into those dead eyes. She pointed her filigreed finger at the beast.

"Fire."

The HDFS *Blood, Sweat, and Tears* and her entire escort unleashed their fury. Grapeshot, missiles, novabolts, and torpedoes armed with nuclear warheads flew toward the hydlord.

And the *See No Evil* fought back. Its dozens of tentacles,

twitching with whiskers, spewed ink from pulsing vents. A rain of ink washed over the fleet, sizzling over force fields, burning through at spots. Inkblots slammed into hulls. Once it touched the starships, the ink began crawling across the hulls like living creatures of tar, seeking entry through bores and pipes and ports. Damage reports flooded the *Blood, Sweat, and Tears*. A few viewports went dark as ink blotted out the sensors.

But the *Blood, Sweat, and Tears* kept flying. Through the dark rain she charged. Ink ripped open chunks of her hull. Casualty counters spun madly through digits. Screams sounded from deeper in the ship. A few hyds seized their chance and leaped onto the dreadnought and her escorts. As ink burned holes through hulls, hyds laid eggs inside, infecting the ship with parasites. Humans often referred to hydrians with male pronouns, but hydrians were hermaphrodites, able to change gender throughout their life. Even powerful male warriors could lay eggs. And now they were disgorging their foul brood into human warships.

"Fire again!" Einav cried. "Aim everything at the hydlord!"

Another round of raking fire hit the *See No Evil*. Nuclear warheads exploded against the blind hydlord. Tentacles ripped off. Chunks blasted open in the galactopod, exposing the meat inside. An eyestalk burst, scattering confetti of skulls. But the beast still lived!

The titanic alien was close now. Only a few klicks away. Its deformed beak opened, dripping blood. Its rows of teeth spun and ground like chainsaws. The creature was as large as the *Blood, Sweat, and Tears*. Its remaining tentacles reached out, grabbed the dreadnought, and squeezed.

The hull creaked.

Klaxons wailed.

The bridge shook and more viewports shattered.

Somehow the beast was still alive--and they were in its

grip.

* * * * *

Addy was down in the engine room, trying to keep up with Einav's impossible demands. One moment, the crazy lady wanted to charge forward full speed. Well, that took a lot of juice for the engines. The next moment, Einav wanted to fire a full cannonade. And Addy ran and scrambled again, spinning winches, shoving levers, even manually moving pipes, trying to direct the energy from stern to prow.

"Dammit, Einav, slow down!" she shouted.

The *Blood, Sweat, and Tears* shook as blast after blast hit her. Creaks and moans ran through the dreadnought. Everything was rattling and moaning and breaking. A pipe burst, spilling out a stream of gravitons. Nearby engineers floated into the air as gravity went crazy around them.

Murphy, the chief engineer, was still unconscious. Addy must have punched him too hard. So she had replaced him as leader, shouting at mechanics, directing them here and there in a frenzy. The *Blood, Sweat, and Tears* shook again. Booms rolled through the ship. Were those the cannons firing? No--blasts against the hull! Probably those inkblots. They not only corroded metal, they also hit the ship with huge kinetic energy. Another pipe burst in the engine room. This time steam burst out. Two mechanics screamed as the steam washed over them. They ran and fell, skin bubbling and peeling.

"Medics!" Addy shouted. "I need medics down in engineering!"

A reply came over the nixnet. "We'll be there as soon as we can. Casualties everywhere!"

A floating, holographic screen showed Addy a schematic of the ship. Decks were breached along both the port and

starboard. Dammit, this whole ship was falling apart. Addy
needed to--

The ship jerked madly. The dreadnought was a mile long,
but she shook like a starfighter flying through a nebula. Addy fell
and banged her elbows hard on the deck. Toolboxes overturned.
Two giant gears, larger than wagon wheels, detached and rolled
across the engine room. Power died to one of the exhaust ports.
The lights shut down across the engine room, plunging everyone
into darkness.

"What the hell was that?" Addy said.

She pushed herself up. The main lights were dead, but the
backup batteries kicked into gear. Nixnet flickered back to life,
showing her schematics of the ship, crew vitals, and a view from
the outside sensors.

A hydlord was gripping the dreadnought. The *See No Evil!*
He was crushing them in his tentacles!

Dammit! Addy wanted to be out there in a starfighter,
bombarding the beast! Or at least on the bridge, firing the raking
cannons. She had always been a combat soldier. A warrior! But
down here, she reminded herself, she was doing important work
too. In a battle, fighters were the fists. But noncombat soldiers
were the brains, the lungs, the heart, the body that kept those fists
flying. Addy, an infantry grunt by trade and temperament, was
serving in her first noncombat role. She was seeing battle from a
new perspective. It wasn't as glorious, perhaps. Nobody wrote
songs about the noncombats. Nobody praised military cooks,
sappers, armorers, janitors, clerks, and all the other professionals
who kept an army fighting. No Hollywood actors portrayed the
humble mechanic toiling in the bowels of a warship; they all
wanted to play the heroic captain. But down here in this engine
room, Addy saw soldiers just as courageous, motivated, and
proud. They might not be firing guns, but with every pipe they
welded, every piston they installed, every leaky tube they patched

up, they kept this great machine fighting.

I can kick ass from here too, Addy thought.

The hull creaked. More pipes burst. A piston overturned and began pumping across the floor, moving in jerks like some deranged newborn giant, hammering through workstations and shattering all in its path. The piston slammed into a mechanic, crushed him, and kept going until it hit a steel bulkhead and finally died. The holograms flickered, showing more damage across the ship. Entire inner decks were creaking and cracking. The tentacles kept tightening, crushing the dreadnought like a tin can. The cannons were firing, but the hydlord was smart. He positioned his tentacles to avoid the bores, and there was nothing the ship could do.

But there is, Addy thought. *I can still fight from here.*

"Engineers!" she cried. "Listen to me! You will reverse the propulsion field, direct the power to our shields, and flood them with energy."

They stared at her, aghast.

"You can't!" said Murphy, finally waking up from his nap. "Dammit, the propulsion field emits *fifty times* the power of our shields. You'll burn our shields up!"

"Well, good morning, Mr. Sunshine," Addy said. "That's exactly the plan."

The bald engineer scowled and stomped toward her. "I won't allow it. Who the hell are you anyway? Security, arrest this woman and--"

Addy delivered another uppercut to his chin. Just like last time. Once more Murphy spun around like a ballerina, then crumpled and hit the deck. Let them court-martial her later. Addy didn't care.

Everyone was staring at her. Addy stared back. "Well, go on, move! That means now, soldiers!"

They rushed to do her bidding. Addy activated her jetpack

and rose in the air. She floated above her crew, directing them here and there, reconfiguring the engine room in ways it should never be assembled.

"No time to weld--just shove that part in!" she shouted at one man.

"Forget bolting the cables down!" she told another. "String 'em! Faster, soldier!"

As the engineers worked, the hydlord kept shaking the dreadnought. More components popped and cracked. The ship was crumpling.

"All right, reroute propulsion power to shields!" Addy said. "Now!"

The mechanics stared up at her, hesitating. Addy cursed, swooped down, grabbed the winch, and turned it herself. Power thrummed, the deck trembled, and electricity crackled through the air. The mechanics winced. A few hit the ground and covered their heads.

"Here goes nothing," Addy muttered, shoving down a lever.

Power surged.

The ship's fusion core flared, filling the entire dreadnought with light. Power that should be streaming out the exhaust now flooded pipes all along the hull, crackling and searing and flaring out into the shields.

Sensors shattered. Cables fizzed and burned and flailed like snakes. Enormous energy flared around the dreadnought, wreathing the ship with light like the corona of a star.

The blind hydlord screeched. The flaring shields burned his tentacles, eating through carapace and flesh and bone. He couldn't even release the ship. His tentacles melted, sticking to the hull like burnt meat to a pan, withering up. Armless, the creature tumbled backward in space. His stumps burned.

Addy pulled the lever back. The power left the shields,

returning to the exhaust ports. The last sensors shut down. Addy couldn't see what was happening outside.

"Did we get him?" she whispered. "Is he dead?"

A growl sounded behind her.

Then another growl from overhead.

Hisses and whispers filled the dark engine room.

In the dim light of the backup lamps, Addy saw tentacled shadows. Red eyes. Creatures scuttling near. Hydlings. Newborn larvae, each as large as a man. They must have just hatched from eggs, and with ear-shattering screeches, they attacked.

CHAPTER TWELVE
Necroflayer

On the bridge of the *Blood, Sweat, and Tears*, the crew had felt Addy streaming power through the dreadnought. Electricity raced through the bridge, flooded the control panels, and sizzled through the air. Two viewports shattered. The hairs stood on Marco's arms, then sizzled away into smoke.

"Addy, what the hell are you doing down there in engineering?" he shouted.

She didn't answer. Damn the woman!

But whatever she was up to--it was hurting the hydlord! Marco watched as the great tentacles ripped off, shriveled up, and withered on the hull like overcooked bacon on a hot pan. The *See No Evil* tumbled backward in space. The carapace shattered across the hydlord's head, falling off to reveal the creature inside. The blind squid sneered and bared thousands of sharp teeth.

"Fire," Einav said.

An unnecessary command. The gunners were already unleashing their torpedoes.

The barrage hit the blind hydlord. His head burst open like an overripe fruit. The blast even took out dozens of nearby hyds.

Cheers rose across the deck. Crew members jumped and hugged and pumped their fists. Einav merely smiled thinly. Sparks blazed across her white uniform. Her gilded buckles and filigreed starhand shone like molten gold. The viewports bathed her with starlight and firelight. Marco looked at this idol of light and power, in awe of his leader. Like she sometimes did in battle, she seemed to him more than human, a battle angel risen from history to smite the enemies of humanity. Marco knew her better than that, of course. He knew the real Einav, the earthly woman, a human with foibles and flaws and frailties. Yet sometimes, like this time, he understood why Einav Ben-Ari inspired so much courage in warriors, why they called her the Golden Lioness.

"Well done, Addy," Einav said. "Addy?" She frowned. "Addy, do you read me?"

"I've been trying to reach her over nixnet," Marco said. Fear gripped his chest. "Oh god, she must have flooded engineering with so much power."

Einav turned toward one of her crew members. "Get me a visual down in engineering."

The young officer pursed his lips and tapped on holographic panels. "The cameras are dead, ma'am, but I can get an audio feed. Streaming to bridge speakers now."

Marco and Einav listened. They heard grunts. Snorts. Screeches. Then rattling gunfire.

"Hydlings," Marco said. "Hydlings on the ship!"

"Security, get down to the engine room!" Einav said.

The security chief's voice crackled over nixnet. "Ma'am, the enemy is boarding from multiple locations across the ship. I'm organizing a squad to head down to the engine room."

Marco drew his firearm. "I'm heading down there."

He took a few steps. Einav grabbed his arm and glared at him. "Brigadier Emery, you are a bridge officer."

"Einav, I'm no use up here. You know it. My wife is in the engine room, surrounded by hydlings. She's probably terrified, surrounded, maybe . . . maybe dying. I'm going down there."

Einav nodded and released him. Marco ran.

* * * * *

Down in the engine room, Addy was having the time of her life. She was firing a pistol with each hand, laughing, blasting aliens apart. This was more like it!

A hydling leaped from her right. Addy pulled the trigger, blasting its brains out. Another hydling swooped from above. She fired again, knocking it back in the air. It fell into a nest of churning gears that promptly crushed it. More hydlings scuttled underfoot. Addy rose high on her jetpack and rained down hellfire on them.

She liked hydlings. They weren't much bigger than her, they grew no carapace, and they were fun to kill. The bigger they got, the tougher they were. The larvae were good sport.

Around her, engineers and mechanics raised makeshift weapons. Blowtorches. Wrenches. Hammers. Drills. They hacked and slashed at the advancing hydlings. The alien squids leaped at them. The larvae grabbed one mechanic and ripped him apart. They grabbed another and bit him in half, then feasted on his innards. The other mechanics screamed in horror, but they did not flee. They fought. With power tools, even just with fists, they fought back the creatures.

Nearby, a cluster of hydlings bundled into a ball. Ten or more of the squirming creatures locked together, tentacles interweaving, and rolled across the deck. Together they formed a terror as large as a full-grown hyd.

Addy flew toward a bulkhead, jetpack thrumming. A hot pipe ran overhead, delivering steam to the pistons. Addy holstered her guns, pulled on her thick work gloves, and ripped a chunk of pipe off the wall. She aimed it like a cannon, bathing the rolling ball of hydlings with concentrated steam.

This steam was designed to move one-ton pistons. It made short work of the hydlings. Their tentacles shriveled off, and the ball of them collapsed onto the deck. They bubbled and cooked and filled the deck with a sickeningly-sweet smell.

"Steamed squids tonight!" Addy said.

More hydlings scuttled across the deckhead above. Addy drew her pistols and fired upward. Squids fell and slapped onto the deck. Addy fired a few more shots, putting bullets in their heads. They twitched, hissed, drooled, and died.

"Anyone else?" Addy shouted. "Huh?"

She spun in the air, jetpack ablaze, guns hot in her hands.

"Who else wants some? Anyone? Ah, there's one!"

A hydling was crawling across the deck, several tentacles missing. Addy fired from above, hit the wretch in the head, and it crashed down dead.

"Yeah, that's right!" she cried. "This is Addy Fucking Linden. You come onto my deck, you die!"

She laughed, adrenaline pounding through her. Her eyes stung. Several dead mechanics and engineers lay on the deck. Young men and women who had given their lives to save this ship. Joy of victory and grief for this loss mingled through Addy.

She looked down at her surviving crew. Pride swelled her chest.

"Soldiers of the engine room! I've fought with infantry on alien worlds. I flew with starfighter pilots against enemy fleets. But never have I seen soldiers braver or nobler than you. We've won the day--but at great cost. We will not forget the fallen. With their life, they bought us victory." She raised her fist. "Victory!"

"Vict--" they began just as Marco burst through the door.

"Addy, I'm here!" He ran into the engine room, an assault rifle in hand. "Where are they? Where are the bastards? Ah, there's one!"

He fired at a supine hydling.

"It's already dead!" Addy said. She flew down toward him. "They're all dead. We already won the battle."

Marco looked around and blinked. "But . . . I came to save

you."

She smacked the back of his head. "Dumbass."

"Ow." He glowered. "Save me some next time. Sheesh."

She smiled and pulled him into a hug. "Love you, baby." She kissed him on the lips. "I love you so much."

Marco drew his handgun.

"Poet, what's wrong?" She kissed him again. "Don't you--"

He fired a plasma bolt over her shoulder.

Addy spun around, gasping. A hydrian loomed behind her, tentacles raised, a bullet in its head. The alien wobbled and fell backward.

Marco blew on his barrel and holstered the gun.

"Saved your ass." He winked. "Thanks for saving me one."

* * * * *

On the bridge, Einav surveyed the battle around her. A sphere of viewports surrounded her, and while some had shattered, she still got a good view of space. A hundred warships or more had fallen. On some of those ships, hundreds had died. The casualty counters were offline. Perhaps a good thing. If they ever updated, they'd likely be in the thousands. Maybe the tens of thousands. This was a massacre.

Two hundred starships still flew. Maybe more. Ragtaggers. Warships. Plucky little starfighters. They were all still fighting together. Even in the horror there was hope.

Many hyds still flew. Thousands of them. But two of the three hydlords were dead! *God's Nightmare*--the strange, mutated one, formed of three triplets joined together. *See No Evil*--the blind one with the whiskers. Both were gone, and the hyds they had commanded flew in disarray. In the shoal, Einav realized, there were no battlefield promotions. Hydlings could eventually grow into hyds, and hyds could eventually grow into hydlords. But it took the creatures time--and lots of food--to reach the next instar. Most never advanced beyond hyd. Each hydlord was like a general, rare and powerful. And now the enemy was down to one last commander.

"But where is the final hydlord?" Einav said, looking around. "I could have sworn there were three."

Her crew looked with her, scanning the viewports all around. Thousands of hyds spread all around, creatures of the second instar. Unlike the smaller hydrians, who were naked, hyds flew inside galactopods of thick chitin. They were larger than hydrians, roughly the size of Joey. Hydlords were far, far larger. The smallest hydlord was the size of a blue whale, and some grew much bigger. Where was the third hydlord? There should be one more.

Addy and Marco limped onto the bridge, back from engineering, covered with dark hydrian blood and ash.

"I left engineering with Chief Murphy," Addy explained. "He woke up again, and I felt bad for the bastard. Didn't want to knock him out a third time."

"So you just left him with an engine room full of dead squids, broken machinery, and repairs to last till Christmas," Marco said.

"Guys?" Einav said. "Have you seen the third hydlord?"

Marco frowned and stepped toward her. "How do you lose a hydlord?"

Everyone stared around, seeking it. Had it retreated? The battle still raged, the human warships fighting the galactopods, but they saw only the smaller squids.

"That's odd. Look over there." Addy pointed. "That group of hyds."

Marco and Einav stared too.

"I see it," Einav said. "In that quadrant of the battle, the hyds seem more organized. They're taking proper military formations. The other hyds seem scattered and confused. But not those ones."

"Almost as if somebody is leading them," Marco said.

Addy shoved him. "Stop butting in. This is my discovery."

"I wasn't--"

"Shush!" Addy said.

Einav stepped closer toward one viewport, squinted, and tilted her head. Something was odd about the middle of that hyd formation. Something about how their tentacles moved, how their eyes seemed opaque. The galactopods there seemed almost . . . smudged.

Then she gasped.

Her eyes widened.

"What is it?" Marco said.

Einav pointed. "Look! Tilt your head! Gaze into the distance. Try to unfocus your eyes."

It was like one of those old stereograms the ancients had found so fascinating in the twentieth century. If you looked just right, smaller shapes faded, and a large shape leaped out in three dimensions. Among those hyds was a hylord. A huge beast, twice the size of the last one. No, it wasn't just *among* those hyds. It *was* those hyds! A few hundred of them, at least. It was made of smaller hyds!

No, that too was inaccurate. It was . . .

"Camouflage," Einav said. "Its carapace is covered with camouflage! With lifelike images of small hyds! It's hiding in plain sight."

Addy gasped. "I see it! Ooh, it's a big one. Good. Let's kill it."

The *Blood, Sweat, and Tears* was in poor shape. Einav knew that. Her hull was breached in multiple spots. Entire decks were exposed to space. Hundreds of her spacers, many with critical roles, had floated dead into space. One exhaust port was blown open. Many cannons were bent or shattered. The remains of *See No Evil*'s charred tentacles still wrapped around the ship like withered ivy around a rusty metal pole. Einav wasn't sure *Blood, Sweat, and Tears* had another fight in her. Yet fight she must, for so long as the enemies of Earth still breathed, Einav would strike at them.

One of her crew looked at her. Einav recognized him. Max Waller. He was a young comms officer, well known across Earth. He was the only officer in the Phoenix Fleet with Down Syndrome. Until him, it was thought no people with Down Syndrome could serve as bridge officers. But young Waller had achieved the impossible. Now he voiced what everyone was thinking.

"We won't take another hit, ma'am," he said. "We're falling apart."

Einav looked at the courageous young officer. She swept her gaze across the smoking, cracked bridge, looking at her other officers too. One by one. All courageous. All had fought their own battles to serve here on the bridge of a flagship.

"Back in the Alien Wars, they called me the Golden Lioness," she said. "This lioness does not give up. She does not back away from a fight. So long as this lioness has a single tooth, she will bite. And should she lose her last tooth, she would claw. And should her claws shatter too, she would lunge upon her enemies, and with her toothless gums and clawless paws, she would pound them into the dust. Even if it meant her death. Tonight you are all lions. You are descended from warriors! Your grandparents fought the scum, the marauders, the grays. The blood of heroes flows through your veins. I do not know if we fly to victory or death. But one thing I do know. We do not flee! We fly to battle and we sound our roar! Onward, *Blood, Sweat, and Tears*! Onward, Phoenix Fleet! Onward, heroes of Earth! At that hydlord--full speed ahead!"

Addy raised her fist and let out a deafening cry, "Let's cook some squid!"

* * * * *

Blood, Sweat, and Tears' engines rumbled. To compensate for one of her damaged exhaust ports, her side thrusters engaged. The dreadnought was slower than usual. Skittering. Leaking steam and air. Like a wounded, limping lioness, the warship charged. For glory. For death. For one last battle.

The camouflaged hydlord saw them approach. His tentacles flared out, and his mouth opened in a furious roar. Silent was that roar, for no sound traveled in space, but it cast out gravitational waves that knocked back nearby hyds and shook the charging *Blood, Sweat, and Tears.* In his fury, the hydlord lost his camouflage, revealing the true color of his carapace. He was the color of dried blood and lined with coiling lines of sickening yellow. Runes were engraved into his shell, spelling out his name. Here flew the *Necroflayer.*

He was larger than the other two hydlords. Larger than both combined. His tentacles spread for miles. His mouth could devour warships. His skin bubbled out through cracks in his carapace. The tips of his fleshy tentacles burst out from their armor like toothpaste from tubes. He seemed prepared to reach the next instar in a hydrian lifecycle--to grow from a hydlord into a hydprince.

As far as Einav knew, there was only one hydprince in the Milky Way galaxy. His name was Ninazu, and he still feasted on Mars. She would not allow another to take form here above Earth!

Blood, Sweat, and Tears flew closer. Other ships joined her. The *Brimstone Fury,* another dreadnought, swooped in from the starboard and joined the charge. The *Ragnarok*, third of the mighty dreadnoughts, flew in from the port side. With them, they brought dozens of frigates and corvettes. The Phoenix Fleet flew in all its strength. Three hundred ships had risen from the sea. Perhaps only a hundred now remained, but the strongest among them--the three dreadnoughts--still flew.

They charged closer to the *Necroflayer*. The beast loomed before them, tentacles spreading so wide they could engulf the fleet.

"Full raking fire!" Einav cried.

Every ship in the Phoenix Fleet, from mighty dreadnought to tiny starfighter, opened fire together. The projectiles streaked forth, lighting up space. Down from Earth, it would look like a great comet hurtling across the sky. The fusillade pounded the hydlord, chipping off armor, burning flesh, ripping a tentacle free. The colossal beast rumbled and roared.

Even little Joey, damaged as she was, emerged from *Blood, Sweat, and Tears'* hangar bay. She was firing her plascaster at the enemy. Einav glanced at Addy and Marco. They still stood beside her on *Blood, Sweat, and Tears'* bridge.

"Joey, what are you doing out there!" Marco cried into his minicom.

"Fighting!" she replied over the nixnet. "Einav called out everyone to fight."

"That's our girl!" Addy said, grinning.

"Be careful, Joey," Marco said. "Please be careful."

As much as she liked Joey, Einav was focused on her dreadnoughts and frigates. They kept bombarding the hydlord. The *Necroflayer* danced and flailed in space as the barrage tore at him. For a moment, Einav dared to feel hope.

But then *Necroflayer* regained his momentum and launched a counter-attack. The gargantopod lunged forth, tentacles spewing not ink but thousands of hydlings. The larva squirmed through space, splattered across warships, and began eating through their hulls. Alarms sounded across the *Blood, Sweat,* Tears and the other fleet ships. Enemies were boarding! Hydlings were crawling in!

Addy sneered and drew her katana. "Time to slice up more squid for dinner."

Marco drew his handguns. "Stay behind me, Addy. I'll keep you safe."

"Shut up, Poet!"

"Form an arrow formation!" Einav ordered her captains. "*Blood, Sweat, and Tears* will take the center. *Brimstone Fury*--fly off our starboard, stem aligned with our stern. *Ragnarok*--fly off our port side, mirrored position. Carriers! Form pyramid clusters above and below. All other ships, expand around us in rings and keep hitting that hydlord!"

Squeals and screams sounded deeper inside the *Blood, Sweat, and Tears*.

Hydlings were already inside the dreadnought. And moving fast. Einav saw them on the holographic schematics. Hundreds of them. The *Necroflayer*'s foul brood was spreading like a disease.

"Marco, Addy?" she said. "Keep them off my back."

Addy licked her blade. "With pleasure."

"Eww, Addy," Marco said. "There's squid guts on that thing."

"Lick it too, Poet. It's good luck." She brought the blade closer to him.

He shoved her aside. "Keep that disgusting sword away from me."

Einav stared ahead, eyes narrowed. The *Necroflayer* was taking heavy damage. His carapace was falling off in chunks. His tentacles flailed. They grabbed a few starships and crushed them. But the rest kept firing! The great exoskeleton cracked and crumbled, exposing . . .

Einav gasped. "He's already growing another exoskeleton. He's trying to become a hydprince."

"Here they come!" Addy cried, her eyes shining with delight.

A score of hydlings squirmed onto the bridge, tentacles flailing madly. With a battle cry, Marco and Addy leaped toward them.

"Concentrate your fire on the hydlord's head," Einav told her captains. "The new carapace there is weak. No nuclear warheads. We're too close. Hit him with conventional torpedoes and neutron fire."

The ships continued firing. *Necroflayer*'s tentacles kept lashing, grabbing ships, hurling others into the distance. Hydlings covered half the ships in the fleet, squirming inside.

From the corner of her eye, Einav glimpsed Addy swinging her katana, cutting hydlings down. Marco was firing a plasma pistol with each hand.

A hydling leaped onto a bridge officer. It was Max Waller, the young officer with Down Syndrome. He fell, screaming as the larva ate him alive. Addy swung her katana, chopping the hydling in half. But it was too late to save poor Waller. He lay dead. He had died in battle. A hero.

Einav shoved aside her grief for now. She stared at the *Necroflayer*. The bombardment was hurting the hydlord. But it wasn't enough. The gargantopod was moving closer. The armored tentacles reached toward them, blades spinning in the suction cups. The hydlord--or was he a hydprince by now?--took on new camouflage. His new exoskeleton displayed a mimicry of smashed human starships. Sick bastard. The creature was mocking them.

The *Blood, Sweat, and Tears* was losing power. Half her gunnery crew was dead. Her cannons were cooling off. Einav raised her chin and inhaled deeply. Was this the end?

A voice filled nixnet. "Hey, Marco, buddy! Whoo! I got

your back, bud!"

Einav looked up. A huge cannon was flying through space. Engines propelled the bore forward, and a cockpit perched on top. Wyatt sat inside, whooping and loving every moment. The *Spacehog*'s huge cannon began to spin, unleashing hell at the *Necroflayer.*

Behind Wyatt, emerging from the shadows of the hyds, came the Ragtag Fleet in all its filthy, rusty glory, all firing their devastating guns. Anti-matter bolts slammed into the hydprince, destroying the alien's very atoms. Quantum funnels burrowed into the titan like worms, sucking up flesh, then disgorging it halfway across the galaxy. Biological weapons lurched through space-- hideous aliens the size of boa constrictors, their jaws full of fangs. Like snakes from a can, the living missiles landed on *Necroflayer* and carved their way in.

And from below, light was rising like the dawn. Round, rocky ships like asteroids rose, turning to reveal innards full of crystals.

Geodes. Geode ships!

The Menorians were here.

* * * * *

"Aurora!" Einav cried, tears leaping into her eyes. "You're alive!"

The Menorian appeared on a floating screen. The benevolent, purple octopus stood among the crystals that controlled her ship. "We ride the waves at the turn of the tide! Menoria flies in aid!"

Einav laughed. "You did manage to escape Mars! You did survive! Thank God."

New hope blazed in Einav. Her friend was alive!

Aurora was Princess of Menoria. Not queen yet. She could

not summon the full fleet of her world. But after losing her personal fleet over Mars, she was back! Back with a hundred more ships! The geodes gathered light, then blasted out blinding beams, carving through the hyds.

The three fleets worked together. The Phoenix Fleet of Earth. The Ragtag Fleet of the asteroid belt. And the Geode Fleet of Menoria. Together they bombarded the *Necroflayer* until the creature burst open and exploded like a dark supernova, spreading clouds of ink across space. Some of the noxious tar hit nearby starships. A few Firebirds crumpled in the sticky black grips. Some ink slashed the *Blood, Sweat, and Tears'* prow and began corroding the armor, but not enough to break through.

Across the bridge, crew members cheered. Addy sliced through the last hydrian on the bridge. Severed tentacles slapped against the viewports and trailed down, leaving ooze.

"Victory!" Addy cried, somewhat prematurely.

Einav knew this war wasn't over yet. Thousands of hyds were still outside. Hydlings still crawled through the ship. The *Blood, Sweat, and Tears* was falling apart.

But yes, they had scored a victory. A great victory. Two hydlords and one hydprince--slain! The battle would soon continue. But for a moment, Einav allowed herself to take a breath. To smile. To feel some hope.

We can do this, she thought. *The cost will be great. The sacrifice nearly too much to bear. Tens of thousands of brave soldiers died here this night. And millions died on Mars. More might die before the end. But we can hurt them. We can kill them. We can beat them.*

She raised her chin, eyes damp.

"We can win," she whispered.

That was when she saw it.

She lost her smile.

She stared in silent shock, feeling the blood drain from her face.

It's over, she thought. *Earth. Humanity. It's over.*

They covered space, dropping out from warp speed. Not just on this battlefield--but all around Earth. Countless hyds spread into the distance. Hundreds of hydlords flew among them, overseeing the smaller warriors. Above them all, descending toward Earth's north pole, loomed Hydprince Ninazu. He had engorged himself on Mars, feasting on the living flesh of that world. The ancient god was now the size of a small country.

Big and small, there were billions of them. They surrounded the globe.

They drew us into a trap, Einav realized. *They pulled our fleet away from Earth. Surrounded us. Then sent in the main force.*

The shoal was here in all its might. And Einav did not know if Earth would survive the night.

CHAPTER THIRTEEN
I'm Here

From up in space, Einav watched it happen.

Billions of hydrians descending toward Earth.

Her eyes were dry. They had shed too many tears. Her heart felt dead in her chest. It had shattered so many times. It was October 28, 2270. The day of the prophecy. The day of the Hydrian Holocaust.

From *Blood, Sweat, and Tears'* bridge, they all watched. Officers shed tears. Prayed. One man fell to his knees in terror. But not Marco and Addy. Not Einav. They did not cry, did not tremble. They had seen too many wars.

Einav knew what her friends felt. She felt it too.

Rage.

Not red, flaming rage, all burning wild and loud. No. This was a cold, silent rage, more dangerous by far. This was rage tinged with terror and grief. This was a rage that would never stop burning. That consumed the soul.

Hundreds, maybe thousands of hydlords were descending toward Earth. Full hydlords--gods of the void. Some had emerged from warp right by the planet, shaking and cracking spacetime. They were already touching down, landing in forests, oceans, and cities. Serving their lords, countless hyds stormed down like so many hailstones.

Above them all, commanding the invasion, loomed Hydprince Ninazu. He descended toward the North Pole like an unholy god. His carapace was falling off in chunks the size of cities, revealing hundreds of eyes on his dark flesh. After engorging himself on the people of Mars, he was transforming into the final instar in the hydrian lifecycle. He was becoming a hydking. Earth would be his throne, and from here, he would rule the galaxy.

Earth was only a hundred thousand miles away. Just down the block. Reports began streaming in. Some were military reports from officers on the ground, speaking over nixnet. Others came over the regular internet. Videos from civilians. They floated on holographic screens around Einav. Their voices filled her ears, echoing like haunting ghosts.

"Oh God, they're landing!"

"The hydrians are on Earth!"

"We need help! Somebody help!"

Dozens, then hundreds, then thousands of videos floated around, shrinking to thumbnails. Einav watched it happen live all around her. A hydrian landed on a school, tore the roof off, scooped out children, and devoured them. Hydrians rampaged down city streets, grabbing, crushing, and consuming people. Hydrians clung to the Statue of Liberty, ripping her down. They filled the sea and bubbled up onto the shore. They toppled skyscrapers, rummaged through the remains for survivors, and gobbled them up.

On the bridge of the *Blood, Sweat, and Tears*, they stared in silent horror, barely believing. This had to be a nightmare. This could not be real.

Commander Harris, tall and steely-eyed, walked across the bridge. He stood by Einav and stared down at the world.

"And so the world ends," said the grizzled captain of the *Blood, Sweat, and Tears*. "In fire and darkness. Never thought I'd see the day, Admiral."

Einav looked at him. He was a gruff man in his sixties. But compared to her, he was young--not even half her age. He had not even been born during the Alien Wars. He had not seen the conquest of the marauders or the devastation of the scum.

"The day the world ends?" Einav said. "No. No! The world does not end today. Today the new world begins! This is the hour of our greatest defeat. But it will become the hour of our greatest courage. We are lions! We are warriors! They can destroy our ships. They can invade our world. But we will fight back! We will win!"

Marco, her dearest old friend, approached her. He looked at her, and there was something hollow in his brown eyes. Something haunted. Something that nearly made Einav break down and weep.

"Can we win, Einav?" he said softly.

Einav looked at him. Then looked at Addy. Then passed her gaze across everyone on the bridge. And when she spoke, she broadcast her words to the fleet. At first she spoke softly, yet with every word, her voice gained power until she was shouting.

"I know you're afraid. I know you're grieving. I know that millions are dying. But we've not lost this war yet! We fought them in space. And we will fight them on land. We fought them across the galaxy. And we will fight them here on Earth. We fought them on the red planet and we will fight them on the blue. We will never stop fighting! We will fight from starships, and should our starships fall, we will fight them from tanks on land and ships upon the sea. And even if those mighty machines of war should shatter, we will fight them on our feet. And should our very feet give up beneath us, we will crawl through the mud, clawing and biting and still fighting. Still fighting! We are lions! We are lions, children of Earth! Roar with me! Fly with me--to war!"

Many hyds still flew around the human warships, the remnants of the three hydlords' hosts. It no longer mattered. Right now, all that mattered were the people on Earth. And that was where they must fly.

"Commander Harris, turn this ship around," Einav said. "Take us back to Earth. We'll fight our way through. Fleet! All captains of the fleet! Rally around the *Blood, Sweat, and Tears*. Defensive cluster formation. Our planet needs us. Fly!"

This time nobody cheered. This time nobody had hope. They were flying to their deaths in battle. They all knew that. Did Einav? Was her hope merely a fool's hope? Should she order this fleet to flee to the stars? Should they seek another world, try to rebuild humanity far from the scourge of the shoal?

No, she decided. No, the shoal would spread from Earth. It would consume this planet first. But Earth would not be the last. Einav and her crew could, perhaps, shelter on another world. Live for years, maybe even generations in peace. But sooner or later, the shoal would arrive there too, and every world in the Milky Way would fall to them, and all life would be snuffed out. Aside from the foul, unholy life of the squid.

No, they could not run. This was where they would make their final stand. Where they would defeat their foes or die fighting.

Marco and Addy understood. She saw it in their eyes. They were thinking the same thing.

As the ships began to move, plowing through hyds toward Earth, Marco stepped closer to Einav. He held her hand.

"To the end," he said. "To victory or death. Together."

Addy took her other hand. "Together."

Einav's eyes stung. In all this horror, she still had them. Her friends. She held their hands tight.

"Together."

* * * * *

The Phoenix Fleet had suffered heavy losses. They were

down to a third of their size. They were not far from Earth. Normally, they could fly there within moments. But now countless hyds lay between them and their world. The journey home would be far longer and harder.

Einav hoped that, for now at least, the enemy would focus all their effort on Earth. That only the hyds of the three dead hydlords would still plague the fleet. She was wrong.

While many hydlords had already touched down on Earth, hundreds still filled space, and each commanded a fleet of the smaller hyds. Countless red eyes turned toward the human fleet. Jaws opened with lurid grins, baring fangs the size of trees, and tongues emerged to lick slavering chops. Red eyes gleamed like pools of blood. A million hydrians or more turned toward the limping, battered Phoenix Fleet.

Alarms wailed across the *Blood, Sweat, and Tears'* bridge. All the holographic screens from Earth vanished--both the military ones on nixnet and the civilian videos.

"What's happening?" Einav said.

The new comms officer shook his head, helpless. "A signal is washing over us, Admiral. It's battering our firewalls. It's coming from . . ." He gulped. "From that thing over the north pole."

Static sounded from the speakers, then screeching feedback. A hologram appeared on the bridge of the *Blood, Sweat, and Tears*, life-sized.

A hologram of Erafel.

The hybrid had changed. His skin, once pinkish, had become gray and veined with black. His eyes were sunken and rimmed with purple bruises. Those eyes glittered in their sockets like obsidian tinged with firelight. His chest was bare, revealing many scars and welts and gashes. From the waist down, his tentacles had grown bits of chitin like scabs. But he was only half hydrian. The carapace was not forming properly, and as he slithered on the appendages, chunks fell off and vanished in wisps.

Erafel's enormously long fingers uncurled. Each finger had many joints and was as long as an arm. An azoth shard was embedded into one of his palms. Einav remembered Joey blasting that chunk of azoth out of Ninazu's mind. The godstone, Erafel called it. It had sunken into Erafel's hand like a piece of shrapnel. The flesh around it was rotten and oozing. The entire hand dripped. Yet the unholy light of the crystal thrummed around his hand, keeping the rancid flesh intact.

Addy snarled. Instinctively, she swung her katana, but the blade merely passed through the hologram harmlessly.

Erafel laughed. "Ah, Addy Linden, impetuous and stupid as always. And if it isn't Marco, my old pupil! I enjoyed tormenting you back then, and I enjoy it even more now. Ah . . . and there she is. The Golden Lioness." Erafel slithered closer to Einav, his beady black eyes glinting with amusement. "Still alive, after all this . . . I'm impressed."

"At least one of us still lives," Einav said. "You look like a walking corpse."

Erafel laughed--a sound like snapping bones. "Yes, I am in many ways undead. I cannot die the death of mortals. In that sense, we are alike, Einav. Both cursed with long, strange life. Both with shards of eternity in our palms. Both leaders. Both warriors. You've been an excellent adversary, Einav Ben-Ari. But you've lost. I give you one last chance. Surrender to me. Kneel before me! Be mine. And I will spare your life."

"No thanks," Einav said.

He bared his teeth and squirmed closer. His foul face thrust toward hers. His tongue emerged from his rotting mouth and licked his sharp teeth. He was only a hologram, but Einav could practically smell him.

"You're an attractive woman, Einav. Your skin--so fair.

Your hair--so golden. Your body--"

"Stay away from her!" Marco said, stomping closer.

Erafel ignored him. He leered at Einav. "Your husband died long ago. Be mine instead. Kneel at my side. As my concubine, you'll have wealth and power. Like Hart, if you serve me, you'll live in luxury."

Einav grimaced. "You sicken me. You foul bastard."

He hissed, his eyes leering. "Yes, perhaps I sicken you. But if you resist me, you'll die, Einav. You'll die screaming. You'll die a long, tortuous death. So will your friends." He glanced at Marco and Addy, scoffed, then looked back at her. "Kneel. Wear the jeweled collar I place around your neck. Live in my court among my pretty things. And I'll spare your friends too."

"Don't do it!" Addy said. "I'd rather die."

The rest of the crew raised their chins, defiant. They were all with Einav.

Erafel growled and snapped his teeth at Addy. "Then you will die. All of you!" He glanced back at Einav as if hoping she might change her mind.

"Crawl back to your master, Erafel," Einav said. "Crawl back to Ninazu and tell him this. A lioness does not surrender. A pride of lions begs for no mercy. You might have conquered many worlds. But this time, you've messed with the wrong planet. I'm coming for you, Erafel. And for your master. I'll kill you myself. And before the end, you'll be the one to kneel."

"Burn!" Addy said.

Erafel's eyes bugged out. His jaws dropped lower and lower like a snake's jaw, revealing rows of teeth. "Then die!" he shrieked, his voice like shattering glass, filling the bridge.

"Get this hologram off my bridge!" Einav said.

Finally, the comms officer managed to restore the firewall. The hissing hybrid vanished in a swirl of light. But his voice still echoed through the *Blood, Sweat, and Tears.*

Die . . . Die . . . Die!

* * * * *

With the hologram gone, Einav focused on the scene outside. Standing on the bridge, surrounded by viewports, she could barely see space. Only the endless sea of hydrians. The aliens seemed to stare right at her as that terrible voice echoed.

Die . . .

And then countless hydrians stormed through space toward the Phoenix Fleet.

Einav stared at them, chin raised. She had lost most of her fleet battling ten thousand hydrians. Now millions flew toward her.

Die . . .

Across the bridge, the crew prayed, whispered, and held one another. One man ran toward the door.

"I need to be with my wife," he muttered. "I--"

"Return to your post!" Einav shouted. "Bridge crew--at your stations! All ships, fly! Fly! To Earth!"

The engines roared.

The Phoenix Fleet charged forth into the shoal--a couple hundred ships, leaving a trail of fire, racing into an alien ocean.

"If this is our end, let it be a legendary end," Einav said. "In ages to come, should any humans still live, let them remember the last flight of the phoenixes."

"To Earth!" Addy cried.

"To Earth!" said Marco, fist in the air.

Onward they charged, engines lighting the dark, cannons booming and blazing, the brave soldiers of Earth, the last survivors of a great fleet. Last flight of the phoenixes. One last battle before the endless night.

Clustering closer together like an ancient cavalry, they

plowed into the enemy lines.

Blood, Sweat, and Tears' prow rammed into hyds, scattering their galactopods through space. The other ships charged right behind, plowing through the alien formations, their cannons firing, their crews not turning back, not losing heart. Hydlords loomed above them like storm clouds. Ink rained, sizzling on hulls, melting through metal. And still the phoenixes flew! Still the fleet charged onward!

Firebirds shattered. Corvettes burst open. A frigate crumpled and burned. And onward the survivors flew! Storming through the hydrians. Cutting deep into their storm. Last flight of the phoenixes--for death. For death! For death in battle. For death over a blue world. For the death of soldiers. The death of phoenixes and a dream that someday they could rise from the ashes.

The enemy lines thickened. Hydlords linked their tentacles together, blocking the passage to Earth. Another frigate shattered. Then the *Brimstone Fury*, a great dreadnought, cracked open and spilled out air and kicking spacers. The *Blood, Sweat, and Tears'* prow crumpled and more decks burst open. Chunks of the ship careened into space. Again and again tentacles lashed them, breaking off pieces of the dreadnought.

"The ship is falling apart!" somebody cried.

"Shields are down!"

"Our chassis is cracking!"

"Our core is unstable!"

Great cracks and booms reverberated throughout the ship. The very foundations were ripping.

This was the end.

Marco and Addy held each other, tears in their eyes, saying their goodbyes.

But Einav was not ready to die. Not yet.

She raised her starhand.

On the palm, the Mariner's Tear shone with purple light. No two azoth crystals were alike. Some were small and opaque, others pure as lavender moonlight. Some came from the mines of Corpus; they could bend spacetime, allowing starships to travel the galaxy. Some grew in the twisted minds of hydrians, and their dark light spread their wickedness. The Mariner's Tear was fairer than them all. It was the brightest azoth crystal Einav had ever seen, the purest, the finest. It had once glowed in a ship of the ancients, the great mariners who had sailed the Milky Way and built the Tree of Light. For a million years, it had glowed in a shipwreck on a lost world, and now it shone in the palm of her ivory hand. A miniature star fused hydrogen into helium in the heart of the *Blood, Sweat, and Tears*, releasing enough energy to power a starship the size of a town, and the Mariner's Tear was mightier.

Einav tilted back her head, holding out her starhand, and let the power surge. This power flowed from the quantum battery in her prosthetic--but also from a well deep inside her. The power of her soul. Of her memories. Of her lost loved ones. Of those she loved who still lived. It was the heart that powered the Mariner's Tear, and that made it greater than any engine. As the human mind was more complex than any star or galaxy, so was the human heart mightier than any force of nature. And Einav's heart brimmed with love. For her friends. For her country. For her species. For Earth. For the stars themselves.

The Mariner's Tear shone with blinding lilac light, and the light flowed from the starhand across the bridge, through the crumbling halls and decks, through engine rooms and exhaust pipes and the great, churning fusion core below. Along every path the light took it healed. It soothed the dying. It gave hope to those who still fought. It grabbed bulkheads and hulls and held them together like gossamer. The force of the Mariner's Tear spread from stern to stem, holding the ship in one piece as *Blood, Sweat, and Tears* flew on. Einav held the dreadnought in the palm of her hand.

Off the flagship's port side, the *Brimstone Fury* cracked in two. The tentacles pulled her apart like jackals dismembering carrion. Hydlords reached inside to scoop out spacers. *Brimstone Fury*'s fusion core overflowed and burst, blazing with white light. In her death, the great dreadnought indeed released the fury of fire and brimstone. The explosion tore hydlords and hyds apart. It washed over nearby human ships too, burning corvettes and searing open a frigate. But even as so many starships burned out, the *Blood, Sweat, and Tears* flew onward, wreathed in the light of the Mariner's Tear and powered by the heart of her admiral.

By their starboard side, the *Ragnarok* was firing her cannons, storming at the enemy. She was of equal size to the *Blood, Sweat, and Tears*. Yet oceans of ink washed over her, ripping open her hull. Hydlords grabbed her, crushed her, and her air leaked out and her water spilled into space. Her fusion core overflowed. And another blast of blinding light lit the battle, ripping apart nearby galactopods and warships alike. Indeed the dreadnought ended like the Ragnarok of legend--with light and devastation and great death.

Of the three dreadnoughts of the Phoenix Fleet only the *Blood, Sweat, and Tears* remained.

Another frigate exploded.

And another and a few more corvettes.

Every few seconds, another ship winked out. As they flew onward to Earth, the fleet was crumbling, shedding ships like scraps of flesh off a body. Like the great fish of *The Old Man and the Sea*, they kept losing bits of themselves. And as she flew onward, Einav felt that her soul too was chipping away, shedding its last vestiges of mercy and hope, leaving only a cold, hard, metallic core, a sphere that vibrated to the tune of vengeance.

She wanted to kill.

She no longer felt hope. No longer felt mercy. Even her grief had hardened and transformed. All she wanted to do was hurt them. Hurt Erafel. Hurt Ninazu. Hurt Hart for his betrayal. This is what the enemy had done to her. They had peeled off and burned every other part of the woman she had been. They had turned her into a terrible weapon. A doomsday weapon. And she would bring upon them their doom.

They flew another thousand klicks. And another ship burned.

They plowed deeper into the storm of the shoal. And the last of their Firebirds shattered.

Earth loomed ahead, so large it covered the prow viewports. But Einav no longer recognized her planet. Earth was no longer blue but black. The squids surrounded her world. They scuttled across her cities. They filled her seas and darkened her forests with their ink. The god Ninazu had landed on the pole and gripped the planet, sending his tentacles farther and farther south like living longitude lines on a macabre globe from the mind of a maniac.

Then, between the hydrian hosts, Einav saw something on the planet.

Blazes of light. Fire. Explosions. Streaks of missiles flying from land to land.

Were the hydrians burning the world? No, theirs was not the way of fire. They were creatures of water and darkness. This was the light of the Human Defense Force. Of lines of heavy armor. Of artillery booming. Of bombs exploding against the monsters from the void.

The ground forces were fighting! And like those flickers of light on the planet, Einav felt hope flicker.

"Earth lives," she whispered, then raised her voice. "Earth lives!"

Marco and Addy looked at her, eyes so empty. They were

holding each other, pale. There was almost no hope in their eyes.

"Earth lives," Einav told them. "Say it with me. Say it! Earth lives!"

"Einav, Earth is gone," Marco said softly.

She grabbed his arm. She pointed. "Look. Look! We fight! We still fight! Say it with me. Earth lives!"

He raised his chin, and his eyes burned with cold fury. "Earth lives."

"Say it louder!" Einav said. "Everyone on this bridge, everyone in this fleet--say it with me! Earth lives!"

"Earth lives!" they cried.

Another ship and another exploded. The *Blood, Sweat, and Tears*' cannons boomed, knocking back hyds and hydlords. Even with only a handful of corvettes left, they flew onward through the storm.

"Earth lives!" they cried. "Earth lives!"

The cannons unleashed nuclear warheads. Blast after blast lit up the night. Each bomb was a hundred times mightier than the weapons dropped on Hiroshima. With the terrible fury of technology, they cut their way through the shoal, destroying the enemy lines until it was just ahead.

An open pathway to Earth.

The sky was right below. A dark sky. A sky with no blue that remained. A sky of squids. But between the storm clouds the light of Earth's fighting men and women still shone.

Of the mighty fleet of Earth, only a handful of ships remained, *Blood, Sweat, and Tears* largest among them. Joey flew at her side. So did the *Spacehog*. So did the geode ship of Aurora, loyal to the end. So did six or seven other ships. That was all. Those were the tattered remains of Earth's might in space.

"Your orders, ma'am?" asked Commander Harris.

"Fight," she said. "Kill. Kill every squid you see. Fight to the end. We take down as many of the bastards with us as we can.

We go down in glory."

* * * * *

As the warships unleashed the last of their arsenal, the hydrians surrounded them. The tentacles lashed them. The ink covered them. Another frigate and another burned. A great hydlord slammed into *Blood, Sweat, and Tears*' stern, and her engines sputtered, and the gravity of Earth grabbed the dreadnought.

And then they were falling.

Falling through smoke into the sky.

The mighty dreadnought crashed through the atmosphere, ionizing the air. Great walls of flame soared around the ship. Whatever remained of the hull plowed through flying hyds, and *Blood, Sweat, and Tears* kept plunging. Other starships crashed down with them, falling apart, burning up in atmospheric entry. But Einav's starhand still glowed. With her force of will, she kept her ship together, wreathing her love and care around *Blood, Sweat, and Tears* as the dreadnought dived toward the ground.

Einav didn't know where they were falling. Didn't know what land lay below. All was smoke and squids.

Even she, wielding the Mariner's Tear and the strength of her woeful soul, could not battle the great forces of gravity and kinetic energy that were tearing at the ship. The exhaust system tore free from the underbelly and burned up. The prow peeled back to reveal the chassis, and fire leaped into the decks to consume all within. Liquid fire flowed through the ship. Casualty counts soared across the bridge, and then the holographic screens vanished. The computer systems were shutting down.

Finally the viewports themselves shut down as the sensors on the hull burned up. The bridge plunged into pitch blackness. The illusion of floating in the open vanished. The bridge was located in the ship's deepest, most secure layer, buried within thick walls. Now as the ship crumpled and tore apart, the crew rattled around in a metal sphere, trapped. The air stopped flowing. Life support died. They were free-falling.

Only the glow from Einav's hand now lit the bridge. She could see only those nearest her. Marco. Addy. A few bridge officers. They tried to reach her, but they were flying through the bridge, tumbling, rising and floating and falling, hitting the walls.

She caught a few with her light, pulled them close. Marco and Addy held her.

"I got you," she whispered to them. "I got you, my friends. I--"

And then the bridge jolted madly and the walls cracked.

Fire and stone and melting metal leaped around them.

They slammed into the Earth and scraped across the land, plowing through rock and root, soil and stone, wood and water. Whatever remained of the *Blood, Sweat, and Tears* rumbled and ripped across the landscape, tearing open the planet. And still Einav held onto her friends.

"I'm here," she whispered, holding Marco and Addy close. "I'm here . . ."

She felt small arms hold her. Her son, her dear Carl, looked at her, eyes damp.

"I'm here," she whispered to him, holding this ghost from her past.

Lailani huddled against her, a broken little soldier. Kemi was there, a stalwart friend. Caveman stood by her, big and brutish and loyal, and so was Jackass, a soldier she had let down, the first soldier she had lost. And then they were all there around Einav in the darkness--Texas and Elvis and St. Pierre and all the rest of them. The soldiers of the Dragons Platoon and the armies she had led in war. All her soldiers. All her children. She wrapped them all in her embrace.

"I'm here . . . I'm here."

And now that hard sphere inside Einav shattered, and her grief flowed out and her tears streamed down her cheeks. Because she had loved so many. She had led millions in battle. And she had lost so many children. She was alone with their ghosts and her grief. And as ruins of the *Blood, Sweat, and Tears* rattled in the darkness, their faces all floated around her, then faded . . . Faded . . . Leaving her alone.

But no.

She was not alone.

Marco was still there at her right-hand side. Addy was still there as ever at her left. They held her in their arms.

"I'm here," Marco whispered.

"I'm here," Addy whispered.

As Einav wept, they held her, and finally the glow from her starhand faded. She had given her all, and now she could only be held.

And then--a crash.

A terrible jolt.

The universe seemed to be ending. Every bone in Einav's body seemed to be cracking.

Without the power to hold the bridge together, she thought they would die.

But she lived. And she realized they were no longer moving. The *Blood, Sweat, and Tears*--or whatever remained of her outside the bridge--had stopped.

Einav blinked. She was on her knees. Held within the embrace of her friends, she looked up, and she saw light. A crack had opened in the deckhead above, and a beam of sunlight fell upon her, piercing the smoke and ashes. A bird glided overhead.

"Earth lives," she whispered. "Earth lives!"

CHAPTER FOURTEEN
Wrecks

Marco groaned. He must have blacked out. Now he was coming to and everything hurt. His toes. His joints. His face. His bones. His insides. Even his goddamn eyebrows hurt. Marco hadn't known that was possible. Worst of all, a terrible weight was pressing down on him. Constricting him. He could barely breathe, and his bones were creaking under the mass.

I'm trapped under a chunk of bulkhead, he thought. *I'm being crushed to death.*

Addy's voice sounded above him. "Ugh. That was a rough crash. Luckily I landed on something soft. Hey, Poet, where are you?"

He moaned beneath her and shoved her. "Get off me! God, you weigh a ton. I thought a bulkhead fell on me."

She gasped. "I'll show you a bulkhead!" She began punching him.

Marco crawled out from under her. Joints creaking, he rose to his feet. Physically, thanks to the Methuselah Scrum, he was only in his thirties. But right now he felt every one of his 148 years. He was bruised and battered, his hair was charred, but he was more or less in one piece.

He grabbed Addy's hand and helped her up. She stood beside him, cracked her neck, and winced. "Oh man. If you hadn't cushioned that fall, Poet, I'd have broken every bone in my body."

"If Einav hadn't wrapped us in her azoth field, we'd be splattered across the deckhead," Marco said. "Where is she?

Einav?"

He looked around, waved aside smoke, and coughed. The bridge spread around him, a scene of ruin. Every viewport had shattered. Every workstation had overturned. A crack spread across the deckhead above, letting in beams of afternoon light, cold air, and an ashy drizzle. Somewhere in the distance a crow cawed. Some bridge officers pushed themselves up, coughing and bruised and bloody. Some lay on the deck, wounded or dead. Where was Einav?

"Einav?" Marco cried.

He walked through the bridge, seeking her. He helped a few survivors rise. Commander Harris was already on his feet, pulling others up, then kneeling to administer aid to the wounded. A bandage encircled the gruff commander's head, and blood matted his hair, but he was dedicating his all to helping others. Marco wanted to help. But he also must find his leader.

Marco turned toward Addy. "Guard the bridge. I'm going to look for her."

Addy slammed a magazine into her rifle and shouldered the gun. "Got it."

Marco looked at her. Even after falling from the sky, Addy stood tall, strong, and proud. Bruises and scratches covered her, but her back was straight, her chin raised. Her World War II helmet sat askew on her head, the words HELL'S PRINCESS scrawled on the green metal. But she was no demon from hell. She was an angel from heaven, a battle angel, full of wrath and righteous retribution.

"What are you looking at, Poet?" she said.

"You. I love you, you nut."

He stepped toward her, pulled her into his arms, and kissed her on the lips. She grabbed his hair and kissed him back with equal passion.

"Love you forever, Marco," she said.

Marco explored the rest of the bridge. It was a large chamber, roughly the size of an old movie theater. A few hatches had torn off, revealing battered corridors full of dust and mangled metal. He saw footprints in the dust. Female footprints, he thought. He followed them.

The footprints led him down the corridor, then stopped by a service hatch with a ladder inside. Marco hesitated for a moment, remembering the last time he had entered an elevator shaft. It had been on the *Pride of the Lioness*, if he recalled correctly. He had encountered hydlings inside. A shudder passed through him, but he plowed ahead, entering the hatch. Fresh air wafted from above, and a drizzle damped his hair. He climbed the ladder.

Normally it would be a long climb--several stories tall--to the top of the *Blood, Sweat, and Tears*. But several of the upper decks had simply . . . slid off. Marco emerged onto a mangled ruin. This had once been an interior deck. Now it served as the top of the ravaged *Blood, Sweat, and Tears*, legendary flagship of the Phoenix Fleet. Charred chunks of curled-up bulkhead, broken gears the size of houses, and severed tentacles covered the ruin. No bodies remained. The fall from the sky must have blown them off or incinerated them.

He was facing the stern of the ship. The huge exhaust ports thrust out below him, charred and cracked, one missing entirely. Beyond them, a boreal forest spread toward blue hills and a misty horizon. Above the clouds, barely visible, one could make out the shape of hydrians. The great squids hovered in the sky, their red eyes mere smudges like dying stars seen through a storm. A distant rumble sounded. At first Marco mistook it for thunder, but it was the rumbling of a hydrian far above. The sound rolled across the landscape, and the trees shook in a cold wind. The hydrians were above the clouds, it seemed, and could not see the land below. The ship's survivors were hidden.

Marco turned away from the stern, wanting to see how

badly the prow was damaged. A gasp fled his lips. His eyes widened. A mountainside soared before him. The *Blood, Sweat, and Tears* had crashed into the mountain, burying herself into the soil and rock. Half the ship seemed to be embedded into the mountainside.

Then Marco saw her. She stood a hundred yards away upon the ruin of the *Blood, Sweat, and Tears*, gazing into the distance. Einav Ben-Ari.

Her back was turned to him. She still wore her white outfit. Simple white trousers. A white shirt with golden buckles along the side. Her hands hung at her side, one made of filigreed ivory, the glow of its crystal dimmed. A gust of wind lifted her dirty blond hair and billowed it like a banner. Around her slender waist still hung the golden belt she had purchased at Darktech Cove, each coin along the chain engraved with another animal.

Marco approached her. When he came to stand at her side, she did not look at him. She didn't even seem to notice him. She simply gazed into the distance, and Marco followed her gaze. He saw the forest sprawl into the distance. A river snaked below, and mist wreathed the mountains. Again a rumble rolled down from above. Marco shuddered.

Finally Einav spoke, her voice soft, but still she did not look at him. "They're communicating with one another. They ripple the very sky with their voices. They're searching for us. For any human."

Marco's eyes widened. He pointed. "Look! Smoke. Smoke rising from the forest! Part of our ship? Or maybe other ships crash-landed too. Einav, we have to find them. To find other survivors."

She turned to look at him. And God, her eyes! They were as green as this forest and as haunted as the memories of this broken Earth.

"We are not survivors, Marco. We do not have the luxury

to think of ourselves as survivors." She clasped his arm, almost painfully. "We are soldiers."

He nodded and raised his chin. "We are soldiers." He looked around him. "So let's, um . . . go search through the wreckage for other soldiers."

Einav smiled. At first it was a small smile. A sad smile. But then it grew into a true smile that showed her teeth, that reached her eyes, that banished some of the darkness there. She embraced him and laid her head on his shoulder.

"I love you, Marco Emery. My brave soldier. My best friend. I'm glad you're with me. Here at the end of one world and the beginning of another."

* * * * *

Cory Hart, King of Apeworld, stood on his palace balcony, watching the world end.

The hydrians descended upon Jerusalem. Thousands of them. They landed on the ancient limestone walls, draping their tentacles across the parapets. They plopped down onto domed temples and wrapped around minarets. A colossal squid gripped the Wailing Wall, while others squirmed along the souks, shattering the merchant stalls. They filled the sky like storm clouds and squirmed across the hills.

The same thing was happening all over the world. As Hart stood here on the balcony of Hart Hall, holographic screens hovered around him, broadcasting scenes from across the globe. Hydrians wriggled their way down Champs-Élysées. One hydrian tried to land on the Eiffel Tower, poked itself, squirmed, then wrapped around the base. Squids surrounded the Golden Gate, splashing in the water, wrapping their tentacles around the bridge, and pulling it down. People fell into their waiting mouths. A hydlord embraced Christ the Redeemer while its children rampaged along Copacabana, gobbling up beachgoers. One lobster-red hydrian perched atop Matsumoto-jō Castle, roaring and flailing as soldiers fired at its carapace. A golden hydrian wrapped itself around the sphinx, while others climbed the pyramids and reached into their hidden tunnels.

"The world is ending," Hart whispered. "It's over." A tear rolled down his cheek. "I tried. I tried to save it. I tried to do the right thing." He fell to his knees and lowered his head. "O, Earth, I'm sorry."

"Cory?" A soft voice from behind him. "Cory, what do we do?"

He turned around. She stood at the balcony door, her back to the bedroom. Heather. His beautiful wife. Their children clung to her, eyes wide with terror.

Be strong for them, Hart thought. *Protect them.*

"Heather, take the children down to the bunker. We'll be all right, kids."

They were weeping.

His daughter pointed. "Daddy, the monsters are here . . ."

"It'll be all right, sweetheart. Daddy will keep you safe."

Heather trembled. "Cory, they're everywhere. What--"

"Get the kids down into the bunker!" he cried, voice cracking.

The kids whimpered. His daughter reached out to him.

"Cory, aren't you coming?" Heather said, tears on her cheeks. The grunts and squeals of hydrians sounded across the city. The shape of their tentacles danced in Heather's eyes.

"I must stay to fight," Hart said. "To lead the soldiers. Get into the bunker. You'll be safe. I'll protect you."

"Cory . . .," she whimpered.

He stepped closer and pulled his family into his arms. He kissed them one by one. Then he whispered into Heather's ear, "I'll look after you. Always. I promise. Now go. Be strong for the kids. I love you."

Sniffling, Heather left the bedroom with the children, taking them down and down below the palace to the bunker far below.

Hart did not join them. No, he had spent too many years cowering in that bunker. Down there he was useless. Maybe up here, maybe . . . Could he still do something? Anything?

He stood on his balcony, gazing upon the horrors. The hydrians were rampaging across the Old City of Jerusalem. They slithered over the Church of the Holy Sepulchre, profaned Golgotha, and wrapped around the Tower of David. They draped across the city walls. From here, Hart could see a hydrian crawling over the Gate of Mercy. The city boasted eight ancient gates dating back to biblical times. This was the gate through which Jesus had entered Jerusalem. The Gate of Mercy had been sealed in 1541, filled with bricks. The double archways remained. The gatehouse still stood. But nobody had entered or left since. According to ancient traditions, when the messiah arrived in Jerusalem, he would walk through the Gate of Mercy. Now Hart watched a hydrian's tentacles slam at the bricks, ripping open the blocked gateway, and chortling.

Is this the messiah then? Hart thought. *A squid?*

"They're destroying everything," he whispered to himself. "Our city, our world, our faith." He lowered his head. "What have I done?"

A deep voice rose. That voice that had been haunting Hart for a year now, speaking from the crystal, echoing in his mind day and night.

"You did the right thing. You warned me of Ben-Ari's assault. You served Ninazu well, my son."

Kneeling on the balcony, Hart raised his hand and looked at the crystal embedded into his palm. The skin around it was inflamed. But the crystal itself--the hydstone--was dark. Erafel's face did not shine as always within.

Hart blinked. How--?

A hand touched his shoulder. Greatly elongated fingers coiled across Hart's shoulder, so long they draped halfway down Hart's chest. Each finger was like a snake.

Hart gasped and spun around. Erafel stood there! In the flesh! Right there on the balcony!

On his knees, Hart gasped at the hybrid. He had seen Erafel a thousand times in the crystal. Had seen him a thousand more in his nightmares. But never until now in real life.

He was even more hideous in person. Erafel's beady black eyes glittered in dark sockets, and black veins spiderwebbed across his gray skin. Below the waist, his tentacles were trying to grow exoskeletons like the larger hydrians, it seemed. But it looked more like scabs that kept crumbling, falling onto the balcony, then regrowing. Like Hart, like Einav, Erafel had a crystal in his palm. The meat around the stone was rotten.

"Yes," Erafel hissed. "I'm like you, Hart. I too have an azoth stone in my hand. Mine came from the broken mind of Ninazu. The godstone, I call it. With this gem, I'm always connected to my lord. A part of his mind. I whisper to him. And he whispers to me. We are joined. And you, Hart . . . You are one of us."

Hart shuffled closer on his knees. "Please, Erafel. Please, I beg you. Call off the hyds! They're . . . they're eating people. Oh God, I saw them eat people. It was Einav who attacked you! Einav! I served you. I only ever served you." He clasped Erafel's hands. "Please spare this planet. Take me if you must. But spare this world."

Erafel looked down upon him. "Oh, my child . . . I already own you."

Hart struggled to his feet. "Yes. Yes, you do. So--"

"Get back down on your knees, worm." Erafel shoved

him down. "You are not worthy of standing in my presence. I named you King of Apeworld. And this is how you repay me? Sending your fleet against me? Fighting my hydlords?"

"It was Einav!" Hart cried. "It was Einav Ben-Ari! I warned you, Erafel! Don't you remember? I helped you!" He prostrated himself and began kissing one of those scabby tentacles. "You must believe me."

Erafel slapped him with the tentacle. "Look at you. Groveling ape! Pathetic simian. At least Einav has some pride. You sicken me, ape. What use are you to me? I thought you could command Apeworld for me. But you cannot keep your fellow apes under control. So Ninazu will devour your world."

"I can be of use!" Hart said. "Ninazu said he . . . he wants slaves, right? Female slaves, yes? I can get him some. The most beautiful women! And . . ." Hart pushed himself back up to his knees. "And I can get you women too. The most beautiful ones you like. They'll serve you well. Yes, yes! I can help you. I can get them for you."

And Hart saw it then. A glitter in Erafel's eyes. A hunger in his gaze. A slight flicker of his tongue licking his lips.

Yes, so he does have a weakness, Hart thought. *He does still have a man's desires. He craves human flesh and not just for eating.*

"What are you saying?" Erafel scoffed. "Instead of being a king you'll be a pimp?"

"I'll be whatever you need me to be. I'll supply you with the riches of this world. Gems and gold and jewels. Women of every shape and color. What's a ruined, ravaged Earth worth to you, Erafel? Where's the joy in ruling over a pile of ashes and bones? Earth has such wealth! Such treasures and joys of the flesh! I was king once. I know where to find the sweetest of wines. The sweetest of female flesh. Spare this world, and I'll show you its wonders. I'll provide you with all the carnal joys of humanity. If only you spare Earth!"

Erafel seemed to be considering.

Good. Good! He could be reasoned with! He could be bribed!

"How do I know you're sincere?" Erafel said.

"I promise you!"

"You might simply be groveling and lying to save your fellow apes." Erafel's dark eyes blazed. "You might be planning to betray me."

"Never, my lord!"

"Then prove it," Erafel said. "Prove to me your devotion. And instead of destroying Earth, I will enslave it."

"What proof do you need?" Hart said. "Say the word and it's yours. Do you want gold? Diamonds? Rubies? I have them all! Do you want the Rolex from my wrist? It's yours! Do you want women? I have many fine women on my staff. Take them!"

A shrewd look came into Erafel's eyes. With a foot-long finger, he tapped his chin.

"Maybe we can make a deal," Erafel said.

"Yes. Yes! Anything! Anything your heart desires." He pulled the Rolex off. "You like this, huh? Take it." He pulled off his school ring. "Here! It's a real ruby." He hesitated, then pulled off his wedding ring. His eyes dampened, but he held it out. "It's gold. It's . . ." His voice cracked. "Just take it."

"No, Hart. I'm not interested in your baubles. Those are toys for apes, not demigods. But there is something I want you to give me. . ."

A chill ran through Hart. He looked up into his lord's eyes, and he saw hunger there. Cruelty beyond measure. Evil. There was pure evil in those eyes, and they were bottomless pits, for his evil had no end.

Then Erafel spoke, and wicked delight filled those eyes like fires burning flesh. "I want your wife."

Hart froze. That chill got colder. Like ice, it spread

through his chest, freezing his ribcage, clutching his heart and lungs.

"What?" he whispered.

"I want your wife," said Erafel. "I want Heather Hart. I want her to be my concubine. My lover. My slave. And I want you, Cory Hart, to give her to me."

"No," he whispered. He stumbled backward until his back hit the balcony railing. "No. Anything but that. Heather did nothing wrong."

"Oh, but you did, Cory Hart." Erafel slithered closer on his tentacles. "You did much wrong. You failed to control this world of apes. You failed to contain Einav Ben-Ari. You failed my trust. The only way to regain my trust is to make this sacrifice. The ultimate sacrifice. Give me your woman to be my mate. I'll place my seed inside her belly, and she'll bear my spawn. Only then will I know that you serve me fully. That you would do anything for me." A wicked smile twisted his lips. "God stopped Abraham before he could sacrifice his son. But the new god of Earth will not stop you."

Hart realized he was still on his knees. He rose to his feet, then turned away from Erafel. He gazed over the railing. He could see the hydrians race over Jerusalem. Soldiers were fighting them now. Guns boomed and fire raged. Smoke rolled over the city. It was like this around the world. From pole to pole, from desert to forest to northern ice. A sudden urge rose in Hart to climb over the railing, to leap into the fire, to vanish, to escape this nightmare. But would he fall right into hell, passing through fire into fire? He had done so much evil in his life. If God was not dead, would he judge him in the world beyond?

"It's the only way," Erafel said softly, placing his hand on Hart's shoulder again. "The only way to save the world."

"But my kids . . ." Hart hesitated, licked his lips. "Will my kids . . ."

Erafel shrugged. "Do with them as you like. Keep them. Get rid of them. I don't care. They're too young for me. Maybe in a few years, when your daughters are older . . ."

Rage flared in Hart, blazing madly, blinding him. He saw red. He leaped at the hybrid. "You bastard!"

In his fury, Hart tossed his fists. He kicked. He screamed and pummeled his foe. Erafel merely stood there, laughing. It was like punching a wall. Every blow against Erafel's crusty skin bloodied Hart's knuckles until finally he fell to his knees, fists bleeding.

"Yes, good, good," said Erafel. "Rage is such a splendid feeling, isn't it? Finally you're showing some backbone! This is the man I want to see. Go now! Fetch me your wife. Bring her to me. And together, Hart, you and I will rule this world."

Hart didn't care about ruling the world. This world was a nightmare. But if he refused, the hydrians would keep rampaging. And this world, nightmarish as it was, would end. Was it not better to live under the hydrian heel? Einav would tell him that it was better to die on your feet. That was all well and good for a soldier. But what of Hart's children? What of billions of children across Earth? Should they "die fighting" too? What was the life of one woman--even a woman Hart loved--to save billions of lives?

I can save them, Hart thought. *I can still stop this slaughter. I can save the world--or what remains of it. I just have to sacrifice the woman I love. And my soul.*

"Just . . . not the kids, all right?" Hart said.

Erafel nodded. "All right, Cory. All right."

Tears in his eyes, Hart led Erafel through the palace. To the elevator. Down and down past the palace floors, then underground, plunging lower and lower into purgatory. At the bottom, they walked down a hall carved into the living rock, buried deep below Jerusalem. There were no guards. Earth was demilitarized. A part of their earlier deal. A deal meant to keep the squids away. A deal Einav had broken.

Finally they reached the blast door to the Hart family bunker. Hart wondered if Erafel, with his enormous hands and great strength, could have ripped the door right off the hinges.

But he wants me *to open it,* Hart thought. *He wants me to prove my loyalty.*

And that day deep below Jerusalem, Hart proved his loyalty. He turned the combination lock on the blast door. The lock clicked.

But he was not proving his loyalty to Erafel like the chimera thought. He was proving it to Earth. To billions still alive. Billions he was saving.

Hart pulled the metal door open.

Heather was inside the bunker. She was sitting on the concrete floor, playing a board game with the children, most likely an attempt to soothe their fear. She looked up at him. Then she looked at Erafel. And terror filled her eyes.

"Heather?" Hart said. "Heather, come here please."

She rose to her feet. "Cory . . . what is that?" She was looking at Erafel. Her eyes reflected the half-man, half-squid.

"Heather, come here," Hart whispered.

She took a step back, sheltering her children behind her. "Cory, what is that thing?"

"Please. I'm sorry, Heather. You must come here."

The children cried. They clung to their mother.

"Kids, you have to let go," Hart said, his tears flowing.

"Cory!" Heather cried. "Oh God, Cory!"

Swaying on his bundle of tentacles, Erafel entered the room. The children screamed. Heather tried to flee behind the desk, but Hart grabbed her arm. He pulled his wife. Dragged her toward the monster. She fought him.

"Cory!" she cried. "Cory, what are you doing?"

"I'm sorry," he whispered, tears falling, weeping but still

pulling her. "I'm sorry, Heather, I'm sorry, I'm so sorry. I love you so much . . ."

As he sobbed, he pulled her toward the beast. And the creature reached out. Those long, long fingers wrapped around her. The hybrid grinned and licked his chops.

"Mommy!" the children cried.

Hart had to grab them. All three of his beautiful children. To pull them back. To hold them in his arms, hugging them, trapping them. They screamed and tried to break free, tried to reach their mother.

"Stay with me, kids," he said. "Stay with me. Mommy will be fine. She'll be fine."

"No, no, Mommy!" they cried, wriggling in his grip, reaching out to her, but he tightened his arms around them, almost crushing them, weeping onto their tousled heads.

"She'll be all right. Mommy is all right. Mommy is all right . . ."

"Cory!" Heather screamed, kicking and reaching out to her children. But Hart held them tightly as Erafel dragged her away. The chimera pulled her into the hallway. Heather's eyes were bugging out in horror. Her mouth hung open, just screaming, just making that horrible, wordless, endless scream as Erafel dragged her farther and farther . . . until they disappeared in darkness.

Hart remained in the bomb shelter, kneeling on the floor, holding his children in his arms.

Long after Heather had disappeared, long after the stench of Erafel faded, long after Hart lay in bed that night, he could still hear her scream. And he knew he would hear it forever.

CHAPTER FIFTEEN
Giants in the Mist

Marco and Addy trudged through the boreal forest, mud sluicing around their boots.

"Ah, Poet, I tell ya, this is the life!" Addy inhaled deeply and grinned. "The great outdoors! The smell of pines. The soothing rain. The birdsong."

Marco grimaced and shooed aside midges. "The bugs. Don't forget all the bugs."

"Oh, shut up." Addy shoved him.

He wobbled in the mud, his arms windmilled, and he fell onto the ground. Mud splashed.

Addy looked down at him, then burst out laughing. "I didn't push you that hard. I--whoa!"

Marco grabbed her and pulled her down into the mud with him. She landed with a splash.

"You were saying?"

She gasped. "You dirty little bastard!" She lifted a handful of mud and threw it at him.

He threw back a handful. "Serves you right."

Soon they were mudslinging back and forth, covering themselves with the stuff. If any animals were watching, they must have wondered at these two strange humans who had fallen from the sky.

Finally, when both husband and wife were exhausted and sopping with mud, they leaned against each other. Marco slung an arm around his wife. Sitting in the dirt, he looked around him.

Pine trees soared. A hawk glided overhead below the mist. Mushrooms sprouted all around, birds sang, and a handful of deer bounded down a nearby slope.

"You're right, Ads," he said. "It's beautiful here. I missed the outdoors. We used to hike in the woods all the time. Remember when--"

A grumble sounded in the distance. The forest shook. The birdsong ended. For a long time the rumble continued like thunder. It was an organic sound like thunder yet oddly metallic and mechanical. A sound like creaking machines and the grumbles of beasts in deep metal caverns. A sound that sent chills down the spine and seemed to shake the stone foundations of the world. Finally the terrible rumbling ended, but the birds remained quiet.

"A hydrian," Addy whispered, reaching for her gun.

"He's miles away, by the sound of it." Marco pushed himself up, then helped Addy stand too. "We better get going. The others might be in danger."

They kept trudging through the forest, covered in mud. The pines soared and mist flowed between their boughs. It was November but not yet frozen, and carpets of needles crunched underfoot where the mud gave way. Normally Marco might have enjoyed the trek. Hiking had been a passion of his before the wars. But that rumble still echoed in his ears. When the trees parted on a hilltop, Marco gazed into the distance. On the horizon, he saw the vague shape of hydrian. From here, it was only a smudge in the fog, its tendrils like tornado funnels. It was moving across the land, heading westward until it disappeared in the distant haze beyond the mountain.

"This land is crawling with them." Addy spat. "The fuckers are here in Canada. Bastards!"

Marco looked around him. "Are we in Canada?"

When the *Blood, Sweat, and Tears* had crashed, they had fallen through a storm of hydrians, smoke, and fire. Their tracking instruments were all dead aside from a few simple compasses. They could be anywhere.

"Yeah, this is Canada all right," Addy said. "The boreal forest. I'd recognize it anywhere."

"We could be in Alaska. Or Russia. They look similar."

"No, Poet. We're home. I can feel it in my bones. We're home."

"Lucky crash, huh?" Marco said.

Addy slipped her hand into his. "I never imagined our homecoming like this, Poet."

"I suppose there aren't many big, open spaces left on Earth anymore," Marco said. "Canada is one of them. The rest of the world must look worse. Swarming with hydrians. I remember seeing the videos from above. They were covering cities. They probably only sent a few scouts out here to the wilderness."

"A good thing for us," Addy said. "We can regroup here. Build an army. Hide among the trees. Then pounce in attack!"

Marco raised an eyebrow. "An army, Addy? I thought we were looking for survivors. Other shipwrecks. Not an army."

She stared at him, her blue eyes hard. "I'm not done fighting."

Marco caressed her cheek. "Addy, maybe we need to find a little cave. To hide. To ride out the storm. Maybe, instead of fighting, we just need to survive."

"No, Poet. No." She placed a hand behind his neck and stared into his eyes. "We are soldiers. Don't forget. We fight. Are you with me?"

He looked into those blue eyes he loved. Eyes so proud yet so haunted, so brave yet so pained.

"Yes," he finally said. "I'm with you. Not only as your husband. But as your fellow soldier. We fight together, side by side. Like we always did."

A smile broke through her stern facade, and her eyes

softened. "My brave little Poet. Yes, we've always been fighting side by side. Since we were kids."

"I love you, Addy."

She kissed his lips. "I love you more. Even if you taste like mud."

They kept walking. Einav was back at the *Blood, Sweat, and Tears'* shipwreck, searching the dreadnought for survivors--and for weapons. For now, the shipwreck formed their makeshift camp. At least until they could find better, more hidden shelter. Einav had sent the married couple out to scout the forest for other shipwrecks. Not only the *Blood, Sweat, and Tears* had crashed here but a handful of her escort ships as well. More than anything, Marco hoped to find his beloved Joey.

"Let's climb that hill." He pointed. "Maybe we'll see something from the top."

Addy groaned. "Climbing? Hill?"

He raised an eyebrow. "I thought you liked hiking."

"Yeah, hiking downhill. Nobody said anything about going uphill."

"Just pretend there's a hot dog tree on the hilltop." He began trudging uphill, then groaned as Addy leaped onto his back.

"Carry me!" She wrapped her arms around his neck.

He groaned. "God, how old are you?"

"I'm four. Carry me!"

He took a few heavy steps, carrying his wife, and grimaced. "God, you weigh a ton."

"Shut up. I'm petite. You know I only weigh 115 pounds."

"On the moon, maybe." He shook her off. "Walk from here."

"Fine." She rolled her eyes. "If you push me."

He positioned himself behind her, placed his hands on her backside, and began shoving her uphill.

"Ooh, Marco." She looked over her shoulder and waggled

her eyebrows. "You sly dog."

He removed his hands. "I'll just climb by myself. You can rest here."

He kept hiking uphill. Addy walked at his side. "Fine, you win. I'll walk."

He raised an eyebrow. "Are you imagining a hot dog tree on the hilltop?"

"I'm imagining shoving you downhill from the hilltop. Now that's a motivator!"

They climbed on. Soon Addy was huffing and puffing and wheezing. Marco glared at her.

"How can you fight aliens for hours without breaking a sweat, yet you can't even climb a little hill?"

"Because fighting is fun."

Finally they reached the hilltop, where they found a crown of pines and mossy boulders. The landscape swept around them, hills and valleys rolling toward a distant haze and snowcapped mountains. A stream ambled between the trees like a ribbon, sparkling gold where the sunlight hit it.

"We got a good view from up here, all right," Marco said.

Addy spat. "And if anything is lurking in those woods, it has a good view of us."

"We're covered with mud, pine needles, and sap. I'd say it's pretty decent camouflage."

Addy dumped a fistful of mud on his head.

"Hey!" Marco bristled.

She shrugged. "You said it's decent camouflage."

From the piny hilltop, they scanned the wild. A few scattered fires burned here and there, raising plumes of smoke. Most must be smoldering chunks of the *Blood, Sweat, and Tears*, ripped off during atmospheric entry. Others might be smaller starships that had crashed into the forest. Marco must explore each one of those smoky pillars.

He hoped Joey was somewhere here in the wilderness. Last he had seen Joey, the little black starship had been hurtling toward Earth, wreathed in fire and hydrian tentacles. She had vanished into the storm. Most likely, she had perished along with hundreds of other starships. Again and again, Marco had tried calling her on his minicom. She never answered. But he maintained hope that she had managed to enter the atmosphere, to survive the fall from the sky, and land somewhere around here. Maybe she was hurt. Maybe she needed him. He scanned the forest, hoping to see a chunk of darkness, but if she had fallen here, she was buried among the trees.

Then Marco noticed something. Another distant hydrian was moving along the horizon. A big one--a hydlord by the looks of it, probably as large as this hill. But it was hard to tell from this distance, and the beast seemed smudged like a gray cloud fallen onto the land. Suddenly two tiny pinpricks of red light ignited in that distant smudge, staring across the distance. Right toward the hill. Toward Marco and Addy. Both froze. Could the creature see them? For long moments it stared, but then those red eyes faced away, and the smudged behemoth trudged onward through the rain, finally disappearing beyond the horizon into a sea of mist.

"There!" Marco pointed. "See that, Ads?"

She squinted, then gasped. "A blueberry patch!" She smacked her lips and rubbed her belly.

"Not that blueberry patch!" Marco snapped. "Look past it. See that line of broken trees?" He sniffed. "I smell a whiff of smoke. A small ship crashed there." He coughed and waved his hand in front of his face. "There's a lot of smoke, actually."

Addy lowered her cigarette. "Huh?"

Marco glared. "Where did you get that?"

"A magical bluebird, wearing a tiny tuxedo, flew down from the treetops and handed me a cigarette." Addy slapped the back of his head. "My pocket, dumbass. Where else?"

"Well, put it out. I don't want any hydrians to smell it."

"Oh wait, I got something else in my pocket." She reached inside, then pulled out her hand, middle finger extended. "Put this out."

Shaking his head in disgust, Marco trudged downhill. Addy followed, smoking her cigarette. The brush was thick, the mud slippery, and many boulders and thickets blocked their path. They walked for an hour, talking about this or that. At times, it felt almost like the old days, hiking in the backwoods of Ontario. Despite it all, this was still a beautiful planet, and walking here reminded Marco of what he fought for. Was there any hope to save this world? Could they indeed fight from the ground, liberate this beautiful planet?

"Addy, come on, hurry up."

She looked up from the blueberry patch, lips covered with blue juice. "Coming!"

Finally they reached the path of broken trees in the valley. The ground was scorched and littered with scraps of metal. Marco recognized bits of an exhaust system, a scrap of hull, and undetonated artillery shells.

"Cool!" Addy said, stepping toward one of the warheads, a lit cigarette in hand. A few sparks flew in the wind.

"Get away from that before you blow us up!" Marco said, pulling her back.

They kept walking, following the trail of shattered trees for about a kilometer. Finally they reached the shipwreck. The ruin smoldered on the forest floor. Was it a shipwreck? For a moment, Marco thought it might be a giant cannon, perhaps ripped free from *Blood, Sweat, and Tears*' hull, which had tumbled down here. But then he saw the cannon sprouted mangled exhaust ports, a stubby wing (presumably the second wing had snapped off), and a shattered cockpit.

"The *Spacehog*!" Marco said, racing toward the wreck.

Addy ran close behind him. They reached the ship. It was a crumpled wreck. The cannon seemed in surprisingly decent shape, but the parts built around the cannon--the actual ship--had fallen apart.

"Wyatt!" Marco said.

He climbed the wreck toward the cockpit. He looked inside and winced. Nothing but smoke, shattered glass, and charred clothes.

Addy climbed up beside him. She shook her head sadly. "Poor Wyatt. Burned to a crisp. Completely incinerated. I'm sorry, Marco."

Marco frowned. He lifted the burnt clothes, expecting bones to spill out. But there was nothing inside the clothes aside from dice, a deck of cards, and a pack of cigarettes.

"Poor, poor Wyatt," Addy said. "Even his bones burned to dust. He'd want somebody to put those cigarettes to good use."

She reached for the box. Marco slapped her hand away.

"Ow!" She glowered. "What the hell, Poet?"

"Stop robbing the dead."

Addy groaned. "He's not dead, dumbass. I was messing with you. Bones won't burn to dust while the clothes are just charred a bit."

Marco felt himself flush. "I knew that." From up here in the mangled cockpit, he looked around the forest. He coned his hand around his mouth. "Wyatt! Wyatt, you here?"

Addy smacked him again. "Quiet! Hydrians, remember?"

A distant voice rose. "Marco, buddy! That you?"

Marco squinted. He saw him then. The shaggy, bearded man was bathing in a nearby river. Marco and Addy hopped off the *Spacehog*, trudged between the pines, and reached the riverbank.

"Yo, buddies!" Wyatt said, rising from the water.

Marco gasped and covered Addy's eyes.

Wyatt looked down, looked back up, and covered his privates. "Oh, sorry about that, buddies. Forgot my clothes in the cockpit." He shook himself wildly. His beard and long hair whipped back and forth, spraying water.

Addy grimaced and wiped water off her face. "Why didn't you just bathe with your clothes on?"

"Hey, lady, do you shower with your clothes on?" Wyatt grinned and raised a handgun. "Don't worry, I keep what counts with me. I--"

Suddenly the bearded outlaw inhaled, aimed his gun, and fired over Addy and Marco's heads. A boom shook the land, raising birds into flight.

Marco and Addy spun around, drawing their own sidearms, expecting to see a hydrian. Instead they saw a deer stumble downhill and fall dead, a bullet in its neck.

"Fresh meat tonight!" Wyatt said. "It's camping night on planet Earth!"

Slowly Marco's heartbeat slowed. He stepped closer to the shaggy, sopping outlaw. "Wyatt, Einav is alive. We're organizing everyone in the wreck of the *Blood, Sweat, and Tears*. She's beyond those hills, maybe two klicks west of the river. Have you seen any more survivors?"

Wyatt sucked his teeth. "Not as such. I did see another ship go down yonder. A corvette by the looks of her. Probably ten miles away. Bit of a walk, and it's getting dark. What say we skin this deer, have some dinner, keep going in the morning?"

"How about you put on some clothes?" Addy said

Wyatt covered his private parts again. "Sorry, lady. I'll just rush off to grab my garments. Keep your eyes averted!"

He ran by them, heading uphill toward the *Spacehog*. As the grizzled outlaw was getting dressed, Marco raised his minicom and called Einav.

A hologram of their leader materialized in the forest

beside them. While Marco and Addy were covered with mud, and Wyatt was a hairy bear of a man, Einav exuded elegance. Somehow, even after crashing down from the sky into a post-apocalyptic world, the woman managed to look graceful and composed. She stood straight, a calm confidence in her green eyes. Her golden hair hung across her shoulder in a loose braid, gleaming in the sunlight. Marco understood why they called her the Golden Lioness. She indeed appeared to him as a lioness taken human form--a queen who was noble, strong, and fair, yet if you wronged her, she was perfectly capable of ripping your throat out. It was no wonder why, for generations, people had followed Einav Ben-Ari to war. Why Marco had dedicated his life to following her.

"Hey, Nav Nav!" Addy said, waving.

"Hello." A thin smile touched Einav's lips. "So, did you two find anything but mud?"

"We found Wyatt," Marco said. "I, um . . . can't show him to you. Not until he pulls his pants on."

Einav tilted her head.

"Long story," Marco said.

"It damn right is!" came Wyatt's voice from behind the trees.

Marco cleared his throat. "Anyway, Wyatt saw a corvette go down about ten miles northeast from here. We'd like to go investigate. We might not make it back to headquarters tonight."

Einav considered. "It's a long walk in the woods. I wish we had a shuttle."

"A shuttle would only draw hydrians," Marco said. "We saw a hydlord on the horizon. The enemy is out there in the forests. Not many of them, thankfully. I imagine they're focusing on the cities."

Einav nodded. "We got a radio working. Picked up some signals."

Marco raised an eyebrow. "You got a radio signal? What is this, the twentieth century?"

Einav smiled. "Some enthusiasts still use radio."

"The way some nerds like you still read paper books, Poet," Addy said.

"Said the woman wearing a World War II helmet and carrying a sword," Marco said. "Talk about a walking anachronism."

"Anyway!" Einav said before the married couple could come to blows. "The signal is spotty. Barely more than crackling. But sometimes we pick up snippets of news. The enemy is definitely focusing on our cities, not the wilderness. That's probably why we're still alive. The HDF is fighting. But from what I can tell, it's not looking great. We need to find all the survivors we can. Organize. Then get into the fight."

Marco nodded. "All right. We'll go looking for more survivors. But we won't be back until tomorrow. Can you wait that long?"

Einav bit her lip. "I don't like you two spending the night out in the woods. In November."

"Addy and I used to go camping all the time up here in Canada," Marco said. "Even in the fall. We haven't lived in Canada in many years, but it's in our blood. We'll be fine."

Addy wrapped Marco in her arms and squeezed. "I'll keep him warm for you."

Wyatt suddenly appeared, fully dressed, and wrapped his arms around the couple. "So will I."

Einav smiled. "Hi, Wyatt. Watch over those two for me, will ya?"

The big man saluted. "Sure will, ma'am. I keep my buddies safe. If anyone else is still alive out there, and I reckon they are, we'll find 'em."

* * * * *

The sun would be setting in an hour, so they made camp. Marco and Wyatt dressed the deer, while Addy built a campfire. She constructed a makeshift rake from branches and vines, then began to roast hot dogs.

"Where did you get those hot dogs?" Marco asked.

"Same place as my cigarettes. My pocket."

Marco blinked. "You walk around with hot dogs in your pockets?"

She shrugged. "Never know when they might come in handy."

As Wyatt slung some deer meat over the fire, he looked at Addy. "You don't want some venison?"

"Oh, I'll eat the deer," Addy said. "This is only an appetizer."

Wyatt's eyes widened. "You're eating three hot dogs!"

"Don't underestimate her," Marco said. "She'll eat the hot dogs, she'll eat half the deer, and then she'll ask for dessert."

"What hot dogs?" Addy said.

The guys looked at her. The hot dogs were gone, and Addy was licking her fingers.

Wyatt blinked. "Well, I'll be."

The sun set as the deer was roasting. Marco expressed some concerns about lighting a campfire with hydrians roaming the land. Wouldn't the squids see them? But Addy reminded him that many scattered fires were burning in the forest following the *Blood, Sweat, and Tears*' crash. Theirs would not stand out.

Addy guzzled down a chunk of venison, then reached for more. "This is good stuff."

Wyatt glanced at Marco. "You weren't kidding, buddy."

Addy wiped gravy off her lips. "I just wish we had some beer."

Wyatt's eyes widened, and he gasped. "You know, I think I might!" He raced toward the shattered cockpit of the *Spacehog*, then returned with a six-pack.

"My man!" Addy said, giving the outlaw a high five.

Soon they were sitting around the fire, drinking beer. Clouds hid the stars and moons, and only the firelight lit the night. The crickets fell silent as a distant rumble shook the land. The very pillars of the earth seemed to creak and moan. It reminded Marco of being at a concert and feeling the bass ripple through your chest and under your feet.

"Another hydlord," Marco said. "Creepy sounds, those bastards make. Up in space, I could only hear their rumbles when they vibrated through their tentacles into our ships. But here on Earth, they send their rumbles everywhere. Through the air, the trees, the rocks, the soil, and my bones."

"I look forward to hearing their death squeals," Addy said, patting her rifle.

Marco gazed into the darkness. "The HDF is fighting out there. We saw some of that from space. I feel guilty sitting here, drinking beer, safe, while others are on the front line."

"Not me." Wyatt sipped his beer. "I've always been one to fight from the shadows. Even in the HDF, I never liked that doctrine of charging headlong into battle. Noble? Who cares. Always seemed like a bad way to fight and an excellent way of getting yourself killed."

Marco's eyes widened. "You were in the HDF?"

Wyatt shrugged. "Why not?"

"*You?*" Marco said.

Wyatt laughed and scratched his shaggy, grizzled hair. "Yep, imagine it! Me with a crew cut. Ha! Nah, wasn't my thing. Only lasted about a year before they kicked me out."

"But the HDF doesn't even conscript anymore," Marco said. "You volunteered?"

Wyatt shrugged. "Eh, I did and I didn't. See, I was a country boy. Born out in the wilderness of Saskatchewan. Grew up hunting and fishing and living off the land. Ran away from home when I was fifteen. Lived in the woods for a while, traveled the country, did odd jobs. But I always carried something with me." He took a bundle of leather out of his pocket. "This."

The grizzled outlaw unfolded the leather, revealing ancient medals. They gleamed in the firelight.

"I recognize those," Marco said. "That's a Star of Valor from the Scum War. That's a Bronze Sun from the Marauder Uprising. Addy and I fought in those wars. But we're Methuselahs with long lives. You weren't even born, Wyatt."

"They belonged to my grandpa," he said. "I carried them with me whenever I went hunting. Whenever I traveled the land. He was a hero, my gramps. So when I turned seventeen, I tried to be like him. I joined the army, his beloved HDF. And . . . I fucked up." He took another swig of beer. "I overslept, I got in trouble, I punched my commanding officer, I stole, I lied, I raised hell. My gramps was a major. I was a major screw up. They tossed me out onto my ass. I found myself on Ganymede, a million miles from Earth, penniless, nothing but the clothes on my back."

Marco put a hand on the man's shoulder. "I'm sorry, Wyatt."

"Ah, don't worry about it, buddy. Best thing that ever happened to me. I was too broke to fly back to Earth. So I hitchhiked across the galaxy for a while. Did more odd jobs. Scrubbed space barnacles off decks. Then did some security jobs for smugglers and bounty hunters. Finally I joined a gang." He rolled up his sleeve. "See this tattoo?"

Marco gasped at the snarling mushroom with big teeth and angry eyes. "The Basidio Boys!"

Wyatt covered up the tattoo again. "Yep, and a bunch of bastards they are too. Never did well with those mushrooms either. Nah, I ain't much of a team player. So I ran again. Became independent. I won the *Spacehog* at a poker game and set off on my own. Did some time fighting as a mercenary for an Altairian warlord or two. Then for a while, I did some bounty hunting. A bit of enforcing for a loan shark. But I always preferred being a gun for hire. Ha! This is the first job I've done for free."

"Welcome to the club, bub," Addy said. "I've been doing this shit for free for a hundred years. But so long as I can afford beer and deer, I'm happy."

"You can't afford them," Marco said. "Wyatt gave you both."

Addy gasped. "You're right! I'm gonna have a talk with Einav and demand she pay us. But not now." She yawned and stretched. "I'm hitting the sack."

It was a long, cold night. Marco took first watch, pacing around the fire. He held a starflare, a modern plasma assault rifle. A bandoleer of plasma packs hung across his chest. The familiar weight of the weapon and ammo comforted him. He remembered himself as an eighteen-year-old private, holding an antique T57 assault rifle, the kind that fired actual bullets. Weapons had come a long way since then. So had he.

I'm no longer that scared boy, he thought. *I've fought a thousand battles since then. Whatever comes out of this darkness, I'll be ready.*

Yes, he was older now. Braver, perhaps. Mentally stronger, probably. Certainly more experienced. Yet a part of him missed the boy he had been. A boy who had dreamed of becoming a writer. Who wanted nothing more than to hide in his library among his books. Would that boy recognize this man here in the forest, an old veteran with a beard and battle scars, holding a weapon that could unleash a hundred times the devastation of those old bullets? And would that boy be proud of the man? Or would he weep?

I never wanted to become a soldier, Marco thought. *I only wanted to hide among those books.*

But the monsters kept attacking. And he refused to die. War after war forged him into this soldier. They made him stronger, but Marco felt that they had killed a part of him. A part he missed. A part he could perhaps never get back. It was his innocence the monsters had slain.

And the monsters were still out there. Every once in a while, those grumbles shook the land. They still sounded distant. But not as distant as before. Marco kept scanning the darkness for red hydrian eyes, but he could see nothing beyond the firelight. A few steps in each direction the forest plunged into pitch blackness. The fire was burning low. Barely more than embers glowed now. Marco felt isolated in a shrinking bubble of light and warmth, and all around him swarmed the monsters. This tableau, he thought, could represent Earth herself--a small orb of light, surrounded by terror, fading in the dark.

Was there any hope?

Marco remembered the words of the Oracles of Hypnos long ago. That had been a century ago now. He had visited their cave, hoping to learn the outcome of this war. They had foreseen the hydrians destroying Earth. But they had seen hope too. A child. A child descended from him and Kemi.

But Kemi was dead. In Darktech Cover, Marco had bought his little "reanimation" kit. He had probably wasted his money. It was only a scam--just like Addy's mystical helmet and Einav's belt of magical coins. Perhaps hope was like this fire, dying in the darkness. Yet as Marco huddled by the dying light, seeking the last wisps of warmth, he clung to his last wisps of hope too. They were all he had left.

Another growl sounded.

This one was much closer.

Marco stopped pacing, shouldered his rifle, and stared into the darkness.

For a moment--silence. An eerie silence. No crickets chirped, no wind rustled the pines. He could see nothing, hear nothing. But a smell hit his nostrils. A smell like raw fish and worms tinged with the acrid, burning stench of space.

Marco knew that smell. A hydrian.

"Addy!" he cried. "Wy--"

A roar drowned his words, and from the darkness, the beast pounced.

* * * * *

It was a hyd--only the second instar in the hydrian lifecycle, far smaller than a hydlord or hydprince. But even a hyd was a formidable beast. The creature towered, as large as *Tyrannosaurus rex* and just as mean. The firelight danced on its monstrous face. The red eyes bugged out, the pupils mere pinpricks. The jaws opened wide, lined with swords the size of elephant tusks. That mouth could swallow a man whole. The tentacles flared out, the suction cups spinning with blades. Chitin covered the alien like a medieval suit of armor. It was a creature that had evolved for one purpose and one purpose only--to kill.

Marco took in this hellish vision within a single second. By the next second, he was firing his starflare.

White-hot plasma bolts, flaring to blue around the edges, pounded the alien. The hyd screeched and reared. Chunks of its exoskeleton flew off. One shard shot toward Marco and scratched his cheek, drawing blood. He ignored the searing pain and kept firing, bombarding the alien.

The beast would not take this lying down. Even as the plasma bolts pummeled it, the hyd swung a tentacle at Marco. The appendage was anaconda-sized. It wrapped around Marco and lifted him off the ground. The claws in the suction cup sliced him. Marco shouted in pain. He kept firing, washing the beast's face with plasma. But thick nictitating membranes protected the eyes. The mouth widened, prepared to swallow him whole.

"Hey!" Addy cried. "Over here!"

Marco glimpsed her standing on a boulder, holding a bazooka over her shoulder. The hyd hissed, eyes narrowing.

"Addy, wait, don't--" Marco began.

She fired.

A grenade slammed into the creature's mantle and exploded.

Pain.

Pounding, all-consuming pain drove into Marco. The shock wave ripped him free from the tentacle. He hit the ground, moaning. His ears rang. He could barely see. Somehow, lying on his back, blind and deaf though he was, he managed to raise his rifle and keep firing.

"Don't worry!" came Addy's voice, barely audible through the ringing. "Marco, I used the mini grenade. Marco? You okay?"

"I am not okay!" he shouted, scampering backward. Slowly his vision and hearing were returning. "You almost killed me, dammit!"

"I saved your life. Now shut up and keep firing!"

Marco pulled the trigger, but his plasma pack was empty. Cursing, he removed the empty pack and slammed in another. As his vision slowly returned, he saw the damage Addy had wrought. A huge chunk was missing from the hydrian's mantle, revealing burnt meat and pulsing veins. But the head was still unharmed, and the alien was still alive.

"Where the hell is Wyatt?" Marco shouted.

"No idea!" Addy said.

She tried to load another grenade. But that took a few seconds--an eternity in battle. A tentacle swung toward her, wrapped around her, and lifted her. Marco fired his gun, hitting the base of the tentacle again and again, trying to sever the digit.

He managed to chip off some exoskeleton, but he barely even singed the flesh within. Marco was loading a third plasma pack when a tentacle lassoed him. He screamed and kicked, but the tentacle lifted him.

The hyd now held Addy in one tentacle, Marco in the other. The creature was chuckling, holding his two delicacies aloft. Their arms were pinned to their sides. They could not fight. The hyd opened its mouth wide, ready to feast.

And then Marco saw Wyatt.

The hirsute mercenary had returned to the *Spacehog*. The ship had crashed, shattering her cockpit, wings, and exhaust. But one part remained intact--the huge cannon that formed her main fuselage. Wyatt now stood in the remains of the cockpit, a mad look in his eyes. He rubbed his hands together, chuckled, then grabbed a lever.

"Wyatt?" Marco said, still trapped in the tentacle. "Wyatt, buddy, what are you doing?"

Addy's eyes widened. "Wyatt, no!"

"Cover your ears, buddies!" Wyatt said, laughing maniacally. "This is gonna get loud!"

He shoved down the lever.

Marco's arms were still trapped. He couldn't cover his ears. He went slack, sinking into the tentacle's embrace as best he could.

The *Spacehog* roared.

The enormous bore spun at insane speed, hurling a barrage of bullets the size of beer bottles. They had no warheads. They flew with pure kinetic energy. The fusillade slammed into the hydrian's head. And that head burst open like an overripe watermelon in a hippo's mouth.

Marco thumped onto the ground, ears ringing. The tentacle holding him had snapped right off the alien. Marco wriggled his way out, then ran toward Addy. He found her on the ground, still trapped in a tentacle. He pulled the severed appendage off her.

"Addy, are you all right?" he shouted. He could barely hear himself. It felt like his ears were stuffed with cotton.

She was yelling something back at him. He could barely hear. Dammit. Marco had suffered hearing damage in battles before. These days, you could repair eardrums as easily as fixing a cavity in your tooth. But until he could see a doctor, he imagined that his ears would keep ringing.

He pulled Addy to her feet, and she hugged him.

"Ooh yeah, did you see that?" Wyatt said, strutting toward them. "Blew his whole damn head off!"

"You almost killed us, you son of a bitch!" Addy said.

"Both of you almost killed me!" Marco said.

They turned toward the hydrian. Not much was left. Just a mangled mantle and a few severed tentacles. The campfire crackled with fresh light. A fatty chunk of hydrian had fallen onto the embers and burned brightly, painting the grisly scene with red light.

"We can't stay here," Marco said. "The noise will have alerted other hydrians. We got to keep going in the night. Find a new place to set camp."

Addy yawned. "But I'm tired and we have a campfire."

"Addy, we're not sleeping next to a disgusting, stinking, mangled corpse."

"I'm used to it," she said. "I sleep next to you every night." She mussed his hair and kissed his cheek. "Ah, I'm just kidding. You're not mangled."

Nevertheless, they walked onward in the night. The forest was pitch black, and they dared not use flashlights. Wyatt found a pair of night-vision goggles in the *Spacehog*. They were a true godsend. The outlaw led the way, seeing in the dark. Marco and Addy walked close behind, holding onto a rope that dangled from

Wyatt's belt. Even with the rope to guide him, Marco kept bumping into trees and stumbling over rocks. Several times he fell flat into the mud.

Finally they emerged from the forest onto a riverbank. The clouds parted, but they could not see the stars. Hydrians orbited Earth like an exoskeleton around the planet. Only their red eyes lit the world. Was there any beauty left, any hope for dawn in this endless night?

They made camp along the tree line, hidden among the boles. Wyatt took guard duty, but no matter how hard he tried, Marco could not sleep. He lay beside Addy, and whenever he closed his eyes, he just saw the hydrians and heard the ringing in his ears.

CHAPTER SIXTEEN
Out in the Cold

The next morning, Marco, Addy, and Wyatt walked through the forest in search of more survivors. Within an hour, they found another shipwreck. And not a human one.

From a distance, it looked like an asteroid had fallen onto the planet. A huge round stone--roughly the size of a suburban house--sat in a smoldering crater. Trees lay shattered and burnt around it. The boulder was cracked open, revealing lavender crystals inside. When the companions walked around the crater, they saw a big missing chunk from the "asteroid." Crystals the size of men filled the cavilty.

"The world's largest geode?" Wyatt said.

"A starship," said Marco. He had seen this ship before.

When they walked nearer, they saw the alien inside. She was a purple mollusk, similar in appearance to an Earth octopus, though longer-lived and more intelligent. Marco recognized her at once.

"A hydling!" Wyatt said, aiming his handgun.

Marco pushed the man's arm down. "Cool it, buddy. She's a Menorian. Not a hydrian. And a friend of ours." He raised his voice. "Aurora!"

The mollusk looked up. In her eight arms, she held multiple tools. She had been trying to repair her crystalline ship, it seemed. When she saw the humans, her skin changed colors rapidly, turning yellow, then pink, then deep blue. Stripes in different colors appeared and faded across her.

"Menorian language," Marco said. "They communicate with colors. Hang on. I think my minicom can translate."

He fished the little computer from his pocket. It recognized Aurora and translated her colors. A voice emerged in English.

"Marco! Addy! And a friend I don't know. I'm so glad to see you! For too long I was lost in this dry sea."

They entered the crater and approached the cracked geode-ship. Aurora hopped out, leaped toward them, and hugged them one by one. For a moment, Marco couldn't help but cringe. The octopus hugging him reminded him of a hydrian's crushing embrace. But he reminded himself that Aurora was an old, dear friend, someone who had fought at his side throughout many battles.

"Where's Einav?" the Menorian asked. "Is she . . ."

Her skin became a melancholy blue. Marco didn't need his minicom to know this symbolized sadness.

"She's all right!" he said. "She's back at camp. We're here searching for survivors. Have you seen anyone else?"

The Menorian nodded. "Yes. A ship. A small corvette. It crashed about a league north across the river. I don't know if anyone survived. I saw plumes of smoke as from campfires." She turned pale gray. "I should have gone to check, but I fear walking alone on dry land. I am a being of water, and the great dryness frightens me."

Addy examined the broken starship, sucking her teeth. "Any luck fixing your ship? I wish I could help. But I have no idea how this thing works."

"Alas, the engine crystals had shattered," said Aurora. "I tried to cut new gemstone facades with the right angles, but they must be calibrated to the atom. Without proper tools, this skill is beyond me. I fear she'll never fly again."

"We'll keep you safe on this strange world of dry land,"

Marco said. "Will you come with us?"

The octopus nodded inasmuch as an octopus could nod. It was a gesture Menoria had learned during her many years among humans. "With you I will dare. Before we go, take some of the crystal blades from my ship. They're powerful weapons."

Addy's eyes widened. "Crystal blades?"

Aurora disappeared among the towering crystals of her starship, then returned a moment later, carrying three daggers with gilded handles and crystal blades. The crystals were pale lavender.

"Azoth?" Marco said. "These must have cost a fortune."

"Not pure azoth," said Menoria. "Not the kind that propels starships across the stars. This is a special kind of azoth that grows in underwater caves on one of Menoria's moons. It cannot bend spacetime, but it can concentrate sunlight into a searing beam as powerful as any bullet."

With one tentacle, she pointed a dagger at a nearby boulder. The blade seemed to suck up the light around it, plunging Aurora into shadows. The light concentrated within the crystal blade, which shone blindingly. Then the light beamed out, hit the boulder, and shattered the stone.

"Oh baby!" Addy said. "I want!"

Aurora handed her one of the lightblades. Marco and Wyatt each took one too.

"They don't work at night," Aurora said. "That is their great flaw. But during the day, they are mighty."

The group walked through the forest. The Menorian, despite her fear of dry land, was remarkably adept at walking over roots, logs, and boulders, moving more easily than the humans with their clumsy two legs. For several hours, they hiked. The humans had packed leftover venison, which they ate for lunch, along with blueberries they had saved from the patch. Aurora carried seashells in a pack, which she devoured, crunching the shells in her mouth.

"Food's gonna become a real priority sooner or later," Wyatt said. "We'll have to spend time hunting."

"And diving for seafood," Menoria said. "I do not eat land animals."

"Not to worry," Marco said. "There are plenty of rations back at the *Blood, Sweat, and Tears.* A whole warehouse full of them. I believe I've seen frozen crab and cans of tuna in there too, Aurora."

Wyatt raised an eyebrow. "The food survived the crash?"

"Wyatt, those are vacuum-sealed, preservative-drenched military rations. They can survive a nuclear holocaust."

"And they're delicious!" Addy added.

After lunch, they kept walking. In the afternoon, they reached the shipwreck they had seen from a distance. The HDFS *Bianca*, a saucer-shaped corvette, lay shattered in a valley. Here the companions found two dozen survivors. Aside from the helmsman, who had perished in the crash, the entire crew had survived. They had built a makeshift camp around the crash site, complete with a palisade, tripwire attached to warning bells, and three hydling skulls mounted on sticks. They all had weapons and plenty of them.

That evening, as they all sat together around campfires, Marco felt a little more hopeful. Here in the forest, they were up to twenty-eight survivors. That included Marco and Addy, Wyatt, Aurora, and the *Bianca*'s crew. And over three hundred still lived back at the *Blood, Sweat, and Tears,* hunkering in the shipwreck. It wasn't an army. But it was a start. It was humanity surviving, regrouping, preparing to fight back.

"A hundred thousand of us fought the hydrians in space," Marco said softly. "Only a few hundred remain."

"No," Addy said. "Billions remain. All around the world. We'll all fight back. We'll rise up. Like we did to the marauders and the cyborgs. We'll win back this world."

Marco looked at her. She sat by the campfire, nursing a beer. She had washed off the mud in a nearby stream, then immediately covered her face with war paint. She had woven her hair into two braids. They spilled out from under her antique helmet, the one which could supposedly summon a World War II brigade. Even as she relaxed by the fire, her many weapons hung across her back, for Addy never truly rested. She was always on guard. Always ready to fight.

Marco knew her story. Addy Linden had been fighting all her life. She had been born to a drug-addicted mother. On the day of her birth, she had gone into withdrawal. Throughout her childhood, her father had spent his days in jail. At school, Addy had ended up in the remedial class. A child betrayed by the world. Forgotten. Bullied. A child who had learned the world was out to get her. It would have crushed most kids, but Addy had become a fighter. And she had been fighting every day since. It was the honor of Marco's life that Addy had chosen to fight at his side.

He held her hand. "I love you, Addy. More than I can say with words."

She frowned. "What do you want? You're not after my hot dogs, are you?"

"I'm serious, Ads. I just wanted to tell you. You're the bravest, strongest, most wonderful woman I know."

She growled and grabbed his collar. "You forgot sweet!" She twisted his collar, then laughed, poked his nose, and kissed him. "Love you too."

Next morning, the entire group headed back toward *Blood, Sweat, and Tears*, ready to join the larger community of survivors. But halfway there, when cresting a hilltop, Marco noticed another group of shattered trees. There were no plumes of smoke, but it looked like a crash site all right.

"We should check it out," he said.

Addy groaned. "Poet! Last ten times you went to check out a crash site, it was just chunks of *Blood, Sweat, and Tears*."

"It could be her." His voice dropped. "Joey."

Addy sighed. "Marco, you know that she probably didn't survive, right?" She put a hand on his shoulder. "It was crazy up there. Almost every ship was incinerated down to atoms."

"My Joey is alive," he said. "I know it."

They walked toward the shattered trees. Among them, instead of Joey, they found a chunk of mangled metal. It looked like a piece of an engine with some scraps of hull. Cables spilled from the wreckage like dead serpents. Marco lowered his head.

"Just some bits of *Blood, Sweat, and Tears*," he said. "You were right, Addy."

She put a hand on his shoulder. "I'm sorry, babe."

"I really thought we'd find her this time. I really thought she made it." He looked into Addy's eyes. "She was real to me. I know that to everyone else, she was just a machine. Just artificial intelligence. But I believe she had a soul. A consciousness. I believe she was alive. And it feels like losing a friend."

Addy hugged him. "I know, Poet."

As she embraced him, Marco looked at the shattered chunks of engine and hull. And he frowned. Gently, he freed himself from Addy's embrace and knelt by the wreckage.

"No, this isn't a piece of *Blood, Sweat, and Tears*," he said. "Look at this engine. It's a corvette class engine. And . . ." He gasped. "This piece of hull! There's ultrablack pain on it! Just a few smudges, but it's definitely ultrablack."

"Oh, Poet, I'm sorry," Addy said.

"It *is* Joey!" Marco said. "But where's the rest of her?"

He walked between the trees and found another chunk of metal. It looked like a ventilation pipe. Marco walked onward and found a charred seat. A seat from a cockpit. His seat! It was Joey all right. Bits of her lay strewn across the forest.

Addy removed her antique metal helmet. "RIP Joey."

"She might still be alive."

"Marco--" Addy began.

But he ran onward, finding more parts of her strewn among the trees. Bits of hull. Mangled bulkheads. Half of the yoke. Gears, bits of a landing skid, and the airlock handles. Finally he discovered the chassis. It was little more than a charred lump of mangled metal. Marco stood for a moment, gazing down at the ruin.

Wyatt trudged up toward him. He slapped a hand on Marco's shoulder. "Aww, buddy, I'm sorry. It's a hard thing to lose a ship."

Marco stepped into the wreckage and began rummaging, pulling back chunks of bulkhead, tossing aside burnt pipes, and ripping out cables.

Wyatt glanced toward Addy. "What's he doing?"

"He's gone crazy," Addy whispered. "I always knew someday he would."

Marco looked back at them. "I'm not crazy, guys. Joey's body is wrecked, yes. But her brain--the computer that runs her artificial intelligence--is inside her black box. She might still be alive."

Addy stepped into the crumpled chassis. "Poet, she's gone. You're going through denial. I heard about this. There are steps for grief. The first one is denial. The second step is admitting powerlessness over your addiction. The third step is turning control over to a higher power, while the fourth step is--"

"Addy, that's the AA program," Marco snapped. "Shut up and help me look for Joey's black box. I think we're standing in the prow. I think. It could be the stern."

They rummaged around the wreckage for a while. Wyatt and Aurora helped. Finally, among the ruins, Marco found it. Joey's black box. It was about the size of an antique microwave, built of reinforced graphene and steel. It was far too heavy to lift, and it had sunk into the ground to its top.

"Damn!" Marco said. "The hinges are bent. The door is jammed. We can't open it."

Wyatt cleared his throat. "Pardon me. I might be of some assistance." He pulled a crowbar from his pack.

Addy's eyes widened. "Whoa! You carry around a crowbar?"

"I'm an outlaw, honey. I always carry a crowbar."

Addy grinned. "I love the way you think. I already carry around a lock-picking kit. I should add a crowbar to my arsenal."

Wyatt pointed at her belt. "I notice you always carry around a pair of handcuffs."

"Those are for Poet."

Marco cleared his throat. "Excuse me! Little help?"

"Right away, bud." Wyatt shoved the crowbar into the black box. It took a few attempts, but finally the shaggy outlaw managed to crack open the lid.

On the inside, the box was much smaller. Most of the bulk was in the thick box walls; they were designed to withstand virtually anything. Nestled inside among soft wrappings was Joey's central computer. Marco cupped it gently in his hands. The computer was the size and shape of a human brain, encased in a silvery membrane with a few input and output ports. The membrane was translucent, showing Marco a complex network of electronic neurons. The computer was still glowing. The neurons were firing.

"She's alive!" Marco said. "Joey is alive!"

Addy patted his shoulder. "Poet, you're going through stage four. Talking shit."

"Oh, quiet! Make some room. I'm plugging her into my minicom."

They stepped out of the burnt chassis. Marco found a

large, flat boulder, where he set down Joey's brain and his minicom. Wyatt, Aurora, and a few other survivors sat down for lunch, while others stood guard. Marco felt a little guilty about holding everyone up, but Joey deserved it.

He was missing a few data cables, but Wyatt carried those too in his pack of infinite possibilities. Marco plugged Joey's brain into his minicom. If he were right, she'd be able to communicate through the little device.

For a moment, nothing happened.

Marco stared at the minicom. "Come on. Come on, baby . . ."

Then the minicom pinged. The little computer recognized Joey's brain! Data began streaming back and forth!

A graphic appeared on the minicom's screen: a wide-eyed, scared emoji, clutching its cheeks. Joey's voice emerged from the speaker.

"Where am I? What's going on?"

Marco tossed back his head and laughed. Tears of relief flowed down his cheeks.

"You're alive, Joey. Thank God, you're alive."

"Marco? Marco, is that you?" Joey said.

"It's me, Joey! It's me. Can you see me? Look through the camera, Joey!"

Addy sat down beside Marco. She slung an arm around his shoulders. "Poet, now you're hearing voices. That's not even one of the phases. You have to let her go."

"Oh, shut up, Addy!" He held the minicom near his face. "Joey, connect to the camera. Do you see me?"

The emoji changed. It became a pair of huge eyes. "Marco? Marco, I see you! What happened? Where am I? I can't feel anything. I was crashing."

"You did crash," Marco said. "But you survived."

Addy winced. "Eh. Kinda."

"Guys?" Joey said. "I can't feel my wings. I can't feel my cockpit. I can't feel anything. Guys, why am I outside in the forest? *Why don't I have a body?*"

"Sorry, Joey," Marco said. "I don't know how to put this, but . . ."

"You're nothing but a brain," Addy said.

Joey's emoji turned its eyes toward the mangled heap of metal on the forest floor. "Is that . . . is that me?"

Addy shoved Marco. "Why did you show her that?"

"I didn't do anything!"

"You aimed the camera at the wreck."

"I was just sitting here!"

Joey's emoji began to cry pixelated tears. "I'm a burnt, mangled ruin. Look what you did to me, Addy."

Addy leaped to her feet. "Me? I'm the one who rescued your brain! Marco had given up on you."

"I did not." Marco groaned. "Ignore Addy. Joey, we'll get you a new body. I promise. For now, the best part of you is saved. Your soul."

Addy shrugged. "Meh, I always thought her best part was her pantry."

"I can tell from your hips," Joey said.

Addy smashed a beer bottle and raised the broken half. "Watch it! I killed my own brain with alcohol, and I can kill yours."

"So that's why you know about the AA steps!" Marco said. She punched him.

"Ow!" He rubbed his arm. "What did I do?"

"Do you know why people climb mountains?" Addy said. "Because they're there. Do you know why I punch you? Because you're there."

He tapped her head. "But you're not all *there*."

The group of survivors kept traveling south through the

forest. Marco and Addy walked hand in hand. Wyatt trudged along, whistling a tune, his rifle slung across his shoulders. Aurora squirmed alongside the humans, her tentacles competently navigating the forest floor. The survivors of the HDFS *Bianca* walked with them, two dozen in all. Last but not least, Joey nestled in Marco's backpack.

* * * * *

That day, they found even more survivors.

A Firebird had crashed into a lake. They found the pilot on the shore, fishing, reading a novel, and living his best life. He seemed almost disappointed to join the others.

Not two klicks away, the group came across an escape pod. It had launched from *Blood, Sweat, and Tears* during the dreadnought's fiery crash through the atmosphere. Five spacers had sheltered inside. When Marco found them, the five were sitting around a campfire, roasting a porcupine. Quills stuck out of their arms, jammed in with tiny barbs. They seemed happier than the pilot to join the group.

Throughout the trip, Marco kept communicating with Einav over nixnet. The connection was fickle. Normally, nixnet relied on powerful servers inside dreadnoughts and smaller servers in satellites. All those were offline now, but minicoms could also communicate peer-to-peer in a pinch.

"Should we keep searching for survivors?" Marco asked her that afternoon. He stood in the depths of the forest, while Einav was back at the mountain, sheltering in the ruins of the *Blood, Sweat, and Tears.*

"No," Einav said. "I want you back at camp. My other rescue teams located three other escape pods. And they found a few more Firebirds and another shattered corvette. I think that's everyone accounted for."

Addy leaned toward Marco's minicom. "Other teams? Einav!" She placed a hand on her heart. "You don't trust us?"

"To scan an entire forest on your own?" Einav said. "No."

"I can find more people," Addy said. "I'll find more than any of those other loser rescue teams. Poet, come on! We're heading back north."

"No," Einav said. "Guys, our scouts report movement of hydrians in the east. I worry of an impending assault. I want everyone back at the *Blood, Sweat, and Tears*."

Addy gasped. "Now you have scouts too! Oh, you wound me!"

Marco groaned. "Addy, you can't do everything by yourself."

"I never pretended I could. That's why I make you wash the dishes."

They kept walking through the afternoon. It was slow going. Rocks, brambles, and mud slowed their passage, and some survivors were wounded and could only limp. When the sun set, they were still a few klicks away from the *Blood, Sweat, and Tears*. Walking at night was dangerous. The hyd had attacked Marco, Addy, and Wyatt in the darkness. The others reported attacks at night as well. Perhaps it was wisest to make camp, set a guard, and hunker down till dawn. But the safety of *Blood, Sweat, and Tears* beckoned. In the shipwreck, there would be cabins to shelter in, hundreds of people around them, and many more weapons. Not to mention those rations. So they decided to press on in the darkness. They lit flashlights, keeping the beams low. Nobody wanted to alert any hydrian that might be flying above. They trudged on through the dark. Aurora needed no flashlight. The octopus shone with soft purple light, and her eyes gleamed like two silver lanterns.

"Poet, you're leading us the wrong way," Addy said.

"I know exactly where we are." He pointed his flashlight ahead. "I recognize that tree."

Addy rolled her eyes. "A tree's a tree."

"Trees are all different," Marco said. "Like people. Some are graceful, beautiful beings like me. Others are hideous, gnarled nightmares like you."

In the darkness, he managed to dodge her fist.

"Poet, I swear, I--"

A rumble rolled over her words. A hydrian rumble.

At once, Marco and Addy stopped bickering and shouldered their rifles. Behind them, the footfalls of the others fell silent. Rattles and clicks sounded as soldiers drew their weapons. Aurora raised one of her daggers. It still held a charge from yesterday and shone in the night.

The forest was silent. Even the wind died. The crickets stopped chirping.

"Addy?" Marco whispered. "That wasn't your stomach, was it?"

Then, with a deafening shriek, three hyds leaped from the forest ahead. One from ahead. Two from the sides.

An ambush.

The humans (and one Menorian) opened fire.

Marco filled the night with plasma bolts. Addy, bless her heart, was firing her antique T57, firing plain old bullets. Wyatt laughed as he unleashed a neutron machine gun. The bore spun and sprayed and lit the forest as bright as day. Behind them, the others were shooting various laser pistols and plasma blasters. Aurora fired her dagger's single charge, searing through a hyd's shell.

The hyd in front collapsed. Marco's plasma, Addy's bullets, and Wyatt's machine gun weaved together into a terrible spear of destruction. The fusillade shattered the alien's head and destroyed the pulsing pink brain.

One down, two to go. The remaining two hyds plowed into the group of humans. One was a blue, warty squid with one eye and a barnacle-covered mantle. The other sported a red exoskeleton, and its mouth was toothless--whether due to disease, injury, or senescence, Marco did not know. Judging by their many scars, both hyds had clearly seen battle before. And both were hungry for human flesh.

The blue hyd grabbed one of *Bianca*'s survivors. She was a navigator with silvery hair. The squid lifted her overhead, then tore her in two. Her insides splattered onto the forest floor. The blue squid licked up the gore like a dog licking scraps.

The red hyd leaped onto a spacer, engulfing the man within his cavernous, toothless mouth. The alien didn't need teeth. It tossed back its head, gulped its prey down, and belched.

The hyd in front of Marco suddenly twitched, then thumped back onto the forest floor. The brain was exposed and mangled. It was definitely dead. Sometimes, dead hyds still twitched until they cooled off. At random, Marco chose another hyd to fight--the blue one with one eye. The creature was still licking the navigator's entrails from the forest floor. Wincing in disgust, Marco opened fire.

His plasma bolts slammed into the creature. But on his own, without Addy and Wyatt's firepower, he wasn't doing enough damage. The armored kraken was plowing through human survivors, lifting several in its blue tentacles. The beast bit off a man's leg, then sucked out the blood like a man sucking meat from a crab leg. Some survivors tried to fight back, but in the chaos and darkness, they could barely aim. The scene alternated from pitch blackness to searing light whenever Marco fired his gun. Each time the light flared, the hyd was closer to him. Closer. *Closer.*

His gun dinged. Out of ammo! Darkness fell.

The blue devil chuckled. Hot, rancid breath washed over Marco. It stank like rotten meat. He slammed in another plasma pack, fired again, and once more light flared. The hyd was right on him! The jaws opened like a gate to hell, ringed with bloodied teeth. Marco filled that mouth with hot plasma, and the beast recoiled and shrieked. But it still lived! It spat out plasma and roared. Why wouldn't the damn thing die?

And why wasn't anyone helping him? As the blue hyd spat out fire, Marco glanced behind him. Addy and Wyatt were fighting the red, toothless hyd. They had their hands full. The other survivors weren't much help either. One man was wriggling away, his left leg gone. A few spacers lay dead. Others had lost their nerve and cowered behind trees. A few did try to fight, God bless them, but their handguns did little damage against thick hydrian armor. Against the blue beast, Marco stood alone.

The blue hyd kept advancing. Marco took a step backward. His back hit something.

"Watch it, buster!"

That *something* was Addy, he realized. They stood back to back, firing their weapons. He fired at the blue hyd, she at the red one.

The blue terror, mouth charred, lashed its tentacles at Marco. He fired a squirming limb, melted the carapace, and burned the flesh within. Good! But not good enough. The beast had plenty of tentacles to spare. One wrapped around Marco and lifted him high.

Marco kicked and punched but couldn't free himself. The blue hyd hoisted him into the air, then whipped him around like a rag doll. Even as his head spun, Marco glimpsed the toothless red hyd. It had grabbed Addy! Wyatt lay nearby, unconscious, maybe dead.

From the air, Marco fired down plasma. Not at the hyd grabbing him. But at the one crushing his wife. From up here,

Marco could aim more successfully at the creature's eyes. It took an entire plasma pack, but Marco managed to melt the red hyd's nictating membrane. After that, burning the eyeballs was a cakewalk.

Blinded, the red beast opened its toothless mouth in a wail. Toothless and eyeless, it wasn't happy. In agony, the crippled creature dropped Addy.

At once, Addy scrambled to her feet, drew her katana, and charged at the maimed monster. With a battle cry, Addy leaped into the air, then thrust her sword into the hyd's burnt eye socket. The blade drove into the brain.

Addy landed on her feet. The red hyd twitched, whimpered, then fell down dead. Two tentacles slammed into Addy, knocking her down and burying her.

"Goddammit!" she cried, struggling to free herself.

Marco, meanwhile, was still in the air, struggling against the hyd who gripped him. The cobalt kraken was chortling. With its other tentacles, it lifted other survivors. It devoured one--a gunner with a white beard. The ravenous alien gulped the man down, licked its chops, then turned its eyes toward Marco.

He was out of ammo. He had another plasma pack on his bandoleer, but the tentacle was wrapped around his chest, hiding the ammunition. Hanging in midair, wriggling within his foe's grasp, Marco was helpless.

Sudden light flared.

Not the harsh light of a plasma gun or laser beam. Lavender light. Glittering like a nebula.

A blast of energy slammed into the hyd that gripped Marco. The alien's head exploded. Chunks of exoskeleton flew every which way. The brain splattered. Marco winced as soft flesh and sharp shards of carapace hit him.

He thumped onto the ground and wriggled free from the tentacle.

"Can people please stop firing heavy artillery at hydrians while they're holding me?" he shouted. "Addy, was that you?"

But no. He saw Addy lying on the ground, still trapped under the dead red hyd.

The purple light softened, and Einav Ben-Ari walked onto the scene, her starhand raised. The azoth crystal on the palm shone. Her green eyes shone just as brightly, and her golden hair billowed on waves of warped spacetime. Wreathed in light, she seemed like a goddess descended from Elysium fields. Around Marco, some of the survivors knelt.

"Come, follow me," said Einav. "More hyds are moving through the night. There is safety in *Blood, Sweat, and Tears*. Safety for now."

Marco approached her and saluted. "Thank you, ma'am. For saving my life. Our lives."

She returned the salute, then pulled him into a hug. "I missed you, Marco."

Lying nearby under red tentacles, Addy cleared her throat. "Hello! Trapped woman here! Anyone planning on helping me?"

Marco and Einav pulled the tentacles off her. Then Marco reached down and helped Addy to her feet.

"God, you weigh more than the dead hyd."

"Shut up!" She punched him. "That squid weighs much more than 115 pounds."

"Yes, Addy, you weigh 115 pounds like I'm six feet tall."

She snorted. "You wish."

One of the hydrians--the first one they had shot down--suddenly rose with a growl. Half its brain was missing, but it opened its slavering jaws. So it wasn't dead after all. And then it did something Marco had not heard a hydrian do in ages. Something he had nearly forgotten they could do. The hyd spoke.

"We know you . . ." The creature chuckled. "Einav . . . Marco . . . Addy . . . We see you . . . Filthy apes! You will die!"

Marco stared into those terrible red eyes, and inside them, he saw the shoal. Billions of hydrians, swarming across the land, gulping down forests and oceans.

"Who are you?" he said. "Can you speak directly to Ninazu? Can--"

A *boom* shook the forest.

A shell burst into the hydrian's head. The beast wobbled and fell back dead.

Addy lowered her bazooka. "That took care of that."

"Addy, dammit, I was trying to interrogate it," Marco said, his ears ringing anew.

"Oh, please, you know what all these squids say." Addy mimicked a talking mouth with her hand. "Die, apes. Die, apes." She scoffed. "It's all they ever say. Well, look who's dead now." She kicked the carcass.

Einav looked over her shoulder. While the married couple had been bickering, their leader had walked quite a few paces away, heading deeper into the shadowy forest.

"Come on, everyone!" Einav said. "Follow me to camp. It's dangerous out here. Take the wounded. Leave the dead."

"I'm not leaving the dead," Addy said.

Marco nodded. "I have to agree with my wife. They deserve a proper burial."

Einav pursed her lips, then nodded. "Fine. I'll help you carry them. We'll bury them at headquarters. But we must hurry. More hyds are coming."

* * * * *

It was nearly dawn when they reached the *Blood, Sweat, and Tears*' ruin. The dreadnought had once been a mile long. Now she was a third that length. The rest had been lost in the crash and scattered across the landscape. But the reinforced inner decks, along with the stern, had survived the crash. More or less. The remains were cracked, warped, and full of holes, but if you squinted, you could still see the rough shape of a starship. The entire wreck had crashed into a mountainside, lodging itself into the soil and stone. The stern stuck out into the forest. The rest was buried in the mountainside.

While Marco had been exploring the northern woods, Einav had made changes to the camp. A palisade of wooden spikes surrounded the shipwreck on three sides. On the fourth side, the mountain offered natural protection. Torches crackled along the stockade, and Marco thought he could make out snipers in makeshift guard towers.

"Why the wooden wall?" he asked Einav. "From their second instar up, hydrians can fly." He thought for a moment. "Actually, the hyds that attacked us in the forest weren't flying. I don't remember them even having propulsion rings on their carapace."

"There seem to be multiple types of hyds," Einav said. "Until now, we've mostly fought hyds in space. Those ones were flying inside galactopods with propulsion systems. The hyds in the forest are ground troops. Hydrian infantry. Our stockade is for them."

Addy examined the wooden spikes, sucking her teeth. "They'd plow right through that."

"Indeed," Einav said. "And make a lot of noise. Enough to rouse us inside the shipwreck. We haven't been idle. We expect a full assault. We've been preparing."

The group walked through the forest, finally reaching the wooden palisade that surrounded the shipwreck. A gateway rose ahead, lit with torches. Beefy guards stood here, holding machine guns. Marines, by the looks of them. A battalion of them had flown in *Blood, Sweat, and Tears*, though most had perished in the battle and crash. The survivors wore tattered uniforms and stern expressions.

As the ragged survivors approached the gates, the guards snapped to attention. One stepped forward and gave a crisp salute.

"All hail Einav Ben-Ari, the Golden Lioness!" cried the chief of the guards.

"Hail the Golden Lioness!" shouted the other marines.

Einav smiled uncomfortably. "Please, no need to hail or shout. Going forward, a simple salute will suffice."

The chief guard saluted again, this time silently. Einav returned the salute. Two burly soldiers opened the heavy wooden door, and Einav and her companions stepped into the compound.

A section of forest had been cleared away around the shipwreck. Tree stumps sprawled into the shadows. A few scattered campfires glowed here and there. Survivors were roasting deer and fish and boiling water.

Addy patted her pocket and eyed a nearby campfire. "Anyone got a rake?"

"Addy, not now," Marco said.

Past the clearing rose the mountainside, rocky and severe, soaring into darkness. And there was the shipwreck. Chunks of the *Blood, Sweat, and Tears* had shattered in atmospheric entry, and another good chunk was buried in the mountainside. What remained, sticking out from the mountain into the night, was still massive. The structure was larger than the Sydney Opera House.

"The shipwreck has become the headquarters for our rebellion," Einav said. "We've been welding the cracks shut. Putting sensors on the outside to watch the forest. And we've got machine gun nests inside the exhaust ports."

"So no chance of hiding, huh?" Marco said. "The fire, the guards, the wall . . . the hydrians will see this for miles around."

As they walked toward the shipwreck, Einav looked at him. "Hide, Marco? Yes, we could hide. We might find a cave or two, and some of us might cower there for winter. Maybe we'd even survive till spring. Or we could disperse across the world, every man for himself. But I prefer to make a stand. A final stand. The *Blood, Sweat, and Tears* has fallen from the sky, but her crew still fights. I still fight. This is where we fell. So this is where we stand."

Marco nodded. "This is where we stand."

"This is where we stand!" said Wyatt.

"This is where we roast hot dogs!" Addy said. Marco rolled his eyes.

Dawn rose above the mountain, draping the camp with soft light. Looking around, Marco saw weary, wounded survivors. People who had fought among the harshest battles Marco had ever seen, and he'd been a soldier for generations. People who had seen Mars destroyed, seen tens of thousands of soldiers die around them. People who had lost friends, family, but not hope. Yes, past the trauma in their eyes hope shone like this sunrise. Even as they suffered, even with all this death and despair all around, they stood tall. They exemplified the nobility in humanity. The reason Marco fought for his people. As Einav walked by, they rose to their feet. They saluted.

"Golden Lioness," they whispered.

"There she walks, the Golden Lioness."

She's the one who gives them hope, Marco thought. *And she gives me hope.*

Addy slipped her hand into his. "I have a good feeling, Poet. We're gonna win this."

Marco was not so sure. They were only a few hundred survivors. And who knew how many hydrians Erafel would send their way? A sudden urge filled Marco to run with Addy and Einav. To hide. To survive. He crushed that urge. No, he would not simply survive in a cave. What kind of life was that? Better to die on his feet, fighting for Earth.

But hopefully, he fought and won.

They reached the shipwreck, climbed a rope ladder, and entered the shadowy headquarters of Einav's rebellion.

CHAPTER SEVENTEEN
Red Eyes in the Woods

The day at *Blood, Sweat, and Tears* passed in silent anticipation. The hydrians did not like daylight. Since crashing onto Earth, nobody had reported attacks during daylight. The hyds preferred the darkness. During that long, tense day, the survivors saw the forest stir--trees swaying and cracking, boulders rolling, birds fleeing. They heard the grumbles in the sky and saw shadows swarm above the clouds. The enemy was in the woods and sky, mustering. An attack was coming. Not just a few hyds this time but a concentrated assault. Marco feared the coming night. He might not live to see another dawn.

There was much to do all day, and everyone had a job. The mechanics were trying to get *Blood, Sweat, and Tears'* graviton generators up and running again. The fusion core had melted and leaked across space; it would never work again. But if they could get the smaller generators working, they could power a rudimentary force field around the shipwreck.

Or at least that was what Addy claimed. She spent all day rushing through the bowels of the shipwreck, bossing poor mechanics around. According to the doctors, she had been born with neonatal abstinence syndrome, and she had spent her childhood in the remedial class at school. Her brain came with some challenges, but in some areas, she was brilliant. Show her a machine, and she could figure it out, tweak it, fix it, repurpose it. She struggled to read a book more complicated than *Freaks of the Galaxy*, but with barely so much as a high school degree (she had only graduated thanks to Marco's help), she could work engineering miracles. Even to this day, a century into their marriage, Marco was learning more about her challenges and her brilliance. Every day, she annoyed him. But also surprised him and delighted him. And every day he loved her more.

The others were busy at their tasks too. With her eight arms, Aurora spent the day disassembling, cleaning, and reassembling rifles that had survived the crash. By nightfall, every survivor would be armed. For his part, Wyatt took over artillery operations. He led a crew into the dreadnought's armory, where they found several heavy Zeus-class missiles. Each was seven feet long and tipped with a heavy warhead. Only by miracle had they not exploded in the crash. Wyatt, a lover of explosives big and small, quickly began rigging up a makeshift cannon to fire them. Commander Harris, the great-grandnephew of Marco's friend from bootcamp, took command of the *Blood, Sweat, and Tears'* surviving marines. The grizzled, gruff officer was positioning his fighters across the shipwreck, valley, and mountainside, readying them for face-to-face battle with the hydrians.

Across the camp, everyone had a job to do. Those who were too old or hurt to fight were not idle. Some dug trenches. Others tended to the wounded. There was even a priest among the survivors. That day he buried the dead, then moved among the living to pray and offer comfort.

For his part, Marco spent the day rigging up a lighting system for the coming night. Hyds had natural night vision. Some human soldiers carried night-vision goggles, but not many. Come sundown, Einav's army would need lights. Marco enlisted a team of twenty young spacers, all survivors of the *Blood, Sweat, and Tears.* Their officers had died in the crash, and they were eager to serve under the famous Marco Emery, hero of the Alien Wars.

"We're going to light up this valley," he told them.

Spotlights would be nice. They had none. They considered

running electric cables around the defensive palisade, stringing a few overhead, and adding light bulbs. They searched the shipwreck, but they couldn't find nearly enough electric cables. Or light bulbs. Must they resort to torches? Then Marco remembered something. Most warships, in their armories, carried flares. They could be used by marines deploying to dark worlds. Sometimes they provided illumination in space--perhaps for a crew working on hull repairs. Marco found a cache of flares. His team spent the afternoon adapting grenade launchers into flare guns.

As sunset approached, Marco ordered his team to distribute the flare guns across the camp. Taking one flare gun with him, Marco went in search of Einav. He couldn't find her. He went down to engineering--a cavernous deck inside the shipwreck. Addy was there, cursing at her mechanics.

"Einav?" she said. "Nah, haven't seen her. Now make yourself useful, Poet, and grab that--Poet? Poet, get back here!"

He searched the ship's bridge next. But the bridge, buried deep inside the ruin, was abandoned. The bunks? The warehouse? He called Einav's minicom over and over, but nixnet was on the fritz again.

Finally an idea struck Marco. He knew where to look.

He walked through *Blood, Sweat, and Tears* until he reached one of the enormous exhaust ports. The pipe was so large you could fly a small starship inside. Several troops were here, setting up machine gun nests. Wyatt was among them. The hirsute outlaw was rigging up a spinning platform for one of the guns.

"Hey, buddy!" He gave Marco a fist bump.

Marco exited through the exhaust port, climbed the scaffolds along the outside rim, and made his way to the top of the shipwreck. More survivors were here, patching holes and cracks and setting up artillery stations. A few snipers were already in position, aiming their rifles at the forest below. Marco walked among them. He found Aurora behind a barricade, holding no fewer than eight guns, one in each tentacle. The Menorian looked at him and spoke in colors. His minicom translated.

"I intend to kill a few squids."

Marco patted her on the head and kept walking. Soon he reached the mountainside. The *Blood, Sweat, and Tears* had crashed here, burying a good chunk of the ship inside the mountain. A wall of soil, rock, and uprooted trees rose ahead of Marco. He climbed the mountainside, digging his hands into nooks and crannies. On the way up, he saw the marks of hands on the mountainside. One normal hand. One hand with enormous power; the fingers had left holes in solid stone. He was on the right track.

Finally, about a hundred yards up, Marco reached a platform of stone that thrust out from the mountainside. The outcrop formed a natural balcony overlooking the valleys, forests, and rivers. Somebody had set up an entire command post up here. Three light artillery cannons stood like sentinels, bolted into the rock. A spotlight rose beside them, plugged into a generator. (*Ah, so we do have a spotlight!* Marco thought.) Several minicoms stood on a boulder. There was also a central computer, a trench, battle rations, and a hatch leading underground.

The hatchway was made of steel, its handle shaped like a snarling lion's head. It was funny, Marco thought. Even now, at a time of war, humans cared for art and beauty. There was no practical need to install a hatch shaped like a lion's head when a simple handle would suffice. But that was the way of humans. Even as the world burned, humanity cared for beauty. Perhaps at times of war beauty meant more than ever. Where did this hatchway lead? Marco didn't know. Perhaps it delved through stone and soil, eventually leading into the *Blood, Sweat, and Tears*. The shipwreck lurked below, lodged into the mountainside.

He found Einav standing among the cannons, gazing into the distance. The cold November wind billowed her hair and pinched her cheeks pink. She stood alone. The setting sun reflected in her eyes. She seemed like a golden statue, a gilded prophet risen from the biblical age. Marco suddenly felt like he was walking on hallowed ground. These were legendary times. Times of history being forged in the ruins of the world. There she stood. His leader. His judge. His best friend, golden in the sunset.

* * * * *

For a moment, Einav seemed not to notice Marco. Then she looked at him and smiled sadly. "There's something that always seems melancholy about November. It's not cozy like October, when we still remember our days of summer. It's a time before the long winter. A time to prepare. A time before the true cold. And this will be a long, cold winter."

Marco stood at her side. He gazed toward the east. The boreal forest spread beyond the clearing into dark mist. Suddenly Marco gasped. The trees were rustling! A few trunks were falling. Red eyes shone among them.

Marco pointed. "The hydrians!"

"Yes, there they are," Einav said. "They've been moving through the forest for quite awhile now. As we're preparing, so are they. They will attack soon. Tonight, I imagine."

"It's almost dark. We should get back to the ship."

Einav kept gazing at the forest. "I'll stay up here for a while," she said softly. And something in her voice sounded so young to Marco. He had almost forgotten that Einav was not just the legendary leader, the Golden Lioness, the heroine from history, a leader forged by 150 years of hardship and warfare. She was all those things, to be sure, but she was also a woman. A human soul. A human who longed for comfort, love, companionship, and safety.

Marco had not known Einav in her youth. When he had

met her, she had been a twenty-year-old ensign, already an officer
and leader. Oh, during the Pax Terra, that long century of peace, a
twenty-year-old would be considered young. A youth. Practically a
child. The Alien Wars had been different. During those hard
times, children had grown up fast. They became soldiers as soon
as they could hold a gun. A twenty-year-old was already an old
soul, a hardened soldier.

Marco had never known Einav the child. What had she
been like? She came from a proud military dynasty. Her father had
been a colonel in the HDF. Her grandfather too. Her ancestors
had fought the Nazis in the forests of Europe. The Ben-Aris had
been soldiers and leaders since the beginning. Einav Ben-Ari had
been groomed for command. Marco knew that. But had she
always wanted this? Had she ever just wanted to be a regular girl?
Was a part of her still a regular girl, trapped within her suit of
armor?

He stepped closer. "I'll stay with you, if that's all right."

She smiled at him and slipped her hand into his. "More
than all right. Thank you for being here, Marco. I love you more
than you'll ever know. You and Addy both."

A memory from long ago resurfaced in Marco's mind.
Which war had it been? The Marauder War? The Gray War? That
he no longer remembered. It had been a century ago. But he
remembered Einav entering the cockpit of their little starship at
the time. The *Saint Brendan*, he thought. She wore pajamas. He
remembered that, because it was the first time Marco had seen
Einav without a uniform. Seen her not as an officer but as a
woman. That long night, they had talked. About what might have
been. About how it might have looked--had they ended up
together. As more than officer and soldier. As more than friends.

They had never mentioned it again. Not in all the many
long years since. But sometimes, when she touched his hand,
when she glanced into his eyes this way, Marco wondered what

she was thinking. Did she still sometimes contemplate that "what if?" Did she still sometimes imagine "what might have been?" Or was even that memory from long ago a false memory, something he misinterpreted, misremembered?

Or maybe, deep down inside him, did Marco harbor these thoughts? Was he projecting them on her?

I love Addy with all my heart, he thought. And he meant it. There were many things Marco doubted. His hope in this war. His faith in God. His own sanity, sometimes. But one thing he never doubted: his love for Addy. He loved his wife with every fiber of his soul. With every beat of his heart. With every cell in his body. To this day, after a century of marriage, whenever he looked at Addy, he loved her even more. And should he live another century, his love would only grow.

And yet, now, as Einav held his hand, as he saw the softness and vulnerability in green eyes that were normally so stern, he realized that he loved Einav too. He loved her as a soldier loved his officer. As one loved his oldest, most loyal friend. And for that memory from long ago, in the cockpit of some long-lost ship in a nearly-forgotten war, and the echo of what might have been.

Whatever we are, this is perfect, he thought. *It's the honor of my life to have spent these long years with her. With Einav. Just the way we are.*

"I was thinking, Marco . . .," she began, and his heart skipped a beat. Had she too remembered that night long ago? Would she bring up the awkward tension between them?

"Yes?" he said, lips suddenly dry.

"We should call Addy up here. And have dinner together. Here on the cliff."

He exhaled in relief. He was suddenly ashamed of his thoughts. No doubt he had misinterpreted her touch, her look. His cheeks flushed and he nodded.

"Yes. One last dinner before . . . before the end."

"Before victory." She smiled, and now her smile was warmer, that famous Ben-Ari smile that showed her teeth and lit up her eyes. "Have some hope, Marco. We might still win."

Marco checked his minicom. "Nixnet is back online. The mechanics are doing their work. I'll call Addy for dinner. I just hope she doesn't insist we eat hot dogs."

A rumble sounded.

For a second, Marco tensed, sure it was a hydrian. But it sounded more like a rumbling engine. Suddenly Addy rose toward the stone outcrop, wearing a jetpack.

"Did somebody say hot dogs?"

Marco sighed. "Who needs nixnet?"

Addy grinned. She held out a pack of hot dogs in one hand, a rake in the other. "I got dinner covered."

Marco looked at Einav. "Don't worry. I have some rations in my pack."

Addy landed on the outcrop of stone. She stared at the three cannons. Her eyes widened. "Whoa. Are those Sultan Stingers? The new 2270 model? Those guns are badass!"

"We had some on the *Blood, Sweat, and Tears*," Einav said. "They were inside the armory, packed in foam and plastic. They're normally meant to deploy onto alien worlds during land invasions. I figured they'd be of good use up here."

Addy patted one of the bores. "Sweet."

They sat down for dinner. Addy carried a insta-fire kit in her pack. She unfolded it, and a campfire leaped up on the outcrop. Addy busied herself slinging hot dogs onto her rake prongs, then roasting them. The firelight danced across her antique World War II helmet and the many guns, blades, and grenades that covered her body. Einav still wore her white uniform with the golden buckles. As for Marco, he had found battle fatigues in the shipwreck. Good old olive drab. He had donned them for battle. He carried his starflare assault rifle across his back, and his flare gun hung from his belt.

"Was there ever an odder trio in the galaxy?" he wondered aloud. "Once more, the three of us must save the world."

"Hey, we're the pros," Addy said. "We've been doing this for 150 years. When aliens invade, who you gonna call? The Alienbusters!"

Marco blinked at her. "What?"

"I made up a name for our trio. We're the Alienbusters."

"Addy, we're not twelve."

"I am. Mentally at least." She bit into a hot dog.

Marco nibbled his rations. The box claimed it was honey-garlic chicken breast and steamed garden vegetables. Tasted more like cardboard.

"Ah, to hell with it," Marco said, tossing the military ration aside. "Ads, pass me the rake."

She sniffed and wiped her eyes. "I thought you'd never ask."

Soon all three friends were eating hot dogs. Their campfire burned on the stone outcrop like a lighthouse overlooking the dark forests below. The sun sank below the trees. Normally while they shared meals, the trio reminisced. Such was the way of Methuselahs. But tonight they ate silently. Merely being so close together was comfort enough. Marco could not imagine surviving such dark days without his two closest companions. He had lost so many loved ones, but he still had Addy and Einav, and with them at his side, every day of life was a blessing.

The sun fell behind the horizon. The clouds still hid the sun and stars. The trio rose to their feet, walked to the edge of the outcrop, and gazed into the darkness. They could no longer see the forest.

"I don't see any red eyes among the trees," Marco said.

"They're out there," Addy said. "I can smell 'em. They smell like worms and jellyfish washed onto the beach."

Marco unslung his flare gun. "May I?"

Einav nodded. "Over the trees."

Marco aimed the gun above the dark forest. The flare shot upward, then burst into light like a star. It was designed to hang in the air and burn for hours. Light bathed the treetops. Marco tapped his minicom, messaging his fellow flaremen.

His team was ready. A score of flares flew from across the camp. In the sky, they ignited and shone. A few floated above the forest, while others lit up the camp. Orange light flickered across the dark forest, clearing, and shipwreck.

Now Marco could see the forest. The trees were rustling. Cracks sounded as several trunks fell. Grunts and squeals rose from the shadows below the treetops.

"Man those cannons," Einav said.

Marco and Addy needed no encouragement. Each ran to another cannon. Marco was familiar with these weapons. Sultan Stingers were classic guns. Their bores were seven feet long and large enough to stick your fist into. Stingers had been popular back during the Alien Wars. Those old versions had fired plain old bullets. These modern Sultan Stingers fired novabolts, same as the projectiles Joey had once fired.

While Marco and Addy had been searching the forest for survivors, Einav had set up her command center here on the stone outcrop. The Sultan Stingers were bolted into the rock and loaded to the gills with novabolts. Each cannon stood on a round stand. Steelglass bubbles protected the gunner while allowing full visibility. The bores could swivel in every direction other than down. Unless the enemy sprang up beneath your feet like a gopher, you could hit him.

Marco hopped onto one stand, Addy onto the other. They grabbed the handles that controlled the cannons. Each handle had buttons, allowing the gunner to move, aim, and fire. As Marco held the gunnery controls, tingles ran through him. There was nothing quite like holding onto a cannon powerful enough to blow up a house. Sultan Stingers were only light artillery, of course. They were tiny compared to the enormous cannons the *Blood, Sweat, and Tears* had once fired. But Marco still felt that intoxicating sense of ultimate power at his fingertips.

It felt good. He was scared for the battle ahead. He was always scared before a battle, even now, an experienced officer. But at times like these, he thought back to his childhood. To running scared down the streets of Toronto as the scum chased him. Of watching helplessly as the alien centipedes devoured his mother. He was no longer that frightened little boy. He was a man in a uniform with a big gun at his command. He had vowed long ago to never run from battle again. To always face the monsters and slay them.

The trees kept rustling and cracking. And Marco saw them now. Red eyes in the forest. Tentacles flailing. The enemy was moving closer.

Einav did not hop toward her own cannon. Not yet. She ignited the spotlight mounted on the stony outcrop. A beam blasted upward, lighting up the clouds. The glare of that beam revealed hyds--thousands of them--lurking above the clouds, visible now in silhouette. The aliens squealed. Tentacles reached down like tornado funnels. Red eyes blazed behind the cloudy veil like fiery comets.

Across the camp below, voices rose in terror. Marco felt the same terror grip his chest. The humans were only several hundred strong. What hope did they have against so many monsters?

Einav spoke into her minicom. Her voice ran out from speakers on the outcrop, rolling across the camp.

"Hear, O Earth!" she cried. "Hear, warriors of humanity! Tonight is a night of squids. A night of blood and battle and death. But tonight too is a night of valor. A night when our courage shines bright, and our ferocity lights up the dark. Stand tall, warriors of Earth! Stand proud! Stand with me! I am Einav Ben-Ari. Tonight I roar at your side. Tonight we are all heroes! We will win!"

In the camp below, they looked from side to side. They were still afraid. Even from up here, Marco could see the terror in the soldiers below.

Marco raised his minicom. His voice thrummed from the speakers. "I am Marco Emery. I fought in the Alien Wars. I fight with you! We will win!"

"I am Addy Linden!" cried Addy. "I liberated Earth from the marauders. And I will liberate it from the squids. I fight with you! We will win!"

The trees crashed across the forest. Hydrians scuttled forth. The beasts burst from the forest, eyes flaring, tentacles flailing, swarming toward the defensive walls. More hydrians emerged from the clouds and came diving down, jaws open and salivating.

"Say it with me!" Einav cried. "We will win!"

"We will win!" cried the hundreds of heroes.

"Fire!" Einav shouted.

The first hydrians reached the walls. And the forces of Earth fired their guns.

CHAPTER EIGHTEEN
The Mists of Time

The hydrians surged from sky and woods, and the humans answered with devastating fire.

The boreal forest lit up with the light of battle. The defenders on the parapets fired their plasma rifles. Inside the *Blood, Sweat, and Tears'* exhaust ports, Wyatt commanded the artillery force. His gunners unleashed fusillades of shells and plasma bolts. Across the shipwreck, snipers fired everything from bullets to grenades. Down on the ground, Commander Harris was leading the marines in battle. They were firing from the wooden walls, trenches, and pillboxes on the foothills.

Atop the outcrop of stone, overlooking the battle, the trio of Methuselahs fired their Sultan Stingers. Novabolts surged forth, searing white, comprised of neutrons packed into spears of pure destruction.

They were only a few hundred defenders at the wreck of the *Blood, Sweat, and Tears*, but they unleashed enough firepower to make an artillery corps proud.

So far, the attackers were all hyds--hydrians of the second instar. They weren't as large and devastating as hydlords, the third instar. But they were certainly bigger and meaner than the little hydlings, the larvae of the species. The hyds were the shock troops of the shoal, big and brutish. Each beast weighed several tons and could swallow a man whole.

Hyds, the companions had learned, came in multiple varieties. Broadly, they could be divided into two main types.

There were the "infantry hyds" who were built for ground assault. Their tentacles were stronger and tipped with clawed "feet," allowing them to move swiftly across land. Then there were the "flying hyds." Their bodies sprouted organic propulsion systems. Dark, hard rings extended beneath their mantles, spinning rapidly around blazing cores. These were the hyds that had attacked the fleet in space, and they seemed equally comfortable flying through air. It was similar to some species of ants, which produced both walking and flying varieties.

Thousands of hyds of *both* types now surged toward the human headquarters, rising from the forest and swooping from the clouds.

The human fusillade pounded the alien horde. Carapace shards flew every which way. Severed tentacles careened into the distance, knocking down trees. Dislodged hydrian teeth peppered the ground and impaled the wooden palisade. The dark blood of the beasts flowed. Countless died, but countless more replaced them, squirming over the corpses. The squids shoaled onward into the humans' fire.

Even as the barrage continued to pound them, the hydrians returned fire. Their tentacles pointed forward, bulged, and spewed inkblots the size of basketballs. The storm of ink splattered the camp. Some inkblots hit the palisade and began consuming the wood like liquid termites. Some ink droplets sprayed human defenders and began eating through their armor, uniform, and skin.

The flying hyds rained down an inkstorm. Splotches battered the steelglass canopies that protected the Sultan Stingers. Marco winced, expecting the steelglass to shatter, but the transparent barrier held. He yanked the handles, pitching the cannon toward the sky. Ink slid off the canopy and hit the rocky outcrop, sizzling and charring the stone. With his bore pointed straight up, Marco opened fire. His novabolts soared and slammed into hydrians above.

Addy and Einav followed his lead. Severed tentacles rained. One slammed into Marco's canopy and rolled off. Another draped across his cannon's bore like a wet sock on a clothesline. A hyd's corpse crashed down only feet away. The armored squid was the size of an elephant. On impact, it cracked open like an overripe lemon, spurting blood.

For a moment, the rain of ink eased. Marco glanced toward the forest clearing below. The hyds were swarming over the fortifications. The wall of wooden spikes did little to hold them back. Commander Harris was leading a courageous defense. The gruff officer and his troops fought from wooden guard towers and deep trenches, firing bullets and plasma. Many hyds fell but others kept climbing over their dead. Their tentacles reached over the stockade, grabbed soldiers, and hurled them into the distance.

Marco knew the barricades wouldn't hold for long. Harris was a tough old fighter, and his soldiers were just as brave, but they were falling fast. Besides, even as the crawling hyds stormed the walls, many flying hyds kept descending, bypassing the palisade and trenches altogether.

Marco kept firing upward. So did Addy and Einav. More and more hyds crashed, hitting the mountainside, the clearing, and the shipwreck. And more kept coming. The great swarms bubbled up from the forest and oozed from the sky. Ink splattered the camp, eating wood, stone, and flesh. The trio kept firing. Great streams of novabolts lit up the night, searing through hydrian shells and cooking the flesh inside. They slew many. They slew scores of the beasts. But for every hydrian felled, several more swarmed from shadow.

Several flying hyds descended toward the outcrop. The trio fired upward. Novabolts soared skyward, expanding and blazing with white light, pounding the enemy. The searing bolts of neutrons devastated the creatures. But three hyds survived the barrage and landed on the stony outcrop. With screeches, they scuttled toward the three humans.

Marco swiveled his cannon, bringing the gun to bear on the charging beasts. A hyd leaped into the air, jaws open wide and spraying saliva. Marco fired. The novabolts pounded the alien only meters away, burning through its mouth and blasting out the back of the head. The creature slammed down and skidded across the outcrop. Its corpse thumped into the Sultan Stinger.

Another hyd swooped from above. Marco tried to raise his cannon. It was stuck! The corpse was jamming the gears! Marco kicked the dead hyd, tugged on its mantle, and tried to free the cannon. Finally the gears moved again. He swung the bore upward and opened fire just as a hyd landed on the cannon.

White light and pink flesh exploded everywhere. Marco knelt inside the steelglass canopy, covering his head with his arms. When the light cleared, he found his cannon buried under another alien corpse. He fired again. Novabolts carved through the dead hyd, soared skyward, and seared another squid. Marco was doing well, killing a lot of the aliens. But more kept landing. They were everywhere. How long could he keep this up?

Einav and Addy were being mobbed too. They could barely hold back the creatures. The alien corpses piled up. Soon they'd be buried in dead squids.

One hyd managed to grab Addy's cannon. With a mighty tug, the alien bent the thick metal bore. Addy cursed and fired anyway, a decision she instantly regretted. The entire muzzle exploded. Blue fire leaped across the stony outcrop. Addy yelped and jumped back as her control panel flared and sparked.

"My cannon's dead!" she cried. With a snarl, Addy grabbed her bazooka and turned the weapon toward the enemy. "Bring it on, bitches."

Laughing, she fired a shell.

Tentacles were disassembling Einav's cannon too. One beast tore gears off her Stinger, crippling the weapon.

Through the inferno, Marco gazed down toward the clearing. The defenders were falling fast. The enemy had broken down the walls and was charging across the field.

Einav spoke into her minicom, and her voice boomed from the speakers. "All troops, fall back into *Blood, Sweat, and Tears*! Harris, pull your soldiers back! Everyone--into the shipwreck!"

"What?" Addy cried. "No way! Addy Linden doesn't run from a fight."

Giving her bazooka a rest, Addy raised a plasma rifle in each hand. She opened fire, roasting a nearby hyd.

"I gave my orders!" Einav said. "Addy, cover us. Marco, head with me to the hatch."

She pointed at the trapdoor in the stone, the one with the lion head knob. Marco left his cannon to the squirming hyds. He ran, firing his assault rifle, leaping over and around tentacles. Alien jaws rose around him like gateways to hell. He kept running, dodging snapping teeth, bathing the beasts with plasma, until he reached the hatch. He yanked it open.

"Einav, Addy, get in!" he cried.

Addy was busy firing her twin rifles. "You guys first."

Einav ran toward the hatch too. Hyds leaped toward her. She held no gun. Instead, Einav lifted her starhand and uncurled the fingers, revealing the glowing azoth crystal on the palm. The purple light flared. The hyds squinted and squirmed. Einav raised her hand, and the hyds levitated from the ground. She thrust her palm forward, and the hyds flew back and slammed against the mountainside.

"Damn," Marco whispered, gazing in awe at his leader.

Einav reached the hatch. "Hop in, Marco."

He wanted to argue, to insist he remain outside until

Einav and Addy were safe underground. But he could imagine them bickering endlessly, each insisting on remaining outside the longest, risking life and limb to save the other two. So Marco swallowed his pride.

"Fine, I'll go first."

He entered the hatch. He found a shaft leading downward through the living rock of the mountain. Rungs were bolted into the stone. Marco descended, and a moment later, Einav entered the hatch too.

"Addy, get your ass in here!" Marco shouted up the shaft.

His wife was cackling above, firing her rifles.

"Addy, in!" Einav said. "That's an order."

Addy fired a few last rounds, leaped into the shaft, and pulled the hatch shut.

As they climbed the ladder, the hatch suddenly flew off its hinges. A tentacle reached down the shaft. Addy shouted, drew her sidearm, and fired upward. Marco winced as bullets pinged through the shaft, banging back and forth between the walls.

"Addy, you're gonna kill us!" he shouted.

The tentacle wrapped around Addy, and she yelped and clung to the ladder. Einav scampered up and grabbed the tentacle with her starhand. The ivory fingers glowed, cracked the chitin, and sank into the flesh. The tentacle pulled back, sizzling. Addy fell and hit Einav, and Einav fell and hit Marco, and soon all three were falling. Marco tried to grab the ladder. His fingers banged against the metal rungs. Damn it hurt! Finally Marco grabbed a rung and clung on. Einav landed on his head, and Addy slammed into her, and they all lodged together inside the shaft.

"Ow," Addy said.

"Ow?" Marco groaned, crushed under the two women. "You're the one on top!"

They kept climbing down, moaning with pain, until they reached another hatch and dropped into the wreck of the *Blood,*

Sweat, and Tears.

* * * * *

The shadowy innards of the *Blood, Sweat, and Tears* spread into echoing shadows. The shipwreck creaked and moaned, and with every distant boom of the cannons, bulkheads twisted and dust fell from above. This part of the ship had lodged into the mountainside during the crash from space.

The dreadnought's austere, well-lit decks had become a labyrinth of warped metal, flickering shadows, and mangled bulkheads. Not much had survived the crash intact. Marco imagined himself walking through the bowels of some rusting metal giant.

"We'll head to the artillery stations in the exhaust ports," Einav said. "Sounds like Wyatt and his boys are still fighting there. We'll join them."

Marco pointed above. "What about that hatch? Lots of hydrians above."

"Stand back," Addy said. "I got this."

She hefted her bazooka.

"Addy, wait!" Marco said.

Einav pulled him back just as Addy fired. A shell flew up the shaft and burst. The entire shaft twisted and collapsed. Rocks from the mountainside tumbled down, blocking the passageway. Addy blew on her bazooka.

"You were saying, Poet?"

He winced and rubbed his ears. They were ringing again. He kicked aside a rock.

Rumbles sounded all around. The deck tilted. The hydrians were shaking the very mountain. Spacers ran down the shadowy tunnel, carrying assault rifles. When they saw Einav, they halted and snapped to attention.

"Come with me," Einav said. "To the stern!"

She led the way, and Marco ran close on her heel. The others followed. As they ran, the ship shook again. Cracks raced across the deckhead. Rocks tumbled down and dust filled the air.

"They're trying to bring the whole mountain down on us!" Marco shouted.

A huge crack raced across the deckhead, exposing massive boulders. The cracks widened. The boulders rumbled and threatened to tumble down.

As they ran, Einav raised her starhand. The Mariner's Tear glowed. With the power of her stone, Einav raised a spacetime funnel, bending reality to keep the ceiling in place. The survivors kept running.

They reached the stern, which stuck out from the mountain. The upper decks had shattered in the crash, the core had imploded, and the engine room had fallen apart. But the enormous exhaust ports of the *Blood, Sweat, and Tears* still stuck out the stern. There were three of them--pipes so enormous mammoths could stampede down them. Or hyds.

The trio ran down the pipe, guns aiming the way. Other survivors raced behind them. Finally they reached the exhaust port's rim. From here, they gazed out into the night.

The shoal covered the land. Thousands of hyds bustled over the stockade, trenches, and clearing. They were climbing the foothills now, heading toward the shipwreck. More were descending from above.

A team of brave warriors stood inside the exhaust port, bombarding the enemy. They fired light artillery, grenades, plascasters, and any other weapons they had. A few soldiers, God bless 'em, were firing simple handguns. Wyatt stood among the troops, teeth bared and hair wild, firing a huge machine gun. Bullet casings flew every which way. Aurora was firing a weapon in every one of her eight arms. The Menorian wielded pistols, rifles, and crystal daggers. Commander Harris and his troops were racing up from the foothills. So few of them remained. The brave infantrymen leaped into the exhaust port, the hyds hot on their tails. Battered and bleeding, Harris and his boys spun back toward the enemy and kept firing.

Einav, Marco, and Addy ran to join the defenders. They shouldered their assault rifles and fired at the oncoming horde. There was no need to aim. Wherever they fired they hit something.

Like shooting squids in a barrel, Marco thought.

Tentacles draped down from the exhaust port's upper rim. The trio fired at them. A hyd dropped from the rim, shell cracked, and scampered into the pipe. A barrage of fire knocked the squid out onto the swarming horde. The monsters were everywhere, surrounding the opening. A tentacle reached inside, grabbed a soldier, and yanked the man out. Blood splattered.

Was there no end to the beasts? Marco stared across the field, and in the firelight, a horrific sight churned his belly. A towering shadow was lumbering through the forest, crushing trees like a man might crush blades of grass. The creature was gargantuan, a kraken larger than any animal living on Earth. This behemoth could put blue whales to shame. Its tentacles were like redwoods, its mouth a horrific cavern full of red flesh and teeth the size of telephone poles.

A hydlord.

The creature still wore its galactopod shell. Runes larger than men blazed upon its mantle. The cuneiform spelled out the monstrosity's name: ROTSPAWN.

"He seems nice," Addy said. "His skull would make a great trophy."

She loaded a shell into her bazooka and fired. Marco, Einav, Wyatt--everyone in this exhaust port--fired on the advancing hydlord. The bombardment slammed into *Rotspawn.*

Flames leaped across the behemoth, fell onto the forest, and the trees ignited. The titan kept advancing, shaking the earth, roaring as the barrage pounded it.

Still the kraken advanced. The hyds, who had seemed so monstrous only moments ago, now appeared to Marco like mere bugs. Their hydlord towered over them. The smaller squids moved aside, hissing and bowing, making room for their master.

Rotspawn emerged from the forest, flattening a few last pines. The defenders of the *Blood, Sweat, and Tears* bombarded the creature. The hydlord shrugged it off, aimed its bloated tentacles, and disgorged ink.

Dark globs flew toward the shipwreck. There was enough ink flying their way to fill an Olympic swimming pool. Marco cringed, pulled Addy back, and shielded her with his body.

"Get off me!" she said.

Einav stepped forward, raised her starhand, and blasted out a massive shield of spacetime. The hemisphere ballooned, protecting the stern of the *Blood, Sweat, and Tears*. Ink splattered the force field and dripped to the forest clearing. Einav stumbled back, swaying on her feet. Marco caught her before she could fall.

"My starhand battery is almost drained." Einav's face was pale. "I might not be able to do that again."

The hydlord kept advancing. It would need a while to rebuild its stores of ink. Even without that weapon, *Rotspawn* was a mighty foe, large enough to destroy the *Blood, Sweat, and Tears* and everyone within.

Marco still held Einav in his arms. He looked into her eyes.

"We can't hold them back, Einav. We can't win this. We have to escape. Addy has a jetpack. She can fly to safety and carry you. The rest of us can retreat into the forest or mountains. We might survive in the wilderness."

"No." Einav freed herself from Marco's grip and stood on

her own. "I will not escape while a single human still lives. Here is my final stand."

"I'm staying too," Addy said. "I don't run from a fight."

"There's no shame in living to fight another day," Marco said.

"There will be no other day," Einav said. "We could perhaps make it a few miles. They would hunt us down. Maybe we'll survive until dawn, but not much longer. No, Marco. I'm staying. If we fall here tonight, then here is our end. This is our fortress. This is our Masada. This is our final stand. Victory or death are our only two options."

"Victory?" Marco said. "What chance do we still have?"

Addy fired another shell at the approaching hydlord. Rotspan was getting closer. Wyatt, Aurora, and the others were bombarding the behemoth, chipping its armor, but nothing seemed to slow it down. Marco fired another plasma pack at the kraken. For all the damn good it did. They might as well be shooting a mountain.

"We still have a chance." Addy tapped her head. Her helmet rang. "We have this."

"What, your brain?" Marco said. "You're going to come up with a cunning plan?"

"Not my brain, brilliant as it is," Addy said. "My helmet! My antique, magical World War II helmet. You remember what they told me in Darktech Cove, right? It can summon a World War II brigade."

Marco rolled his eyes. "Addy! That's just a scam. Just nonsense to make money. Like saying crystals can heal you."

"Hey, you know crystals healed me that time a snake bit me," Addy said.

"Addy, that was a nonvenomous snake! And you killed it by throwing my mineral collection at it."

"See? Crystals saved me. And this helmet will too. I can

feel them, Poet. Those old soldiers from centuries ago. I can hear them sometimes when the helmet is on."

"So you're hearing voices now," Marco said. "That's encouraging."

He fired another plasma pack. *Rotspawn* was reaching the foothills now. The hydlord grabbed onto the mountainside and began climbing toward the shipwreck. Scores of spacers still stood in the exhaust port, firing everything they had at the behemoth. But the hydlord and his hyds kept advancing.

"Addy," Marco said, "I seriously doubt your helmet--your cheap helmet, might I add--can summon an infantry brigade. What did you spend on it again? Three hundred credits? What could a trinket that cheap actually do?"

She blushed. "Um, Poet, I . . . sort of lied about the price. I spent a million credits."

Marco nearly choked on his saliva. "A million credits? Addy! That's our life savings! That's more than what Joey cost!"

"I know, I know. But Poet! It can summon a brigade. It's a Darktech artifact. The real deal. And the soldiers it can summon are real too." She took a deep breath and raised her chin. "And I'm going to prove it."

She stepped toward the edge of the exhaust port.

"Addy, stop!" Marco rushed toward her. "What are you doing?"

She looked at him, a sad smile on her lips. "Our last stand, Marco." She grabbed him and kissed him hard on the lips. "I love you, Marco. I love you forever. You're the light of my life. I'll see you again. In victory or death."

"Addy, wait--" he began.

But she kickstarted her jetpack and flew out into the darkness.

* * * * *

As Addy flew into the storm of hydrians, she knew she might never see Marco and Einav again. Her husband. Her leader. Her two shining stars. But Addy knew that should she fall tonight, she would see them again in the world beyond.

But hopefully that would not be for many years. Because dammit, she was Addy Linden, Bane of Marauders, Slayer of Squids. She had fought a thousand battles. She had slain a million foes. And she wasn't ready to die yet. There was some fight in her yet!

Her jetpack roared. She rose on jets of fire, a grenade launcher in each hand. All around her spread the shoal. The hyds swarmed across the forest below. They filled the sky and they covered the mountainside. Ahead rose *Rotspawn*, the great galactopod of a hydlord. The other humans were still back in *Blood, Sweat, and Tears*. Out here, in this storm of darkness, Addy Linden flew alone.

Amazingly, the hyds paused. They stared at her. Their eyes darted back and forth, their tentacles rose, and they hissed. And then something happened that sent shivers down Addy's spine. The gargantuan *Rotspawn* opened his mouth and spoke.

His voice was like rolling thunder. The waves of bass ached against Addy's chest.

"Who . . . are . . . you?"

She raised her chin. "You might have heard of me. I invaded the lair of the Scum Emperor on Abaddon. I raised Earth in rebellion against the marauders. I crawled across the ruinous world of the grays, faced down Queen Nefitis, and ended her reign. I destroyed the Dreamer and shattered his nightmares. I faced down the starlings and freed Earth from their grip. Who am I? I'm Addy Fucking Linden, heroine of Earth. And you can go to hell."

She fired both launchers, hurling two grenades at

Rotspawn.

As explosions rocked the towering beast, Addy placed a hand on her helmet.

When she had bought the helmet at Darktech Cove, she had found a folded letter inside. It was crumbling and yellow with age, a memento from the soldier who had once worn this helmet. Addy had read the note over and over, memorizing the words.

I write this now in the fields of France. My brigade has fallen, and I'm among the last who live. Brave men fought under my command. Brave men paved our way to the east. Brave men fell upon this field. Our souls will live on. Our courage will shine again. Into this helmet, I place technology no man has dreamed of. A visitor from the stars, a luminous being like an angel, gave me the gift of space and time. A hole in reality. A hole in my helmet. Should you need us, future reader of these words, we are here. Call us from the fields beyond time. Speak to us these words: "Rise again from sorrow and sing the song of freedom!" And we will rise.

From the mists of time, Colonel Henry Locker.

When Addy had bought the helmet, she had thought the hole was a bullet hole. But over and over, she had contemplated the words in the note. A hole in reality. A hole in my helmet.

So she had run tests. She passed graviton scanners over the helmet, and the scanners maxed out. The helmet was bending spacetime.

A hole in reality. A hole in her helmet.

A wormhole.

No, this was no usual World War II antique. It was a wormhole generator. Addy removed the helmet from her head, letting her two blond braids flutter in the wind. She raised the old green helmet overhead. The wind whistled through the hole. Flying here amidst the shoal, Addy whispered the code to activate the device.

"Rise again from sorrow and sing the song of freedom!"
For a moment, nothing happened.

The watching hydrians chuckled. They resumed their
advance. Bombardment flew from the *Blood, Sweat, and Tears*
behind Addy, hitting the creatures, unable to slow them down.
The human defenders were running low on ammo. Low on
fighters. Low on hope.

Then, in Addy's hands, the helmet began to thrum.

The "bullet hole" seemed to swirl, breaking Addy's
intuitive understanding of physics. The hole expanded and
expanded. Or was the helmet around it shrinking? Her hands were
changing shape, fingers growing longer and thinner until they
almost seemed like Erafel's hideous paws.

With a cry of dismay, she dropped the helmet. It tumbled
down toward the forest clearing below the shipwreck. Her hands
shrank back to their previous size.

The helmet thumped onto the dirt. A few nearby hyds
recoiled, hissing at the artifact. The hole was growing larger and
larger. Soon it was larger than the helmet itself. The helmet was
still there, and it was still the usual size. Yet the hole was
somehow bigger than the entire helmet it was in. Addy could not
explain it, nor ever draw a picture of it. Or even describe it
properly with words. It was beyond what her brain could
comprehend. Somehow the very laws of reality were changing.
The wormhole expanded, sucking up rocks, tree trunks, and bullet
casings. The hyds all retreated, fearing to fall into this black hole
that opened on the battlefield.

Then, from inside the black hole--the sound of metal
rumbling. The thunder of rolling tanks. The shouts of soldiers. A
trumpet gave its clarion call, and a dim voice rose as if from a
world beyond. "Charge!"

They emerged from the mists of time.
Soldiers.

Soldiers in olive drab, steel helmets on their heads, M1 rifles in their hands.

Flying above, jetpack thrumming, Addy stared down in wonder. It was real. She had known it would work. Awe and wonder flowed through her, and her eyes dampened.

A Sherman tank rumbled out from the wormhole, then another and a third. Green jeeps roared forth, soldiers with machine guns inside. From the mists of time they charged to battle. Warriors of the Second World War. Heroes from centuries ago. At their lead, Addy saw a tall officer with a grim face. His helmet was missing, revealing graying hair. She recognized him from the insignia on his uniform.

Colonel Henry Locker. The owner of the helmet Addy had purchased. A helmet to summon him and his men from beyond space and time.

The officer stared around at the macabre tableau. His eyes widened and he took a step back. But then those eyes narrowed. His face hardened. And he raised his fist.

"Soldiers, we have been summoned!" he cried. "Fight!"

With battle cries, the ancient army surged forth to battle.

The infantrymen stormed the forest clearing, firing their rifles. The tanks rolled forth, muzzles lighting the night. Howitzer cannons rolled out the wormhole, adding their fire to the barrage.

The bombardment slammed into the hyds. The aliens seemed stunned and confused. They faltered backward. They made a half-hearted attempt to fight back. Their tentacles slammed into a few ancient soldiers, hurling them into the air. Their jaws devoured others, while their ink consumed still more.

But the soldiers kept coming, surging through the wormhole from the 1940s to the 2270s. Scores, then hundreds, then thousands. More tanks rolled forth, cannons booming, tearing into the alien swarm.

Then, with roaring engines, out flew the planes.

Addy stared in wonder. A military buff, she recognized those planes.

"Hawker Hurricanes!" she said, gaping.

Their propellers whizzed. Their engines roared. They shot out from the portal and soared above the forest of hydrians. Each plane carried machine guns, rockets, and bombs. They kept coming like a swarm of hornets, so many Addy lost count.

Their pilots had trained to fight the Nazis and Japanese. They had never seen the horrors of the hyds. But not a single pilot turned to flee. As one, these antique fliers opened fire. Some Hurricanes fired rockets across the sky, destroying hyds in the air. Others raced above the forest, strafing the crawling squids. A squadron flew rings around *Rotspawn*, bombarding the hydlord like the planes attacking King Kong.

Watching from the sky, Addy cheered, tears of wonder and relief running down her cheeks.

"Earth rises to fight!"

From Earth's past of heroism, heroes rose again. And the hyds fell before them.

The battle raged, though victory did not yet belong to humanity. The hyds were regrouping, striking back. Tentacles grabbed Hurricanes and slammed them down. *Rotspawn* grabbed a tank and hurled the enormous machine through the air. The tank slammed into a platoon of infantrymen.

Jetpack thrumming, Addy dived toward the battle. She was ready to kill. To charge with her ancestors. To fight among heroes.

CHAPTER NINETEEN
The Golden Lioness

Standing in *Blood, Sweat, and* Tears' exhaust port, Einav gazed in wonder at the scene. An army from the Second World War-- emerging to fight! The Sherman tanks boomed. The M1 rifles crackled. The Hurricanes roared through the sky, strafing the enemy.

Einav understood how it worked. Addy had not just bought any old antique helmet but a wormhole generator. It had opened a portal to the past--and pulled out this army. Somebody must have installed this wormhole back in the 1940s. Who had it been? A twentieth-century scientist? Some time traveler from the current era? An alien intelligence? Einav did not know. Maybe she never would know. But this was real, not some hologram or illusion. The hyds were actually falling back.

"It's like magic," Marco said. He stood beside Einav, watching with wide eyes.

"It's technology," Einav said. "As Arthur C. Clarke said, any sufficiently advanced technology is indistinguishable from magic."

Marco shook his head in wonder. "Amazing. So Addy's helmet is the real deal. She was right."

"If the helmet is real," Einav said, more to herself than to Marco, "maybe all technology from Darktech Cove is real."

She looked down at her belt. She had bought it at Darktech Cove. A golden chain encircled her waist. From it dangled golden coins, each engraved with a different animal.

According to the label, if you ripped off a coin and placed it under your tongue, you would transform into that animal. Einav had never believed that. She had bought the belt of coins for aesthetic value. It matched the golden buckles on her shirt, the color of her hair, and the filigree on her starhand. She also thought the coins gave the belt a Middle Eastern flare, appropriate for her heritage. Yet now she wondered. Could this belt actually do as advertised? Could its magic be real?

Down on the field, the World War II army was fighting for its life. The bodies of soldiers and hyds alike were piling up across the field. In the sky, the Hurricanes were firing rockets and machine guns, battling the terrible flying hyds. Rain and fire rained. It truly was a sight to behold--warriors from the ancient past emerging to battle aliens from another galaxy. Einav would never see anything like this again.

Here in the exhaust port of the *Blood, Sweat, and Tears*, the gunners were running low on ammo. Wyatt's machine gun unleashed another belt of ammunition, then stopped spinning. Across the jutting stern of the shipwreck, the light artillery was petering off. Marco tossed down his plasma rifle.

"I'm out." He drew his handguns instead. "This is all I got left."

Aurora was down to firing three rifles instead of eight. "I'm almost out of ammo too," the Menorian said.

Einav fingered her belt. Could it be?

She looked up at the others. Wyatt, Aurora, Harris, and a score of other defenders looked back. And of course Marco was there. He was always there.

"We will join Addy and her phantom soldiers," Einav said. "One great final assault into the enemy horde."

Aurora flared bright red. "Yes!"

Wyatt drew twin pistols with jeweled hilts. "Hell yeah!"

Commander Harris nodded sternly. "Yes!"

Marco turned toward Einav. "On your order, Einav. We're ready."

Once more, Einav looked at her belt. The golden coins chinked. Which coin should she choose? The fierce mother bear? The deadly she-wolf? The proud eagle? As she contemplated, the Hurricanes above blasted back several hyds, and a beam of sunlight shone through. The light ignited one of the coins.

The lioness.

Of course.

Her last name, Ben-Ari, meant "child of lions" in Hebrew, and many claimed that Einav looked like a lioness. The Golden Lioness, they would call her during the Alien Wars. She grabbed the golden coin, ripped it off the chain, and held it up. The lioness on the coin gazed back at her, eyes gleaming.

Here goes nothing, she thought and placed the coin under her tongue.

The coin dissolved. Liquid gold filled her mouth and ran down her throat. Warmth filled her. The gold flowed through her veins, along her bones, and into her mind, tickling all over. A shock pounded through her. Her muscles contracted. She pitched forward, landed on all fours, tossed back her head, and cried out in pain. Every bone in her body seemed to be shattering and reforming.

Around her, she saw the others fall back. Wyatt crossed himself. Marco gaped.

"Einav?" he whispered.

She tossed back her head again, and this time when she called out, no human voice left her throat but a roar. A deep, terrible roar that filled the exhaust port, echoing. The pain eased, fading to a tingle. And Einav felt strong. Stronger than she had ever felt in her life. Limber. Powerful. Bursting with vigor.

Standing on all fours, she looked down at her hands, but she saw paws. Fur covered her right paw. In human form, she had no left hand. Instead, she wore her starhand, a masterwork of filigreed ivory embedded with azoth. The prosthetic had changed shape, becoming an ivory lion's paw adorned with golden motifs. The azoth gemstone still shone there.

Einav raised her head and looked at Marco and the others. Wyatt fished out a mirror from his magical pack of everything, and Einav gazed at her reflection. A golden lioness stared back with green eyes. A huge lioness, easily quadruple her human weight, and fangs gleamed in her jaws.

And then Marco did something that shocked Einav nearly as much as her transformation.

He knelt.

"Golden Lioness," he said.

The others knelt before her. "Golden Lioness!"

But even as they knelt, they held their guns. They were ready. Einav walked toward the edge of the exhaust port. Her muscles rippled. Her entire body coiled with pent-up power. She placed her front paws on the port's ledge, puffed out her chest, and gazed down upon the battlefield. The tanks, jeeps, cannons, infantry platoons, and planes were battling the hyds everywhere. Addy fought among them, flying at the vanguard, her jetpack spewing fire.

Einav let out another roar, louder than before. It was so loud everyone on the battlefield heard and looked toward her-- even through the din of explosions and flying bullets. And with that great roar, the Golden Lioness leaped out of the *Blood, Sweat, and Tears* and into the battle.

Behind her, Marco let out a roar of his own. So did Wyatt and the others. They leaped out the exhaust port, landed on the mountainside, and ran behind her toward the enemy.

Einav ran down the mountainside, moving faster than she had ever run, feeling stronger, fiercer, more alive than she had felt in years. Again she roared, and her cry echoed down the mountainside. Hyds turned toward her, hissing, and raised their tentacles. They fired inkblots. Einav leaped from side to side, dodging the assault, then vaulted off a boulder, pouncing toward one of the giant squids.

Even as a lioness, a large and fierce predator, she was small compared to a hyd. The armored squid was the size of a mammoth. Yet she leaped onto the alien nonetheless, slashed her claws, and shattered the protective membrane over its hideous red eye. She bit into the eyeball, crushing it between her fangs.

The alien squealed. Einav kept clawing, ripping open the carapace around the eye, exposing more flesh. The creature buckled and its tentacles flailed. Einav would not release it, clawing and biting until she cracked open the skull.

The hyd thumped down. Einav spat out chunks of flesh and bone and brain. Blood covered her golden maw. She stood atop the corpse, let out a deafening roar, and leaped toward the next hyd.

The alien swung its tentacles. The lioness dodged them, skidded across the ground, leaped up, and grabbed one tentacle where it met the body. She crunched the armored limb between her mighty jaws, severing it. Then a second tentacle and a third. The hyd still lived. It lunged at her, jaw opening wide. The creature's jaws were far larger than her own, but Einav would not retreat. She let out a roar of challenge, raised her ivory paw, and the azoth crystal glowed. She swung that paw, her starpaw, slamming it into the hydrian's face. Teeth flew. The jawbone ripped off the alien. The hyd thumped down, and she was on it at once, biting its head, ripping out chunks of skull, until the alien lay still.

"For the Golden Lioness!" Marco cried, running down the mountainside. Only now were the humans, on their slower feet, reaching the battlefield. Marco fired his twin pistols. Wyatt, Harris, and the others ran with him, shooting their own sidearms.

Aurora joined the humans, firing her crystal daggers.

Addy saw them. She soared high on her jetpack, fired a grenade at a flying hyd, then swooped to join them. She gazed at the Golden Lioness charging through the field.

"Einav? Einav, it is you!" Addy raised her fist and her voice echoed across the battle. "Hear, O Earth! The Golden Lioness fights with you!"

The troops all cried out together in glory--both the soldiers from the twenty-third century and those from the twentieth. The Allied warriors gazed in awe at the Golden Lioness leaping in their midst. They saw her claws and teeth tear their foes apart. And they cried out with those who knew her.

"The Golden Lioness! The Golden Lioness!"

The troops rallied around her and began beating back the hyds. The squids fell dead or fell back. Ahead loomed their hydlord, the foul Rotspawn. Tank shells had cracked his carapace. The bombs from planes had blasted chunks in his mantle. The infantry had perforated him with bullets. Yet the kraken still lived.

The Hurricanes swooped to strafe the hydlord. Rotspawn leaped up, grabbed a plane with one tentacle, and slammed it onto the ground. Tanks blasted off the hydlord's armored fins. Yet still the dark god lived.

Einav raced across the battlefield, leaping over dead hyds and around charging soldiers. She sprinted between several rumbling jeeps, leaped over an artillery crater, and kept going, heading ever closer toward the towering monster. And towering the beast was. Rotspawn loomed as large as the Statue of Liberty.

The Golden Lioness zigzagged across the battlefield. Inkblots slammed down around her, searing the soil. Hyd tentacles lashed at her, and she slid below them or leaped above them. Jaws snapped all around, and she dodged the teeth. Hurricanes flew above, and bombs fell onto the lines of hydrians. Through the flames the lioness ran. Finally she reached a row of tanks that were bombarding the hydlord. She leaped onto one tank, raced across its bore, then soared into the air.

The azoth crystal in her paw shone, bending the fabric of reality, propelling her upward. A beam of light fell between the clouds, illuminating her as she soared. The light glimmered on her golden fur and claws. Rotspawn rumbled before her, his enormous mouth opening wide. His tentacles scooped up tanks, grabbed planes, and pulled them into his crushing jaws. Before him, the lioness seemed minute, no larger than a bee attacking a buffalo.

A bee killed my mother, Einav remembered. *A single bee killed a mighty woman. And a mighty woman can slay a god.*

Upward flew the lioness until she reached the head of the hydlord. There she swung her starpaw, infusing it with all the power inside her, with the trauma of her many wars, with the strength of her mother, with the might of her ancestors coursing through her veins, and with the memory of her lost soul. The battery was dead, yet Einav Ben-Ari carried within her a greater power. In her burned the souls of people she loved. In her blazed the light of Earth. With this light, she swung her mighty starpaw, slamming her heart and soul and rage into the hydlord. And Rotspawn's jaw shattered. His teeth flew into the distance like the pillars of a shattering temple. His very skull cracked, and the hydlord crashed down dead and shook the earth.

Trees collapsed. Cracks raced across the land. And from the battlefield rose cries of triumph. The soldiers cheered, calling out her name. But not her human name. Upon the field of victory, they cried out: "Golden Lioness!"

Seeing their hydlord fall, the hyds lost heart. The humans attacked with renewed vigor, pounding the smaller squids, driving them back into the forest, and felling them from the sky. The Golden Lioness stood upon the carcass of the hydlord, her snout covered in blood.

She looked east across the forest, seeking more hydlords. But she saw none. The hyds were routing, and the tanks and planes chased them, bombarding the aliens as they fled. Addy was flying above the fleeing swarm, dropping grenades, laughing and living her best life.

Standing atop the hydlord corpse, the Golden Lioness spun around and gazed back toward the mountain. During the battle, she had mostly focused on the forest and clearing. But the hyds had attacked the mountain too, descending the slopes toward the *Blood, Sweat, and Tears'* ruin. The stony outcrop where Einav had set up her command post thrust out above the shipwreck.

And there, upon that ledge of stone, stood a familiar figure. With her sharp feline eyes, Einav saw him clearly even from this distance. He was a half man, half squid. From the waist up, he was human, his skin ashen, his face gaunt, his hair long and gray. From the waist down he was a hydrian, his dark tentacles clutching the mountain. The ashes of battle rained around him. His thin lips were a tight line, his eyes little black beads. His elongated fingers draped at his sides like spiders. In one of those hands pulsed a wretched crystal, embedded into rotten flesh. The shard from a god's mind.

Across this great distance, Erafel stared at the Golden Lioness. She stared back. He was wreathed in shadows, while she stood in a beam of light. He was a squid and she a lioness. He commanded a great shoal, and she a civilization of heroes. One of them would become the ruler of this world.

But it would not be decided today.

For a long time the two foes stared at each other, a chimera and a lioness, shadow and light, despair and hope. Then, finally, Erafel gave her a little nod. His eyes glittered like shards of onyx, and in her mind, Einav heard his voice.

"We will meet again, Einav. You won this battle. But I will

win the war."

Then he turned and scuttled up the mountain.

Einav let out a great roar, head tossed back, and the power of the coin flowed away from her. Once more her body broke, twisted, reformed. She reared onto her back paws, and they became feet again. She had not done anything to release this power. Perhaps the magic simply ran out. Einav took a deep, shuddering breath, and she was a woman once more. A woman standing atop the corpse of a great slain hydlord. She stared again at the mountain, but with her human eyes, she could barely see Erafel. Just a tiny black speck like a spider scuttling up the mountainside.

"Stop him!" she cried. "Bombard that mountain! Stop him from fleeing!"

They heard her call, and they relayed her order across the force. Tanks bombarded the mountainside. Planes dropped bombs onto the slopes and peaks. When the dust settled, they found no sign of Erafel. Had he fled? Or had the bombardment incinerated him? Einav, Addy, and Marco scoured the mountainside for hours, seeking him while planes flew overhead.

He was gone.

"He's toast," Addy said. "Probably just scattered atoms in the dust."

Yet Einav was not too sure. His words echoed in her mind. "We will meet again . . ."

* * * * *

The battle was over.

The last hyds fell back, leaving a smoldering forest strewn with the dead. It began to snow. The flurries danced like ghosts

over the corpses, then buried the fallen in white shrouds. Einav
walked across the battlefield. The dead lay all around her. Hyds.
Heroes from the present. Heroes from the past. The wounded lay
here too. Some missing limbs. Others missing faces. Some burnt.
Others broken. Medics leaned over some, fighting their own
battles against death. A priest prayed over other men, easing their
passage.

Einav had won another battle. She won most battles she
fought. And every victory ended like this. With death and despair.
With screams and tears.

Through the snow, a tall officer in olive drab approached
her. He wore no helmet, and frost glistened on his short, graying
hair. Colonel Henry Locker, a man from beyond time, gave Einav
a crisp salute.

"Ma'am."

She was shorter and thinner than him. Physically, she
looked younger. Despite her advanced age, she could pass for his
daughter. She wore no recognizable military uniform, only her
white outfit with the gilded buckles. Yet he recognized her
command. She returned his salute.

"Colonel Locker," she said. "You saved our lives."

"It's my duty to fight monsters," said the officer.

Einav realized how bizarre it was. She was talking to an
apparition. A ghost. A soldier from the Second World War. Yet
no, this wasn't a mere ghost. He was as solid as she was.

"You're . . . real, aren't you?" she said. "Not just a trick.
Not just a hologram. An actual soldier from the twentieth
century."

"Indeed I am, and as I look around me, I struggle to
believe this place is real." The colonel shook his head in wonder.
"Monsters from space . . . What year is this?"

"It's 2270," she answered.

The colonel blew out his breath in wonder. "When the

woman from space visited me, when she gave me my helmet, I never imagined it was real. Someday they'll need you, the woman told me. The people of a future Earth. Someday they'll call you. And you did."

Einav frowned. "Who was this woman?"

"She came in a bizarre machine. A time machine, she called it. She stood no taller than my shoulders, and her hair was short. She said her name was Rowan. Rowan Emery. I never learned more. Do you know her?"

Einav thought back to the prophecies. To the words of the Oracles of Hypnos. To the promised descendant of Marco and Kemi. A girl who would one day save Earth. Who was already fighting with them, though she had not yet been born.

"Know her?" Einav said. "Not yet. Not yet . . ."

The colonel glanced around him at his men. The soldiers were gathering all around. Soldiers with stern faces. With haunted eyes. Many were so young. Only teenagers. They had survived the beaches of Normandy and the hellish ruins beyond.

"We must be returning home now," said Colonel Locker.

Einav put a hand on his shoulder. "Must you? We won one battle here, but many more battles lie ahead. I sure could use your help."

"I sure would love to stay," said Locker. "But back home, they need us too. We're fighting our own monsters there."

"I know," Einav said softly. "My ancestor fought in that war too. He's still fighting, back in your time."

Locker's eyes widened. "Really! What's his rank? What regiment is he in?"

"The partisans of Lithuania," Einav said. "In your time, he's just about to escape the Vilna Ghetto. He's the only Ben-Ari who survived the Nazi inferno."

Locker's face paled. Then his eyes hardened. "Yes. We must soon return to our time. You're fighting terrible monsters here in 2270, ma'am. But back in my time, the monsters we fight are far more evil. Farewell, Einav Ben-Ari, the descendant of a hero."

And then he swirled away like one of the flurries of snow, vanishing into the haze. All his army--the infantrymen, the medics, the wounded, the dead, the tanks and the planes and cannons--they blew away like so much snow. Even their piles of bullet casings vanished. Only the smell of gunpowder and their tracks in the snow hinted that they had ever been here at all.

Without the twentieth-century soldiers, the field seemed to empty, the remaining army so small. Barely two hundred survivors remained. Some were shabby outlaws of the Ragtag Fleet. Others were HDF officers who had survived the slaughter. A few were Martians. Some were Earthlings. And two were Einav's oldest, dearest friends. Marco Emery and Addy Linden.

As the snow fell over the fields of dead, the survivors gathered around Einav. To one side sprawled the forest of broken trees and dead hyds. To the other side rose the mountainside and the shipwreck. It was a pocket of victory. An oasis of solace. A graveyard where hundreds of brave humans had fallen. And beyond this valley, all around the world, the enemy still swarmed. Einav wasn't getting much news from the rest of the world. She wasn't even sure where in the world she was. But from what snippets they had received while crashing down, she knew that hydrians were swarming over cities. That they orbited the planet like a shell. That Ninazu perched upon the north pole, growing from hydprince to hydking, gripping the planet in his tentacles.

As they gathered around her, Einav spoke to her people. "We won a victory today. A great victory. But many more battles await us. I know that we are few. Most of us fell on Mars. Or in space. Or here on this very battlefield. We are the last few survivors of what was once a great fleet. I know we're weary. I know the pain and fear are almost too great to bear. But I know that if we survived this battle, if we survived Mars, if we survived the shoal in space--we can keep surviving! We can keep fighting! I don't know if the Human Defense Force still fights elsewhere on this world. I don't know if across Earth, people are rising up against the squids, or if this world has fallen, and here where we stand is the last corner of freedom on Earth. I don't know. But I believe. I believe that there are others who fight. I believe that the Human Defense Force still stands, that it's stronger than the enemy has imagined, stronger than even I imagined. In times of despair such as these, there is no force mightier than the human spirit. It's stronger than diamonds. Sharper than blades. Brighter than the sun. We faced the enemy and beat him! And we will face him again, and again, and again, and we will keep beating him! We will fight, my friends. We will fight onward. We will raise this Earth in rebellion, and *we will win*!"

"We will win!" Addy cried, fist raised.

"We will win!" Marco shouted.

"We will win!" cried the survivors, and their voices filled the valley, echoed through the forest, and rose on the snowy wind into the sky.

That snowy wind blew across the boreal forest and the icy plains. Beyond the mountains, the tundra spread northward under the storm. The wind howled, the snow fell thick, and the land cracked and moaned. But even here were hydrians. They moved across the snow in lines like ants. They rumbled across the sky, stirring the snowy wind. Many of them were heading north. Heading toward their king.

Beyond the vast frozen plains, beyond fields of ice where nothing grew, he reigned. The northern pole was his domain, and there he rose like a mountain. Taller than any mountain on Earth. A creature of a size that should not be. A hydking. A god. And his name was Ninazu.

His mouth was a canyon. His eyes were red temples. His

tentacles spread out, as wide as mountain ranges, spreading southward along the globe like longitudinal lines. From his throne of ice, he gripped the world in a planetary embrace. As his billions of children feasted, Hydking Ninazu smiled.

The story continues in…

If I Forget Thee, Earth

A Prayer for Earthrise V

NOVELS BY DANIEL ARENSON

Earthrise: The Original Series

Earth Alone

Earth Lost

Earth Rising

Earth Fire

Earth Shadows

Earth Valor

Earth Reborn

Earth Honor

Earth Eternal

Earth Machines

Earth Aflame

Earth Unleashed

Earth Remembers

Earth in Darkness

Earth, Our Home

A Prayer for Earthrise

Hear, O Earth!

Earth of Gold and Light

East of Earth

The Shores of Eternity

If I Forget Thee, Earth

On the Milky Way Rivers

Mintari

A World of Dinosaurs
Where Dinosauars Roam
March of the Dinosaurs

Alien Hunters

Alien Hunters
Alien Sky
Alien Shadows

Kingdoms of Sand

Kings of Ruin
Crowns of Rust
Thrones of Ash
Temples of Dust
Halls of Shadow
Echoes of Light

The Moth Saga

Moth
Empires of Moth
Secrets of Moth
Daughter of Moth
Shadows of Moth
Legacy of Moth

KEEP IN TOUCH

www.DanielArenson.com
Daniel@DanielArenson.com
Facebook.com/DanielArenson
Twitter.com/DanielArenson

www.ingramcontent.com/pod-product-compliance
Lightning Source LLC
Chambersburg PA
CBHW020528020726
47494CB00006B/1677